Stories

5/23

In September, the Light Changes

IN SEPTEMBER, THE LIGHT CHANGES

THE STORIES OF

ANDREW HOLLERAN

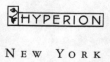

NEW YORK

"Sunday Morning: Key West" was first published in *The Faber Book of Gay Short Stories* edited by Edmund White (London: Faber & Faber, 1991).
"Petunias" was first published in *Poz* magazine (New York: August 1998).
"Someone Is Crying in the Chateau de Berne" was first published in *Christopher Street* magazine (New York: September 1980).

Library of Congress Cataloging-in-Publication Data

Holleran, Andrew.
    In September, the light changes : the stories of Andrew Holleran/Andrew Holleran.—
1st ed.
        p.   cm.
        Contents: Sunday morning: Key West—
The hamburger man—Petunias—Someone is crying in the Chateau de Berne—Blorts—
The man who got away—The ossuary—
The penthouse—The boxer—The housesitter—Amsterdam—
In September, the light changes—Joshua and Clark—Delancey Place,
The Sentimental Education, Innocence and Longing.
    ISBN 0-7868-6461-3
    1. Gay men—United States—Social
life and customs—Fiction.
2. Americans—Travel—Foreign countries—Fiction.   I. Title.
PS3553.03496I5   1999
813'.54—dc21   98-43997
                                                                  CIP

Book design by Holly McNeely

FIRST EDITION

10   9   8   7   6   5   4   3   2   1

"Sometimes in life all we need is a change of weather."

—*Marcel Proust*

CONTENTS

In September, the Light Changes

❦ THE OSSUARY

LEAVING MEXICO CITY FOR OAXACA WE GOT LOST—circling, for over an hour, a neighborhood near the airport because we were confusing, we realized after stopping to ask directions for the fifth time, the word *derecho* (straight ahead) with *derecha* (to the right). "You see the importance of vowels," said Mister O'Connell. Finally a beautiful woman, seeing us go by her window yet again, like clothes in a dryer, took pity on us, ran out to our car, and told us to look for the sign that said "Puebla, Cuota." And, after giving her the carnations we'd bought outside a church, we found the highway to Oaxaca while Mister O'Connell sat in the backseat crying, "*That* was an angel! Literally an angel! An angel of God!"

No one was sure whether he meant this literally or figuratively since he seemed to be lingering in churches long after the rest of us had seen the altarpiece and were ready to go—having to be physically prodded, as he sat slumped in the back pew, staring into space or resting with his eyes closed, praying or in a trance. At first I thought he was just taking a load off his feet—Mister O'Connell had become fat—but when I finally asked him outside the cathedral in Mexico City why he was lingering, he said that he was happiest now in churches, or convents, or monasteries, and that last fall in Madrid, after visiting the museums, he had found a church not far from the royal palace, and had sat there for hours watching society ladies say their rosaries. This should not have surprised me, though so far as I know he did not attend church in New York. On Sundays he went to prison instead, where the young man who came and went in his life, sometimes answering the door of the apartment on East Eleventh Street when you least expected it, was incarcerated—for a reason no one dared ask. We didn't dare ask because there was something very private about this dignified, heavyset man who caught the bus for Sing Sing every Sunday morning in a dark suit and tie. (Sundays were very busy for him: Mass, prison, an AA meeting in the evening.) The man in 4B, we gathered, had a past. Though he now worked for a travel magazine, Mister O'Connell had worked for *The Catholic Worker* when Dorothy Day was alive, and had become more secular with each successive magazine, till now he was at *Conde Nast Traveler*. (Mister O'Connell, someone who had known him before us said, was "the beautiful ruin of a long Catholic education.") He always seemed to be in a rush, at any rate, except when he distributed homemade cakes to the people on his floor at Christmastime, and then he would sit and visit; otherwise, one had to catch him in his booth at Odessa, where sitting with him as he ate a huge plate of pierogi was like having a private tutorial—his mind, his manners, were so fine; a pleasure that appealed to young men of sensitive bent who knew they could enjoy Mister O'Connell's company without ever having to worry he would put a hand on their knee, since he was much too Catholic, and old-fashioned, for that, and interested only in Ramón.

This year the enthralled Celt was a medical student who had just moved in across the hallway from Mister O'Connell's small rent-controlled apartment—a tall, disheveled youth with blond hair and a gymnast's physique who was about to start his studies at Columbia, and who now kept exclaiming over the brand-new ribbon of concrete, the engineering marvel of the toll road to Oaxaca, which we had all to ourselves as we crossed bridge after bridge through the dry, empty mountains. All of us exclaimed, actually, as we drove south, we were so relieved to finally be on our way; yet something—the stress of leaving Mexico City, the spell of the arid, empty countryside we had driven through for hours, or just the fatigue at the end of a journey—reduced us all to a strange silence when we found ourselves seated that night on the second floor of a restaurant overlooking Oaxaca's central plaza. Everyone stopped talking, and felt sad, all of a sudden, as if a bolt of melancholy had struck us dumb. Some people explain such sudden cessations of conversation by the passage of an angel through the room; Mister O'Connell said it was probably the fact that beneath us in the crowd of people circulating round a gazebo in which a small brass band was just putting away its instruments was our exact fantasy of Mexico. "Perfection always depresses," he said.

There were four of us at table—Mister O'Connell, myself, a lesbian from Marietta, Georgia, whom we had met while checking into our hotel, and the young medical student who lived across the hall from Mister O'Connell in Manhattan. Beneath us was a much larger crowd amid the trees, gazebo, benches, and lampposts—mariachis in studded black suits with their violins and trumpets, waiting for some party to begin, young children elaborately dressed, the girls in frilly white dresses and bows, their parents and grandparents, teenagers in clumps of their own sex, ice cream and balloon vendors, women selling textiles and ceramics on the sidewalk opposite the cathedral. It was like that mural in the National Palace in Mexico City of Chapultepec Park come to life—a stage play in which one tried to figure out the actors, and what parts they were playing, and what play. "There is a line from Neruda," said Mister O'Connell, patting his lips with the linen napkin after taking a small bit of guacamole on his bread, "describing a *paseo* just like this."

"Which one?" said the med student.

"The one where he compares the homosexuals cruising to a necklace of palpitating oysters," said Mister O'Connell.

"Neruda is so brilliant," said the lesbian from Marietta.

"The trouble is, from up here I can't quite tell who's palpitating and who's not," said Mister O'Connell.

"Well, he is, I think," said the med student, pointing down at a young man in white who had just entered the square from the southwest corner. "And they are," he said, indicating two men with buzz cuts conferring while they looked over each other's shoulders at the crowd going by. "In fact, they were in the post office. They're Canadian."

"And who are *they*?" said Mister O'Connell of two men who had just come onto the terrace and were walking toward the table in the corner—the first a tall, silver-haired man in a green blazer with a lavender scarf around his neck, the second a short, dumpy man in wrinkled shorts and a gray T-shirt whose black beard and vulpine face gave him a rather sinister aspect. No one spoke. "This is why we travel, is it not?" said Mister O'Connell. "It's like a mystery by Agatha Christie—the other guests."

"I quite agree," said the lesbian from Marietta. "I think I saw those two in San Miguel. I've been running into many of the same gringos wherever I go. Tell me," she said, turning to Mister O'Connell, "are you enjoying Mexico?"

"*Now* I am," said Mister O'Connell. "This is entrancing," he said, waving a hand at the shaded square below. "But the capital! My God! When I left I said to myself: No matter what happens to you for the rest of your life, there will be one good thing—each morning you awaken you can say, 'I am not in Mexico City.' "

"Was it that bad?"

"Appalling," said Mister O'Connell. "I hadn't been in thirty years—and what used to be a lovely, Parisian city is now so polluted you can taste the air. Another sad spectacle of a culture converting itself to the American model, when its own model, while different, was superior in many ways. I cannot understand it. Must everyone on the planet own a color TV and a station wagon?"

At this point yet another couple came onto the terrace, a man and woman in their fifties or sixties, who were escorted to the last table with a view of the plaza down below.

"And who is that?" said the lesbian from Marietta.

"That is a man I used to know in New York," said Mister O'Connell, "when he was an editor at the *New York Review of Books*. He is such a bibliophile that when we went to Egypt together he stayed in his room and read a book about the pyramids rather than go see them. We no longer speak, however. We had a falling out."

"Over?" said the med student.

"John Cheever," said Mister O'Connell. "Odd duck," he muttered, staring at the square below as the man and his wife passed behind him.

I suppose we were all odd ducks; anyone who travels is—stripped of their context, their native habitat, people seen abroad are like words used in an unfamiliar way; you have to figure them out, removed from their usual setting, as if you'd never seen them before. The next day we went to the pyramids of Monte Alban; Mister O'Connell took the tour in Italian, to hear the language, and, he told me when he returned, to be near a handsome man with a thick black mustache, who was wearing a pink polo shirt. Later, in the dry, sunny stillness he fell into another trance—and finally off the ledge; but he was not hurt and was in good spirits when we got back to the hotel we had chosen near the main square after two others more popular with foreigners refused us because they were full. The most expensive—a converted convent up the street—we only visited after dinner to look at its gardens and courtyard. To our surprise, the couple we'd seen in the restaurant the night before—the tall, silver-haired man in the blazer and the sinister man with the black beard—were at a table in the small courtyard when we turned into it; the tall, distinguished one, his face quite angry, was saying to the other in an intense voice that carried easily over the plash of the fountain as we passed: "*Give me the bone!* I want it and I want it now!" Mister O'Connell turned to us with raised eyebrows, as he placed a hand at his throat, and, when we had reached the colonnade on the other side of the fountain, turned to us and said: "What do you suppose *that* meant? 'Give me the bone!' What were they talking about?"

"They're probably archaeologists," said the med student.

"*Lo dudo,*" said Mister O'Connell. "In Peru, yes, Peru is full of bones, they are constantly discovering skeletons in tombs, the dry, desert air is a perfect climate that preserves both textiles and the contents of ossuaries, but Oaxaca is not a place one comes to for bones. Of that sort. No, I wonder if we have not witnessed something else. An obsession of a cruder sort. For some reason, that little exchange reminded me of Robert de Peu."

"Robert de Who?" asked the med student.

"A very handsome Texan who lived in your apartment before you. A bright, wonderful young man who arrived in New York full of ambition and dreams and then got waylaid when he met a man on Fire Island his first summer there. A very tall, dull, nice but otherwise totally unremarkable insurance salesman from New Jersey whose sole distinction was an exceptional appendage," he said. "For which Robert dropped out of the Ph.D. program at NYU so the two of them could take a cruise around the world that lasted six months. When Robert got back, he was a nutcase, a shred of his former self," said Mister O'Connell. "There was no point in his enrolling in classes. He had lost all joie de vivre, and muscle tone, his eyes had a mad, haunted look, he was ill-tempered, thin-skinned, cynical and bitter, *and* a total alcoholic who had to clean friends' apartments to support himself. It goes without saying, he never finished his dissertation on Gertrude Stein!"

"Why?"

"Because he was obsessed! Addicted! Because he had reduced life to mere aesthetic considerations! Because he, too, demanded a bone—in many places just like this—in just the way that man in the courtyard did. And of course the man who had the bone ended up boring him to death. Waking up in hotels in Kuala Lumpur, Aswan, and Singapore with that lump, facing him every night across one of those little tables with the snow-white linen and nine courses—all because later in the cabin he knew he would get his bone. By the time the ship docked in Long Beach, Robert de Peu was, I'm told, incoherent! He had been drinking constantly for six months. He was a wreck, a ruin. Which is what happens when you let that particular carnal obsession rule your life, as it has apparently that man over there," he said, nodding at the couple across the courtyard, still in deep argument, as the man pounded his hand against the table, and his imperturbable companion sat there with a smile on his lips. "Seneca called sexual desire 'a cruel and insane master.' There's living proof!" he snorted. "The things you come upon in Mexico! Could it be more *Night of the Iguana*? This country draws some truly deadbeat Americans."

Or so he thought till later that evening, when just the two of us were left on a bench in the Zócalo, reluctant to go in, even though the mariachis were all putting their violins and trumpets into their cases and the Indian women who had spent the day selling statues and painted goblets were walking home with their babies on their backs and their toddlers hand in hand, and the waiters had come out and taken in the chairs and tables before the restaurants, and the man selling balloons was walking forlornly away, his face a mask of fatigue, and the two Canadian boys we'd seen earlier were the only foreigners out, still walking by, looking behind them, stopping to confer with an air of suppressed excitement. ("I assume it gets gayer as it gets later," sighed Mister O'Connell, "like everything else.") Even we had decided there was no point in sitting there any longer when the tall, silver-haired man in the green blazer walked into the square alone and sat down on the bench across from ours. "I would guess La Jolla, or Marblehead," murmured Mister O'Connell as we looked at this handsome man of about sixty-five. Crossing his legs, now this way, now that, surveying the square with a distracted, impatient air, he seemed to be reviewing mentally the scene in the courtyard—part of which we had witnessed—or some other problem that was making Oaxaca beside the point. Eventually, since there was hardly anyone else out at that hour, when he had calmed down somewhat and allowed his gaze to focus on the foreground, his eyes came to rest on us: Mister O'Connell and myself, sitting right across from him. At which point Mister O'Connell smiled and gave a little wave.

The man nodded curtly, but that was enough for Mister O'Connell. "Enjoying Oaxaca?" he called across the space between us. The man seemed dumbstruck by the question, either because it had never occurred to him, or he could not find appropriate phrases to express what he really felt. "*I* know," said Mister O'Connell, "it's a mixed bag, like all of Mexico, though I find, given the changes the country has undergone, it's a miracle something as charming as this still remains. I'm rather *over* Mexico myself, this is my sixth visit in thirty years, and if I ever come back, it will not be within three hundred miles of that metastasizing tumor called La Capital. Were you in Mexico City?"

"Just to change planes," said the man.

"Lucky you," said Mister O'Connell. "I don't know how long it can go on."

"I don't either!" said the man in a tone of clipped fury.

"I mean Mexico City," said Mister O'Connell.

"Oh," said the man.

"You meant something else," said Mister O'Connell.

"Well, yes," said the man, standing up, coming over and sitting down on our bench as a streetsweeper came up to his bench with a broom. "I'm afraid I'm embroiled in a little situation of my own that has made me indifferent, momentarily, to Mexico. I'm having difficulties with my—traveling companion."

"Believe me," said Mister O'Connell, laughing, "you are not alone. It happens to the best of friends eventually. One travels with others at one's peril. There's nothing like a trip to ruin a friendship. One must be very careful. What, exactly, is the problem?"

"It's simple, really," said the man. "He has something I want."

Mister O'Connell looked at me.

"And he won't give it to me!"

Mister O'Connell looked my way again with a roll of the eyes, then turned to the man and said, "I'm so very sorry. But—I suppose you must ask yourself—is this thing really so important to you?"

"Yes!" said the man.

"I see," said Mister O'Connell, with downcast eyes.

"And he knows it," the man said. "Which is why what he's doing is so cruel!" Then he blurted out: "And he's a Jesuit!"

"A Jesuit?" gasped Mister O'Connell.

"Yes," said the man. "Of course he only teaches at a college in Missouri, and the reason he's a Jesuit is because thirty years ago he wanted to get a deferment to avoid Vietnam, if you ask me. But still! He's behaving very oddly for a priest."

"Indeed," said Mister O'Connell.

"He said he refuses to give it to me till our last night in Mexico, and then he said I'm going to have to *make* him give it to me."

Mister O'Connell's jaw dropped.

"Give what?" I finally said.

"My lover's bone," said the man. "The bone from my lover's ashes I scattered on Monte Alban today. Donald had just finished reading from the *Book of Common Prayer,* which is the reason I asked him along in the first place. I'd finished scattering the ashes according to the instructions my lover left, I'd done all he asked— after waiting six years, because I just couldn't bear to do it, to part with his ashes. And then Donald leans down, picks up a piece of bone, about two inches long, and puts it in his wallet. I said: '*What* are you doing? Put it back!' And he just smiled and said: 'Protestants like you always have a problem with relics.' I told him I was not a Protestant. And he said, 'Well, then, you agnostics,' and I told him I was not an agnostic. I told him I was a scientist. I told him I was not even a Christian. I am an atheist. He said he knew plenty of people who were scientists *and* good Christians and *I* said they were lying to him. Anyway, he kept the bone and won't give it back to me! Said I'll have to force him to give it back on our last night in Mexico. Then I slammed him against a wall of one of the pyramids, and threatened to kill him, but that only made him happy."

"Why?"

"Because he's a masochist, and now he can't wait till I threaten to kill him again, which I refuse to do, of course. But when I ask him nicely for the bone he says something like, 'Now is not the right time.' Well, when is the right time? I could strangle the shit."

"Oh no," said Mister O'Connell, "it's what he wants you to do."

"I know that," said the man. "By the way, my name is Richard."

"How do you do," said Mister O'Connell, introducing himself and me, and then, rather than make the small talk that accompanies introductions, he returned immediately to the subject they had been discussing. "Couldn't you steal the bone instead while he's asleep?" he said.

"*Steal* the bone? It's *my* bone! Or my dead lover's! Anyway, I tried that but he's hidden it somewhere, it's not in his wallet, where I saw him put it when he picked it up. I looked. I must say the whole thing leaves me feeling very edgy. This is *not* what I had in mind for my farewell to Larry."

"And in such a sacred place," said Mister O'Connell.

"Exactly," said Richard. "Larry always felt Monte Alban was a source of great energy."

"You've been here before, then," said Mister O'Connell.

"The year we met," said Richard.

"And that was . . . ?" said Mister O'Connell.

"1962," said Richard. "We were together thirty years. And it's taken me six to be able to even think of giving up the ashes. Which I thought I had done," he said. "Till Donald picked up the bone."

"*Why* do you think he did it?" said Mister O'Connell.

"I don't know," said Richard. "Years ago, I slept with him. But I had no desire to do it again, and I think he always held it against me. People like him are not used to other people *not* being interested in them."

"You mean—"

"He has what the Taiwanese call 'instant fame.' Or at least the biggest dick in Minneapolis. I think it's bothered him all these years that I didn't want to sleep with him again, much less become romantically involved, and now it's almost as if he's flirting—he's like a seven-year-old girl who takes something from a seven-year-old boy and makes him chase her around the room. It's just so silly. Unless he has some mystical angle on it I don't know about. I refuse to ask, frankly, because I'm furious. It's just not done. You do *not* pick up someone's bone whose ashes have been scattered and put it in your wallet. The scattering of ashes is a sacred moment. *Why* does he want that bone? And why should I even have to ask?"

"Shall *I* ask him?" said Mister O'Connell. "You don't want to, you're too angry, but I could. Come with us tomorrow, we're going to the ruins at Mitla—in the next village. They're marvelous, the bus leaves at ten. I'll chat him up there."

The next day we all set off in a van for Mitla, which, when we got there, turned out to feature another church, with an open-air market next to it where women swarmed our vehicle to sell us painted ceramics, plates, and dolls. "I feel like food left out on a picnic table in a cloud of flies," Mister O'Connell muttered as we walked along. "It is demoralizing after a while." The ruins themselves were strangely impressive, however—much smaller, less grand, than Monte Alban, but somehow more evocative: the dull red paint still on part of the temple, the precolonial frieze, the big, square courtyard where the victims were sacrificed, the tiny room one was allowed to enter where the priests had stayed. I sat in a far corner of the courtyard and watched a busload of French tourists take over the site for an hour, and then drive off, and then spotted Mister O'Connell walking deliberatively across the open sunlit square of earth. "You can feel it here, can't you," he said. "It's that little room, that dull red color, it's much more Maria Montez than the other, something happened here, you can actually imagine it, and it was blood sacrifice," he said with a sigh, sitting down beside me. "And the church," he said, looking at the twin domes that rose directly behind the ruined temple. "You know, the Spanish built their cathedrals right on top of the temples they tore down, to let the Indians know: *This* is your religion now. It could not have been more arrogant or brutal. What Europe did in the name of religion is astonishing. And now what is our religion? Travel packages. Two weeks in Cancún. *Seinfeld*. MTV. The point is, Dostoyevsky was right—if God is dead, then everything is permitted. The world is only recently awakening to that fact. Oh, Mexico," he said, lying down on the stones. "It has so much more history than we do, and it's such a big, big mess."

"He's coming this way," I said.

"Who?" he said.

"The Jesuit."

"Ah," said Mister O'Connell, sitting up. He waved. We watched the priest walk slowly across the grassy rock-strewn courtyard, pause to look into the entrance to a burial chamber, and then resume his way toward us in the dry, white sunlight. "The Jesuits are the reason Pascal wrote the *Provincial Letters*," said Mister O'Connell in a somnolent murmur. "They were very slippery creatures even then. They're awfully smart. And you know where intelligence leads you . . . ," he said.

"Where?" I said.

"Directly into S and M," he said.

"That's what he looks like, actually," I said. "A man in a leather bar, utterly average, though there is something louche about him, something sly."

"Very evocative, don't you think?" called Mister O'Connell when the Jesuit came near.

"Very," said the priest.

"I was just saying the Spanish always built their churches on the foundation of the temple they tore down. Rather cruel."

"Rather," said the priest. "But then the human race has been politically correct only a very short while."

"So true. Weren't you people in fact expelled from Mexico in the last century?"

"Almost," he said. "Persecuted, certainly, and confined. But some of us remained."

"Mexico has had this schizoid history," said Mister O'Connell. "Both very devout, and rabidly anticlerical, depending on the period. I am so impressed by the few churches we have visited, how they are still used, by all kinds of people, all ages, both sexes, all hours of the day. In the National Cathedral I saw a young man take his baby to the foot of a statue and press the hem of the saint's robe to the baby's lips. They are still very devout, whereas we are so very rational. I asked a friend only last month, a Presbyterian minister I know, if he believed in God, and he laughed, and said: 'That's a very Catholic question.' Can you imagine? A very Catholic question! I should have thought it was a very human one. But in the United States, science, or applied science, rules. Do you actually have a parish and a flock?" he said.

"I teach," said the priest. "Linguistics. Foucault."

"Ah," said Mister O'Connell. "Not two of my favorite subjects. Is this your first time in Mexico?"

"Yes," said the priest, sitting down beside us.

"You must admit it has *quite* an ecclesiastical history," said Mister O'Connell.

"It really does," the priest said.

"And a pre-Catholic one," said Mister O'Connell. "And that's why it's fascinating. Or used to be. I'm afraid it's becoming too second world, too American, now. A bit too much hustle and bustle. Mexico used to be different. Now it's all leaded gasoline and soap operas on TV."

"Well, that's history, too," said the priest.

"And what is your history, if I may inquire?" said Mister O'Connell. "How do you know each other, you and your friend?"

"What is this, confession?" laughed the priest.

Mister O'Connell went white and smiled. At that point someone waved at us from the van and we realized we were leaving. "The caravan moves on," said the priest, and we got down from the wall and crossed the blazing courtyard in silence, several yards

apart. "You *don't* interrogate a Jesuit," muttered Mister O'Connell as we drove back into town. "Did you hear that? 'What is
this, confession?' I know when I've met my match. This is obviously going to be tougher than I thought," he said, and he was
silent till we got back to the hotel.

The hotel was a rather small four-story building right downtown between a jewelry shop and a bank—which explained, perhaps, the presence of soldiers with machine guns on the sidewalk
nearby. Its atmosphere was not that of the luxurious converted
convent, or even the bougainvillea-covered pension popular with
Americans up the street. Its atrium was plain and the people in it
mostly silent: a mix of German youths reading their guidebooks
before setting out for Monte Alban, American women traveling
in groups, with visors and sensible shoes, writing letters beside
cups of tea, and Mexican businessmen reading the contents of
their briefcases. It was a hotel whose noise was that of maids and
janitors, the slap of pails and mops, and echoing voices as they
cleaned rooms that were quite spartan—simple furniture, a ceiling fan perpetually revolving, not the slightest decoration—and
redolent of disinfectant, a bit like a hospital; very clean, with
gleaming tiles and just-washed floors. Mister O'Connell's room
was on a short, dark hall with a broom closet leading to another
smaller courtyard. The med student thought they should change
rooms, after our first night there, so he could sleep late during
the day—since Mister O'Connell was not going out at night, and
the med student was, wandering around Oaxaca at two in the
morning trying vainly to find a gay bar—but Mister O'Connell
showed the med student how to close the shutters and the double
doors, draw the curtains and stuff pillows round his head, so that
whatever noise the street produced would not penetrate. Latin
cultures were always noisy, said Mister O'Connell, if you were not
very careful.

Unable to sleep, the med student and I went to the plaza to

watch people. When we went to wake Mister O'Connell after his nap a few hours later, we found him still in his underwear, and he went right back to bed while we sat down on a bench in the corner. "Do you like your room?" I said. "Like it!" he said. "This room is my *dream* of Mexico. This room is *right* out of Graham Greene," he said as he lay there watching the ceiling fan revolve overhead. "This room is made for the dark night of the soul. It's the room all Americans are secretly seeking when they come to Mexico, even though they think they want the Hyatt. This room is a confessional," he said. "It reeks of God."

The med student said all he could smell was Lysol.

"God *is* Lysol," said Mister O'Connell. "Both at the beginning, in childhood, and at the end, when one has put away things of the flesh—when the hospital bed has to be fumigated and the corpse cleaned. God *is* Lysol," he repeated, waving a hand in the direction of the ceiling fan. "I can understand perfectly why Morris stays in the hotel and reads about the ruins rather than going to them. It's the room that does it. It's the room that casts the spell. It's the room that asks Pascal's question—why *do* men leave it, to go out?" He sat up. "Have we eaten all those cheap coconut cookies we bought in the market this morning?"

"Yes," I said.

"Then that answers Pascal's question," he said, falling back with a sigh. "We must go buy cookies. I shall commune with the dead after dinner. I shall have my religious crisis here later tonight."

I said he must be thrilled having a Jesuit so close at hand.

"Not really," he said. "Ten years ago, yes. But I've heard so many stories about them now. A friend of mine in Los Angeles has a Jesuit friend who comes to visit—they go to nude beaches together and pick up men. Can you imagine? The last one they saved, inadvertently, from suicide, it turned out. He had gone to Black's Beach to drown himself. My friend and the Jesuit, I must say in all fairness, were probably the two best people he could have met at that moment—a therapist and a priest! God works in mysterious ways. They brought him back to their tent, *and* a more hopeful view of life. But to go to a nude beach in San Diego to pick up men—is not my idea of a priest. Even if God may have sent him there."

"Isn't that a bit sentimental?" said the med student.

"Not at all!" said Mister O'Connell. "That is just how God acts—through other people. All we can possibly know of God is embodied in other people! God can only be other people!"

"Sartre," said the med student, "said, 'Hell is other people.' "

"Well, of course," said Mister O'Connell, "though I think what Sartre meant was, 'Hell is other tourists.' Or, 'Hell is being a tourist.' "

"Do you really feel that way?" said the med student.

"Don't you?" said Mister O'Connell. "Don't you have these terrible moments when you are traveling abroad, far from home, of absolute panic—when you suddenly realize you *are* far from home, that you are basically nobody, or simply a rootless little consumer with precious few elements of identity who ventured too far out on a limb, and the limb is now about to crack?"

"No," said the med student.

"Never?" said Mister O'Connell. "You never have these moments when you are traveling of realizing that you have sinned, sinned greatly, and the only thing you can do is return home immediately and do penance?"

"What sins?" said the med student.

"The sins you are evidently too young to have accumulated," Mister O'Connell said, "but which I suspect you inevitably will. The sins that cluster like stamps on your passport when you have traveled a great deal," he yawned. "When I was young that's all I wanted—lots of stamps on my passport. That was my sin. I should confess to the Jesuit—though I'm very old-fashioned in these matters. I find this one a bit much."

"And slightly sleazy," I said.

"Sleazy's the word," said Mister O'Connell. "Whatever his original motives for picking up the bone, to use it now as a tease is beyond the pale! For that's what he's doing. So foolish, considering the man has no desire to sleep with him. And there's the irony. It is the atheist who refuses to be corrupted by the presence of a large reproductive organ. Rara avis. You'd have to go far and wide to find someone like that, especially in these times, which grow, as you know, more and more pornographic. So pornographic I often think a religious revival must be just around the corner. The country used to have them every twenty years. But now that science, and the entertainment industry, are regnant, it is hard for the religious impulse to express itself. We believe, alas, only in the here and now."

"But what else is there?" I said.

"The not-here-and-now," said Mister O'Connell. "The so-called other world. The one we can neither see nor hear. The one where presumably those we love who have gone before us hover and watch. The land of the dead. You are young, dear boy, you have not had much experience of death, I presume, or rather, the only deaths that have any impact, of those we love. Well, someday you will experience *that*. Till then, enjoy. After that, join the club. What do you suppose he will *do* with the bone?"

I said I couldn't imagine.

"It is the first thing that has interested me in a long, long time."

"But you travel so much," I said.

"Oh," said Mister O'Connell, with a wave of his hand. "Travel is completely pointless."

"Pointless! Why?"

"It's just another form of consumerism," he said, yawning. "People buy trips now the way they buy automobiles and blankets. They get on a plane, are transported to some hotel, like the one in Ixtapa, or a beach in Vietnam, and all they've done is exchange the scene they saw on the television screen or the magazine cover for the real thing. Cancún, Bali, Miami Beach. What's the difference? The experience of traveling—which used to take weeks, months, which used to be full of danger and difficulty—is gone. There is no traveling anymore. There is only container cargo. And the cargo is tourists. Unless drug smuggling is a form of travel," he said, putting a finger to his lips. "*May*be if you're landing at Kennedy with twenty condoms filled with cocaine in your lower intestine, any of which may burst and kill you instantly, you feel a sense of adventure—more, anyway, than the poor slobs in Manhattan who are going to buy the cocaine and use it. But that's it. Otherwise, it's over."

"Over?"

"Because of television, dear boy, and the jet plane. To come down from one's room in Machu Picchu, as I did last November, and see the concierge watching Bobbie Batista on CNN describe a freeway pileup in Atlanta—it's over. There is no travel anymore. There is no there to go to. The whole world is now Atlanta. It worries me. I often wish there would just be a *flood*—to just wash it all away. Tell me—if you were God, would you spare the earth because of one good man, or would you drown it because of one bad man? You could go either way, it seems to me."

"What are you talking about?" said the med student.

"The fact that we are so decadent," said Mister O'Connell. "That Americans are so rich, and bored, and trivial, and selfish, and therefore doomed."

"Intellectuals are always saying that," said the med student. "But America just goes on eating hamburgers, having babies, and building shopping centers. The West is booming."

"Not in my view," said Mister O'Connell.

"But you're not Bill Gates, are you?" said the med student.

"No," said Mister O'Connell. "I'm not Bill Gates."

"So *you* may be decadent. But that doesn't mean the country is."

"But it does, it does," said Mister O'Connell. "Because I've had all the advantages. I was the middle-class son! I was given the education. And here I am in a hotel in Oaxaca wondering why a Jesuit with a big dick picked up the bone of a man whose ashes were scattered by his homosexual lover beside the pyramids of Monte Alban. I am a biopsy of the larger culture. In a democracy decadence does not arrive when the aristocracy becomes effete—it shows up in the life of the average man. Americans," he said, "are too damn sophisticated. You'd never know we once had sumptuary laws. You'd never know the Puritans had rules about how you could dress. Now we've got Marky Mark on the bus shelters in Calvin Klein underwear—and queens who actually buy the stuff! We've come a long way, baby. To the point where the only thing interesting anymore is what the Jesuit plans to do with that bone."

"What do *you* think he means to do?"

"I don't know," said Mister O'Connell. "There's no telling what people do with ashes nowadays. Now that cremation is so à la mode. You could write a book about the things queens have done. A friend of mine was left ten thousand dollars to scatter his lover's ashes in twenty separate places! By the time he was done, he had racked up a hundred thousand frequent flier miles, *and* a new boyfriend from Sri Lanka. Queens consider ashes a reason to party! The Church, on the other hand, has never liked the idea of cremation. And she has always been very fond of relics. Churches are built on relics. A church must have one to be consecrated. So perhaps that's all it is. In an age when you no longer go to the grave, or hear the clods of earth striking the coffin, in an era when I can no longer distinguish between a funeral, a cocktail party, and an encounter group, we may be facing nothing more than a Jesuit's natural respect for relics. An ancient respect for bones the rest of us have lost. We must consider all the possibilities," said Mister O'Connell.

"Which are," said the med student.

"One," said Mister O'Connell, holding up a finger, "he took the bone merely to flirt. Two, the Jesuit could not bear to see a man's mortal remains left on the ground for the wind to scatter, even at a place as dramatic as Monte Alban. Three, it's because it *was* Monte Alban, a pre-Christian shrine, that he could not allow it. Four, he thinks someday Richard will want a memento, something to remember his lover by."

"That's quite creepy," said the med student.

"Not at all," said Mister O'Connell. "Just because you were raised in a country that has quite banished the presence of death from its culture—bones are a big part of human history, dear boy, a big part of human history. The bones of the saints—don't get me started! Battles, cities, crusades, massacres, history itself, have all centered on bones. Peru is loaded with bones."

"I somehow don't think anyone wants his lover's femur sitting on a shelf next to the stereo."

"Be that as it may," said Mister O'Connell, "I want to know *why*."

"But I thought you were going to ask him."

"I was," said Mister O'Connell, "till he mocked my natural tendency to interview people. Once they do that—once they put up the warning flag—I can go no further. I will not be rude. He fired a shot across my bow, this afternoon at Mitla—queen to queen—and that is that. I respect boundaries. One must."

"Then how are you going to find out?" said the med student.

"*You* are going to ask him," said Mister O'Connell, sitting up.

"Me?"

"You're young, you're attractive, you have universal appeal—*everyone* is attracted to you. You have that thing a young gay man has when traveling which puts travelers' checks to shame, you have that quality which *does* make travel an adventure, even in the age of container cargo—you have desirability. Good looks. Work it! My time is past, *you're* on the dance floor now. It's the sort of question I see most naturally occurring in a postcoital embrace."

"If he's trying to get his seventy-something friend to sleep with him," said the med student, "I don't see why he'd want to go to bed with me, at twenty-seven."

"Oh how I wish I was twenty-seven," said Mister O'Connell, "and could do it for you."

"Do you?"

"Of course," said Mister O'Connell. "*I* saw you, dear boy, in the square last night get looked at by that handsome Mexican father walking the two-year-old. He didn't look at *me.* I foolishly went nowhere when I was twenty-seven. I was so addicted to Manhattan at the time, I wouldn't even go to Brooklyn, much less Brazil. I was too busy being gay. And now that I am traveling again, I'm too old to be part of the *paseo,* the way you were last night. *Be* part of the *paseo,* dear—sleep with the Jesuit!"

"I find him unattractive in the extreme," said the med student.

"That's not the point," said Mister O'Connell. "The point is to use your gifts while you have them." He fell back on the bed. "Take it from one who knows. A few years ago I read the life of J. R. Ackerley, the British writer, who discovered Japan when he was older, and realized how much he liked the people and their manners. I'm half *afraid* to travel now, half afraid to—"

We stopped to listen to the maids in the hallway; they went on.

"Discover *my* Japan," said Mister O'Connell. "The place that will make me realize I should have gone there sooner."

"Well, why don't you find that place now," said the med student with a calm, unflappable air, "so you can start enjoying it?"

"Because that is the moment when you are destroyed!" said Mister O'Connell, sitting up. "When the sea you have been walking through, like the Israelites escaping Egypt, suddenly comes crashing down upon you. When you finally understand just how and why it was that you wasted your life! Most people cannot bear to face such truth! This is why I won't go to Portugal!"

"*Por*tugal?" said the med student.

"Yes," said Mister O'Connell. Then he said in a quieter voice: "I have a suspicion that Portugal is *it*."

" 'It'?"

"The place I should have gone when young. Though of course," he said, standing up, "it is quite possible this place does not exist at all. The point is, we are here, now, in Oaxaca, whose square I find a little bit of heaven, and we have a mystery to solve—why the priest pocketed the piece of bone. Please think about your assignment and reconsider," he said to the med student, and with that we all went out to have dinner. It was early. We first chose one of the restaurants on the square and drank beer while we watched the crowd circulate, and the soldiers with rifles outside the bank finally jumped into the back of a truck that came down the narrow street and drove off. The shops were closing up. A concert was beginning in the square on a stage in front of the church—two singers accompanied by a quintet of guitar players. It got darker. The lights came on. Men with clusters of balloons wandered around through the crowd of children, grandparents, tourists, teenagers. It was impossible not to feel a sense of anticipation, that something wonderful would happen in the square that night, that you would meet someone and fall in love. Instead, we went up to dinner in the same restaurant. As we were walking to our table, the Jesuit and his friend were leaving theirs; and just as we were sitting down, the Jesuit made a slight detour and came over, leaned down beside Mister O'Connell, and said: "The reason I did it, I'm not sure. I don't know why I did it. It was one of those things I can't explain, except perhaps that I could not bear to see him left in a foreign place, so far from his own country, because of some New Age superstition. I can't tell that to Richard without hurting his feelings, and so I'm going to keep the bone until I do know what is best, and if it makes him angry and no longer a friend, then that is that. So now you know," he said with a smile.

"Yes," said Mister O'Connell, with wide eyes.

"Good. Because I knew you were a *knower,*" said the Jesuit. "Good night. Have a safe journey home."

And with that we all sat down, and for some reason fell into the same sad silence we had been overcome by the first night we got there and stared down into the square; a silence even I cannot explain, unless it was one of those sudden pockets of depression that people fall into when they're tired of travel, and far from home, or it really is an angel passing through the room.

THE BOXER

NOBODY IN THE HOUSE KNEW EACH OTHER. We'd all answered an ad, placed by the two men who rented the rooms upstairs. It was the first house I'd ever shared with people not related to me by blood and there were times, sitting in the parlor in the afternoon, taking a break from my reading, when I wondered who had lived here before, when the place had been occupied by a family. For someone, somewhere, the rooms were full of memories. All I could see was one of those two-story frame residences built in the teens or twenties in Iowa City on a street too near downtown for its own good. It had two bay windows, a small front porch on which a swing hung, rusted and unused, and an enormous kitchen whose window looked out on a naked pear tree, its branches growing straight up, as if underwater. The pear tree looked exotic, especially in the evening, set against the pink glow of a winter sunset with a hard, bright scimitar of a moon caught in its startled branches, like a tree in an illuminated manuscript.

There was nothing Persian about the house, however. The town's business district had eaten away everything to the rear of its forlorn wooden frame, eroded the slope behind us into a huge gray blister of a parking lot, and it was now part of that decrepit no-man's-land where the commercial stops, like some lava flow, and the residential begins. The owners of the house had long since rented it out and gone, like good Americans, elsewhere.

In the house that winter was a gaggle of grad students: a Japanese mathematics major who disappeared each day after breakfast; two men upstairs pursuing doctorates in psychology; a poet; and I. None of us used the parlor. The two psychologists lived upstairs, the poet, mathematician, and I below; the only time we met was when we collided in the kitchen, or had to tell the psychologists that their dishes were piled up so high in the sink the grease and sauces on them had congealed into a paste that was attracting flies, which appeared miraculously in the dead of winter. The psychologists upstairs were close friends, but quite different in appearance and personality. Morton was short, husky, outgoing, and cheerful. Hal was tall, thin, pale, with gaunt cheeks and dark gray eyes that looked bruised or shadowed. He kept irregular hours. The telephone was in the parlor, that unused room, and in the middle of the most silent, sunny, snowy afternoons, when a call came in for him, I would shout up the stairs "Hal!" expecting to hear no reply, but he would call back and then appear, rubbing his eyes, awakened from sleep, and come downstairs to take the call, like an animal roused from a cave. He worked with mentally disturbed patients at the local veterans administration hospital, and it was that to which I attributed the air of gloom and depression he carried around with him; some sadness or profound loneliness or acquaintance with the cruelest mental affliction, translated into a low, hoarse voice, gray eyes, and the disheveled air of someone who sleeps through crisp winter afternoons in a midwestern university town. Early that autumn there was a string of young men coming to the house asking for Hal—people he had met in the local bars, or former patients, I wasn't sure which—but after a few weeks, they stopped and began phoning instead, perhaps because Hal was no longer living there alone, as I gathered he had that summer.

I was not sure if I disliked Hal because I suspected he was more intelligent than I, or because he always had a tragic expression on his face, or because he did not do his dishes; but the way I expressed it to myself was to suspect that he felt himself so above it all—people *and* dishes—he regarded human life as mere illustrations of principles of psychology, which enabled him to know exactly what was really going on, even if we lesser mortals did not. It irritated me further to see that Morton, his short sidekick, and a young woman with long red hair who came to the house both seemed to be in awe of Hal, as if they knew a person I did not—far finer than I could imagine, well worth deferring to and loving. But I said nothing. Everyone was polite—and because we all had different schedules, and because the house, while not a mansion, was fairly large, we seldom saw each other those first six weeks.

My own room was a closed-in porch that was lined with six windows, no doubt a pantry used for preserves at one time because it was small; it was cheaper than the big bedrooms upstairs, and because it was off the kitchen, it was cozy. It was habitable only because of the space heater I would put on, falling asleep to its low electric hum and bright orange glow, as if I were a piece of bread in a toaster. Living there one could not avoid what went on in the kitchen, and since it was in the kitchen that people sat down for a cup of coffee, a meal, a conversation, I was aware of most people's comings and goings. I don't think anyone entered or left the house by the front door.

The poet lived in a big room off the parlor; but because a mere curtain separated him from the parlor itself, his rent was not much more than mine. The mathematician lived in the front. The real bedrooms were upstairs. The few times I went up there to deliver a phone message I saw that Hal had pinned sheets over the windows in his, and Morton kept his shades always drawn; both rooms were littered with clothes, books, bags of potato chips, empty Coke bottles, and study lamps that were never turned off and burned in the dark corners like so many candles in a monastery. This was graduate school and not a monastery, however, and Morton had covered the entire ceiling of his bedroom with a collage of playmates of the month whose honey-colored breasts drooped down toward the astonished viewer, like putti on the ceiling of a rococo chapel in Bavaria. There was not a single piece of art in Hal's room except a poster advertising a boxing match in Waterloo the previous summer between someone named Enrique Toronja and a man called Billy Piston. Everything else was books and papers.

It took me a while to realize that the young man who most often called Hal, at all hours of the day and night, was the boxer Billy Piston; for a while he was just a man on his way to Miami, Florida, who called sometimes in the middle of the afternoon and sometimes late at night, when Hal was most often out having dinner with Morton or the woman with red hair, or at work. He often spoke over the obstacle of the operator trying to place a collect call and prevent any free communication in the process. He often signed off by shouting: "Tell Hal I'm in Mobile! I'm going to Atlanta!" Or: "Tel Hal Billy called! I'm cool!" Or: "I need Hal! It's important!" And with that melodramatic note— and a tirade against the stubborn operator—the call would be cut off. Eventually I came to associate him with midday; the chill of that parlor, the snow that lay outside the dirty bay windows. The parlor was so cool, the house so still, when I took these calls, that his voice seemed to burst into the atmosphere of that dusty house with the urgency of a man on the lam. His choked consonants, bad grammar, unfortunate inability to find Hal at home, all became in my mind so pathetic I concluded he must be one of Hal's patients—whose progress I followed toward the lodestar of so many hapless people: the sunlight of South Florida, where I pictured him drifting from bus station to gymnasium, always checking in to tell Hal of his progress. And I wondered how many waifs, how many orphans—even in the bars downtown Hal frequented—Hal took under his wing and gave counsel to out of the goodness of his heart.

The only other person who answered the telephone was the poet; and he was gone most of the fall, until, shortly after the New Year he began working at home. I had never met a poet—and because he kept the curtains drawn across the arch that separated his room from the parlor, I couldn't see what he was doing. Once, when I asked him, in the most polite way I could manage, what a poet did, he quoted Randall Jarrell, who said a poet was like a man sitting in his backyard waiting for a meteor to land in his lap. I guess he meant he waited for an idea, or inspiration. He could not have waited more decorously. He kept regular hours and told me that the following fall he was entering law school to please his father. He resembled a lawyer already: Neatly dressed in corduroy pants and Shetland sweaters and Hush Puppies, he led a life far more organized than anyone else's in that house. Even the Japanese mathematician stayed up late playing pinball at a nearby bar, and moaned, laughingly, about it afterward. The poet said he could not understand such a waste of time. He rose each day at eight, cooked his own meals and washed the dishes and pots immediately afterward; kept his food in a neat corner of the third shelf of the refrigerator, boiled eggs in advance and wrote his initials on the shells in ink. He never asked to borrow even a teaspoon of cooking oil. In fact, he was always very reserved, and when you saw him coming home across the parking lot, from his weekly poetry workshop or daily swim at the gymnasium, you would have guessed him to be a business or chemistry major. That's why it surprised me one day when he showed up with a student with very thick glasses and a big nose, dressed entirely in every piece of clothing sold at Iowa Book and Supply to boosters who wanted to advertise their allegiance to the university; a student who looked, in his ten-foot black-and-yellow striped scarf, like a human bumblebee, who took one glance at the parlor of our house and said, in the most acidic, terminally jaded voice I have ever heard: "Why didn't you *tell* me you were living in a play by William Inge? This is beyond *Picnic*, this is *Dark at the Top of the Stairs*! Tell me, is everyone living here as sexually repressed as I am, or am I jumping to conclusions?" And the poet burst out laughing. "No, I'm serious," the bumblebee said, his voice changing in pitch but not acidity, as he unwrapped the scarf from his neck, "Where are Roz Russell and William Holden? When does the picnic begin?" But I did not hear the answer because the poet, blushing to the roots of his hair, mumbled something and led the bumblebee into his chamber, and drew the curtain closed, whereupon I heard nothing but the latter's strange cackling till they left.

The poet, in other words, seemed embarrassed by the bumblebee and essentially smuggled him in and out of the house; the only reason I knew he was there was that incredible nasal drone when he first came in the kitchen, the "Where is Kim Novak when we *need* her?" and "Come back, little Sheba, come back! If you *dare*!" to which the house inspired him. Without the bumblebee the poet was reserved and taciturn. When Morton walked into the kitchen one day when we all happened to be taking a break and unfolded the playmate of the month he had just received in the mailbox—a brunette playing with a garden hose beside a car she was washing—the poet glanced briefly at the photo and said nothing, while the mathematician flushed. "How'd you like to solve that equation, Hiroshi?" Morton

grinned, his watery eyes gleaming. Hiroshi replied: "Very much."
The poet began to eat his soup. "Not your type?" Morton said,
glancing at him. He did not wait for an answer, but passed on
through the kitchen with the centerfold flapping at his side, like
a proud father about to show off his new baby, and went upstairs
to add her to the Wagnerian harem he had plastered on his
slanted ceiling.

It was ironic that the woman who came to the house so often—
the daughter of an army general who lived in Hawaii—was a
plain young person with poor posture, freckles, and a thin mouth;
not one of those honey-colored nymphs who kept Morton company through the long winter afternoons. The women Morton
wanted resembled, in real life, the sorority girls whose trays I
cleared at the student union when I worked as a busboy on the
weekends; one Sunday I noticed Morton at a table in the corner,
staring at them as he ate his apple pie and they gossiped in a
cloud of cigarette smoke, and then went off after stubbing the
butts out in squares of uneaten Jell-O without once even glancing
at him. In real life Morton had Charlayne, the army general's
daughter, who surprised me often in the middle of the day when
she came downstairs, after studying with Hal, or making love
with Morton, or both, and then sat quietly in the kitchen having
a cup of coffee. I was not sure what she did up there. The life that
went on upstairs might as well have been occurring on Mont
Blanc. Shrouded in clouds, cut off by the thickly carpeted stairs,
we heard and saw nothing but what came down in the form of
precipitates: hunger or the need to communicate. The refrigerator
and the telephone were all they needed of us; and the rent checks.
There were whole weeks we did not speak that winter. The only
sign of life on Mount Olympus was the heaps of dishes that eventually accumulated because we refused to do anyone's but our
own. Then the miraculous flies made one of us talk to Morton.
Morton talked to Hal, and one gray afternoon I would return

home to find Hal at the sink, or bathtub, washing them. Then, in February, he, Morton, and Charlayne suddenly began to use the kitchen—really use it, cooking, eating at the big round table rather than upstairs—as if some massive project they had been working on was completed. All of us were thrown off by this startling invasion of the Cloud People. The poet—who, between stanzas, came out to eat crackers and cheese, tapioca, cereal, carrots, anything he could find; writing seemed to increase his appetite—refused to come out of his room because he had no desire to fraternize with them; and as his hunger deepened, I imagined, so did his dislike. One day they descended en masse while we were at the table reading as we ate. When they began assembling their meal Morton said to the poet, while his bacon sizzled: "How are you finding the program here?" "Good," said the poet. "Are you writing?" said Hal in his husky voice as he put bread in the toaster. "Yes," said the poet. "Well, you must be," said Morton, "because you sure haven't brought any women back to your room." There was a silence. "Oh, is that the image?" said the poet finally, patting his lips with a paper napkin. "*La vie bohème? The poet and free love? Tales of Hoffman?*" "Well, one image," said Morton. "The one I have, at least." "But it's quite outdated," said the poet as he stood up. "It's like saying a writer should ship out on a tramp steamer bound for the Far East," he said, taking his dish to the sink. "But there are no tramp steamers anymore. It's all containerized cargo these days. One of my favorite poets is Wallace Stevens, and he sold insurance." And with that he washed his bowl, and left the kitchen.

The Cloud People began to talk about the poet as if I were not there, or as if, because I was reading, I could not hear. "He never dates," said Charlayne. "I've never seen him with a woman, he goes around town only with that weird guy with the nine-foot Iowa scarf. Let's just ask him." "No," said Hal. "But it's so obvious," said Morton. "But is it obvious to him? Do you think *he* knows?" said Charlayne. Morton said: "I doubt it. He's too well-defended." "Well, shall we tell him?" said Charlayne. "I've tried," said Morton, "in my way. He said he was here to write, not date, that his girlfriend was in Chicago. It was all evasion. I'm not sure he can admit it to himself. Why don't you ask him?" "I'll do more than that," said Charlayne, standing up. She released her long red hair from its rubber band, and shook it out so that it fell onto her shoulders, undid three buttons of her shirt, and walked out of the kitchen.

Twenty minutes later Charlayne came back and sat down at the table. "Well?" said Morton. "I did everything but take my blouse off," she said, taking a bite out of a saltine. "But my being alone with him in his room meant nothing to him whatsoever. I might as well have been his mother." "What did you talk about?" said Hal. "My life in Hawaii, what it's like to be an army brat, you guys, the weather. He keeps the world at a distance with this sort of cocktail chatter—this well-bred small talk, this verbal cleverness that masks all his true thoughts. He's very glib. On the other hand, he genuinely may not know what I was doing in there."

A moment later, carrying his laundry bag over his shoulder, his coat and cap and gloves already on, the poet entered the kitchen, crossed to the back door, turned, and said: "Next time, you can attach electrodes to my penis, or use a tape measure to measure blood flow and erectile stages. I'd be glad to help you with your project now but I'm afraid I've already got one load going at the laundromat, and have still another to do. You know. The competition for the dryers is so stiff!" And with that he went out the door.

The next day we were at lunch without the trio upstairs. "You know what a professor told me once," the poet said as we finished our omelettes. "That it was a shame that people who went into psychology were usually nerds who were messed up themselves and wanted to have their own problems analyzed. You always get mediocrities in psychology. I only wish I'd had this cream pie," he said, glancing at the dessert on his fork, "yesterday. There are certain moments in life when one would so like a cream pie. But one so seldom has a cream pie. When you want it." And with that the doorbell rang.

Since I was closest to the parlor I went out to answer it, not even sure the front door opened; but it did, and there stood the bumblebee, in a blazing yellow Iowa sweatshirt, Iowa scarf, Iowa cap, and Iowa mittens. "I've always wanted to come in the front door," he said in the nasal drone that the cold had made even flatter and more attenuated. "The porch swing, the doorbell. The divine Midwest. America *is* the Midwest. America *is* the heartland. Tell me. Does anyone around here shuck corn? Or make apple Betty? No, that would be too much to hope for," he said, and with that he stepped into the living room and removed his gloves, which he then grasped in his right hand as he proceeded. "I heard about the test yesterday," he said as we walked through the parlor. "I wish she had tested me," he said to the poet as he entered the kitchen. "I would have simply told her the truth." The poet looked at him. "That I am a frigid voyeur," he said, starting to cackle. "That I am the founding member of the Iowa City chapter of Frigid Voyeurs, whose motto is from Henry James. 'Live, live all you can, it's a mistake not to!' If only someone," he said, unwrapping his scarf and sitting down, "would tell us *how*. But they never do." His voice dwindled. "They send us to graduate school in*stead*." He looked around the kitchen, on the edge of his chair, extremely alert, taking it all in, no doubt expecting the poet to whisk him to his curtained room at any second. Instead the telephone rang.

"Answer it!" said the bumblebee when he saw the two of us sitting there without making a move. "A ringing telephone is like a baby crying. It must be picked up! It could be *him*!"

"Who?" said the poet.

"Chad Newsome! Life! An invitation to the dance! Answer the phone!"

"You answer it," the poet said, picking up a piece of buttered bread.

The bumblebee stood up immediately, flung his scarf back, à la Isadora Duncan, and, moving his gloves to his left hand, exited the kitchen. "Hello?" we heard him say in the nasal tone of a secretary/switchboard operator in deepest Manhattan. There was a beat, then I saw him, through the doorway, put his hand over the receiver, turn toward the poet, and say: "It's some lunatic calling from Miami." "The boxer!" said the poet. The bumblebee put the receiver to his mouth again and said: "No, I'm sorry, there's no one here by that name." He turned and said to the poet: "Is there? A Hal?" I went to the bottom of the stairs and called his name up; there was no reply. "He's not here now," said the bumblebee. "Yes, I will. I will. All right. Good-bye," he said. He put the receiver down with a dead, glassy expression on his face. "How too utterly bizarre," he said. "And how divine. Who is this person? Why does he want to speak to someone named Hal? What is he doing on the Gold Coast? When is he coming back to town? When can we meet?" And with that the poet bustled him out of the house as quickly as he could before he had to answer any of these questions in front of me.

That week the Boxer called a lot from Florida; now in Key West, now in Fort Myers, then back to Dade County. We began getting postcards of seagulls, women in bathing suits confronting alligators, white hotels lining flat, dun-colored beaches, with just one or two words on the other side; the longest message was: "Hi! Key West dangerous for a guy like me! Call you Tuesday!" But mostly there were phone calls in that urgent voice. "Long distance seems to get him excited," said the poet one day when he hung up the phone—he did not have to say it was the

Boxer—in the middle of the afternoon, and went back to his room, returning our house to silence.

The house was always—except for the phone calls—hushed and quiet during the day; coming back from class, it often seemed as if no one was home—though once I entered via the front door, and found the bumblebee sitting silently in the living room on the dusty brown sofa, staring at the walls. "Where do you live?" I finally said. "In the dorms," he said. "Why?" I said. "For the food fights," he said, rearranging the Iowa headband he wore around his thick, curly hair. On my way back to my room from the mailbox out front, it occurred to me to ask what he meant, but before I could, he blurted out: "Don't you feel this is the very temple of an all-American family—I mean the one that lived here before you? Can't you feel the antimacassars, the radio broadcasting FDR's fireside chats, the boy and girl going on their first date, the mother making apple Betty? In other words, the exact opposite of my own family in Queens? Don't you feel the vibrations, ghosts, and Jamesian whispers with every ticktock of that clock?" I was about to answer when the poet came in, and, as usual, looking embarrassed, even alarmed, at finding his friend here without him, ordered him into his room behind the curtain.

The poet treated the bumblebee that way every time he visited—as if he were something contraband that had to be smuggled in and out of the house, the way Lenin was returned to Russia in a closed train. The minute he appeared, he was hidden behind the curtain that divided the poet's room from the parlor. At first there would be hardly a sound—an hour later they were producing noises that reminded me of the three witches in *Macbeth*. (The bumblebee didn't so much laugh as cackle.) It was the only time I heard the poet laugh. When he left with the bumblebee afterwards for the concerts and readings they attended, only a faint flush contradicted the composure of his face. Back at the house, the poet was as grave as a judge. He spent hours alone in his room, writing, like Rumpelstiltskin spinning gold from chaff. I wondered what he could be making poems out of. The pear tree whose icy branches he saw through his window? Or the snow that lay in thick margins along the branches of the shrubs that formed a hedge between our house and the next? One afternoon when we met in the kitchen after another phone call roused us both, he looked round with a smile at the room glowing with the light reflected from the snow outside, the icy pear tree, the icicles dripping from the porch roof, and said: "I love a quiet house in the middle of the day. I feel sorry for the Boxer. I don't suppose he even knows where he'll sleep at night."

"Who do you suppose the Boxer is?" I said. "A patient of Hal's?"

"I suspect he's someone he met in a bar," the poet said. "Or a bus station. The Boxer seems to live in bus stations."

"So he's just one of those people Hal collects, a bird with a broken wing."

"I think they collect *him*," said the poet.

"They collect him?" I said.

"You assume Hal is doing them the favor," said the poet. "Giving them free advice, listening to their stories, the problems that no one else wants to hear," he said with the cold expression that turned icier whenever he was discussing the inhabitants of Mount Olympus. "But it's the other way around, really. The Boxer doesn't need Hal," he said. "Hal needs the Boxer." A fly—released from its secret source in the middle of winter—began climbing over the dirty dishes in the sink. "There's something drained about Hal, as if he needs a blood transfusion—some emotional need that isn't being met—some profound loneliness and melancholy and fatigue. Imagine spending the afternoons and evenings with all those schizophrenic old men," the poet said. "I get my hair cut in that hospital. It's only a dollar-fifty—I discovered it by accident one day. I sit there and wait for my turn reading old issues of *Field and Stream,* and *Guns and Ammunition.* Stories about men killing bears and deer and Germans in World War Two. All these ads for rifles and bullets. All these men who went to war and now can barely stand when the barber says, 'Next.' That's where Hal works. So it doesn't surprise me at all that he attracts these young men who may have problems but are in perfect health otherwise. Anyone who's seen Hal's room—all those books on the spinal cord and brain chemistry—could predict a boxer. Who probably never reads anything but a comic book. Who just gets on a bus when he's tired of one town and goes to another. No, I'm pretty sure the Boxer doesn't need Hal as much as Hal needs the Boxer. But the Boxer went away, so now Hal won't come down for his calls." With that the fly came to light on the poet's napkin, and the poet, who had already rolled up a copy of the *Daily Iowan,* smacked it dead.

And then, as in some Vincent Price film, Hal came in the back door, followed by Charlayne and Morton, with his new copy of *Playboy,* already opened to the centerfold. He stopped and held it out for us to see: a blonde woman with a lariat and cowboy hat. The poet got up and took his plate to the counter. "Would you settle a bet for us?" said Morton, turning in the parlor doorway to the poet. "Are you a virgin?"

"Worse than that," said the poet, not even bothering to look back at him, "I'm a frigid voyeur."

"Oh, that explains it," said Morton, and he went upstairs.

It didn't, of course; but the poet made sure he would never have to supply another answer. In fact, he changed his whole schedule so that he would never run into the three people upstairs again. I don't suppose they thought of him much at all. He was obsessed with them, however. When I did find him preparing food in the kitchen, it was at odd hours—and at the very sound of footsteps upstairs, he would stop and listen, to make sure they were not coming down; once, when someone's footsteps did make the stairs creak, he dropped everything he was doing and fled to his room, spilling a whole carton of cottage cheese onto the counter, like a cockroach when the lights are turned on. Indeed, he ate like a household pest now, scurrying back to his room with the meal he had managed to put together before being interrupted, not coming out again till the coast was clear. I couldn't tell if he was afraid of them or just offended. But the only people who used the kitchen for sit-down meals now were Hiroshi and I, and the people upstairs, who began to have vast, noisy dinners whose laughter must have fallen on the poet's ears, as he cowered in his room, like drops of acid. When the Cloud People sat in the kitchen now they talked of papers due, exams to be taken, farewell parties for people at the hospital, while winter waned. Morton was accepted by a clinic in Lincoln, Nebraska; Charlayne was hitchhiking to San Francisco after her last exam; Hal planned to remain at the VA hospital here. If either side was waiting for some final confrontation—some auto-da-fé—it never came; spring arrived instead and loosened the grip of the house on all of us. Sunlight now flooded the parlor by day—real sunlight, not the reflected radiance of snowbanks. The icicles on the back porch vanished drip by drip in four sunny afternoons, the parking lot reappeared as the sun unraveled its carpet of snow, and the wind howled in the big, bare trees across from the county courthouse at night. One day the pear tree bloomed, a frothy mass of white just outside the kitchen window. And the Boxer—as if his presence in South Florida had no meaning now that we had warm weather—stopped calling. Everyone's routine was breaking up. The mathematician came home late on those moist, soft nights of spring from the bars downtown, or another beer bust with his colleagues. People went to farewell parties. One night found us all in the Airliner, in fact—in different booths—even the poet, who, I noticed, was playing a pinball machine as he put away the beers. Shortly after two A.M. we converged in the kitchen to make breakfast after our night on the town, and he chopped up his onion and mushrooms as if he didn't care who found him there. In fact, the poet slammed the refrigerator door shut so hard the little magnets and their messages all fell off, peeled a banana and did not pick up the skin, knocked over the toaster, and finally sat down to his scrambled eggs with a single, loud expulsion of breath—of relief or amazement, I could not decide. Then as Morton, Hal, and Charlayne came in, he said: "Well, well, well . . . ," in a loud voice that was not his usual one.

"We saw you at the Airliner!" said Morton. "So you've finally decided to live a little!"

"Is that what you think it was?" said the poet through a mouthful of scrambled eggs.

"It sure looked like it to me," said Morton happily.

"Ah, Morton," said the poet. "I see you ten years from now going to your symposia in Seattle and Boise and Laramie, Wyoming, delivering your papers, having cocktails in the Boom-Boom Room, taking your secretary to Hawaii for a little fling. But life. I do not see life in your future. In fact, you are all," he said, a fork at his lips as he looked at them with dazed and sparkling eyes, "incapable of life."

"We thought that was your problem," said Morton quietly.

"No—yours," said the poet. "Rarely have I seen three people who *quite* so miss the point as you do. Charlayne, the Groupie. The Lou Andreas-Salomé of South Clinton Street. Offering herself to me to prove a point. And Morton. Freud in plaid pants. And Hal. A figure out of Poe, inflicted with some arctic gloom, trailing, everywhere he goes, even as he washes, now and then, the dishes—a wound that will never heal. *What* a trio," he said, standing up after a speech delivered as if he were merely thinking out loud, in a pleasant voice. "If only you could sing, Morton. But what would you sing? The 'Liebestod'? No, Morton, you may rip out your centerfolds and drink your beer, but do not worry that you will ever be capable of Life. The divine spark is quite beyond you." He went to the kitchen sink and began mechanically—as if the beer was wearing off now—his dishes, as usual. "And Hal—you should have gone south and joined the Boxer."

"The Boxer is a compulsive fantasist who has trouble distinguishing between reality and make-believe," said Hal with a faint smile.

"And what does that make you?" the poet said, turning to look at him. "The Delphic Oracle? Madame Blavatsky?" He put his bowl on the shelf and turned to face them, wiping his hands on the dish towel. "To think," he said, "the Boxer cried out, from darkest Tampa, for love! And never got past the operator."

"Why didn't *you* talk to him, then?" said Hal.

"Because I am a frigid voyeur," said the poet, "and frigid voyeurs do not do such things." He sighed. "That is my cross, I accept it." And with that he left the kitchen and passed through the parlor into his room.

The next day it was as if everyone had left the house—as if no one lived there, an impression heightened by the open windows, the curtains moving in the breeze, the dusty, sunny silence of the rooms. That afternoon I sat with the poet in the living room as he waited with his suitcases for the taxi that would take him to the train station. The windows were open, and I was reluctant to go to work; so I prolonged our farewell by asking him if he would miss anything about his year in Iowa City. "Miss anything?" he said. "I'll miss the pear tree. The kitchen. This house, oddly enough. The phone calls from the Boxer. I certainly won't miss them," he said, raising his eyes to the stairs. "I'm afraid for me the year was something of a waste." At that moment a horn honked in the street and we stood up and took his suitcases. We walked out the front door, past the rusted porch swing no one had used, down the steps, and over the brief walk whose slabs were so ill-aligned that rows of dandelions now grew between

them. He held his hand out to me and we shook. "By the way,"
I said as he got in the taxi, "what happened to your friend? The
one with the Iowa scarf and cap and sweatshirt?" He rolled down
the window and smiled: "He's living in Tampa. With the Boxer."
And with that the taxi went forward—down the tunnel of green
trees that gave to the street in front of our house such a genteel
and all-American air, and sheltered families more tightly bound
together than our own.

⌒ T H E   P E N T H O U S E

THE FIRST TIME I SAW ASHLEY MOORE he was floating over
Central Park in a balloon—in an advertisement in the *New York
Times* for Saks Fifth Avenue. He had just won the Coty Award at
the age of twenty-six and they were featuring his line of clothes
in their stores that year. Even though Ashley Moore was not his
real name, or even the first he'd attached to a label, he had, by
creating a designer dress that secretaries could afford, become
successful—after a series of flops—at a very young age. In the
photograph he is wearing a tuxedo and a smile as he tips a bottle
of champagne into the glass held by one of the models wearing
his dresses (a pair of twins he used to go dancing with at the
Twelfth Floor)—so handsome he looks like a thirties movie star;
he and the Chrysler Building, someone said at the time, were the
two most beautiful things in New York.

And, the day I saw that advertisement in the paper, he was
rich and famous, too—too famous to go to the places I did,

though one night at the Everard Baths that same year I heard a
ruckus, turned a corner, and saw Ashley standing in the hallway,
saying to a very handsome, dark-haired man with a thin mustache, who was lying on a bunk in a room with the door opened:
"What is this? I can't even get you on the phone, and here you
are reading the *Post* stark naked for everyone with the price of a
locker to *shtup*." That was the first time I heard Ashley's unnerving voice; as hard and flat as a frying pan he had just used to hit
you over the head. ("Next to Ashley," someone said, "Thelma
Ritter sang bel canto.") The man in the room was the Prince, I
learned later—Ashley's soon-to-be-ex-boyfriend, a beautiful Jew
who indeed used to read the newspaper at the baths while waiting
for someone to stop in, and who eventually, after opening up a
sandwich shop in Soho, met an accountant and moved to a suburb
in New Jersey—as far from Ashley as he could get. Ashley would
never have gone to the baths for any other reason; at least I never
saw him there again. He was living at the time with a famous
decorator in a part of town on the Upper East Side a friend used
to call "the Land of Ormolu," and his social life was fairly private.
Even when they came to Fire Island, for instance, they vanished
moments after walking ashore from the seaplane; nor did Ashley
ever dance at the Sandpiper, or stroll the beach—he remained all
weekend inside a vast oceanfront compound people called "the
House of Pain" (because meals there were as formal as state dinners) in a harem of one, completely invisible to the outside world.

The world that he worked in, however, was becoming increasingly visible in the late seventies, which is when I saw it for the
first time after a friend got a few of us invitations to a fashion
show Michaele Vollbracht was having on a covered pier on the
Hudson River, where we sat down a few rows from the elevated
runway. The place was mobbed. The lights dimmed. Rows of
gaunt, grave people leaned forward with expectant faces. The
music began. The models walked out in sequined clothes with a

circus motif, turned, walked back again. There were lights, music, a sense of drama, and a well-dressed, attentive audience. "But no script," said my friend when it was over, echoing my thoughts. "It was everything you get in the theater except the play. They had nothing but the clothes on their backs."

"That's fashion," said the publicist who had brought us.

"I think it's mostly about evening," a woman was saying to a TV reporter in the aisle to our right. "I think it's a very American collection, rooted, of course, in couture, but still very much of New York of today. I think it's about the past *and* a new way to be modern."

"Oh please. This show isn't about anything," the publicist muttered to us as we filed past her, "but selling rags. At least Ashley never pretends that it's anything else."

He knew Ashley, and his was the next show he took us to: Ashley's last, as it turned out, in a large room at the Fashion Institute of Technology. He had just sued his backers for a large sum of money, and whether or not he knew the outcome of his lawsuit that night, you could tell he was mocking the whole milieu. Not only was there no music, drama, production values, or theme—the audience arrived on what, once you walked past a curtain, turned out to be the runway itself, so that you found yourself suddenly being stared at by everyone down below; a reversal of roles that was by no means a pleasant surprise for everyone—though Ashley, when I glanced down at him, seemed to be getting a kick out of the momentary shock on the arriving faces. Down on the floor, out of the glare, one walked among the dresses on mannequins as if in an atelier—dummies people ignored as they drank white wine and gossiped. It was Ashley's way of saying: no more spectacle, no more va-va-voom. These are the dresses, on dummies, inspect them if you like. The lawsuit against his backers had already been filed; when it was settled a month later he had no real reason to produce another line of clothes—financial, that is.

When asked if he missed his old life—it's rare for someone to retire at the age of thirty-two—he said: "You know? I *did* it, and I don't miss it." For a few months I don't think he even noticed its loss; like some star that sends light out far into the galaxy long after it has collapsed, his face was still in all six windows of I. Magnin's in San Francisco, and May Cohen's in Jacksonville, Florida—where, like an actor taking his show on the road, he went, the winter after his last fashion show, to emcee a charity auction, and to decorate a house in the annual tour of designer homes, and, in Huntsville, to chair a fashion show for a diabetes foundation. In Denver he went to the gay rodeo, in Milwaukee he appeared on a talk show, and then one day, after that gave out, he returned to Manhattan, to find that his career was not even talked about. ("I *used* to be famous," he always told his tricks.) And so, just when his colleague Halston went on to introduce Ultrasuede and make appearances with Liza Minnelli, Elsa Peretti, and Victor Hugo at Studio, Ashley moved downtown and retired to a penthouse.

The penthouse he rented commands the north side of Abingdon Square, like some fortress castle, overlooking what was the heart of gay life in 1980, the Village. The previous owner had been a drug dealer named Norman Pearl—a man who would flood the terrace in winter and hold ice-skating parties where all the guests, on LSD, went whirling around to Donna Summer. The building had a canopy, a mirrored lobby, and a doorman, and the triangular park across the street gave it a sort of Upper East Side elegance; while only a few blocks away were things the Upper East Side did not have—the abandoned piers along the river where sex could be had at all hours of the day and night, and, a few blocks in other directions, back-room bars like the Toilet and the Strap. Ten stories up, on the terrace of the penthouse, however, one felt above it all.

And you were: The penthouse itself was not large, but the

terrace, five times its size, had views of the river and harbor. On a summer night, sitting inside while the wind buffeted the canvas awnings, people felt, surrounded by its white candlelit walls, as if they were in a house on the coast of Turkey; or, gazing down at Wall Street's lighted towers from the terrace outside, as if it weren't a cottage at all but a ship that had been anchored off a steep, volcanic island just east of the World Trade Center, an island you might swim to on the right drug. In other words, the place was enchanting; the reason people went when he asked them—the penthouse.

He had them come over, I suspect now, the way a decorator furnishes a library with books that the owners will never read but which are an essential element of the decor. It's not that Ashley was unread—he could quote by heart Somerset Maugham—but he must have felt some desire for an intellectual life (if only the ambience) when, the first night he had twenty of us to dinner, he looked up, seated on a pillow underneath the spot-lighted Hurrell photograph of Joan Crawford that hung above the mantelpiece, and said: "This is what I like. I want my table surrounded with writers and drag queens and hustlers and professors. You know? Berlin in the thirties. Paris in the twenties. I want the *mix*." Some mix! Louis, who worked the door at Studio 54 two nights a week and was so obsessed with fashion models he had constructed a little altar in his bedroom to a Bruce Weber discovery he was stalking named Jeff Aquilon; his roommate, a limousine driver equally obsessed with Jackie Onassis; a novelist who'd not published a thing since his first book eight years ago; a professor from Rutgers writing a book on Edith Wharton; a drag queen named Honeypot Larue whose boyfriend was a bouncer at Xenon; a drug dealer named Doctor Love who'd burned down a town house on Bank Street after the landlord caught him manufacturing angel dust there and kicked him out; a young decorator who spent most of that summer recuperating from a chin implant that kept shifting; two even younger graduates of FIT who, after a year spent selling clothes at Macy's, decided it would be easier to work as hustlers; Victor, the author of a book on Hollywood's treatment of homosexuals, whose lectures in local bookstores Ashley attended dressed like a beatnik at Deux Magots, with a black beret and scarf round his neck, until Ashley started having people over to see the slide show in his penthouse—the only person Ashley deferred to on the subject of the movies (though that had its limitations: "I never sleep with people who know more about the movies than I do," Ashley always said when someone asked if he and Victor were lovers).

The penthouse was perfect for such an evening—even if Ashley had not invited the people who came there. ("You know," he said to Victor after hosting his thirty-eighth birthday party, "your friends are nicer than my friends.") It was nearly devoid of furniture—some potted jade plants, a mirrored wall against which eight gilt ballroom chairs guarded a low, black-lacquered table, and big white canvas pillows guests sat on when they ate—and therefore easy to use for lectures and soirees. "The seventies were about lounging," Ashley explained to us in that hard, flat voice our first night there, just days after that decade's expiration. "It was about banquettes and Quaaludes. The eighties will be about conversation. That's why I got these chairs where you have to sit up straight, and sparkle. I expect everyone to sparkle," he said to his visitors, striking them dumb with fears of inadequacy instead. As for the chairs themselves, or the rent on the penthouse, there was one rule: One asked no questions. When someone gasped, "Where did you *get* these chairs?" he was ignored. ("Why should I tell him where I got the chairs?" he said in that steely voice. "He can't afford them. What's the point?") You learned very quickly: His cat didn't like being touched, and Ashley didn't like being queried on any subject. This introduced a certain tension. When that same evening the decorator asked Ashley, over dinner, why Gloria Vanderbilt had been turned down by the co-op board of River House, Ashley put down his chopsticks, glanced at the cat, pointed to the man, and said: "Kill, Doris. Kill!" Then he droned, over our nervous laughter: "Some people want to know how the Incas built those incredible walls in Cuzco, or why fog forms, or how the stars still emit light even after they've died—George wants to know why River House told Gloria to take a hike." And George started to choke so badly on his noodles he had to go to the bathroom and throw up.

We were invited that first night to Ashley's to watch the opening episode of a series on PBS called *I, Claudius,* broadcast that winter, though as the novelist muttered to me when we passed each other in the hall: "This is the closest any of us will ever come to the court of Caligula, and I don't mean what's on TV."

"You got that right," an emphatic voice said; we looked and saw Honeypot Larue powdering his nose in front of a mirror in Ashley's bedroom. "He always makes you wonder—who's next?"

"It's not that," said the professor in a low voice as he joined us, "it's that he doesn't bother to pretend—it's rather refreshing, almost exhilirating, in a way, the refusal to observe the niceties. He has simply stripped away the genteel *politesse.*"

"I agree," said the novelist. "No doubt because he's operated in the business world, a world where politeness has no function, where money is money. That's why he's ended up sounding like—" He stopped, then said: "I'm not sure what it is he sounds like. He sounds like—"

"A gangster," said Honeypot Larue, still fluffing before the mirror.

The novelist and the professor stared at him.

"Look," said Honeypot, "I don't know why you're bothering to figure him out—it's very simple. He's mean! He's a mean queen and that's all there is to it!"

"What do you mean?" said the professor.

"I mean, she's mean," he said. "Look. Here's an example. I ran into him last night on Christopher Street on my way home from the Strap. He said, 'Hi, you!' " He paused, powder puff in hand, and looked over at us. "You know, of course, he doesn't know any of our names—that's why when you see him out somewhere, he always yells, 'Hi, you.' He asked what I was doing. I said I'd just been at the Strap. He said: 'A pretty thing like you wasting your seed there!' And I thought: That's the first nice thing he's ever said to me."

"Nice?" said the novelist.

"That I was a pretty thing," he said. "Hang around, you'll see. You can't enjoy yourself here because you never know what he's going to say next. I think I prefer a slightly more romantic approach," said Honeypot Larue.

"But you see," said Louis breathlessly at our backs, "that's Ashley. Ashley isn't romantic. He has no illusions. Ashley is very direct," he said in a hushed, worshipful tone.

Ashley was very direct. When the professor from Rutgers asked him another question later that evening over dessert, we all went mute. We were sitting on the pillows eating blanc mange when the professor noticed the floor-to-ceiling bookcase behind Ashley filled entirely with bound volumes of *Vogue* magazines stretching back to the twenties, and he said, in the ecstatic voice of someone who has just seen an unexpected explanation for the universe: "Do you mean you do *research* the way I do for an article? You mean you look at old copies of *Vogue* for ideas, you actually study them?" And Ashley, putting down his champagne, gave him that look which only a basilisk has and—after a beat, and a raised eyebrow—replied: "How many ways do you think there are to make *shmatte*?" That was all Ashley ever said about his profession.

His profession actually was increasingly academic. He still spoke of going uptown occasionally to a party at Halston's or Giorgio Sant'Angelo's, or to dinner with Fabrice, but he was no longer working, in a city that does little else during the day. He spoke on the phone with the people who'd helped him during his career—the backers who still wanted to introduce something with his name on it (anything, apparently), the magazine editors, columnists, models, and publicists with whom he'd partied when he was showing a line twice a year. But that was all he did, and when he hung up the phone, he found himself with people who were much more fascinated than he was with fashion and excited to be in the company of one of its names. Our fantasy was Ashley—even if we were all afraid of his turning his attention on us, and could not understand what he was doing with us in the first place, so far from the Land of Ormolu. Then one afternoon it occurred to me. I was riding my bike down the old West Side Highway, eye level with the upper story of the rotting piers that bordered it, when I stopped to watch a man silhouetted in the broken windows of a pier waiting for someone to approach him, and then I looked over at Ashley's penthouse, its green-and-white-striped awnings shining in the sun, like a cruise ship that was indeed anchored off some island to let its passengers go ashore. It was the only tall building over there; there was nothing between it and the river to impede its view of the Hudson and the piers; it seemed to both snub, and preside over, the black roofs beneath it—part of the Village but not quite. And I realized why Ashley was there—for the same reason we were, though I never actually saw him at the piers, or in the bars (one could not imagine Ashley standing in the Ramrod like everyone else, waiting), and never asked him, when I arrived at the penthouse, God forbid, what he had done that day with his wealth, good looks, and freedom . . . even when he complained one afternoon, "The only people who cruise me are middle-aged Chinese businessmen and nine-foot-tall Puerto Rican transvestites," since this obviously was a joke. Ashley was very handsome—a square-jawed, all-American, masculine-appearing, corn-fed blond—though you never knew, when the door to the penthouse opened, whether this masculine-looking all-American would be standing there bare-chested in camouflage fatigues, dog tags, and paratrooper boots, or in a Titian-blue ball gown by Charles James, looking like a debutante on the Cunard line in 1933. Sometimes it was both. ("The trouble with you," we overheard him tell a young art critic that evening, "is that you're afraid to let the *woman* in you out! Haven't you ever been running down the boardwalk in the Pines and felt your tits bobbing? Forget this article you're trying to finish on Matisse—do one on Dovima!")

Nevertheless, whatever he wore you never commented on it—Ashley trusted a compliment no more than he liked a question. You let him lead you without a word into the penthouse in his fireman's boots, gold lamé jockstrap, and diamond earrings to a terrace full of people who were equally speechless and thus looked even more, when they turned toward you, like the cover for an album by the Village People. (The penthouse was often crowded with men who dressed not as what they were but what they were hoping to attract; as if the object of their sexual fantasy was only looking for a mirror image of himself. The FIT graduate who could talk for an hour about what to look for in a moisturizer dressed like a pipe fitter on an offshore oil rig; the novelist like a Puerto Rican boxer on the skids, the drug dealer like an invest-ment banker at Morgan Guaranty, the Edith Wharton scholar like a Hell's Angel from upstate New York.) Then there was the core group—the ever present scattering of men with dark mus-taches and dark eyes, as perfectly matched as a necklace of black pearls: Ashley's type, or rather attempt to replace the Prince (home before the TV with his hubby in suburban New Jersey). "Where does he *get* these people?" the novelist asked one evening.

"He gets them in those Chinese-Cuban restaurants on Eighth Avenue," Louis said. "He walks right in when he sees a cute one, when they're eating alone, and invites them down. I was with him today when he did it! He found one in the elevator in Mario Buatta's building, he finds 'em everywhere, he could find one in the Arctic Circle!" he said with a whoop. "His type is very definite. He found one in Georgia last week! We were returning from Thomasville, through all these white, WASP towns, and when we got to Atlanta, Ashley got out of the taxi, took one look at the men waiting for cabs, and said, 'Mmm, Jews.' You have to look like the Prince to get in bed with *him*."

The bed was in a room you saw when you went to use the bathroom; in the corner, with black sheets and pillowcases, surrounded by a weight bench and bar bells, and high heels scattered on the floor, and curtains stirring at the windows whose light made it a luminous and shadowed lair that made you think of a spider, a spider that devoured its mate, since his consort was never around for very long. Each Sunday that winter when we went over to watch the latest episode of *I, Claudius,* and eat Chinese takeout, we would find the previous boyfriend gone, or looking abashed; few of them lasted any longer than an emperor's sister on the BBC. Those trips down to earth produced a constantly changing cast of characters who paradoxically all looked alike—strangers who were brought up to the penthouse and then dropped just as quickly. None was conventionally handsome, at least compared to the perfection of the Prince. I remember a slightly overweight statistician from Staten Island, a shoe salesman from Bayonne, an orthodontist from the Five Towns, and a Cuban who was famous on Fire Island for his deep voice and donkey dick. But none of them, not even the last, endured. ("He asked me if we were having an affair," I overheard Ashley say one night as he came into the kitchen. "I told him, 'We're having a sexual encounter.' ") The only way to keep going to the penthouse, it seemed, was not to become a trick, or even a favorite; I knew people were doomed when Ashley went up to them and showed them a photograph he'd ripped out of a French fashion magazine and said: "I saw this and thought of you." (Fatal words!) No one survived this sentence; he tasted and moved on; it was unnerving even to be walked to the door, much less have him wait for you in the doorway while the elevator came up— staring at you as he stood there with one arm on his hip and the other on top of the door, like Elizabeth Taylor in the poster for *Cat on a Hot Tin Roof.* The minute the doors closed on the eleva- tor, people let out sighs of relief.

Sometimes Ashley walked out with us when we left the build- ing—wearing Thierry Mugler or Kansai, and a little black leather jacket from Gaultier he'd brought back from Paris that looked confusingly like something sold on the rack in a New Jersey mall. "Whadda ya think? Am I overdressed for evening?" he would ask, not expecting a reply. We didn't know what he expected, especially when he decided to stay with us and prowl the town. (When out with Ashley, we were told to call him "Clem," unless there was a line at the door, whereupon he used his real name and we all got in immediately.) "I know two new wave queens on Fourteenth Street who are having a party," Louis said as we walked out one night. "We could go there. But I hate new wave. I hate the clothes, the music, the look." After a beat, Ashley said: "It has aspects." An hour later, we were there. Of course, the rest of the week he had other, better places to go, one felt: the life we read about in the *Post.* The dinner for Karl Lagerfeld, the party at Lutèce. Whatever was on Page Six. Ashley talked to two women every day—his mother, and Claudia Cohen. What minor gossip the entourage brought back every Sunday night when we assem- bled to watch *I, Claudius* Ashley listened to with a stone face and expressionless eye. There wasn't much he didn't know. The only person he seemed curious about—and listened to—was the novel- ist, and he brought no gossip whatsoever, because he'd spent all day sitting home trying to think of something to write, and didn't even try to provide what everyone thought Ashley wanted.

Nobody could. I was happiest in the kitchen, rinsing dishes after dinner before *I, Claudius* began, while Louis loaded the dishwasher beside me; out of range of whatever it was that made being at the penthouse so nerve-racking. (The novelist dubbed the place "The House of Good Taste and Bad Manners," two things often in conjunction, he said, in New York and Los Angeles. But that didn't explain it.) It was as if Ashley had gone to all that effort to create this beautiful space—the bleached floors and striped awnings, the lilies in a spotlight—like some insect that waits at the bottom of a flower only to devour anything foolish enough to be beguiled by its beauty; as if the beauty was the object, and our appreciation of it a minor detail. He was one of those people who put a great effort into hospitality and then, once the guest has arrived, begins to extract a price for it all. At least that's what it felt like even in the relative safety of the kitchen, while the party went on in the candlelit living room, where Ashley sat surrounded by a circle of men with mustaches and dark good looks.

The Prince was still Ashley's main topic when we met him. "Real men don't move their hands and arms around when they talk," Ashley said to someone one night. "They sit entirely still. Have you ever seen the Prince? He hardly moves a muscle. He's like Mount Rushmore. It makes me crazy." "I saw the Prince," said the bouncer. "In Soho." "People go by his shop just to see him through the window," said Ashley. "He makes sandwiches. He makes cakes. He's a big success. He won't take my calls." One day, lying in the sun on the terrace, he said to the novelist, "I think the Prince was it. I don't think I'll ever have another boyfriend." "Why not?" said the novelist. "Because I'll never find anyone like him. And even if I could—I'd drive him away, the way I lost the Prince. I've got money, looks, fame, and a big cock. Who can have sex with me?" he said, turning to the novelist, his forehead beaded with sweat, his eyes invisible beneath two slices of cucumber, his head covered in a towel wrapped as a turban. "It's not that," said the novelist. "It's not what you are. It's what you're not that's your problem."

"What am I not?" said Ashley.

Everyone held his breath; but the novelist, without even looking at Ashley, said: "You're not—vulnerable. The problem with you, Ashley, is that you haven't got any problems. You're too successful. You have no depth."

"So what should I do?" said Ashley. "Invest unwisely? Dress like Iggy Pop?"

"No," said the novelist, "but—"

"But what?" said Ashley, putting on more Bain de Soleil.

"You need some problems," he said.

"I've had my problems," said Ashley. "I've had my ups and downs."

"You have?" said the novelist.

"I've had lawsuits," said Ashley, "dresses that bombed, friends burning to death on foam-rubber mattresses, hair loss, bankruptcy, boyfriends who wouldn't commit, lovers who ripped my head off when I set the table wrong. I lived for eight years in the House of Pain."

"Well," said the novelist, "you seem to have survived it all with no permanent sadness."

"What's that?" said Ashley. "A bad Tony?"

"It's Lucretius," said the novelist. "Tears are in the nature of things. Which is why this is so hard to take," he said, waving an arm at the terrace. "It has no tragic vision."

"Please," said Ashley. "You get up and you throw some flowers in a vase, or, if you're Jeanne Moreau, in the salad," he said, referring to a movie we'd seen the night before, "you put Chanel Number Nine on your tush, and call a boyfriend for lunch. What's so difficult? The one thing I've never understood is the desire to suffer. Life's bad enough. Just yesterday I had a tragic vision—when I ran into Julio Ramirez. It was a horrible shock."

"Cancer?" said the decorator, leaning forward.

"What cancer?" said Ashley. "He shaved his mustache off."

"*No!*" gasped the decorator.

"They're all doing it," said Ashley. "Armando shaved his off last month. Now his whole set has done it and it's starting to spread. You watch. All it leaves are these thin, wounded little mouths. These prim lips. What people refuse to accept is that they look best one way, and when they find that, like Perry Ellis, they should stick to it—no matter what—till the day they die. It's called 'classic.' But no, people think it's time for something new. So we're going to see thousands of thin, wounded little mouths in the coming months! *Brace* yourself. Have you been to the Boy Bar?"

"No," said the novelist.

"They would die before they grew a mustache," said Ashley. "Everything about them is thin and wounded. Not just the lips."

"There's a new bar on Second Avenue," said the decorator, "that's even worse! It looks like an art gallery—all white, with blinding lights. I walked by it last night. I felt like a vampire!"

"That's how you're supposed to feel," said Ashley. "They don't want to look at you. They want to look at each other. So they turn up the lights. They make every moment last call. Because they know that makes you feel like Bela Lugosi."

"But why?" said the decorator. "It's so mean!"

"Of course it's mean," said Ashley. "They want our apartments. I see them sitting in cafes on St. Marks Place, all in black. They look like a Jules Feiffer cartoon. You want to go up to them and say: 'Are you aware this has been done?' But you don't, because it would be a waste of time. They don't know Feiffer. All they know is *Gilligan's Island.* They've spent their whole childhoods watching TV. It's made them ironic. And thin and wounded. Not just the lips."

"Some of them are cute," said Louis.

"Some of them could sit on my face and I'd be a very happy woman," said Ashley. "But very few. Because there's one problem."

"And that is—" said the professor.

"They would die before they'd grow a mustache. Which is unfortunate for those of us who like them. If women had mustaches, I'd be straight. My idea of a man—forgive me if I'm narrow-minded—involves a mustache."

"But you don't have a mustache," said the decorator.

"Exactly," said Ashley. "Some of these kids are shaving their bodies, too. They've got hair on their head, and hair on their balls, and nothing in between. They're into retro and Nair. Victor runs around with them now. They love Victor. They get to talk about movies *and* be political. I watched his demonstration on West Street yesterday through my binoculars. They were yelling at cops on horses—like Streisand in *The Way We Were*."

"I wouldn't get near a cop on a horse," barked the gay postcard tycoon. "The horse could kick, and ruin your hair plugs."

"Victor goes right up to the nag," said Ashley. "He lives for these confrontations. He loves these kids. He brings them by before the demonstrations. I serve them lunch."

"But what do they *make* of all this?" said the decorator.

"They walk right out and stare at the view," said Ashley. "They don't even see the rest. They couldn't care less about the bleached floors, or the chinoiserie, or the Coromandel. They don't get the references to Chanel. They're like Ninotchka—little Communists. They wear black, Levi's cutoffs, and shoes that would crack a fire hydrant. They look like ICBMs. They're out to kick ass. Something I've never wanted to do, personally. There's other things you can do with ass. So tell me about Proust," he said, turning to the novelist, who had promised to give Ashley a reading list. "What's his *shtik*?"

"His *shtik*?" said the novelist, raising his eyebrows.

"In twenty-five words or less," said Ashley.

"Well . . . ," said the novelist. "Proust is a man who went to a party—and then went home and wrote a book about what was wrong with it. Which is essentially what all novelists do," he said. "We go to a party and then tell why it was awful."

"Like Victor and the movies."

"Yes," said the novelist. "Victor sees movies morally—in terms of homophobia."

"Oh please," said Ashley impatiently. "So what if Franklin Pangborn's a little nelly in *Flying Down to Rio*? Who cares what straight people think about us? I don't care if they understand what I do in bed. *I* don't even understand what I do in bed, I could care less what *they* think about it. Straight people's opinions don't interest me, and the only reason what we do interests them," he said, wiping the lenses of his little dark glasses with white frames, "is because they're so deeply bored. I think you're bored," he said, turning to the novelist.

"I am," said the novelist, sitting up and blushing, as if he'd been found out. "Something is over. I feel I've stayed too long at a party, only I don't know where to go next. So I stay. But something is over."

"So find what's starting," said Ashley.

"Not this new wave stuff!" said the novelist, sitting forward. "I refuse to go to the Mudd Club and wear safety pins in my ears, or go to Roxy and roller-skate to what's left of disco. I think it *all* sucks!"

"Don't be so picky," said Ashley. "So hard to please. It's like the pier. If I see something I like, I take my bike, go downstairs, and race over—he may be gone, or taken, or had a sex change by the time I get there, but I made the effort, and there'll be someone else. It's like fashion. Of the moment. Though I'm working harder at the pier than I ever did on Seventh Avenue. It's difficult to have sex when you can have it any hour of the day or night.

That's why I don't live in San Francisco. As it is, I'm spending too much time on the pier. The pier is not for people with short attention spans. I won't even wait for a table at Mortimer's. What am I doing at the piers? I'll tell you what I'm doing at the piers. I'm looking for the Prince. Who doesn't go to the piers. Who's living in New Jersey. While I'm meeting schmucks."

"I'm not meeting anyone," said the decorator.

"Wait till your chin settles," said Ashley.

"Is that all it takes?" said the professor. "Because I'm not meeting anyone either!"

"Because you have a brain," said Ashley. "You're better off. Listen," he said. "If you end up the same way after sleeping with them that you were *before* you slept with them, why sleep with them? It just means you have to change the sheets."

"But sleeping with them is heaven," said the novelist.

"Whose heaven?" said Ashley. "Heaven is going around the world this fall on the *QE2*. Did I tell you Louis and I are going around the world on the *QE2*? This fall. He'll be my escort. God knows I've got the dresses for a cruise."

No one said a word—torn between their registration of this addition to Ashley's glamour, and the realization that, come autumn, all this would be ending. Then Ashley put the binoculars down and said, "What do you think about salad?" and looked at the entourage.

"What do *you* think about salad?" the professor said, with the beatific smile of a baby, so happy to be at Ashley's penthouse about to have lunch that he had forgotten the cardinal rule.

"What do *I* think about salad?" said Ashley in a dark voice. "I know what *I* think about salad. I want to know what *you* think about salad. I could care less if I ever saw lettuce again in my life."

There was a silence in which all the hospitality had collapsed, like a soufflé, and even the professor's smile curdled on his face;

but then the doorbell rang, and Ashley left the terrace. "Oh, *cooool!*" we heard the new arrival say in a deep voice, "A real penthouse! I've never seen a penthouse! You really live here?" and Ashley reply in his flat monotone: "You could say so. But it's a constant effort. People think you have a penthouse the way you have a T-shirt. But you don't. It's work all day long." And then onto the terrace came Ashley, Victor, and the new face—a big, hairy young man wearing a black T-shirt that said VENCEREMOS, and a yarmulke; the latest object of Ashley's eyes.

Someone who refused to come to the penthouse (and claimed our host was a "disgrace to his profession!") said that Ashley Moore surrounded himself with people he could dominate—that we were all losers—but this seemed slightly reductive. The new arrival, whose father ran a yeshiva, was quite bright; even if all we discussed that day was Crawford's performance in *Mildred Pierce*. No one, at Ashley's, ever discussed serious subjects. Nobody there wanted to. The staffer at the UN didn't want to talk about famine relief in Africa, for instance, or the city attorney about problems facing New York, or Ashley about fashion; they all wanted to listen to the hustlers talk about their johns, or Honeypot Larue tell us why the big, beefy bouncers from Brooklyn wanted to go home with him and not a real woman. The two FIT graduates who had quit Macy's to hustle ("We're still in retail!") but now spent the day sitting at home waiting for the phone to ring; the novelist, who spent the day staring at the walls of his tiny apartment on West Street waiting for an idea; even Victor, and his disciple, the young gay militant, spent that afternoon in a deep discussion of whether this winter's coat for gay men would be the green nylon bomber with the orange lining.

"I remember car coats," said Ashley at one point. "Car coats on men walking their dogs on Fifty-third Street while the dogs peed. With bombers, you can see the butt and basket. With car coats, you were always guessing." I could not imagine Ashley guessing. The most unsettling thing about Ashley, someone said, was that he knew exactly what he wanted in a world where most of us do not.

The latter category, he said, included the people who came to the penthouse; we were like dancers between songs who slow down and even stop while trying to decide if the new theme being introduced is worth dancing to. The novelist was right. The year we went to Ashley's was a strange time: Something was ending, but nothing had replaced it, and Ashley's penthouse seemed like an oasis. Outside, the city seemed increasingly cold—the bigger the dance club, the colder it was. Bond's—as big as an airplane hangar—featured, the night Ashley took us to the opening, not only a row of dancing fountains, but so much fake fog the guests refused to evacuate when a real fire started because they thought it was an effect. At the Gilded Grape we danced beneath ten Puerto Ricans in gilded G-strings on trapezes. At Le Club we ran into people like Ashley's former business partner, now a cable TV hostess, writhing on the floor between the legs of a Turkish wrestler covered in olive oil. ("Listen," said Ashley before the decorator could speak, "don't complain. It keeps her off the street and off the phone.") At Twelve West I walked in one night to find Ashley and Patti LaBelle judging the Mister Blueboy Contest. After the winner (a sobbing bartender from Ohio) was announced, people started dancing to a medley from *My Fair Lady* set to a disco beat. At Roxy they were roller-skating to the music. Even the fashion shows—the novelist said—were empty and meaningless. ("There was a woman weeping," said the novelist when we got to the penthouse one night. "*Weeping.*" "She weeps at all of them," Ashley said. "Except Stephen Sprouse. They had a fight.") Our visits to the penthouse, after all, took up only a small portion of our lives—Sunday nights, the occasional afternoon; the rest of the time we were out in the city, and the city in 1980 was changing.

Sometimes, on a weeknight, I would see the professor—whose

chief activity, now that he was on sabbatical, seemed to be avoiding his book—at a bar like Ty's or the Eagle. It was odd seeing another member of the entourage in these places. We hadn't much in common with each other—only that we went to Ashley's—and since what we had in common could be viewed from so many angles, even remarks about our host were tentative and brief. There was no way of knowing, after all, if the other person admired, or despised, Ashley—found him the acme of glamour or vulgarity. Ashley himself was a hybrid. Raised by a dancer at the Copacabana whose husband—a cowboy she had met on his way to Germany during World War Two—had died before Ashley was born; raised to be, in essence, a showgirl, I wonder if Ashley himself knew what he was. "I'm sorry we didn't have more time to get to know each other," a playwright who'd been Ashley's neighbor on Fire Island one summer said when I overheard them talking on the terrace. "It's just as well," said Ashley. "If we'd spent time together, you'd have seen right through me, and then you'd have hated me."

We were all confused that year—the professor in the window of Ty's, ignoring the room as he stared at the empty street outside, wasn't just a man looking out the window of a bar on a slow night; he was all of us, waiting for something new. Christopher Street was deserted on weeknights now. The young queens preferred the East Village, where, on St. Marks Place, a group called Fags Against Facial Hair had stenciled on the sidewalk the words CLONES, GO HOME. Even at the Cockring, the last of the small dance clubs, whose floor was the size of Ashley's bedroom, they were starting to play music that brought the dancers to a halt, like hunters in a ballet some witch has cast a spell upon; songs so raw, barbed, snotty we would hang our heads and walk off the floor—leaving a single, scrawny youth in baggy clothes bouncing around like a corpse being given electric shocks to bring it back to life. His movements took up a lot of space. The dance looked childish and affected—a spoiled brat's tantrum—as if he resented, not enjoyed, being in New York. Even Louis, who loved every new thing, hung around the penthouse after Studio, unless Ashley wanted to go out. Eventually the penthouse became for us what an embassy must be for frightened travelers in a country undergoing a revolution, a place where it was reassuring, no matter what was going on outside, to hear Ashley tell newcomers as he led them through the room, "There are only two looks now, Chinese and modern. This is a little bit of both." Occasionally he tried to help the people who seemed most stuck. After watching Louis, for instance, who could not live on what he earned two nights at Studio, walk up the beach at Fire Island one day telling friends on blankets that he needed a job, Ashley said when he got back, "The trouble with you is that you know five thousand queens from the Pines and Studio, but what you need to know are five people who can actually give you a job." (Of course no one knew quite what Louis did; the little business card he had printed said merely "Consulting.") Finally Ashley hired Louis himself as an assistant—though all that seemed to entail was hailing cabs when they went out. But the decorator he got a client. The hustlers he recommended to a madam in the East Fifties. The drug dealer he sent to Minneapolis to dry out. The limo driver he found work for with a woman who lived in the apartment beneath Jackie O. And Victor—who still lived in an apartment with a tub in the kitchen—he got a new shower and bathroom, designed by the decorator, though not without demanding a strict accounting of costs before reimbursing him. ("She's the cheapest white woman on the planet!" the decorator fumed. "Those ballroom chairs he has? They're rented from a catering firm! She lives in perpetual terror that she's going to be taken advantage of! She never leaves the apartment unless it's free! I'm writing a book—called *Decorating for Jews*!" "Ashley isn't Jewish," said the novelist. "Who cares?" said the decorator, and stomped out of the room.) The shower and bathroom were the exception—most of what he did was, very astutely, tell people what they should do to get on with their lives.

Even the novelist—whom he respected in a way he did not the others, because, someone said, Ashley wanted to be a writer (and the novelist wanted to be a designer)—needed, in Ashley's eyes, a fundamental change. "For instance, let's start with basics. Where do you live?"

"At West Street and Bank," he said.

"In Bob Ritter's building?"

"Yes."

"The police call that building 'Love, American Style,'" said Ashley as he fastened a small faux pearl clip earring to his ear. "Because it's filled with hookers and fags and freaks."

"That's what I am," said the novelist.

"No, you're not," said Ashley. "You're a Princeton graduate. You're a nice Ivy League boy living *la vie bohème*. You want to live in a place your parents can never visit. Well, you got it. The hallways in that building stink of piss. They're so narrow, you can't even go down them in a hat. You have to exit that building sideways in drag. I lived there in 1969. The apartments are tiny and someone is always throwing up in the mailbox. I have a prop-osition."

"Which is?" said the novelist.

"I may have to leave town at any moment," said Ashley. "Be-cause I'm in a pyramid."

"What's a pyramid?" asked the young yeshiva graduate.

"It's a Ponzi scheme," said Victor, intervening before Ashley could even consider telling the cat to kill him. "You put in five hundred or a thousand bucks, and you get your money back only when you bring somebody new into it. It's a way to double your money."

"The money's the least of it," said Ashley in his hard, flat tone, cutting back into the conversation like a buzz saw. "It's a reason to be social. It's for ladies who lunch. They get to dress up, go out, show off their Bill Blass, and dish. It's the latest version of mah-jongg. But it's illegal. Because the city doesn't want anyone making money unless it gets a cut. You can't go out at night in Thierry Mugler without getting beaten up, and they're upset about pyramids. Go figure. Anyway, they're going to raid one. In fact, they're going to raid ours, because we've got names that will make better copy for Page Six. The district attorney isn't stupid. He knows what makes the news. I've been advised to go away— till Morgenthau cools his chops. I've been asked to design Myra Blanchard's wedding in Montecito. I'm going to do *A Midsummer Night's Dream.* On a hilltop above Santa Barbara. And I want you to move in here. With Doris. I've got her food in the pantry. She's no problem. She doesn't even like to be touched."

"I can't," said the novelist.

"Why not?" said Ashley.

"I'd have to readjust to new surroundings," he said. "Besides, I use the people in my building as characters. I could never give them up."

"So what about you?" said Ashley, turning to Victor.

"I'd feel guilty," said Victor, squirming on his mat.

"Why?" said Ashley.

"I couldn't walk past the doorman," Victor said.

"Because?"

"He's a doorman," said Victor.

"What's wrong with that?" said Ashley.

"No one should be a doorman," said Victor. "I would never know what to say when I walked by him."

"Hello will do," said Ashley. "You don't have to discuss Marx."

"But he's older than I am," said Victor. "He shouldn't be a doorman."

"This is a free country," said Ashley. "Anyone who wants to

can be a doorman. And he makes a lot more money than you two do."

"Money isn't important to me," said the novelist.

"What is?" said Ashley.

"Beauty," said the novelist.

"Beauty!" Ashley barked.

"Creating art," said the novelist. "Or . . . trying to," he said, blushing.

"Forget art," said Ashley. "You need a book that will sell. Then worry about art. Nobody makes art thinking they're making art. It's the wrong way to go about it. The dresses Charles James made that are in the Brooklyn Museum he used to pin up on Puerto Ricans in the Chelsea Hotel. Because he loved to make dresses. First you have to make a dress, then *maybe* the dress is art. With a book, first you have to entertain." He raised his head and looked over at the novelist through the little white-rimmed sunglasses he was wearing beneath a lime green towel he'd wrapped around his head as a turban. "I could write a best-seller in a year," he said. "I would analyze what the current best-sellers have, sit down, and write one. That's what you should do. If you're going to write, write a blockbuster, like Jacqueline Susann. I can see you writing a blockbuster on this terrace. Take my advice—your apartment is holding you back. It's like heroin, rent control. You think you're a success because your rent's a hundred and twenty dollars a month. Don't let me be the first to tell you—this is not enough. You do not put on your tombstone: 'My apartment was rent-controlled.' You have to *do* something with your life."

"I just want a husband," said Honeypot Larue.

"That's all very nice, but don't hold your breath. You don't want a husband for a living. You do something else, and maybe a husband comes along," droned Ashley. "Do something while you're waiting. Do something new!"

"There is nothing new," said the novelist. "That's why you have all those back issues of *Vogue*. There is nothing new."

"There's slightly new," said Ashley. "There's new because they've forgotten what's old. There's new because Aaron just moved into Manhattan, and he wasn't here before." And he looked over at the new face, sweating in his yarmulke under the blazing sun.

The novelist lay there, as immobile as a stone. Then he said: "Why do the police call my building 'Love, American Style'?"

"Because no one even remotely straight lives in it," said Ashley.

"It's going co-op," said Victor.

"If the women's house of detention were standing," said Ashley, "it would be going co-op. And it would be a lot nicer than Love, American Style. You're supposed to look back on your days of struggle as basically a happy time. I don't. I hated every day I woke up in that apartment. I was poor. I hated being poor," he said. "I still can't decide which would be worse in life—to be poor or to have a small cock," he said.

And with that sally the terrace fell silent, while I stared at the source of this philosophy—our host, streaming with sweat like a golden idol, his eyes covered with cucumber slices. Victor closed his eyes and sighed. The novelist and the professor looked at one another. And then I saw the novelist look at Ashley—with a faint grimace I attributed to the brilliant light, but which may have been more than that. A siren was heading downtown in the street below; a tug was pushing a barge up the river; the sky itself was dead white; it was one of those moments of sudden stillness when you realize everything you have been saying, and doing, is a waste of time, and you want to leave immediately. But no one did, till four o'clock anyway, when Ashley had to get ready for the people in his pyramid, scheduled to arrive at six. It was a big surprise when I opened the *Post* two days later and saw the headline: Ashley vanished, it turned out, the way he appeared—in the pages of a newspaper. Only this time it was an article about his indictment by the district attorney.

That was the end of the penthouse—or the seventies, if you prefer. That was the last I saw of Ashley, at any rate. He spent two nights on Riker's Island and the rest of the summer in Santa Barbara. The person he sublet the penthouse to—a tall, angelic-looking man whose chief claim to fame was having produced the Sleaze Ball—alienated Ashley from the landlord somehow, and when Ashley returned to Manhattan in the fall, the penthouse had new locks. Walking past the building the following winter it was obvious someone else had moved in; there were tiny white lights strung along the terrace, and a blue glow under the eaves—a note that might have made sense at some party in the Pines but looked tacky in the city.

Of course, anyone who leaves a city as I did expects to find everything just as he left it when he returns. But though I went back to New York the following decade—sometimes just to buy a pair of shoes I was sure I could find nowhere else—I inevitably learned that Hudson's, on Fourth Avenue, no longer carried them; and the big, dusty room where old Jewish men had shuffled about, telling young Puerto Ricans to climb the ladders and get the shoe I wanted to try on (the one that went with plaid shirts), was now a brand-new gutted space with polished blond floors, white walls, ficus trees in pots, and piped-in disco music. Everything was being upscaled. The same thing happened to Paragon on Broadway; and Unique Clothing. The final straw came the day I returned to Canal Jeans and was told they no longer carried painter's pants; in the strange way we personalize the discontinuation of products in a consumer culture, I felt someone had told me *I* was obsolete. This is a tale about fashion, after all.

The rest of the entourage gradually peeled away from the city during the decade that followed, I learned on my intermittent visits; the hustlers went to California, after trying Seattle—the perfect antidote to New York, they decided; one ended up in San Francisco and the other in Los Angeles. The man who stole the penthouse from Ashley eventually ran out of people to con and left New York for Minneapolis, where he ran a hair salon with Doctor Love. The decorator got a loft, redid it, but was then kicked out by the building's new owner because he had never obtained a proper lease. Ashley moved to a new apartment in one of the turrets of the Ansonia; then to an apartment with a room-mate in midtown, where he began making dresses again, though nothing apparently came of that.

Other things happened, of course—a certain look (jeans, black leather jacket) remained a constant on men downtown, but the draining of energy from the West to the East Village continued. The city decided to renovate parks that had been drug bazaars for most of the seventies. The Zeckendorf Towers went up on Union Square, obliterating one of my favorite views of the city: the clus-ter of spires, floodlit at night, that made one think, looking north from Astor Place, of Dresden. The line of people waiting to get into the Boy Bar got longer and longer. On St. Marks Place, and along Second Avenue, unlicensed merchants began selling old magazines, records, clothes, and books on bedspreads they laid out on the sidewalk, so that walking to the St. Marks Baths you had to pick your way through what seemed to be the scattered contents of a hundred children's closets. Then the St. Marks Baths closed, its two slender black doors vanishing beneath a thick paste of fliers for new wave bands, and people who had gone there started going to the Jewel, a movie house up the street, instead. And then the restaurant mania began—when everyone went out to dinner, since the theater was not worth going to, and they couldn't have sex anymore. And it seemed as if that was all there was to do in New York: eat in public.

Years passed. Then one day, last spring, I ran into the novelist in one of the big, new bookstores that have sprouted all over lower Manhattan, though it took me a few moments to recognize him. Standing at the magazine rack, he looked like a little old man, silver-haired, eyebrows entirely gray, shoulders hunched as he read a copy of *Face,* his mustache gone, revealing, as Ashley predicted of us all, a thin, wounded mouth. Walking out we passed a table on which Victor's book on Hollywood homophobia, just reissued, was displayed. "When was the last time you saw him?" I said when we were on the street. "At one of his lectures at the center," he said. "He asked half the people in the audience to stand up, and when they did, he said: 'This is how many of you will be dead in five years.' He and Ashley had a big fight about Act Up, and they never spoke again."

"And when was the last time you saw Ashley?" I said.

"In the Ansonia," he said. "He had this round room he got some guy to marbleize—and he invited a bunch of people over for drinks, hoping he could get it published in a magazine. I didn't stay very long," he said. "I didn't know anyone there except Ashley. He'd decided to become a decorator, he said. He had the personality of a decorator, I always thought. The eye, the taste, the desire to arrange things. Ashley loved to arrange things. You know how he tried to arrange *us.* Ashley was a control queen," he said as we strolled up Greenwich Avenue toward Eleventh Street. "Then he ran into something he couldn't control."

"When did he get sick?" I said.

"Just after Victor," said the novelist, "and Louis."

"And when did you last see Louis?"

"At Studio. He was wearing an overcoat. He looked ninety-five."

"And what happened to the professor?"

"Never wrote the book on Edith Wharton. Died five years ago in Key West."

"And the guy Louis lived with?"

"Became Jackie O's driver!" he said.

"You see," I said, "there are happy endings sometimes. People's dreams can come true."

"But then Jackie O died," he said.

"Well," I said. "How's the decorator?"

"Lives in a tiny place on Tenth Street," he said. "Never goes out."

"And Honeypot Larue?"

"Works for Merrill Lynch. Vice president," he said. "House on the Island, boyfriend, very muscular, three-piece suits and a beard."

"Honeypot with a beard!"

"Facial hair is coming back," said the novelist. "It had to. There's nothing else you can do."

"And what about you? Do you still go to fashion shows?" I said.

"Oh no," he said as we turned into Abingdon Square. "Fashion seems so tacky now. All these transparent tops. I think it's cruel to the models—some breasts shouldn't be exposed! But people are so desperate to be hip—they'll do anything. All anybody wants now is to push their product. This city has become very bourgeois. Haven't you noticed? It's incredibly boring. This younger generation is the worst of all. They're utterly materialistic. They all want a penthouse," he said as we stopped in front of Ashley's old building.

"Who's in Ashley's now?" I said.

"Some Korean businessman," he said. "I asked the doorman. I went in the other day just for old time's sake. But I couldn't wait to get out."

"Why?"

"Because it brought back all those afternoons sun-bathing with Ashley!" he said. "That awful time! Those lectures about writing like Jacqueline Susann. It all reminded me of how much time I wasted hanging around that place. How much time I've wasted, period. It's a time of life I'm rather ashamed of," he said. "That's why I was so relieved when I finally brought it to an end."

"Brought it to an end?" I said.

"Yes," he said, squinting up at the penthouse. "By turning Ashley in. The professor and I were the ones who called the cops and told them where the pyramid was meeting that day. We had to," he said. "We couldn't stand the vulgarity anymore. It really was all so very vulgar!" he said, with a frown, and then he shook his head and said good-bye.

For a city that counts fashion as one of its leading industries, the people and streets I'd been walking looked remarkably the same—besides the shaved heads and muscles, tattoos and ear-rings. The West Village itself was even more peculiar in that re-spect; watching the novelist walking up Hudson Street, it looked like a kind of ghost town, a stage set in an empty theater. The streets I took on my way to the river were utterly familiar—more restful, dignified, if possible, than before—the houses with their vine-covered grilles and high windows, exactly what had been here before gay men moved in, and then left for a new neighborhood to the north. The West Side Highway, from which I used to gaze at Ashley's penthouse, had long since been dismantled, and with it the piers and rotting warehouses—where now people walked upon the one remaining dock in the open air, the brilliant April sunshine, like figures in some painting by Seurat, on promenade. The whole side of the island was being redone—like a hotel room being made up for a new customer. West Street was torn up, and one had to walk that day along a narrow strip of wooden planks between a ditch and the doorways of the bars. Eventually, if news-paper reports were accurate, there would be some sort of park. At the moment it was still in transition, however, although to make this park the entire infrastructure of the world Ashley had come downtown to dip into had vanished; only the penthouse, still grandly surveying the roofs beneath it, remained, its gray granite shining in the sun, a vessel for another generation's dreams.

❧ Sunday Morning: Key West

He was sixteen the first time he went—he drove down from his hometown in North Florida with the boy next door. They ended up on a beach, a beach he could not identify now, since he now believes Key West has no beaches. There was a beach, at sixteen. He lay down on it, fell asleep in the sun, and got so burnt he had to be hospitalized when he returned home covered with fat, yellow blisters. That fall his friend next door joined the air force, and he went north to a university in New York.

The second time he went to Key West, someone yelled "Faggot!" at him—he was standing beside a fence opposite the cemetery, straddling a bicycle, when two men in a paint-scraped pickup truck went by and tossed the word out the window as if it had been a water bomb or a bunch of garbage. He couldn't remember anything else about that trip. He was astonished by the epithet because, though by now he *was* leading a homosexual life, he didn't think he looked it; but, like being cheated in Naples, it left him with an indelible impression of the place. He did not go back to Key West for fifteen years. He settled in New York and went to Fire Island instead, which had bigger and more beautiful beaches, and met a man there with whom he lived for a while. In other words, like everyone, he had his love. When he went home to Florida during this period, he heard the news of his high school friend next door—now stationed at an air force base near Frankfurt—and thought: Well, this is my air force, my adventure. He was content.

Then everything changed. The next time he went to Key West, his first memory—his friend's snow-white body in beige elastic bathing trunks that resembled a woman's girdle—had faded, but one thing still seemed true: Just getting there seemed to be the point. Key West had always, he thought, obtained most of its allure from the fact that it was the end of the road—specifically, A1A: the southernmost town in the United States, the last in a string of inhabited islands. The uninhabited islands kept going to the Dry Tortugas. By now he knew New Yorkers who had moved there and opened up shops. But he did not intend to look anyone up. He drove down for the day with a friend he was staying with in Miami. They parked the car, got out, went to see the crowd on the dock poised to applaud the sunset while men juggled coconuts and ate fire, and ran into a friend from Manhattan.

The friend from Manhattan who came up to him on the dock that visit was a good-natured drifter who took jobs only long enough to save money, quit, and then live in places like Key West a few months at a time. He was the only gay man Roger knew who had temporary-typed his way across the country—living in towns for two months as a New Face; a secretary with a room at the Y who spent his days in an office, his evenings in the baths, bars, parks, cruising. He looked, in the ruddy light of the big red sun setting behind the Australian pines on an offshore island, as if he'd run out of places to type. Gaunt cheeks, thin forearms, eyes that had a radioactive glow betrayed his inability to explore much more; Key West was obviously his last stop. They shook hands after a sunset that now seemed heavy with metaphor. Then he and the friend with whom he'd driven down went into a bar and, after one look at the Hawaiian shirts, deep tans, men dancing to canned disco music, they turned to each other and without a word headed for the car and drove back to Miami.

That was 1981. He left New York that fall to return home to Florida after his father had a stroke. By that time both the man he'd met on the dock in Key West and the friend he'd driven down with were dead. The boy next door was still in Germany. Roger listened, at the clothesline, to the mother tell him news of her son's trips to Egypt, Turkey, Austria, Sweden (to buy a Volvo), Garmisch (for Christmas vacation) with a vague sense of envy— but when his high school friend returned with his wife and daughter on a visit that summer, Roger watched him clean his collection of antique rifles at a picnic table in the yard next door and could not summon the courage or desire to go over and speak with him. The separate paths they'd followed in life seemed to have brought them to such different places.

He kept most people at a distance those years, in fact—even friends seemed to be nothing more than voices on the telephone. He'd return from the nursing home after feeding his father dinner and hear the phone ringing as he got out of the car in the garage. On the other end was one of his friends from New York telling him someone else was sick or dead. Or one of his friends from New York who now, like himself, lived elsewhere, some of them in California, some in South Florida. One of them—his former lover—went to Key West one winter to take a job in a restaurant, fell down and cracked his skull while drunk instead, and was taken in by two recovering alcoholics. He ended up staying. He complained, "You can't have a drink or sleep with anyone in this town without everybody knowing exactly how much you drank or what you did in bed," but he remained. And so Roger began living in Key West vicariously. They spoke on the phone at least once a week. Roger had no news—nothing happened, at least to him, in his town—but Lee had plenty. The first year he followed Lee's efforts to stay sober, the second year to persuade a man indifferent to him to be his lover, the third year to open a T-shirt shop, the fourth year to keep the business and love affair from destroying one another. Lee's struggles constituted an ongoing soap opera, better than *Dynasty*; Roger listened gratefully from the void of his own loneliness. Some nights on the telephone, the lure of Key West—that irrational appeal that survived even his knowledge of the place; its drunks, claustrophobia, lack of beaches—was so strong, he could almost hear the rustle of the palm fronds beside the porch on which Lee was talking to him. Some nights he ached to be where men cruised one another, had sex, argued, gossiped, talked about the soccer player from Berlin who'd just arrived in town. Instead he followed, on the phone, Lee's move from apartment to apartment, his struggle with the store, the fights and reconciliations with his lover, but declined Lee's invitation to come down. The newspapers said Key West had become a place for men with AIDS to die; it seemed to him the whole world had become that, and the safest place his house.

Then one day, in the winter of 1989, a Greek tanker struck a reef off the Keys—spilled oil, damaged the coral, made the evening news. That night while he sat before the television set with his bowl of spaghetti, NBC showed the reef the tanker had hit; a reef already damaged by pollution and the vandalism of tourists that nevertheless looked very alluring. Outside, it was a cold, damp, penetrating winter night. His sister had been telling him to take a trip. He decided everything would be all right if he could just go swimming in that turquoise sea above that reef—and he called Lee.

Changing planes in Miami the next day, he had a sudden longing to fly to Caracas instead. Then, halfway along the last leg of the trip—a twenty-minute flight in a small plane—he looked out the window and saw the undulating, white-capped, gelatinous sea. The exhilaration he felt died the instant he stepped through the doorway of the airport terminal, however, when he suddenly realized he had not seen Lee in eight years. He need not have worried. Ah, Key West! "No one comes when they're supposed to," Lee had complained of carpenters and electricians. Now Lee was not there. He phoned the store; the man who answered said to take a taxi; he went outside and did just that.

The taxi was driven by a skinny, scarred, sunburnt, silent blond who put up the windows and turned on the air conditioner in the car as they drove into town. His fellow passenger was a man in tasseled loafers, blue blazer, and horn-rimmed glasses—a man connected to an art museum or gallery in some northern city, he guessed, on his way to a gay guest house. They stared out separate windows as the wind-blown, sun-bleached palms went by beyond the glass. A storm was coming. The sky was overcast. The wind was high, the temperature supposed to drop into the fifties that night, the radio said. He got out of the taxi on Duval Street and went into the store.

A short, handsome man in lime-green hot pants saw his bag, came up, and said, in broken English, "Lee come. Wait here."

Lee arrived a moment later. "I was nervous," he said, grinning, blushing. "About seeing you. That's why I'm late."

"I was nervous, too," he said.

"The first thing is to rent you a bike," Lee said. "Leave your bag here. Phan Li will look after it."

"Who's Phan Li?" Roger said after they went out onto the sidewalk.

"My employee," said Lee. "He's a refugee—he came here with his family from Vietnam."

"Oh," he said. "Is he a hard worker?"

"Very," said Lee. "Though all he cares about is dick. He used to work at the dirty bookstore three doors down, so he knows exactly what everyone likes to do, and how big their dick is. It's like living with a government informer in Havana."

"Well, he was very attentive," Roger said.

"A little too attentive," Lee said. "He told the teller at my bank I drank a bottle of vodka last week on my birthday."

"Happy birthday," Roger said.

"I was trying to forget it." Lee laughed.

With that, he held open the door of a delicatessen they entered to have lunch—in a room where gay men had collected like the grease of a million hamburgers, a million love affairs, he felt, as they sat down. It was the first time in seven years he had been in a restaurant where all the customers were men, sitting alone, in pairs, in quartets. He stared, like a child before an aquarium of sharks at Marineland, at the deep tans, ponytails, beards, mustaches, tank tops, backpacks, and Hawaiian-print shirts, as he listened to Lee's stories about his employees ("In Key West, you either wait tables or own the restaurant. There's nothing in between"), his struggle with drink ("I stopped going to meetings"), his lover ("I had to fire him, he was being so obnoxious to everyone. The next week he was diagnosed with AIDS. Now he won't speak to me"), the young German soccer player who worked as a cashier in a health food store ("Wait till you see him, we'll go there after lunch"). Eight years of separation vanished with their hamburgers and lemonades. Lee's eyes remained, however—those azure eyes he'd fallen under the spell of years ago, in the kitchen of a friend's apartment on Second Avenue. He realized—with relief, as he ate his Key Lime pie—that something else was also intact; Lee was still good, still kind, still compassionate; which meant more to him now than years ago, when all that had mattered were the eyes.

"You look the same," said Lee.

"So do you," said Roger.

Then they both laughed. And the kitchen in which they had met, the window, the ailanthus tree outside the window so close one could reach out and touch the branches, the two stools on which he and Lee sat talking till their legs finally touched, came back to him now as he watched over Lee's shoulder those who could still do what he could no longer: eat alone in public. He realized, watching them, that he was now a virtual recluse. One of those middle-aged men who, after a parent he was caring for had died, would go out on a date with another man his age whose parents had also just died—meeting in a restaurant like this, as fragile as flowers, as set in their ways as cement.

"Ready?" Lee said, picking up the check. "We'll go back to the apartment now, and then hit the beach."

The beach was the one he must have gone to when he was sixteen; he remembered the circular cement rest room. The dock that stretched out from the sand toward the half-submerged planks of a wooden seawall was familiar, too, though everything seemed smaller than he had imagined. He lay down in the shade of a thatched roof, a few feet from Lee in the bright sunlight, and said, when Lee asked why he was avoiding the light: "I have to stay out of the sun now. I had three skin cancers removed last summer."

"I had two taken off last week," said Lee, pointing to a patch on his shoulder.

"Then why are you out in the sun?" said Roger.

"I have to look nice for the customers," Lee said. He laughed. "My doctor says people have them removed, and go straight to the beach!"

The beach: beyond the pool of shade, life went on just as he remembered it in the hot sunlight. He and Lee seemed to have picked up, years later, right where they'd left off, on another, northern beach—with the same artifacts: *New York Times*, box of cookies, jug of water, bicycles. He noted, however, one difference: Lee was cheerful in the midst of troubles—his lover's illness, the hospitalization of a friend. Like everyone in the middle of the fray, he had a vivacity those trying to keep it at a distance did not. Odd, Roger thought as he listened to the faint sound of voices, waves, passing airplanes, how the people who have to deal with it daily seem more alive than those who don't. With that, he roused himself and went out onto the dock to swim. The water felt like ice. He sat there on the slimy steps watching a woman in a bathing cap swim back and forth in diagonal lines across the rectangle of water between the dock and the seawall. She did not seem to mind. Nor did a plump German man, who entered the sea via the steps Roger was sitting on, turned over on his back in front of him, and said, "Ah! *Schön!*" Finally Roger went in. He swam fast to get warm, but each time he reached beneath the water to complete his stroke, his hand plunged into the eelgrass growing on the bottom. There's gotta be another beach, he thought as he got out and walked back through the glare.

There was. Watching Lee negotiate traffic ahead of him as they bicycled across town through narrow streets lined with gardens of grape trees, bougainvillea, and palms, to a beach Lee said was better for swimming, he felt a curious tenderness for the person now taking care of his wants. He looked so fragile on the bicycle ahead of him. But then the number of people one matters to in life is small, he thought, and, in the end, the real nonrenewable resource. When they got to Fort Taylor, two men were lying on their backs on picnic tables in a grove of Australian pines, talking in Hebrew. A group of young men in black bathing suits lay on a pile of rocks near the shore, like seals, shining in the sun. They chained their bikes to the trees, and sat down on a picnic bench in the shade. They talked about new friends, old friends, wakes, memorials, blood tests, fear, depression, insomnia, the restaurant, the local gay church, spring break, the invasion of Panama, Manuel Noriega, the drug business, Tennessee Williams, Calvin Klein, Jerry Herman, a memorial service to be held for a man from Chicago on a dock that evening, the local newspaper, George Bush, the importance of hats, their parents, and real estate values as water skiers suspended from parachutes floated by, and an old Coast Guard cutter returned from the open sea. Finally Lee mentioned his lover, who would not speak to him now that he'd been fired from the shop and was dying in a guest house in the Old Town, and the friend in the hospital—an older man he'd met in AA, a man he liked to discuss history and politics with, whose mail he had promised to take him that afternoon.

"I won't take you," Lee said, standing up, "because he's too weak. Let's meet back at the apartment, at five. Unless you meet one of these beauties," he said.

Fat chance, he thought. He put his towel down on the sand between two young men on separate towels of their own, their lithe bodies shimmering beneath a film of sweat and oil. The beauty of the man on his left—tall, long-legged, curly brown hair, blue Speedo—grew on him as the afternoon waned, and he began to feel what he had not felt in a long time: desire. So he plunged into the milky green sea and did his best to catch the attention of the man in the blue Speedo. But when he returned to his towel, the blue Speedo was saying to the other young man: "I liked it, but it wasn't what I'd do with a lamp store. You know? I mean, it was OK for L.*A.*" And his long-legged beauty disintegrated under the same banalities that had neutralized desire twenty years ago on the beach in the Pines. Eventually the two men got up together and left. He imagined their return to a room in a guest house: the embrace inside the door, the taste of saltwater on a sunburnt shoulder, the kisses, the undressing, the shared shower, the water splashing on their backs. He imagined as he lay there watching the sun descend in the sky the wet footprints on the floor, the messed sheets, the long, hot afternoon ending, finally, in sex. Then he took another swim and left the beach. He looked at the empty porches of the beautiful old houses in gardens of delicate palms as he bicycled back to Lee's in his bare feet, happy to have swum, to be alone, for the moment, relaxed at last. But all of that depended on his having Lee to return to, he thought: the problem of loneliness solved. Still, he was just beginning to see the possibilities of the place when he rounded the corner and saw Lee getting off his bike at the gate.

"How was the hospital?" he said, thinking, the moment he said it, that it sounded like: *How was your day, dear?*

"He's coming home tomorrow," Lee said. "I told him I'd take care of him at home till we need hospice." He took out a pack of cigarettes from his pocket and said: "This is why I keep falling off the wagon. I'm now George's main support. The doctor told me he's in the final stages. Sometimes," he said, as they locked their bicycles to the post, "I just wish they'd die." He looked up at him and said, "Isn't that awful?"

"No," said Roger. "I think that about my father, too. It's only normal. On the other hand . . ."

"What?" said Lee.

"I'm terrified that he will."

"Why?"

"Because he's my whole life now," Roger said. "What would I be doing if I weren't caring for him?"

"Well," Lee said, "I'm not allowed to care for Michael. That's where he is," he said as they sat down on the second-story porch of his apartment. "Right there," he said, nodding at the annex of a pink hotel directly opposite—the shutters of an attic window closed against the sun. "The weird part is, I left some things in the room, and now that he refuses to see me, I can't get them."

"Like what?" said Roger.

"Like my camera."

They looked across the street at the pink guest house, the closed shutters, in the late afternoon sunlight.

"I keep thinking it must be hot inside," said Lee. "I keep thinking a lot of things, since I look right at it, every day."

"What does he have?" said Roger.

"It went to his brain," said Lee.

"Toxoplasmosis," said Roger. "The thing everybody fears the most." Together they stared at the closed metallic louvers. Then they returned to the newspaper scattered on the cloth-covered wicker table between them. The palms rustled in the late afternoon breeze. A yellow wagon train went by half filled with tourists listening to a man at the wheel with a microphone. Six o'clock plunged the bougainvillea against the garden wall into shadow. Lee lit a cigarette, and removed his sandals.

"Isn't the problem with Panama a mess?"

"Yes," said Roger.

That evening they had dinner in a little Cuban restaurant around the corner whose waiters, Lee promised, were especially handsome. They were. When they got back to the apartment, they began looking at more handsome men—from Fire Island—in scrapbooks Lee took down from the shelf.

"You know, they carry photographs around with them now in San Francisco," Roger said. "To show what they looked like before they got sick. A friend of mine out there goes to parties for people with AIDS, and sometimes the discrepancy between the photographs and the people showing them to him is so great he starts to cry and leaves."

Lee shook his head.

"I haven't cried once since this began," said Roger. "I don't know why."

"It's because you're cold!" said Lee, and they laughed.

That evening they had trouble sleeping. Lee woke in the middle of the night more than once and lit a cigarette; and Roger, lying awake on the sofa, concluded they were both victims of that malady of middle age—insomnia. Nerves. Something unsettled. Deep down, a discontent. The two questions all survivors faced: What will I do if/when I get sick? And: What will I do at sixty, if I don't? In the morning, Lee said: "Call the excursion boat."

There was nothing to take an excursion to—each captain he called said high winds had made the sea so rough, so cloudy, a visit to the reef was pointless. They spent half an hour trying on shorts instead. Then they went out onto the porch, had breakfast, read the newspaper, till Lee said: "I have to help George check out of the hospital. You go to Fort Taylor. I'll meet you back here at five. Now remember," Lee said, from the doorway, "tomorrow you leave town, and *you* don't have to worry about your reputation. But you do have to leave *me* something to talk about, after you've gone! So do something outrageous!"

"OK!" he laughed as Lee went out the door. Instead, he washed the breakfast dishes, and went back to the porch and sat down at the wicker table to browse through the scrapbooks and wait out the most intense period of the sun. He became mesmerized by the passage of pedestrians and cyclists in the street below, the emptiness of the little garden, the breeze that stirred the pages of the newspaper on the table before him. Time passed. He moved the ashtrays and shells about to weigh down sections of the newspaper as the breeze shifted. What is the point of going to the beach? he wondered. Hidden away here in the shade above the tiny garden, he felt completely content. Finally, even reading the newspaper seemed too much effort, and he turned his attention to the street below, which itself seemed to have expired under the heat of the noonday sun, as everyone lay on the beach. Then he raised his eyes to the shutters on the pink house across the street, and he wondered if they were not the real reason he was still sitting here.

The shutters reminded him of a church on Good Friday—the

hours from noon to three when Jesus was on the cross, and Catholic children were forbidden to play outside. Now the hours of twelve to three were honored indoors for a different, purely secular reason. But still the same lesson seemed to obtain: Someone was always suffering, while the rest of the world went about its business. He stared at the shutters across the street and marveled at the fact that, six or seven years after the first people he knew died, unaware of the cause, or the number to follow them, it was all still, in some terrible sense, a mystery—as blank, as impervious to light, or man's cleverness, as those silver louvers layered one upon the other like the blades of a fan. He sat there thinking of the outrage, the impotence, the deaths past and to come, the denouement no one could have foreseen, like the effect of sun on the skin years after an adolescent sunburn. He sat there wondering why he had not cried till now, not once, and if he would someday. He sat there watching the death room of someone he did not even know, and was still sitting there hours later when Lee came home from the hospital. He looked up, startled, when the door opened.

"How was the beach?" Lee said.

"I didn't go," he said, embarrassed. "I've been sitting looking at these old photographs. It's so cool and pleasant on this porch. I could sit here forever. You have a very nice life here. Tell me," he said, closing a scrapbook, "who are you still in touch with from the old crowd?"

"You," Lee said. "You're all I've got, snookums!"

The words pleased him. They went downstairs together to have an early dinner; they took a long walk to the Truman Annex and back afterward. Tourists in cotton clothes, their hair still damp from swimming, were gathering in the streets as twilight deepened. Lee asked him one more time if he wanted to visit the bars, but he declined. They went home and watched a movie on cassette instead, then went to bed, the two of them on the same futon, accustomed now to each other.

In the morning he awoke just as dawn was breaking; a milky blue light filled the garden below, and was stealing through the cracks in the shutters as if it meant to bathe everything in the splendor and profuse life of the tropics. He looked at Lee—in the pale light surrounding the room—got up quietly, and went out to the porch. The pink house, the silver shutters across the street, were drenched in dew—a dew he imagined as he stood there soaking the bedroom like some miraculous holy water that would dissolve the sickness within. Then he turned and looked back through the open doorway at Lee, asleep on the futon. Next year, he thought, Caracas.

The Man Who Got Away

HE HAD SEX ONLY ONCE BEFORE HE WENT TO COLLEGE—with a man he met at the mall near his house in suburban Philadelphia, an electrician in charge of the mall's power plant, a forty-two-year-old man who was sitting on a bench outside the men's room when he came out. When he got to college that fall, however, he had no intention of pursuing sex with men; there was a gay bar downtown called the My Oh My, but the town was so small, there was no way he could have gone into it without someone seeing him; so he roomed with five other boys, and dated women. It was the late sixties. It was a small town in a valley in central Pennsylvania, founded solely for the purpose of the university, so there was no industry, nothing but the school itself, and there was something so paradisical about the place, the hollow the school was set in was called Happy Valley. He was certainly happy—so happy to be away from home that he stayed in town during his Thanksgiving break, too; his mother, back home, was drinking, and his parents were glad to have him taken care of elsewhere. So glad they surprised him, when he got off the train at Christmas-time, with a brand-new Chevrolet convertible, a car he was embarrassed to drive back to school—since this was the era of the Volkswagen—especially when he drove down to Washington later that year to protest the war in Vietnam, and saw, stuck on the freeway in a traffic jam, not one other General Motors product in view. Still, the trip was a great success; he was standing outside the Capitol on inauguration day when Nixon came out and walked to his limousine, his face covered with makeup for the cameras. He decided to major in history.

He made friends easily in the department; everywhere, in fact. He was very handsome; he had large blue eyes and many blue sweaters that matched his eyes. When his best friend broke up with a young woman who was so beautiful people said she looked like Julie Christie, he drove out to see her in the confidence that he knew she liked him. The day he went, seven other boys drove out, too, like people coming to comfort a woman who has just lost her husband in an accident, and she made him think, as he sat quietly in a wing chair on the edge of the group, of Sleeping Beauty surrounded by the Seven Dwarfs—a vision he surrendered only when, after smoking dope and drinking with his competitors, he fell asleep. When he awoke, the Seven Dwarfs were gone and Sleeping Beauty was stroking his thigh. They went into the bedroom and had sex. He did this three more times but it gave him little pleasure—in a sense, he was Sleeping Beauty—so he stopped calling her and tried to study instead. The attempt was not successful either; his real sexual desires were such a distraction he could barely concentrate on his reading, and not the handsome man in the library carrel next to his; at which point another upsetting thing occurred—one morning at breakfast he read on the Op Ed page of the *New York Times* a column by Anthony Lewis on Israel that he thought was so well written he realized he could never put words together as effectively himself; and he found himself unable to write.

Fortunately, at the time the idea of allowing students to take oral examinations instead of written ones had just become the thing; so he selected his courses on that basis, including one he was sure would be an easy A, given by a Japanese professor of philosophy named Professor Hirosaki. Professor Hirosaki was a short man in his early forties with granny glasses and a round, cherubic face; the queens called him Madame Butterfly, Mitchell would learn later. He knew already that the man had a crush on him. He signed up for independent study with the professor anyway; all he had to do was read Plato and Dostoyevsky and discuss it with him in his office. When the time came for their meeting, however, Professor Hirosaki asked him to dinner in his apartment instead; and Mitchell went there too nervous to talk intelligently about *The Republic* and *Notes from the Underground.* The professor served wine before dinner, which Mitchell drank three glasses of so quickly that his head began to spin; at dinner he knocked his fourth glass onto the white lace tablecloth, at which point he stood up, said he felt very dizzy, and would have to go home. "No, no!" the professor said. "You can sleep here!" But Mitchell refused, backing out the door of the apartment so that he could keep the professor in full view, and, as the professor was insisting, "You can sleep here! You can sleep here!" he fell right down the stairs. That night he slept in his car, two blocks from the gay bar in which he was still too embarrassed to be seen. He went back to reading Dostoyevsky.

One day he closed *The Brothers Karamazov* and realized the moment the book slipped from his hands that he could not remember a single thing he had just read that afternoon; so he began searching for the perfect chair in which to read, on different floors of the library, in different nooks of the student union, even the local laundromat, as if, with the right chair, the right level of noise, the right light, the words his eyes were scanning on the page would pass into his brain and actually make an impression. Instead he seemed to be blocking them out. It was only in the laundromat that he thought he'd found the right set of conditions—the presence of other people, the cozy heat from the dryers, the little pots of African violets set against the grime-encrusted, steamed-up windows on a snowy day—but even there he became aware that the book was merely a prop he could appear to be reading when, in fact, his eyes were focused on a strip of air just above the page where the manager (a business major with a muscular torso who thought the laundromat so warm he went about his business with his shirt off, and, often, a brassiere tied like a bonnet on his head) would pass by, including his concave stomach and his muscular butt, as he went from dryer to dryer unloading clothes for people. This plunged Mitchell only further into despair, till one night he went with the manager to a bar.

The bar the manager liked was one that was popular with people called hippies; young men, often in the arts, who wore their hair down to their shoulders, rings on their fingers, and scarves; they looked to him like the portrait of a youth by Titian he had fixated on in his art history course—a long-faced aristocratic knight with an expression and a beauty that intrigued him far more than the *Mona Lisa*'s. They weren't exactly gay—the gay bar was down the street, behind a topless bar one had to walk through first—but they weren't fraternity boys either. When the manager entered the bar that night, he was greeted by a beautiful long-haired person in a bulky sweater whose sex Mitchell could not determine but who kissed the manager on the lips while Mitchell waited, and who left with the manager an hour later, though Mitchell didn't mind, since that was the night he met Carlos.

Carlos looked like a portrait, too, but not the Titian, not the serene, golden-haired nobleman, but rather the self-portrait of

Dürer—with a high forehead, long nose, and a cold, confident face. He was twenty-seven then, older than most of the people in the bar; an assistant professor of urban planning from Argentina, with a reserved, almost formal manner, until he smiled, and then his eyes nearly shut, the skin stretched as thin as parchment across his face, and something Gothic appeared. There was another contrast: His body was muscular, thick-necked, powerful—his voice was thin and faint. He was completely masculine, however, Mitchell noted; though after being introduced Carlos seemed to take no interest in him whatsoever—a fact Mitchell attempted to correct by following him out of the bar when Carlos left, and, though Mitchell's own car was in the parking lot, standing beside the road with his thumb out when Carlos came by.

The move seemed not to surprise the professor of urban planning; he stopped, let Mitchell in, and asked if he would like to go back to his apartment for coffee. The minute Mitchell walked into the Tudor carriage house and saw the carved tables from Cambodia, the silk kimono hanging on the wall, the framed architectural drawings, his basic disapproval of what he was doing softened and he thought: I'll learn more with this man than I ever will sitting around with my roommates, or even in class. Then Carlos lit a fire, put music on that he would later learn was Pachelbel's *Canon*, and the enchantment was complete. They had sex that night in the middle of a long, steady snowfall, though they were not sexually compatible; after paying thirty seconds' attention to Mitchell's penis, Carlos rolled him over, and Mitchell had to bite the pillowcase between his lips while Carlos enjoyed himself. "This can't go anywhere," Carlos told him the next morning, "you're too old for me, and much too hairy." Eighteen-year-olds, smooth and blond, were few and far between, however, and in the following months Mitchell went home with Carlos many nights by default, and slept with him on his narrow single bed—till one day Carlos went into a straight bar downtown he had taken Mitchell

to a couple of times, in order to avoid suspicion, and the bartender, on greeting him, said, "Where's your boyfriend?" At this
point Carlos told Mitchell they were going to have to break it off,
he was too old anyway, and Mitchell had to beg to be allowed to
sleep at his house, even offering to sleep on the floor if Carlos
would only let him; and, with this state of affairs, the semester
ended, and Carlos drove off to spend the summer on Long Island.

Mitchell was so devastated by the loss he went immediately
into a depression—lying on his sofa for several days, opening his
eyes only long enough to make out the face of John Dean, testify-
ing on TV at the Watergate hearings; when he went downtown
to buy cigarettes, the effort of walking exhausted him so, he had
to sit down on benches along the way to rest. His friends told
him he had mononucleosis. He went to the doctor and took tests;
when they showed nothing, the doctor sent him upstairs to a
psychiatrist; because he dared not tell him about Carlos, the psychiatrist simply concluded, "You obviously don't want to be
here," and sent him down to the doctor, who gave him a vitamin
supplement, and with that he went back to the apartment and
lay down on the sofa again.

Everything seemed hopeless—the Nixon White House, the
country itself, his mother drinking at home, his own future, his
own life now that Carlos was gone. The summer got hotter, while
he kept remembering the winter: lying on the narrow bed in
Carlos's little Tudor carriage house with the dim light doubly
diffused by the gently falling snow and the mullioned windows,
watching Carlos's broad, muscular back as he stood peeing in the
tiny bathroom while bacon sizzled in the pan and Pachelbel's
Canon played on the stereo. But when he opened his eyes, he saw
only John Dean, the prim mouth and horn-rimmed glasses, and
his wife, who looked to Mitchell, through the mist of his depression, as if she had been completely covered in Wesson oil—a
thought that only returned him once again to Carlos, and the

night they'd oiled their bodies and spent hours doing the Princeton rub. So he closed his eyes and sank back into his depression, and continued to lie there, like Sleeping Beauty covered in a growing thicket of thorns, till the third week in August, when Carlos called and invited him to stay a few days with him on Long Island.

He hitched three rides to Pennsylvania Station, went downstairs, and took a train to East Hampton, where Carlos met him, bronzed and blond, in baggy shorts and a beaded necklace, and took him home in a truck with a surfboard in the back to a house in town owned by another professor (of geography, at a college in the Bronx). The minute he walked into the house and saw the four men Carlos's age, professors like Carlos, he knew they wanted him in a way Carlos apparently did not. Carlos was still indifferent. When they got to the beach, Carlos pointed out the surfers to Mitchell, and said a few hours with them each afternoon was better than all the sex to be found in any gay bar; though that afternoon, after their shower back at the house, Mitchell let Carlos discharge his desire for the surfers on his person—which only confused him more. Downstairs at dinner that night, he felt even more out of his depth when he noticed, halfway through the meal, a man underneath the table in a dog collar on his hands and knees, eating out of a bowl; when Mitchell asked if he would not prefer to sit with them, Carlos simply said, "He's fine. Would you like some more mashed potatoes?" And everyone went on as if there was nobody under the table eating dog food drenched in piss as they dined. That night, sitting in the living room as the others talked, Mitchell was ignored—and when the others decided to drive to the Swamp, he chose to go to bed instead, where he lay tearfully wondering whom Carlos was chatting up in the bar and what he looked like. So it was a surprise when he rode back with one of the professors to the city on the train and he realized that this man—a friend of Carlos—wanted him so badly he did not stop talking all the way back to Manhattan.

This gave him a certain confidence—knowing that Carlos's friend, if not Carlos, desired him—and so did the affection Professor Hirosaki evidently felt for him when he enrolled in another of his courses that fall. One evening after their discussion of Plato's *Symposium* he wanted to ask the professor how a person could be so in love that he would eat dog food soaked in urine underneath the table his lover was having dinner on; but he was so embarrassed he asked him instead when they were going to apply Plato and Dostoyevsky to what was happening in America now. The professor laughed, and said that was Mitchell's job, not his. So he did not ask about the man in the dog collar. (He even thought he might have the answer already from what they had been discussing in their seminar—that though Plato felt man could use reason to construct a republic, Dostoyevsky would say that even if man created a state of affairs that was wise and just, people would do something perverse simply to rebel.) The man in the dog collar was not that much of an enigma. Even he now knew what it meant to want someone so much that you would do anything not to be banished from his presence, and he did not equate his professor's crush on him with what he felt for Carlos—a desire so strong that when Carlos told him he was not being offered tenure here, and had taken a job at a small state college in New Jersey that fall, Mitchell was horrified. That August, when Carlos offered him a ride to New York, Mitchell gave up all rational plans for his future and accepted. He had no idea what would happen when they got there—all he knew was that he could be with Carlos for the duration of the trip.

When they got to New York and drove past Christopher Street, Carlos told him, "This is where people hang out who do nothing but look for sex. Some of them do it twenty-four hours a day." This was a life he could not even imagine as they drove past the throngs of men. But that night everything changed. They went first to the apartment of the man whose house they'd stayed at in

East Hampton, and after changing, went out to a bar, where Carlos turned to him and said, "You know how to get back to the apartment. You're on your own," and Mitchell hid himself in a corner by the jukebox, afraid even to light a cigarette because he knew his hands would shake. Thirty minutes later he was asked home by a male model who had an apartment on East Fifty-eighth Street. The next day Carlos dropped off his suitcase there, and drove off to Jersey City, where Carlos had agreed to share an apartment with a dentist. That evening the male model flew Mitchell to Fire Island Pines in a seaplane, and then many things began to happen to him.

They were so absorbing that he forgot all about Carlos—till one night the following winter he saw him at a dance club on Houston Street. Carlos was standing, shirtless, beside one of the speakers, with a red bandanna tied around his forehead, playing a tambourine. In the My Oh My this image had plunged Mitchell into despair. In New York it looked faintly ridiculous, and he did not even go over and say hello. He was surprised when he ran into the professor of geography a year later at another club and the professor asked him, "Do you ever think of Carlos?" because, in truth, he didn't. He was having his own love affair now with the male model; he was working for Halston, taking clothes on tour to cities like Denver and Chicago. He had forgotten about Carlos. Then one afternoon, four years later, his lover, the male model, jumped out the window of their tenth-floor apartment while under the influence of angel dust. And, like the beautiful Julie Christie lookalike who had been visited by seven boys the afternoon he fell asleep in her chair back in college, he was now the one receiving a circle of sympathetic courtiers. Even Carlos came. He brought with him a pale, blond nineteen-year-old garbageman from East Hampton; but the next day Carlos called and said he had brought him only to make Mitchell jealous. Mitchell said, "Oh, really?" He was still in shock and did not care who

Carlos's boyfriend was or was not; but when Carlos called a week later and asked him if he wanted to stay in East Hampton for a while, he said yes.

The minute he got into Carlos's station wagon in East Hampton and drove off with him, he realized to his dismay that Carlos was in love with him, a fact that only made him feel awkward. But he had no place else to go. His lover's relatives had told him to leave the apartment. He was depressed, worn out by drugs, had Lyme disease and no energy. When he got to Carlos's house, he went up to bed. Moments later Carlos walked in, with only a towel around his waist, and said, "I'm going to take a shower now," but the implied invitation in this display of his torso left Mitchell completely cold—the body he had dreamt of back in college now meant nothing to him. "I'm more sexually flexible than I was before," Carlos added as Mitchell lay there. "I'm what they call 'versatile.'" Still Mitchell did not speak. The next morning it was snowing but Carlos went out nevertheless and ran ten miles. There was not an ounce of excess fat on his body. In fact, he looked less fit than gaunt to Mitchell, but Mitchell attributed that to his running. He drank only bottled water, ate broccoli, lentils, rice, and eggplant; he told Mitchell he would have to completely change his diet in order to flush the toxins out of his system, and fast one day a week, for starters. Mitchell at this point was living on cigarettes. He lay there in bed listening to Carlos's prescriptions without a word, thinking, At least he doesn't dye his hair. What Carlos did was squeeze lemons on it in summer in order to turn it blond; even in that, he was organic. Carlos told Mitchell that he was living an unhealthy, self-destructive life; that drug use was out of control in the circles he had fallen in with; that someone on Fire Island, he would not say who, had told him Mitchell had anal warts the previous summer. And with that, Mitchell realized, blushing, that Carlos had been following his career, such as it was, ever since they had moved to New York.

Most nights they sat in front of the television eating seaweed and rutabagas while some program on the Olduvai Gorge or the Georgian influence on American architecture played on PBS; but one night Carlos put on a slide show. Some of the slides he had taken of Mitchell back at school, some with his hair messy, others with his hair combed back. The messy hair made Mitchell look confused, adolescent, vulnerable; the slicked-back hair made him look cold and confident. Carlos kept saying he preferred "this Mitchell"—the one with the messy hair—to "that Mitchell"— the one with the hair slicked back—as the slides progressed.

Outside the snow fell, like bandages someone was applying to his wounds. He felt he was back in the school infirmary. Carlos went to work some days in an architect's office where he made drawings; other days he drew at home; Mitchell could barely read, he felt so exhausted and depressed. He had always explained the meaning of whatever English words Carlos asked him about, but now Carlos's odd constructions irritated him. Nor did he even react to Carlos's announcements that he was going to take a shower. He had begged to be permitted to shower with Carlos at school, he had soaped Carlos's body with the reverence and awe he felt for Pachelbel's *Canon,* but now he let him pad down the slanted floor of the hallway to the bathroom and did not move. One day he saw an ad for a Dean & Deluca store that was opening in town, and decided to go in for an interview. He got dressed in the clothes he had worn all his life since going off to school—a blue V-neck sweater, corduroys, moccasins, a scarf, and an old black overcoat—went into the living room, and asked Carlos if he looked all right. Carlos glanced up and did not answer; he did not have to. Mitchell still had his looks. At Dean & Deluca they told him he was just what they were looking for—someone who could work with rich people planning parties—but when he got back to Carlos, and walked up the snowy path, into the house where Vivaldi was playing as Carlos sketched before the fire, he suddenly decided to go back to the city instead. "You're never going to solve your problems," Carlos said bitterly when he drove him to the train station. "You will go on living from crisis to crisis, and eventually self-destruct!"

That winter he went home to Philadelphia and lived with his parents till he returned to New York in the spring, and he lost track of Carlos; still it was a shock when word came to him through the professor of geography one day on the deck of the Botel at Tea Dance that Carlos was sick. It was early in the plague and it made no sense; Carlos had been living in East Hampton, out of the danger zone, for several years. Carlos had retired from New York City—the world of baths, bars, discotheques, and tambourines; he ate broccoli and brown rice and drank only bottled water. Mitchell had received an invitation to a show of his architectural drawings at a gallery in East Hampton only the previous week. He called Carlos in East Hampton later that fall but did not say anything directly about the bad news; though when Mitchell said he'd learned to take things one day at a time, the last thing Carlos said on the phone was: "I don't live from day to day. I'm living from hour to hour," and he hung up to go to a doctor's appointment. A month later the hours came to an end.

It was all so new then, such a shock, Mitchell had to ask himself what he really wanted to do with the fact that he was still alive; and he decided to go back to school—graduate school—so after his father drove him to the bus station one morning that winter he returned to Happy Valley. The gay bar—the My Oh My—was gone, and in its place a discotheque with a mirrored ball. Little else seemed to have changed, except that he was drinking heavily when he went to see the dean of students. On his way he went into a bookstore and saw a copy of *Civilization and Its Discontents* on a pile of half-price books, which he opened up and read till he came to the paragraph in the introduction that speaks of people who waste their lives pursuing things that cannot possibly provide happiness. When he went in to see the dean, he told him about his years in New York, the tick bite that had ruined his health, but then, rather than try to explain his reason for returning to school, handed him the copy of Freud and asked him to read that paragraph. "Boy," said the dean when he handed the book back, "you got some tick bite! I haven't read that in years!" The dean, he thought when he left, had no idea he was drunk; he had been just drunk enough to play his part well. That night he found a room in one of the fraternity houses that had gone under when the counterculture swept the campus his sophomore year but which had now been taken over by a group of Vietnam veterans who were running it as a rooming house; when he walked in two men were playing pool with rifles. But when a blood drive set up cots in the main room one day, he refused to give blood—he assumed his was infected, that he would die, like Carlos—and, suddenly paranoid, he took his books and moved to the Sheraton, where the old loneliness returned. One night, after coming back from the discotheque, he was so drunk he called the desk at two A.M. and said, "What do you have to do to get a blow job around here?" The clerk said, "I get off at six."

The clerk was a replica of himself ten years before; seventeen and blond and just what Carlos had been looking for all those years. They went upstairs and had sex and when the youth told Mitchell he was moving to New York as soon as he graduated, Mitchell said, "Why?" The next day while walking down the mall in a light snowfall he saw through the fluttering flakes a figure coming toward him that turned into Professor Hirosaki.

"Ah," said the professor, whose hair was entirely gray, "I am astonished but not surprised. Not really. The first time I saw you I knew you would come back."

"Why?" said Mitchell.

"You were carrying two books," said the professor. "The *Genealogy of Morals,* and *As You Like It.* I knew this person was confused."

Mitchell smiled and swayed a bit.

"And now you are drunk," said the professor.

"Yes," Mitchell said sighing.

"Then come to dinner," said the professor.

This time he was too drunk to be nervous, and when the door opened and a Japanese woman who looked about nineteen greeted him—Professor Hirosaki's niece—he felt even safer. "Do not be shocked," said the professor to his niece after Mitchell told them he was a prisoner in the Sheraton (he had run out of money, and was waiting for his father to wire him funds so he could leave). "This country is full of people imprisoned in Sheratons because they cannot pay the bill!" And everyone laughed. "Though I must tell you the news that you are imprisoned in the Sheraton," he said, "is very mild in comparison to something else I heard a few years ago."

"What is that?" said Mitchell.

"It may of course not even be correct," said the professor, "but if it is true—I was horrified—horrified!—when a few years ago I learned you were working for Bill Blass!"

"Halston," said Mitchell, and he went on to tell his host the difference between the two designers—as if he were explaining a fine point in philosophy—and then the story of the last ten years of his life.

"Ah well," said the professor when he was through. "This is what Plato predicted in *The Republic*. Do you remember? Plato said a young man in a democracy would want to be a ship captain, an athlete, a poet, a politician. So much freedom in America! So many choices. Now you are the prodigal son. You feel you have gone astray, in this country where it is so easy to, but you do not know why. The answer is very simple."

"What?" said Mitchell.

"Shit values!" the professor said, and they all laughed. "Shit values!" They all laughed again. "More and more this country is following shit values! That's why I was horrified—horrified—!" the professor said again when he was at the door saying good night "—on hearing you'd gone to work for Bill Blass!"

"Halston," Mitchell said as the door closed. The next morning the money came, along with his father, who drove up, checked him out of the Sheraton, and took him home again. He had just learned he was okay—after moving to Key West and testing negative—when an invitation to a memorial service for Carlos was forwarded to him there. I was cruel to him, he thought, but I couldn't help it—maybe because he was so mean to me. That Christmas a card arrived for him at home in Philadelphia from Professor Hirosaki; his mother opened it and read, over the long-distance wire: "For Mitchell—the one who got away." Then she said: "What does that mean?"

THE SENTIMENTAL EDUCATION

HE WAS A RESPONSIBLE PERSON WHO, after getting two post-graduate degrees, decided he did not want any responsibility. He was otherwise quite conscientious. He was the sort of man who— had you awakened him in the middle of the night—could have told you when his library books were due; he was never late with the rent, or his taxes, and made it a point to vote in every election. But he wanted no part of the work world his education had prepared him for. Instead, he took jobs that paid the rent and no more; went to the gym every day; and spent the evenings looking for sex. He always tried to be kind. The worst thing he ever did was accidentally run over a dog crossing a highway one night as he was driving home to visit his parents in Texas. He imagined himself in heaven having to answer for that cruelty. The second worst thing was leaving three dollars on the table of an apartment in the projects near Fourteenth Street after going there with a young man he'd met in the park, when the young man—to save his honor?—had asked him to leave whatever he thought it was worth on his way out. Since he had only one twenty-dollar bill, and three singles, he chose the latter—he was going to the grocery—which afterward seemed to him an awful, even if unintended, insult. For weeks afterward he went to the park looking for the man to explain, but he never saw him again.

Some of his best friends were hustlers, but aside from that one night in the park—and then only because he sensed the agreement to pay was something the youth needed to convince himself he was not doing this for pleasure—he never hired people, because he connected sex with romance. He suspected at the same time that money was the only thing that differentiated his erotic habits from those of a prostitute. He knew too that Time was passing, and that the people he loved and meant to visit (aunts in Missouri, English teachers, college friends) were getting older— but he was still far enough from both his own birth and death, according to the actuarial tables, that he did not feel the urgency of Time. So when they said, "I'd love to see you," he said, "Okay," and went nowhere. His parents he visited once a year; the others he meant to visit but did not. Instead he remained in the city, and took temporary jobs that allowed him to live on his savings (or unemployment, when he got tired of that particular routine) and devote time to his real desideratum: the pursuit of those sexual relationships he had decided were the most important thing in life.

This urge seemed to play itself out in an endless singles bar of beaches, bars, baths, and rented houses; the sort of places, had he been married, he would never have gone. Instead, he ended up meeting classmates who had married—bankers, lawyers, art dealers—on the street or in the subway, where he was glad to escape them at the next stop, as he felt he had nothing in common with them anymore.

His resumé he did not even bother to assemble. He went to

no class reunions, sent in no information to the editors of those increasingly fat class reports that appeared every five years from the alumni affairs office of his university listing names, addresses, and summaries of lives-in-progress. By about the second or third edition, he noticed a pattern: Those who did write about themselves told of medical school, internships, marriage, children, work abroad, clerkships with judges, businesses begun. The fertile, the fruitful, wrote in. Doctors, for example, always wrote; bankers and financiers moving back to the United States from Hong Kong or London, married couples who wanted classmates to visit them in their new home in Oregon or California, wrote. Everyone else was mum, including himself.

As the years went on, the cheerful beginnings of careers, the marriages fresh out of college gave way to those things that made the class reports read like novels: divorces, deaths, rhapsodies to family life and children, or long, rambling statements of libertarian beliefs by ex-hippies still living in the woods of Michigan. Traces of sadness appeared in unexpected places—accidental drownings, a child born deaf, a suicide.

He, however, seemed to have led a life that could not be put on paper, which was a blank and left no trace, which had neither the successes nor tragedies of the entries in the class reports; just his name, and his parents' mailing address—as if he were still in college, or had never left home. His life consisted merely of going back and forth between New York and San Francisco in those years, searching for a lover. He kept thinking there was a way in which he could be happy, divided between those cities. The first time he went to San Francisco in the mid-seventies, like many people, he wanted to move there immediately. He fell in love with a man wearing a cowboy hat on the airplane on the way out. "Love's Theme" by the Love Unlimited Orchestra was playing on the earphones as his plane floated over the snowcapped Rockies. When he went to the baths on Folsom Street, he heard music he had never heard before—bluesy, country-western bands that sounded like the Allman Brothers but weren't—and spent hours with a bartender from the Midnight Sun. He had sex with a man named Thumper on a promontory at Land's End his last day while an aircraft carrier steamed into the bay before them. He understood immediately what his friend Toby, in Manhattan, meant when he said: "San Francisco gives sex the attention it deserves." They were not neurotic in San Francisco; they were not afraid of sex, and they took their time with it. He kept going back to San Francisco the way pilgrims in the Middle Ages went to Santiago de Compostela, to worship and renew their faith. Friends began moving there and he was welcome to stay with them.

The city changed his friends; sex took over a larger part of their lives, too. It became a staple of daily existence; his friends were always "seeing" someone. And they talked about cars—the cars they wanted to buy when they had enough money—and which part of town they wanted to live in, things no one in New York ever mentioned. They walked all over the city together to Buena Vista Park, Coit Tower, the Castro, and Twin Peaks. His friends were working as either telephone operators or masseurs, or sometimes both. Two became hustlers. He waited for the phone to ring in their white room from which he could see a bridge in the distance and the fog moving in as he listened to his friends negotiate with the men on the line. He met a porn star one of the hustlers had fallen in love with—and sat with them in the porn star's apartment in a high-rise overlooking a bank of fog, a bridge, the bay, thinking he had reached the sanctum sanctorum of gay life: a hustler and a porn star in love with one another, and the cool, white, sunny city spread below. He went to the Golden Gate YMCA and tried not to stare at the men in the locker room; he took a gymnastics class; he drank mineral water, and ate lots of broccoli, and fell in love with a schoolteacher who lived in Oakland.

Each time he went, however, the city was different; and so were his friends. One left after an unhappy affair with a drug addict and moved to Los Angeles. The other went to work for a department store and settled down with the porn star in the suburbs. As for the rest, he thought San Francisco became a bit jaded and self-conscious; either because by 1980 homosexual life was beginning to assume a certain uniformity in every American city—the same clothes, gyms, bars, dance clubs, music—or because the eyes of a visitor, like those of someone newly in love, inevitably adjust to a reality they could not see at the outset. By the end of the seventies he began to think people were behaving in bed the way they did in pornographic films, talking dirty in the same way, displaying their orgasms as if for the camera. He did not know if pornography was beginning to resemble real life more and more, or if it was the other way around. But a certain slickness had set in. One afternoon, while walking back from the grocery past Delores Park, the realization that he might go home with not only his skimmed milk and chicken breasts but any of half a dozen men waiting to be picked up there in the middle of the day all of a sudden distressed him. The blue sky, the sunlight, their beauty, their freedom, and the fact that he and they had arranged their lives to be free at this moment to cruise seemed to him distasteful. Nevertheless he was excited when, back in New York that winter, he learned his friend Toby was about to move to San Francisco. Toby was a librarian whose nine-to-five job updating libraries' computer systems merely served to pay the bills for his real vocation: having sex. The apartment Toby found on Howard Street was so close to the baths and bars south of Market Street, in fact, that he could walk to all of them. So one August when it was stiflingly hot in New York City he went to San Francisco to visit Toby and escape the heat.

Toby shared the apartment with a man who had broken his leg getting out of a sling on acid and was back home in Minnesota to recuperate. So he was alone there during the day, while Toby worked in a library in Oakland. In the evening Toby came home after his workout at the gym, changed clothes, and went out to the bars in which he was still a new face. Toby was hardly home at all, in other words, and during the day his visitor found himself alone in the big, almost unfurnished, sunny rooms.

They had, like so many of the places he and Toby had lived, the look of students' rooms—books, scattered clothes, magazines, mattress on the floor. The light outside was very bright and very clear, like the light on Fire Island in the fall—so bright and clear it etched every surface with a merciless clarity. He ate peanut butter, crackers, and bananas. He never bought food that had to be refrigerated. He washed his shirt, socks, and underwear each morning as soon as he awoke. Then he went outside and draped them over the railing on the back stairs, pausing to look at the alley and the backs of the other houses and buildings stretching in both directions in the beautiful light. In New York there was always laundry behind the buildings, or people sitting in a window, or a man painting sets on a roof, or pigeons. Here there was nothing. The facades looked like the houses in a painting by Edward Hopper; there was not a single person underneath the cloudless sky. When he went back inside, he felt he had lost his last chance to make a connection with another human being. One day he took down a book and began to read.

It was his favorite way to read—in empty houses at the beach in autumn, in farmhouses up the Hudson, or in apartments like this one; he always went to the bookcase to scan the titles, and inevitably found something he wanted to sample. He liked taking his chance on what was sitting on the table beside the bed he was sleeping in at some friend's house in Bucks County; in the bookcases of old books, filmed with salt, or mildew, there were always, among the shipping histories of World War Two, or the memoirs of Churchill, or the handbooks on accounting, odd books he would never think to have brought with him: descriptions of journeys in Ethiopia or India, tales by Henry James, or some romantic novel about women who become doctors, move to Shanghai, and find love in faraway places—the feminists of the thirties and forties before there were feminists. It was the literary equivalent of cruising—he never knew what he would find. He lay down on the mattress on the floor of that apartment the way someone in the lounge of an airport reads till his flight is announced; only in his case, it was until the baths opened. And so, in the middle of the middle of his life, in that blank white city, city of fog and cool silence, he began reading, in an otherwise empty room on a street of pitiless light, Flaubert's *The Sentimental Education*.

The Sentimental Education is the story of two friends who move to Paris from the provinces, take lovers, start a magazine, go to parties, and then return home, years later, to the very place where the novel begins, older and different men. The book has no real plot; it was, he realized after about fifty pages, as the bumper stickers say, *just one damn thing after another,* or rather, what someone else called Life: "What you do when you're planning to do something else." When he was younger he had read *Madame Bovary*—stationed in Germany in the army—but if he saw himself in the woman who had been to a ball, and was forever after trying to re-create the excitement and promise of that one night (much the way he kept coming back to San Francisco to find the joy of his first visit), now, reading this very different book, he began to see that his life, like that of the characters, was simply a bland tale of friendship, affairs, money borrowed and loaned, all of it leading nowhere except to the inevitable disillusionment of age.

It was an easy book to put down, therefore, and pick up again; it was a book that went with the blank light, the emptiness and quiet of the streets outside. It hardly mattered where he paused. He stopped usually to walk downtown to the grocery store to get more peanut butter, crackers, and bananas. Going out when you've been reading is always an adjustment, if not something of a shock, and these excursions were no exception. The little grocery was filled with tourists and street people, and seemed to him shabbier than a grocery on the Lower East Side of Manhattan; everything shabby looked shabbier in California because of the light. There was, also, the knowledge that everyone in the aisles of that little store had gone as far as they could go; as far west, that is, unless they went to Hawaii. California, a professor of his once said, was where everything in America rolled when you tipped it on its side; all that was unattached, all the flotsam and jetsam. Are you flotsam, he wanted to ask the bums he passed on the street as he walked wordlessly home with a bunch of bananas, and a jar of natural peanut butter, or jetsam? And you, madam, talking out loud to the vending machine—are you flotsam? Or jetsam? And he went back to the empty apartment with his lunch, checked on his laundry drying out back in the sun, and picked up Flaubert again.

One day around noon the telephone rang. The caller asked for the roommate with the broken leg. After learning he was healing at his family's farm in Minnesota, the man continued talking in a desultory fashion—a conversation he allowed to continue because he had no one else to talk to—until, all of a sudden, he realized the man (a computer programmer calling from some office in Berkeley) was pretending the two of them had taken two twelve-year-old peasant boys to a hotel room in Quito and were tying them up and sticking dildos down their throats. In less than a minute more, the man across the bay gasped, and cried out; he hung up, walked back through the empty rooms to his mattress on the floor, picked up his copy of Flaubert, feeling vaguely complicit, and thought: What a century.

In the book the protagonist leaves Paris during a political uprising and spends the day with his mistress in the forest of Fontainebleau. That's my life, in a nutshell, he thought. This city is the forest of Fontainebleau, in all its stillness and Mediterranean light, my mistress is the man I'm waiting to meet at the baths this evening, and the political demonstrations in the streets are the crowds, the history, the Life I am always fleeing. A few hours later, to his great relief, night fell. He got up, changed his clothes, after trying on several T-shirts, and walked out so he could avoid Toby when he got home. The baths he went to were so sophisticated that after taking off his clothes and wrapping a towel around his waist, he realized a while later he was the only person who had done this; everyone else wore street clothes. (He had never been to a sex club.) Mostly he walked up and down the narrow, creaking hallways of the old hotel by himself. Only one room was occupied. In it a man stood silently beside an enormous brass bed on which enough surgical instruments for a triple by-pass were laid out, as if for an actual operation. An hour later he saw another open door—but there was a barrier across this threshold: the tanned legs of two muscular young men in white underwear who lay side by side on a bed with their backs against the wall, and their feet braced against the opposite wall. Their sullen, petulant expressions (I dare you to turn me on) he was beginning to think typical of a certain jadedness in gay people, a barrier he had neither the desire nor the ability to cross. Otherwise, to his distress, he found himself as silent and alone in the baths as he had been in the apartment all day, save for the dirty phone call; so he left that bathhouse and walked down the street to another less gloomy and more populated.

There he sat in a warm whirlpool staring at the fish in a gigantic aquarium that formed one wall, and the young men eating hamburgers in their towels at the adjacent bar. I am trapped, he thought, in the Second Empire. Life is bourgeois and hedonistic. When he did enter someone's room in another corridor and lowered himself onto his body, the man sat up in the middle of their lovemaking moments later, looked down at him with doped eyes, and said, "How're ya doin', man?" He wasn't sure, actually; so he stood up, excused himself, and went back to the apartment, grateful this time to find Toby there—uncharacteristically at home—a friend with whom he could watch television and talk.

"There are two possibilities," he said to Toby during a commercial. "One is that some people, a small fraction, always have good sex. And two, that nobody has good sex all the time, but everyone has it now and then, which keeps everyone constantly looking for more. Which is it?" he said.

Toby laughed and continued to stare at the screen.

"I think it's both," Toby finally said. "I do think some people, like porn stars, per*haps,* have good sex—they're human aphrodisiacs. Their partners are *al*ways excited by them. But the rest of us have to make do. Now and then we have good sex, but most of the time we spend looking for it."

"It's like Frederic Moreau," he said, "always obsessed with Madame Arnoux."

"Who's Frederic Moreau?" said Toby.

"The hero, or the main character, of this novel by Flaubert I've been reading—*The Sentimental Education*. I found it in your bookcase. You must have read it."

He handed the paperback to his friend.

"Is this the one where nothing really happens except a lot of little stuff and they end up realizing they've wasted their lives on shit?" said Toby.

"Yes," he said, taking the book Toby handed back to him.

Toby laughed and returned his gaze to the TV screen, where he was watching a rerun of *My Three Sons* because he thought Don Grady "incredibly cute." Then even that tête-à-tête was broken off when Toby decided to go to the bar after all, to look at a bartender who resembled Don Grady, and when it came time for him to say good-bye to Toby (he was returning to New York the next day, when Toby would be at work) he could not think of anything to say. His two weeks on Howard Street had been so melancholy, he could not thank Toby for them; he had hardly amounted to even a houseguest in the scheme of things—he had been someone who just happened to be crashing in the next room. So he simply left a note of thanks the next morning and went to the airport with no sense of saying good-bye; he seemed to be leaving the city the way the fog did, imperceptibly, as if he had never been there.

Eventually, almost by default, he got a permanent job, and when he next went to San Francisco it was on business twenty years later. He stayed in an expensive hotel near Union Square. Toby had died a few years after he had visited him on Howard Street, and he knew no one else in town. The hotel room was enormous and plush and seemed an opportunity he should use; the extra-thick towels, the little wrapped soaps and lotions, the huge bed merely accentuated his solitude, however. He had no desire to walk south of Market, where the bars and bathhouses he had frequented in his thirties had been turned into a homeless shelter, youth hostels, and restaurants popular with yuppies. So he took a walk across town to Coit Tower, and looked at the bay—the beautiful, beautiful bay. He wasn't even sure now why sex had been so important to him; but whatever the reason, the people he might have tried to explain his life to were dead. On his way back to his hotel he stopped in a bookstore and found an edition of *The Sentimental Education* with an afterword by F. W. Dupee he'd never read, and a paperback volume of Flaubert's letters.

The next day, his last, after his meetings were done, he decided to go to Land's End—where he'd had sex on his first visit to San Francisco with Thumper while an aircraft carrier steamed through the Golden Gate with helicopters hovering above it like seagulls circling the mast of a sailing ship. Land's End had changed; like Christopher Street—the other end of this transcontinental pilgrimage—it looked seedy and passé. The few men he passed on the paths, the paths themselves, seemed trammeled and worn. He stood on a promontory looking up the gorgeous coast and tried to remember the thrill the first time he had stood here—like the friends in the novel who remember the brothel they found so mysterious and awesome when young—but he was conscious instead of Toby's remark, years ago, that no one hot came here anymore. He stared nevertheless at the sea where the aircraft carrier had appeared that day, out of the blue—the blue, blue sea—and wondered if Thumper was still alive. Then he walked back through the cypress trees to the corner outside the park where the bus stopped. He who had once believed that sex was the means by which he engaged Life now wondered it if had not been the way he avoided it.

Back in the plush hotel room, sealed off with thick windows, he packed his bag. Then he went to the airport. It was not till he was east of the Alleghenys, in the spectral quiet of the mostly sleeping plane, that he read, under the thin reading light, in a letter from Flaubert to his mistress: "What can compare with the joy of walking up beside someone you had never seen before and know you will never see again?" It seemed as distant a thought as San Francisco.

☙ PETUNIAS

EVERYONE WHO WORKED AROUND THE HARBOR knew he was in
love with Ryan before he knew it himself; they could tell, they
told him later, looking at the petunias. The petunias were in two
big barrels on the deck of the bar and restaurant he was managing
in the Pines that summer. It was a strange establishment—the
cook was temperamental, the headwaiter on drugs, the customers
often obnoxious, and the staff so impatient with them at season's
end that by the middle of September, when people called to make
a reservation at the hotel, they would say there was nothing available even if the place was empty; especially if the accent on the
phone was French. But Morgan was grateful—after an absence of
eight years down South—to be given his old job back when he
needed it; and to be invited by an old friend who lived in Water
Island to live with him. Each morning he walked to work almost
eagerly, down the beach that separated the two towns, as discreet
as the usher at a movie theater, careful not to surprise the men

who were, even at that hour, still wandering Burma Road in various stages of intoxication looking for sex. He went in long before he had to, since the place didn't open till one o'clock, to prepare the menu boards and clean; because it got him out of the house, and into his own little kingdom, even if it was a tiny restaurant he was merely managing for another man; and part of his kingdom was the petunias.

The petunias were red. The restaurant had a small deck with six tables underneath umbrellas that said Cinzano, the two barrels of petunias, and, inside, a bar, three more tables, and the kitchen. The cook that year was a young straight man who was only twenty-three but already had a three-year-old son by a woman in Sayville; his girlfriend this summer was a woman his age who worked in the hardware store. The cook was short and stocky and so at ease with homosexuals he liked to shape the pizza dough into a phallus and then demonstrate his mastery of the gag reflex by slowly swallowing it in front of Morgan. It was something Morgan could no longer do himself. He was not having sex with other people. He had given up booze and sex since becoming unable to have the second without the first. That was why he was back on Fire Island at all, managing a restaurant at the age of forty-four; he had lost his own business in New Orleans when he could not control his drinking; eventually a woman from the IRS had come down from Baton Rouge on her semiannual putsch and padlocked his store along with a dozen others that had not paid their taxes. Destitute, he had no idea what to do after the nuns in a rehabilitation center gave him five dollars and drove him to the bus station, so he telephoned his old boss, the man who owned the restaurant in the Pines, and was deeply relieved to be offered the job he had given up when he'd left eight years ago (to pursue the man he was in love with) and amused to find fliers on all the telephone poles around the harbor when he arrived that said: "Please welcome Morgan back after a triumphant sojourn in the French Quarter!"

The Quarter now seemed to him a sort of nightmare—he was still apprehensive that one day a tourist from New Orleans would enter the restaurant in the Pines and recognize him, since, during his last binge, he had insulted everyone and then half-destroyed the upstairs bar of the Café Lafitte in Exile. But as the first summer came to an end, it seemed as if he had indeed escaped—been taken back by his old community; found some sort of employment, even if he was no longer working for himself; and at least had survived.

It was hard at first, returning to a town where he had been considerably younger and more carefree—hard not to grow depressed watching younger, more successful men arrive and depart every weekend by the boatload—so hard, in fact, he was intimidated by the thought of moving back into Manhattan when the season came to an end, and was grateful when the old friend who lived all year in Water Island invited him to spend that winter with him.

The man who did this was someone he'd known ten years ago—a friend who had himself just suffered a loss, his lover of ten years, an older man who had bequeathed him a house on the edge of Water Island; and it was in this house that he took shelter that winter, and woke up one morning in December thinking this was the only place that made sense to him anymore: Fire Island.

It was a mild winter; he took long walks; they were invited over to dinner with some other people living in the Grove year-round; he made a point of pretending not to hear when Craig began to refer to the two of them as "we" and make plans that sounded very much like those of a couple. He knew that Craig was lonely since the death of his lover and that he was one of those people, like himself, who did not really like to live alone. Still, he had no intention of their being anything more than friends, and it annoyed him to see Craig presume otherwise simply because he was living in his house. Besides this shared fact they were very different people. Craig worked all day doing carpentry. He was good with a hammer and nails; he talked about pipe and drains and insulation and dry wall. He was incurably domestic—and connubial. When he got home in the evening, he loved having someone to talk to. No matter. Eventually it was like watching someone drunk when he was sober—so clearly was Craig in love when he was not. He loathed the fact that as the weeks went by that winter the references to "we" proliferated, and when one day a credit card in both their names arrived in the mail, he felt that was the last straw and resolved to tell Craig he was not attached to him at all.

This point seemed to him important to make, but he didn't know how to do so without being rude, ungrateful, or hurting Craig's feelings. So he stayed in his room longer, waited till Craig had left the house each morning before he came down, took walks that lasted all day and counted the days till the restaurant opened; then he went in a week early to clean up the place and planted the petunias.

He bought the petunias at a nursery once owned by a man he had been in love with—a man who was dead—and put them in the barrels without giving them much thought. It was either petunias or geraniums-and-Dusty-Miller, and since geraniums-and-Dusty-Miller seemed the choice of most people, he chose petunias. He took pride in making the place charming. He hired three young men as waiters—an Englishman, a Frenchman, and an American, as it turned out. They were all in their twenties. His mood improved. He was away all day and much of the evening in the Pines; he hardly saw Craig at all back at the house; each day they went their separate ways, though Craig was still using the connubial "we."

He had not been connubial himself in many years—though he had romance always in mind and had no interest in what was called "sports sex." He had met the love of his life here in the

Pines, in fact, on the dance floor of the Sandpiper, the same night that lover was arrested by the police for using poppers; that lover had died years ago, and his successors had never worked out—after him, he seemed to have fallen out of favor with the gods, and had lived a loveless life for four years, the last three in the Quarter complicated by his hiring hustlers. So that when he returned to Fire Island this time—with fliers plastered around the harbor saying "Please welcome Morgan back from his triumphant sojourn in the French Quarter!"—he was resolved to steer clear of the human mess. Not only was the Pines full of ghosts, he felt like one himself.

Occasionally people who recognized him came into the restaurant and gave their names. Most of them he would not have recognized. Those he did remember were very few, fixtures of the Pines. Years ago, for instance, he would lie on the beach and watch a sinewy, silver-haired man burnt deep brown by the sun take a catamaran out to sea every afternoon—a man whose stamina and fitness (and indifference to the fact that everyone else was so much younger) he admired and whose solitude intrigued him. That lean, silver-haired, sunburnt old man was still sailing his catamaran out through the waves; only now he also walked around the harbor talking out loud to himself. The other man he was glad to see lived on a rise that gave his balcony a view of all the boardwalks and the beach below, where he still spent the afternoons watching the people on the beach and boardwalks through binoculars. His flags were still flying in the breeze, his silhouette still surveying the beach parade. But they were the only two. Then one night a man with a silver beard motioned him over to his table in the restaurant and reminded him of a night he had long forgotten when the two of them had swum out to the man's sailboat anchored offshore and made love all night in the moonlight; when the waiter cleared the table, he found the man's address on a piece of paper with a message saying he would be glad to do it again. Such bouquets thrown up from the past were infrequent, however, and though he was glad of them, he never pursued the invitation. The sailboat was still offshore, but he did not go to it. He was too determined to keep his sobriety, though he was often dumbfounded by the beauty of the young men who still gathered here.

There was disagreement among the survivors of his age and older over the quality of the newest generation. He thought they were quite handsome; they looked to him, at their best, like West Point cadets in training. He stood in the gymnasium behind his little restaurant, talking with the owner, while the men on the benches all around them lifted weights. With nothing more than the swimmer's physique he'd developed in high school, he was now too embarrassed to even take off his shirt and go in the ocean. Otherwise nothing on the Island seemed to have changed, except the fact that no one had mustaches, beards, or even body hair. When the crowd gathered in its underwear one night, carrying torches, and boarded boats for the Invasion of the Grove, they looked like Hitler Youth. The Morning Party was the same.

That weekend a group of men his age who all remembered him—some of whom he'd known twenty years ago—called him over to their table and asked what he thought of the new crowd and, before he could reply, answered for him. "They're all like Stepford wives," one said, "perfectly manicured little facades. Though they don't handle their drugs all that well. They have the right haircut and the right shoes and the right muscles."

"But they don't have *faces*," someone said in a guttural voice. "We had faces. These new guys don't." And they began to reminisce about an era when most male models were gay, and driving out on the Long Island Expressway, you passed, on giant billboards, smoking cigarettes, the same men you would find standing across from you at Tea Dance when you reached the Pines.

At work he turned over in his mind what they had said, though it sounded, on the surface, absurd to him—that one generation (his) would have faces, and another not. Surely to each other, these young men had faces—faces that were profoundly individual, significant, and occasionally heartbreaking.

Three of them, in fact, belonged to his waiters, whom he got to see every day of the week close up—quite separate from the crowd walking though the harbor in phalanxes of friends or glued together at the Morning Party, where the uniformity made them all look interchangeable. The Englishman was handsome but had a personality so practical and brisk he exuded little sexuality. The Frenchman was so sexual that halfway through the summer he was hired by an Italian film producer and taken to the Hamptons. That left the American, a twenty-six-year-old from Long Island who had been living with his grandmother while he studied German, a rather shy person who hung around the restaurant on his time off, had no one picking him up after work, and seemed to spend the rest of his free time back in his room in Steerage.

Steerage was the waiters' dormitory hidden behind a screen of shrubbery a few steps from the harbor. In a town as visually acute as this one, it was just as well that it could not be seen, since it looked like a decaying old motel—a long, wooden building with rows of rooms on each side, with neither privacy nor charm nor cozincss, rustcd chairs and tablcs dccomposing on a littcrcd dcck to the buzz of radios and TVs that were never turned off. He had lived there previous summers, and he knew how hot, noisy, and depressing it all was. Someone claimed the place was kept this way on purpose to discourage people from lingering at season's end; someone else said it was a monument to Love—to the fact that no one was supposed to spend much time there, the assumption being that a young waiter came to the Island to make money on tips, get a tan, and spend all his free time at the pool with boyfriends he had met while on the Island. Ryan seemed to fit into none of these expectations; whenever he had to be called back to work because another waiter (recuperating from some sexual binge) had not shown up, he was usually to be found on the bunk bed in the littered room he shared with a cook, reading *Buddenbrooks* in German.

Ryan was a bright young man who had, like Morgan, majored in history in school; he had never lived in Manhattan, much less taken drugs, gone dancing, and participated in what was called "the Circuit." At twenty-six, he was already starting to lose his dirty blond hair and that made him vulnerable, somehow, in Morgan's eyes. His body was as slender and smooth as his own. He had large blue eyes, a long face, and he exuded sweetness, a quality Morgan valued more than any other. Ryan still did not know what he wanted to do in life—he'd thought of being an actor but had done nothing about it; he wanted to live in Leipzig but had not done that either; he had simply been in and out of college, working in restaurants, living with his grandmother, too shy, if his friend from Long Island was to be believed, to go home with people, interested more in talking than in sex. He did not take Ecstasy and dance, he spent most of his free time reading and was, in short, as sober as his boss, though they faced one another from opposite ends of life on the Circuit.

Morgan wasn't sure what to make of Ryan at first—sometimes he thought Ryan would succeed at whatever he decided to do and sometimes he saw him already dangerously drifting; indecisive, vague, a victim of the same illusions that he had labored under at that age; that there was plenty of Time, and all that mattered was Love. He didn't know how Ryan would turn out. He only knew he enjoyed talking to him and that he was glad to get to work each day because Ryan would be there, even on his day off, hanging around.

He was grateful at the start simply to have someone with whom he could discuss history, or issues in the *New York Times* he read every day with his coffee. Nobody else who worked there would. The one man he knew from Washington, who actually was a deputy-assistant-something-or-other in the Clinton administration, wanted to do anything but that when he came up for the weekend; he stopped in only to ask him where he could get some Ecstasy. Ryan, on the other hand, loved to discuss foreign affairs and domestic politics. That was why the petunias began to flourish; as they talked, Morgan pinched the dead blossoms and leggy stems. Before that the petunias had turned faded and scrawny; bleached by the sun and drought, already exhausted halfway through the season, they had looked merely perfunctory, something put in the barrel at the start of summer and forgotten. Now, looking for something to do with his hands, he started pinching the petunias while they spoke, and Ryan stood there, leaning against the railing, his towel under his arm, watching. Soon the petunias were thicker, healthier, blooming. It was amazing how they bloomed. The two barrels became bright cascades of red that caused people to look as they walked by, while he and Ryan discussed Yeltsin, Clinton, health care, China, affirmative action, everything that was in the *Times* each morning. He didn't realize the meaning of the flowers, however, till one morning the bartender, looking down at him from the balcony of the Pavilion, said, as he watched Morgan pinching the stems as he waited for Ryan, "Sexually frustrated?" Then he realized the others knew he was in love.

They seemed pleased by the idea, even if he was not. Even the bartender smiled from the balcony and said, "Don't get me wrong, I love your flowers!" People who were themselves drinking heavily that summer stopped, swayed, and got teary-eyed as they gazed at the barrels, attempted to grasp their significance, and moved on. The reservations clerk raised her eyebrows when she saw them. They seemed to lift the entire harbor up a notch. People asked him the secret of his success. ("How do you get them to grow like that?" a man called to him; he laughed, and said, "You have to be in love.") Some took photographs. It was as if he and Ryan had gotten married. The only problem in his mind was: Had they? That is, he now knew what the flowers meant—but did their inspiration?

He couldn't say. Between the hordes of muscular young men displaying their prodigious chests to one another, the condoms in receptacles nailed to the trees in the Meat Rack, the jokes, the drugs, the cook baking penises and swallowing them, the men lifting weights as they dissected in flat, jaded tones one another's body parts and those of their dates, the deputy assistant on Ecstasy every weekend, the Morning Party and the man staring at the beach through binoculars every day for hours, it was not a place one associated with romance. It was an exercise in display. It was a party. A party Ryan seemed to have no interest in, however. "I think it frightens him," Morgan said to his older friend Girard one night at dinner. "The way it intimidated me my first year in New York. The first time my lover took me to the Eagle's Nest," he said, his voice rising in surprise as he recalled it, "I would not even let him leave me to go to the bathroom—I followed him. I was terrified of being left alone for even five minutes with all those men! I think Ryan may just be scared," he said, "and he'll stay with me until he gets over his fear of them. And then he'll dump me. That's what's going to happen. But until then, I'm sort of his camp counselor. That's what it is. I'm the nice counselor you take refuge with at summer camp because the rest of the kids are so mean." And they laughed.

It really seemed like that the next day when Morgan said goodbye to Ryan on the dock—he went back to Long Island every Tuesday to visit his grandmother and help fix things in her house—and welcomed him back the next day at the boat. And, when the grandmother came over to the Pines on Ryan's birthday—accompanied by the parish priest—it was Morgan Ryan introduced them to, and Morgan who served the cake at the end of their lunch and bid them good-bye on the dock later that evening, and Morgan who led the waiters in song as they opened a bottle of champagne afterward and toasted Ryan, and Morgan who walked Ryan to the steps of the Pavilion before going home himself. But that night Morgan could hardly sleep, wondering if Ryan had met anyone; and his heart rose when he walked onto the deck of the restaurant the next morning and found Ryan already at one of the dew-drenched tables, stirring a cup of coffee. "What happened?" said Morgan, secretly thrilled. "You were supposed to meet someone! It was your birthday!"

His birthday coincided that summer with something the radio, magazine, newspapers, and television were all proclaiming—the twenty-fifth anniversary of Woodstock, which helped Morgan to remind himself it made no sense that Ryan could be interested in him except as an older brother. He could not imagine anything more stupid than falling in love with someone much younger than yourself. "The young require too much maintenance," someone had told him once. They had a sovereign right—to explore—that no older person could fairly deny them. He was not about to take a role in *Der Rosenkavalier*. Still, following Ryan's birthday he noticed himself becoming possessive in a way he didn't like: waiting for the boat on the day Ryan returned from his grandmother's, assigning him the tables near the bar, so he could see him while he worked, feeling thrilled when the sliding glass door opened on Ryan's day off, and there was Ryan, come to hang out with him and talk, or have Morgan approve his costume for the Leather Party at the Pavilion—torn jeans, boots, and a red bandanna around his forehead. (The other waiters had insisted he go. The next morning he was on the deck watching Morgan pinch the petunias.) Then one day a man in his mid-thirties he had never seen before stopped by, and he and Ryan left together to go dancing, and as he went around the restaurant closing up without Ryan, he was aware he had tears in his eyes. Half an hour later, in the depths of his despair, he heard the only door that was still unlocked slide open, looked up, and saw Ryan coming back. "Look," he said to Ryan—both angry and relieved that he had returned—"I have to tell you something. My feelings for you have become inappropriate."

"I'm in the same boat," said Ryan.

"Do you want to go out back?" he said.

"Yes," said Ryan solemnly.

Out back they lay down on a mat by the pool under the stars and the looming mass of the Pavilion, its outer decks peopled with silhouettes, like the decks of a gigantic ocean liner, and they looked up at the stars till Morgan said: "What are you doing down here with me? Don't you realize what you're missing out on with five hundred handsome men up there?" And Ryan said to him in a calm and level voice: "I'm not missing out on anything as long as I'm with you."

At first he kissed Ryan so hard, Ryan drew back and said, "Hey, hey," as if trying to calm a horse or a dog. Then they resumed. They kissed and held each other for three hours. He kissed Ryan with all the pent-up desire and longing, the deprivation, the loneliness endured, the fear, the suffering of friends, the loss of almost everyone he loved, the joy that this was still possible, that it existed, that it was still there. He kissed him with all the excitement that improbability brings when fate singles you out, because the world he thought was closed off to him forevermore still evidently counted him among the living, he kissed him hungrily, fully, deeply, passionately, with all his years of exile and depression, of faith destroyed and now revived as if it had never been extinguished, his whole body so rigid he was trembling all over, till Ryan drew back, took him by the shoulders, and whispered, "You kiss too intensely." And he said, "Sorry," and kissed him again, immediately, but gently this time while he willed his body to stop shaking, and they settled into a more normal investigation of each other's mouths that was for him merely a fraction of what he wished to do but seemed closer to the parameters of Ryan's desire and concept of kissing.

When he went home that night, he left by the back way, as if he could not expose himself to the stragglers, the lights in the harbor, the dancers still hoping to find, through motion, effort, the communion of music, what he had just obtained in the dark, and when he got to the dunes he found an empty hollow near the beach, lay down flat on his back, and stared up at the majesty and elegance of the stars for another hour, as if they alone knew what he knew now—the secret of the universe. Then he went down onto the beach, took off his clothes, and swam till morning, when he got home and found Craig putting up a fence around his lot. "What are you doing that for?" he said. "To keep out the deer," Craig replied. "So you can grow petunias here. Like the ones you got down by the harbor."

"Don't bother," he said.

"Why not?" said Craig.

"Because I'll never grow petunias here," he said. Then he went upstairs to change his clothes. As he clipped his beard, he could hear Craig downstairs, miserably knocking pots and pans about, suffering what was probably in store for him, too, but in some primitive part of himself he could not feel any pity; love was savage, love was combat, love was survival, and he was in love. Each morning of that week when he set out for work and passed Girard's house, there was Girard, offering him a cup of coffee, insisting he come in and tell him what had been said and done most recently. There was not much to tell. Every night they went back behind the restaurant, took off their shirts, lay down on the mat beside the pool under the stars, and kissed. Was Ryan a good kisser? Girard wanted to know. Not really. Did Morgan have a condom? No, Ryan didn't seem to want to do anything more. ("Welcome to the nineties!" said Girard.) Where did he think it was leading? He didn't know. He knew there were those who snickered when they walked by and saw the two of them out front, pinching petunias as they talked; he also knew everyone else was, like Girard, rooting for him, getting off on it. Each day he went in waiting for the dream to end—it had never worked before, why should it now?—and each day, at some point Ryan said to him, "You gonna hang around afterward tonight?" and bliss flooded his system.

By the second week a certain element of the routine had entered into their lovemaking; he noticed Ryan refused to turn his head sideways for his kiss; but he was very happy. He began each day with a mixture of suspense and joy that—starting the moment he opened his eyes, including his daily cup of coffee with Girard, extending to that moment when Ryan looked up and asked him if he was going to stay after the restaurant closed—reminded him that only people in love are really living. Then one day, a tall, blond man with pitted skin came into the bar, asked for Ryan, and, when Morgan told him Ryan was visiting Long Island, sat down at the bar and drew a map to his house so that Ryan could find him when he got back. And then, a few days later, when the two of them were left alone closing up the restaurant, Ryan turned to him, looking down at the coaster he was turning over in his hands, and said: "I don't know how to say this, but—I think we should stop seeing each other." It was a blow he had always expected, but recently thought he might be spared; as if in life there really are exceptions to the general rule. But he responded briskly. "You're right," he replied in a casual tone. And then he added: "It wouldn't have worked out anyway, since we're both tops."

It was a brusque, dismissive thing to say; Ryan did not reply, and a moment later put down his coaster and slipped out the sliding glass door. Morgan waited for Ryan to be gone for ten minutes before he went out back beside the pool, knelt down on their mat, and began sobbing—so loudly that he woke the manager of the gym, asleep in the corner, and then the head cook, who came out of his room, drunk, and said, when he'd heard the reason for the commotion: "He was only doing it for his job, you silly goose! How could you think otherwise?" at which point the first sheets of rain from a nor'easter forecast all day slapped down on the deck and drove them inside. He could hear the boom of the dance music; then the rain and wind blotted out even that. He ran out to the front of the restaurant, and began pulling in the clay pots of petunias—the two big wooden barrels were too heavy to move—but it was too late; they were pulverized. "Oh God!" the cook said. "The petunias, too!" And he laughed.

The next morning he stayed in bed longer than usual—consoling himself with the idea that at this stage in life one could enjoy the young without possessing them—and when he went downstairs, the storm had passed, flocks of geese were flying south in formation across the sky, the ocean was utterly smooth save for a single line of breakers, and a great, domestic peacefulness lay over everything. He looked out the window at the light. It was the most beautiful day of the season.

↩ BLORTS

I WAS READING THE NEWSPAPER along the strip of asphalt that
serves as a train platform in the town of Sayville, Long Island, the
day Joshua picked me up (though I had no idea at the time it was
a pickup; I learned that years later). The silence around us was
very deep; the sun glittered on the gravel and the railroad tracks
and the fenders of the cars parked in the lot behind the fence; the
few figures going back to the city on a Saturday afternoon had
about them the resignation of the damned—engrossed in their
own books, newspapers, depression over having to return when
all their friends were still at the beach, or just staring into space.
Looking down the tracks, waiting for the train, the gravel and
the rails wavered in the heat. Beyond the parking lot the passing
cars heading to and from the main street of town testified to a
community that had nothing to do with us—we were just passing
through. One felt a momentary void, almost a loss of homosexual
identity, suspended between the two poles of our existence—Fire

Island and Manhattan—watching the cars; the train the only thing that could possibly save us from oblivion and stitch the self together, I was thinking, when a short, very muscular man with a dark beard, crew cut, and heavy-lidded eyes came wandering across the tracks from the direction of the grocery store, slowly eating a carton of yogurt, walked up to me, and asked if I knew when the next train was due. "Four fifty-two," I told him. *"Danke,"* he said, scooping out some yogurt. *"Bitte,"* I said. Then there was a pause as my interlocutor scooped out the last remaining bits of peach from the carton in his hand, ate them, and threw the container into the metal trash can; an act which only deepened the silence around us when it was over, and the gloom enveloping the passengers going back to the hot city. Then the man who had just finished a yogurt sighed, turned to me, and said, "I love going back to the city on Saturday afternoon, don't you? Against the crowd. There's something so overripe about Manhattan on a summer day—as if all sorts of strange fruits were about to drop into one's hands."

"That's from *The Great Gatsby,*" I said.

"Why, yes it is," he said. "Do you read?"

"Yes," I said, "I do. That's why I take the train, in fact. So I can read."

"Me, too," said Joshua in a suddenly thrilling voice. "The train *is* reading. So nineteenth century, so tranquilizing. In fact, whenever it comes round that bend, I always think of Anna Karenina. When she throws herself in front of the Moscow–Petersburg Express. Do you know what I mean?"

"No," I said.

"Good," said Joshua quickly. "That's a good sign. It means you are not mentally ill."

"Well, here's the train," I said as it appeared at the end of the tracks, its headlight incongruously illuminating the bright, hot air. "Now we can read."

"*If* they have any air-conditioned cars," said Joshua as he picked up his black overnight bag with the big shoulder strap. "And if there are no boom boxes and crying babies and teen tramps on their way to score some acid on St. Marks Place. And if the dust-caked windows emit any light. *On ne peut pas oublier, c'est le chemin de fer de l'isle longue.*"

"Do you speak French?" I said.

"I do," said Joshua, raising his voice against the noise of the approaching train. "My grandfather is French, I spent part of my adolescence, such as it was, living with him in Lille. Someday I hope to live to a ripe old age, like my grandfather, who taught me how to cook, and, of course, how to speak French."

"How fluent are you?" I said.

"How fluent am I?" said Joshua. "Well . . . let me put it this way—I can talk dirty in French." There was a pause as we got in line to ascend the steps, and then he said: "On both a dark and a light level."

"Ah," I said in a low voice, embarrassed that others might hear. "And do you do that often?"

"Only when the occasion calls for it," said Joshua. "I don't talk dirty in French with just *any*one—if you know what I mean." And here he laughed a low, husky laugh, raised one arm, and placed his hand gracefully against his throat in a gesture so classic and studied I sensed it was an imitation of Bernhardt, or some famous actress of the silent screen, though in what role I could not say. Then we boarded the train.

The car was air-conditioned, and half empty, and quiet, but we took seats next to one another. Then Joshua removed from his big black bag a *New Yorker*, a *New York Review of Books*, a *New York*, a *Village Voice*, a *Sunday Times Magazine*, a volume of poetry by Anne Sexton, a copy of *Les Liaisons Dangereuses* in French, some essays by Elizabeth Hardwick, and a fat journal. I produced a wan paperback—the aphorisms of Nietzsche. But neither of us read.

We talked instead, all the way back to the city. Just after Jamaica, Joshua said we had passed each other on the beach earlier that day, and I said, "No we didn't. I would have remembered it."

"You don't remember it," said Joshua, "because you didn't see me."

"Why didn't I see you?" I said.

"You decapitated me," said Joshua.

"Oh," I said. "You mean, I—stared at your—"

"Tits," said Joshua, looking down at the massive slabs of pectoral muscle that were displayed in his form-fitting white T-shirt. "My blorts. My iddy-fuggers, as my best friend, Clark, calls them."

Joshua's chest seemed to have nothing to do with Joshua; he was a small-boned, delicate man five feet, five inches tall, with the sensitive face of a young yeshiva student, a small mouth, an aquiline nose, and heavy-lidded brown eyes. Neither his arms nor legs were unusual; it was just his chest—like the armor a Roman general wears in a statue at the Met—though, by the time we reached Pennsylvania Station, I had ceased to think it was his pectoral muscles that made him unusual. It was rather his mind that was impressive—his gift for mimicry, his wit, his erudition. He was so bright, in fact, that when we got off the train and walked up the stairs in the oven of a train station that afternoon I asked if I might see him again. Joshua, however, was evasive. "Weekends I go to the Island," he said. "In fact, I'd be there tonight, except I'm going with my best friend, Clark, to the new Truffaut. We decided we had to see the first show. But I'm sure I'll see you again on the beach. Are you listed?" "Yes," I said. "And you?" "No," he said as we walked to the subway through the tunnel beneath Thirty-fourth Street. "But I'll give you the number. It's BELOVED." He turned to me at the turnstile with that and held out his hand; I took rather than shook it. "Have a wonderful evening," said Joshua. "May it bring you all that you hope and dream for it, in the deepest recesses of your being."

"Thank you," I said, taken aback by the somewhat antique courtesy. "And you, too!" And I watched the small, big-busted man in green army fatigues, white T-shirt, and black nylon bag slung across his shoulder disappear into the crowd funneling toward the A train on a hot Saturday night. Had it not been for the outfit, and his chest, I thought, he would have looked like a Hasid on his way to Brooklyn, some Eastern European student of the Torah. (In fact, this was precisely what he was rebelling against.) There was a strange dichotomy between his body and his personality; or so I thought as I turned and went down another tunnel to the BMT.

Though I called Joshua the following week, I got no answer. In 1973 there were no answering machines; the telephone just rang, mesmerizing an unseen cat, conveying the emptiness of an apartment, implying other parties, other rooms; places the caller was not. Nor did I see Joshua at the beach again in any of the flotillas of men who came walking down the water's edge in visors and dark glasses. In those days not only were there no answering machines, there were not that many muscular bodies either—and we would say of someone that he had an Important Stomach simply because it was flat. Surely Joshua would have been noticeable. But he was not. Nor was he in the city. It wasn't till Halloween week that I ran into him by accident on lower Fifth Avenue, dressed in a suit and tie, coming home from his job teaching fifth grade in Jackson Heights, with a briefcase, and a scarf draped around his shoulders. And then he could not talk because he was hurrying to his gym on Sheridan Square before someone got the calf machine. "I have to work on my calves," he said breathlessly. "Lenny said they need a lot of work, and of course he's absolutely right. My calves are even more pathetic than my forearms, and that's saying a lot."

"Your forearms are perfectly fine," I said.

"You're being kind," said Joshua, putting a hand out to touch my arm and laughing a husky laugh. "My *fore*arms are those of a twelve-year-old *girl*," he said in a sinuous voice that rose and fell in the gathering dusk. "*Who has rickets.* My forearms are not even as big as—no, I mustn't say what they are not even as big as on Anthony Torrescarpa. Not here in front of a Presbyterian church. I must run instead. My best friend, Clark, and I are going to hear Ved Mehta speak tonight, and then eat, what else, Indian. How's the temporary typing going? Knock 'em dead, Red!" he said, and then with a wave, he walked around the corner of Tenth Street and disappeared once more into the mob returning home from work.

I was touched that he had called me Red—since there was not much left in my hair, age had turned it brown; though I missed entirely the reference to a nickname Katharine Hepburn had used for Spencer Tracy in a film, as I missed many things that fall. I felt as if I were missing the city itself, in fact, as I resumed my walk eastward to my apartment on Sixth Street. The people rushing past me on the sidewalk were returning, like Joshua, from jobs I did not have, to apartments which no doubt resembled homes, and some of them carried bouquets of gladiolas, on their way, I supposed, to dinner with friends. The autumn night was still warm enough for people to have left their windows open, and as I walked home across Ninth Street, I could hear voices coming out through the metal grilles, the voices of people having drinks together, or dinner. And when I saw a handsome young man in a khaki-colored suit get out of a Checker cab on University Place with a bunch of tulips in his hand, I stopped and watched him enter an apartment building with the feeling that I had reached the nadir of loneliness. Then I went back to my empty apartment.

The apartment had three rooms, and a brief hall between bedroom and kitchen. None of the rooms was large, but they were all in the back of the building on the fifth floor, and they were quiet and sunny, and the rent was one hundred and twenty dollars—the invisible but chief asset of the place. Furniture I had found on the street—a sagging pink armchair, a sofa, a floor lamp. It was otherwise quite depressing, though I did not think this important; I regarded the apartment as merely a changing room, a place to dress and sleep before setting out again into the city. Four stubby candles, molded to their saucers with wax, lined the windowsill of the bedroom, like candles in a church; waiting for the person with whom I could celebrate the rites I had moved here to observe. I'd thought that having my own apartment, freedom, and youth would be all that was necessary to realize my dream; but in fact, it had proved far more difficult than I had imagined—as elusive as Joshua, for that matter—and the vast majority of evenings I went to bed alone, thinking there was something wrong, something about the city I was missing. That little moment—of turning the light off, before going to sleep alone—always seemed an admission of failure. The next day, I told myself, I would find Him. Meanwhile, the candles on the windowsills gathered dust.

That Christmas, not having heard a word from Joshua or even seen him since Halloween, I went home to my parents in Ohio, and found myself staying longer than planned because I missed the comforts of a house with people in it; and when it was time to go back to the city, my mother seemed so distressed at the idea of my going, I put the painful moment off, and stayed. I had a problem with saying "No," even as a temporary typist: When the woman at the agency called with another job, I was so loathe to refuse her, I found myself on jobs I would have preferred not to take. I was incapable of causing disappointment in another human being, disappointment I was aware of, that is. So when Joshua called one night in January—he had remembered the town I'd told him I came from, and had obtained the number from information—and asked if he could move into my apartment, I said, "Yes," though I couldn't have been more astonished;

in fact, I wondered after hanging up if I'd have heard from him at all if he hadn't suddenly learned he needed a place to stay. Perhaps it was the surprise, I thought years afterward, that explained my assent; or the fact that I was in Ohio for an indefinite stay, and the apartment empty, and empty feeling when I was there; that, and the practical advantage that Joshua would contribute to the rent.

The reason he needed a place to stay, he said, was because he was being fired from his job as a schoolteacher in Queens, and he could no longer afford the one bedroom in his doorman building on Thirteenth Street. "Why?" I said. "Why are you being fired?"

"I am being fired because I slapped a child," said Joshua. "Her parents complained, and I've been suspended, and no matter how the case turns out, I'm finished."

"Why did you slap her?"

"Because she was impertinent," he said.

And that was that; when I returned a month later, I found Joshua and all his things in the apartment. "Thank you for saving my life," said Joshua our first night there. "Thank you for taking me in. I love this place so much, they'll have to *carry* me out on a stretcher."

These words gave me a mild jolt; but the rest of that winter Joshua was hardly ever there. He immediately found another job, copyediting manuscripts at a publishing house, and from work he went to the gym and from the gym he went to a restaurant, movie, or poetry reading with his best friend, Clark. The only time I saw him during the week was when I returned home around midnight and he was already wandering around the room in his underwear and sling-back pumps, setting his alarm clock and apologizing for his drowsiness, and then he did not talk very long. "My Valium just kicked in," he would explain as he lay down on the mattress we'd placed on the floor of the back room, "and I know I'm going under. I always know I'm going under," he said with a yawn, "when I've forgotten the Italian for 'window.'" And with a wave toward that object, he closed the two big doors that separated his room from the kitchen.

When I awoke the next day Joshua was already gone; sometimes there was a note on the kitchen table. ("Please finish the quiche in the refrigerator. It's delicious. From Balducci's.") Or a box of candy, or a magazine with an article highlighted, or some flowers. Joshua wasn't cheap. Whereas I saved my money—so I could stop typing for a while—Joshua spent everything he earned. He bought a futon and a comforter at Bloomingdale's, hired a carpenter to build a bookcase, filled the bookcase with his books, furnished the kitchen with copper pots and pans, and acquired a Russian blue cat ("She's as crazy as I am," he said) that was so shy it hid most of the time and never made a sound. He took friends to the theater, or dinner, remembered birthdays, bought things at Brooks Brothers for his best friend, Clark. He was polite and considerate; when he was home, briefly, on the weekends, he played his music so low I could not hear it, or listened with earphones as he cooked breakfast on Sunday morning for both of us. He was prompt in paying his share of the rent—though never with a personal check; he was so paranoid, he refused to have a checking account, or a listed telephone number, for fear, I surmised, that his family would find out where he was—he did not even use the bathroom much; he showered and changed at the gym.

In fact, he was absent so much of the time that on Saturday mornings I felt, when I arose and found Joshua still there, that I'd detained some exotic bird for an hour or so before it flew off, or he set out on that long round of gym-dinner-movies-dancing, which meant that once Joshua left the apartment, he was gone for ten or twelve hours.

Then one Saturday morning I peeked through the hole in one of the doors that separated the kitchen from his room, like a child on Christmas morning, and found Joshua still on his futon, talking to the cat he was clutching to his naked chest; and when I whispered, "Are you awake?" Joshua raised his head and replied, "More than awake. I've just masturbated for the third time, over a man at the gym yesterday, a visitor from San Francisco with the most incredible mouth, the sort of mouth you don't just want to kiss—you want to inhabit. You want to set up a pup tent and just live there. I can't stop thinking of him," he said, pushing the doors open with his foot. "I came so violently, I frightened Elizabeth," he said, turning over to kiss the cat whose head he held firmly in his hands. The cat emitted the first sound I had heard from it: a small, tentative meow. "*O, mein verrücktes schätzlein,*" he crooned. Then he fell back on the bed and said: "I've got it bad, I can't get this man out of my mind, even Harry Diaz interrupted his lat exercises to cruise him. Harry Diaz!"

"Who is Harry Diaz?" I said.

"Who is Harry Diaz?" said Joshua. "Who is Harry Diaz? Where have you been living the past ten years? In a convent? In Patagonia? You might as well ask: Who is Sylvia Plath? Who is Winston Churchill, or Jackie Onassis? Harry Diaz is—oh, I'll be brief. Harry Diaz is the man I *usually* masturbate over. Tell me, is it hot out today? Or raining?"

"Hot," I said. "Relatively hot—in the seventies."

"Good," he said, sitting up. "Then I can give them tit."

"I beg your pardon?" I said.

"I can give them tit," said Joshua, standing up with the cat cradled in his arms. "I'll wear a tank top." Standing there he pressed the cat against his bosom. "It's nursing," he smiled. "Thank God I'm of use to somebody. Even if that somebody is a miniature lioness with a very small brain. It's been so long since these breasts felt the rough hands of a man," he said. Then suddenly he let go of the cat and it dropped like a stone; a moment later the doors opened completely, and he walked through the kitchen in his sling-back pumps to the bathroom.

Half an hour later, Joshua was gone, turning in the doorway to say, in a blithe voice, "Have a meaningful and productive day!" and I was staring at the cat in the suddenly dead-silent room. I did not see him again till he returned from his excursion to the gym, the health food store, Pottery Barn, Balducci's, a matinee—and then he was home merely to drop his gym bag off, assemble his drugs, and change clothes for a night of dancing. I went down at midnight, got the Sunday *Times,* and went up to bed; and read it quietly the next morning till I heard sounds in the back room, and felt it safe to move about the apartment. Joshua never read the *Times.* He made phone calls instead. The first thing I heard when he got up was Joshua's low, throaty laugh behind the two closed doors, and snatches of dialogue that let me know Joshua was on the phone dissecting the previous night; who was there, who danced well, who left with whom, whether or not the music was good. ("The music was *good,* it wasn't great," he almost always said.) Then, around three o'clock, the two white doors opened, and Joshua found me in the kitchen reading the *Times* over a bowl of granola. "I hope I didn't waken you," he said politely. "I stuffed a sock in my mouth when I climaxed, so there would be no noise." And he walked across the kitchen in his sling-back pumps and went into the bathroom to clip his beard.

Often he sang the blues while he clipped his beard—or a song Lee Wiley used to sing, "Just Look at Me Now"—then he launched into a monologue about the fact that it was impossible to work out in a gym with Harry Diaz, because a) he was so sexy, and b) his definition and size were so superior to everyone else's. "Tell me," he said once, sticking his head out the bathroom door, "do you think the ass *is* improvable? Isn't this where eighteenth-century positivism crashes onto the rocks of a postmodern reality even the twentieth century cannot ignore? Do you think Thomas Jefferson, when he wasn't shtupping one of his slaves, would have considered the gluteus maximus something we can improve? Or something we just must allow to be what it inherently is? Plato of course thought we cannot educate people—we can merely bring out what is already there. Which is why I slapped the little girl. What was already there was just rudeness and contempt. But sometimes when I look at Harry Diaz's bubble butt, I have to ask myself: How can any of us compete with that? I mean, have you seen it?"

"Seen what?" I said.

"Harry Diaz's bubble butt," said Joshua. He waved his scissors and retreated into the bathroom. "I forget you do not go to my gym, and so cannot possibly understand any of these references." And then he began to sing: "I'm not a girl who cares about money, I'm not a girl who cares about fortune and such, oh no, not much, just look at me now!" And then the telephone rang, and with the squeal Jayne Mansfield had used in *Will Success Spoil Rock Hunter?* he darted out of the bathroom and ran to pick up his phone. "Walter Reade Memorial Army Hospital, surgery," he always said in a somber, stricken voice. Then there'd be a pause, and his first explosive seizure of laughter, and with a foot he'd push the white doors shut and I would return to my bowl of granola. It *was* like living with Jayne Mansfield.

Other things certainly suggested this comparison; watching Joshua walk through a crowd on the sidewalk, that's exactly who one thought of—parting the oncoming pedestrians with exactly the same swagger, the rocking back and forth, side to side, as his chest seemed to precede him through space. Though Joshua saw no one—he once passed *me* right by—lots of people looked at him; from the stoop I could see the men turn around. At home there was even more of the big-busted ingenue about Joshua when he was there on Saturday and Sunday: the songs, the sling-back pumps, the towel wrapped around his head like a turban, the little cotton balls Joshua used to remove the Georgette Klinger lotion he applied to his face, the careful clipping of his short, dark beard, and the breathless, sexual laugh beyond the two closed doors. When he left, the toilet bowl was always clogged with those little cotton balls—the only thing, except the occasional hair on the porcelain basin, I objected to; though, rather than tell Joshua he shouldn't throw them in the toilet, I simply removed them with a spatula and tossed them into the garbage. The spectacle of Joshua's toilette was worth the price. I often lingered longer than I meant to in the apartment because Joshua was in the bathroom, singing "Someone to Watch Over Me" as he dabbed the little cotton balls against his neck, and ran on about the other members of this gymnasium on Sheridan Square I had been to only once, I explained to him, when I had just moved to the city and was looking for a gym to join. I mounted the long, narrow stairs to the second floor overlooking Christopher Street, and saw an extremely voluptuous man in a red bikini lying on the calf machine at the top of the stairs, his head back, eyes closed, resting with one arm across his forehead like an apostle asleep in the garden of Gethsemane. The sight frightened me. ("Darling, that was Ramón!" Joshua said when I told him about my only visit there. "He burns hair in Jackson Heights. He's a pussycat! If not a pussy!") I went uptown and joined the McBurney YMCA instead; there the crowd usually consisted of retired men playing handball. And each time I walked past the gym on Sheridan Square my choice seemed to make more sense—for there were always people hanging out the windows between sets, calling things out to the passersby, like prostitutes in Piraeus. They all had big, muscular chests and arms, like Joshua, and were very handsome—but the jokes, the frankness, the musculature intimidated me; I could not imagine exercising in the shadowy room behind these well-built chorus boys in tank tops leaning over the windowsill.

It was quite enough merely to hear from Joshua about the people who went there as he clipped his beard before the mirror in the bathroom, talking about Harry Diaz and the visitor from San Francisco who made even Harry interrupt his lat routine, and the six or seven other people—like Anthony Torrescarpa—who gradually began to form a cast of characters I became familiar with. Some nights Joshua would come home early from the baths, drop his black bag with a dejected air, and sigh: "My en*tire* gym was there. And you know what? I really don't need to hear Jack Hofritz imitate Julie Andrews singing 'Hava Negilah' when I'm at the baths. I can hear that at the gym. Plus the line outside Harry Diaz's door was a little discouraging—it caused traffic tie-ups on the third floor, till Anthony Torrescarpa, who I'm afraid is taking steroids, there is no other way to explain the change, opened *his* door. They all tell me I'm too romantic, but I don't know. I mean, do you think it's right for a man to cheat on his lover? I ask only because that incredible Hot Daddy who works at CBS, Frank Ryan, was lying in a room with his door open, when I know his lover is out of town on a business trip. Am I supposed not to care? He asked me in to smoke a joint, and I said: 'I can't, Frank.' And he said: 'Why not?' And I said: 'Because you're a married man.' He laughed. But he *is*. His lover does Liza Minnelli's choreography. And everyone knows this. Frank shouldn't *be* lying in a room at the Everard asking people in to smoke a joint, while his lover is in Los Angeles. Everyone knows his lover adores Frank. Men are pigs, Red, don't tell me they're not."

"Well, perhaps your standards are too high," I said. "Perhaps you have to accept reality a little more. For instance—did you have sex with anyone tonight?"

"Yes," he said and sighed.

"You had sex!" I said, excited. "With whom?"

"A *real* Hot Daddy. From Newark. Why is it that men from New Jersey are so much nicer than men from Manhattan? That's another thing I can't figure out."

"You don't have to," I said. "The important thing is, you had sex."

"Let's not go overboard," he said. "Let's say we came in the same room."

"But you did come," I said.

He turned at the sink, in his sling-back pumps, his long-john cutoffs, removed the toothbrush from his mouth, and said, "Of course I came. I brought life to the delta," he said. "I was the rain arriving in Khartoum. The Nile rose. Because of me, there will be a harvest this year. Did I come! Of course I didn't come," he said, turning back to the sink and spitting. "That would require a mind-body connection I haven't had since the third grade. But the Hot Daddy from Newark did, and I gave him Rosy Afterglow, big time, as we lay wrapped in each other's arms afterward. That's the only reason to have sex: Rosy Afterglow. The trouble is, one person at least has to come before you can have it. Did I tell you Anthony Torrescarpa and Harry Diaz have started living together? As lovers?"

"Then what were they doing at the baths?" I said.

"Exactly," he said, unfolding the futon. "Exactly. Only I was too polite to ask." He went to the sink, put a Valium on his tongue, and washed it down with a drink of water. "I have two graduate degrees, *and* a letter from Cleanth Brooks at Yale, I speak fluent French, on both a dark and a light level," he said, lying down on his futon, his voice dwindling, "I love my work, even copyediting a novel called *Shalom, My Love,* I have wonderful friends, the biggest blorts for a man my size at the gym, and you know what? I still have no personal life. Is it me, or is it them? Something must be wrong, but I don't know what it is, and I can't find out," he yawned, "because I'm going under, Red, I've already forgotten the Italian for 'window,' " and with that he slipped into the river of Lethe.

Eventually Joshua stopped going to the baths; and we settled

into a comfortable, even happy, routine, broken only by his trips
to other cities—as if he could find there what he could not in
New York. Only San Francisco merited more than one journey;
but even there he went straight to a gym from the airport, as if
he was afraid he would deflate while flying cross-country. In fact,
that was the word he used once while lying on his futon, with
one pump dangling from his foot, and the cat raised high in the
air above his chest: "I'm looking for someone I can deflate with,"
he said. But no such person materialized. The occasional suitor
would climb the stairs—often a sweet, nice man, a typesetter
from West Virginia, a chef from D.C.—but Joshua always found
something wrong with him; primarily, I suspect, the fact that he
liked Joshua. There was no way to tell them their courtship was
pointless. I would pass them on the stairs, on their way to or from
those doomed dates, I would mention them to Joshua and then
get set for the inevitable brilliant analysis of their shortcomings.
The Hot Daddy—that great white whale of Joshua's cruise—
never appeared. And yet Joshua remained hopeful. As the years
passed—and boyfriends, not to mention tricks, came and
went—he remained as optimistic as ever; and on Gay Pride Day,
always set off with me for the parade in a state of excitement and
high spirits—the failure of the system to produce its presumed
benefit (a lover) notwithstanding. "God, Red!" he said joyously
one year when he stepped onto the sidewalk of St. Marks Place
and turned his pectoral muscles to the morning sun, like solar
panels that would supply energy for the march. "Don't you just
love Pride Day? I love being gay! There's nothing in the world
I'd rather be than gay, unless it's lesbian!" And he would squeal
when he saw the tribe gathered together for the march, thrust his
chest forward beneath the lavender tank top, and then march his
blorts right up Fifth Avenue in the brilliant sunshine.

There were days over the next decade, however, when I wished
to strangle Joshua—the sound of the spoon against the metal of

the soup pot he was stirring on the stove behind me, as I sat at the kitchen table reading, enough to produce fantasies of murder. There were times when I regretted ever having allowed him to live with me—when I wondered what my life would have been like without him—when I tried to picture the lover I might have met had he not been always there—when I tired of the brilliance, the verbal extravagance, the lies, the little cotton balls in the toilet and the clipped hairs on the porcelain basin. But, ten years after he'd slapped the schoolchild and asked me for refuge, it was Joshua I lived with. It was Joshua who stirred the lentil soup on the stove behind me, while the wind rattled the windows in their frames on a winter night, and the cat, crouched on the radiator, as beautiful as an Egyptian sculpture, watched us both—the domestic scene (each one of us supposedly wanted to share with a lover) reflected on the surface of her eyes. Eventually I had to face the fact that the time spent looking for a lover usually produces that much more enduring feature of gay life: friends. But I could not say this to him. The closest I came to admitting any of this was when I said, while eating some of his lentil soup one night in deepest January, half-dazed by the hissing of the radiator, the purring of the cat, the coziness of the apartment: "Isn't it amazing? Here I am eating your delicious soup, all because I met you quite by accident one afternoon ten years ago at the train station in Sayville."

"Met me?" said Joshua, turning from the stove to ladle more soup into my bowl. "You didn't meet me," he said. "I picked you up." Then he went back to reading his volume of Anne Sexton poems while he dabbed Georgette Klinger cleansing lotion against his neck with a cotton ball, and the cat looked at me with eyes so clear and direct that when it meowed, it was as if she had said: Always the last to know.

THE HAMBURGER
MAN

MISTER FRIEL DIDN'T HAVE THE VERY BEST GOSSIP—but he belonged to that class of people who know one or two persons who do, and when he got from them a story about Norman Mailer, or Greta Garbo, or Jerzy Kosinski, he brought it to dinner because he was too poor to bring flowers or wine. He told stories instead. He would, at dinner parties on the Upper West Side of Manhattan, tell us that a friend of his who drove limousines for a living had taken Warren Beatty and Diane Keaton out to Long Island recently, or reveal what this same man had heard Mick Jagger say, while being chauffeured out to Montauk, about the tennis sneakers he'd just bought. He knew a man whose beach house Garbo visited; an ex-wife of Norman Mailer. He was able to enliven an evening because that afternoon he had been in the D and D Building when Mrs. Nixon and Tricia had come in to select fabrics. He was a man who had known Tennessee Williams, and the critic Stark Young; could introduce you to Susan Sontag or

Murray Kempton, and when I walked in was telling the people assembled in Colin's big, high-ceilinged living room under a ceiling fan one hot summer afternoon in 1982 what a friend of his who worked at Doubleday had found in Jackie Onassis's desk when he went searching for a pencil one day when she still worked there. "Seventeen pairs of sunglasses!" he said. The guests laughed. There was no way of telling, of course, whether there had been, in fact, seventeen, or five, or zero pairs of sunglasses in her desk, since gossip in New York—gossip anywhere—is seldom exact, because it is a tale passed on from person to person, and each one will do whatever he has to to make it more amusing than it was when he or she received it. (That fall, when I heard the story again in Water Mill, I was not surprised to hear that the number of dark glasses in her desk drawer was twenty-two.)

It was a surprise to see Mister Friel at lunch at Colin's, however, since the last few times I'd gone there for a party he had been absent, and this afternoon when I'd come upon him in the lobby, patting his forehead with a handkerchief in the awful heat, looking for Colin's name on the panel of buzzers, he turned to me and said: "I have no idea what I'm doing here, or why I was asked."

"Why do you say that?" I said.

"Because I'm Colin's hamburger man now," he said.

"What's that?" I said.

"A hamburger man is someone people used to ask to lunch or dinner but he gets demoted," he sighed, "for whatever reason, and is asked for a hamburger instead, usually at the last minute. As in: 'I'm at a pay phone on your corner, do you feel like grabbing a hamburger at that little place on Amsterdam?' I'm quite a few people's hamburger man now, actually. And Colin is one of them," he said, finding the name and pressing the buzzer. And with that we were admitted to the cool, marble lobby, and then, right there on the ground floor, another door opened and we found ourselves ushered by Colin into his big yellow living room.

Mister Friel was a hefty man whose white flesh was always contained within the confines of a dark, three-piece outfit we liked to call his "May-We-View-the-Body?" suit. It gave him a formal air, that of an earlier New York, a more businesslike and disciplined time; though Mister Friel was basically neither anymore, and all that remained of his previous career, really, was his old-fashioned punctuality. It was the other end of punctuality that was the problem; for though he always arrived on time, he rarely wished to end whatever he had arrived for, and seemed happiest sitting in restaurants and lobbies, coffee shops and other people's apartments, talking. Saying good-bye to Mister Friel took a long, long time; many smiles and benedictions, many hugs and pressings of the palm, sighs and fond looks. He had nothing to go home to, actually, since he no longer taught drama or wrote reviews. If the story was true, he'd stopped writing when he'd walked into the office of his editor at *Commonweal* on the day an article was due with a shopping bag full of paper napkins on which he'd jotted down ideas from other magazine articles and books, and indecipherable scribbles on grocery receipts, handed it to the editor and said: "Here, *you* put this together. I can't!" The strain of critical thinking—of making sense of things—had become too much. Now he was a freelancer; a man about town; a peripatetic critic whose intense devotion to all his friends expressed itself in clippings we received in the mail from a variety of newspapers and magazines, with the words: "I saw this and thought of you!" in smiles, and compliments, and the wonderful, tender concern in his beautiful, resonant voice—rather like that of a priest in the confessional, which in some ways he was. Now he sat on the little pink sofa, patting his forehead with a folded handkerchief, gasping not because of the heat, one felt, but the sheer pressure of the three-piece suit.

He had been just as breathless when I had last seen him in the dead of winter at a reception for an experimental filmmaker from

Belgrade—one of his students when he taught drama at NYU (a position he had been relieved of, despite spontaneous student protests, because of his drinking problem). "I'm a teacher who cannot teach," he once said. He worked now as a freelance proof-reader, ruining his vision, we feared, on projects like the collected works of William Dean Howells, in the dim light of his famous apartment—a set of rooms in a Tudor mews on the Upper West Side so filled with stacks of old newspapers and books you could smell the odor of cockroach eggs when you went in. "I rent my eyes to the Library of America," he replied when asked what he did for a living. That was why he usually carried a briefcase stuffed with page proofs—though today he'd left it at home, and seemed eager for the opportunity to talk to other people, to regale them with stories like the one he'd just finished by saying, "That at least is what Jim Dandridge told me," while he reached over to pick up one of the glasses littering a sideboard next to the sofa on which he sat beside a much younger novelist who was as thin and monkeylike as Mister Friel was Rubenesque. "Who is Jim Dandridge?" said Colin as he emptied the ashtrays into a paper bag.

"Who is Jim Dandridge?" said Mister Friel, surprised. "I thought everyone knew who Jim Dandridge was."

"No," said Sarah, a British woman returning to London that evening who had done the research on a recently published biog-raphy of Somerset Maugham.

"He lives in the East Village," said Mister Friel. "He was Frank O'Hara's lover."

"And that's all he's ever been," said the novelist. "Who is he living with now?" he said to Mister Friel.

"Aaron Copland's cook," said Mister Friel.

"That's right," said Colin. "I forgot! You know not only Aaron Copland, but Aaron Copland's cook."

"And the man who drives Aaron Copland's old Mercedes," said

Mister Friel, flushing. Everyone laughed, and Mister Friel beamed.

"But all that is in the past," said Mister Friel. "Today we have a living national treasure in our midst. The man on my left," he said, turning to the young bearded fellow sitting on the sofa next to him. "The author of one of the most beautiful novels to have appeared in a long time," he said, and then, leaning toward the author, in a much lower voice: "I must tell you how much I admired your book."

Now it was the novelist's turn to blush. And, as the others began to talk among themselves about the matinee of *Dreamgirls* two of them had attended the previous day—forewarned by Colin that the novelist didn't like to talk about his work—Mister Friel turned his entire body toward his seatmate. "May I be frank?" he murmured. "May I speak freely? From the heart? What I found extraordinary in your novel, and very rare these days, was the depiction of a character at once extremely sensitive, loving, and passionate—"

The man flushed redder.

"And, at the same time, apart. What Joan Didion has called, I believe, in one of her marvelous essays, *de afuera*. This is the paradox I sensed in your superbly realized protagonist—a man at once in love, with life, and people, and, as all artists must be, I suppose, walled off, apart, surrounded, as it were, by a moat. That is, he moves among us, he is charming," he said as he put the tip of one finger to his lip in a judicious fashion, "he wants to be liked, he *is* liked, even longed for, and yet—correct me if I'm wrong— there is a barrier between him and other people. He is surrounded by a *wall*. Why is this?" said Mister Friel, turning to his fellow guest with the shining eyes of a young boy who has asked his father why God does not appear anymore to men.

"I don't know," said the novelist, who by now was probably thinking that a wall might prove useful if Mister Friel continued to probe this matter. "Isn't there a wall around most people?"

Mister Friel finished off his vodka and grapefruit juice and took another from the sideboard, at which point Colin suddenly realized his guest had been taking glasses from the wrong tray and tried to exchange a plain grapefruit juice for the cocktail Mister Friel was now holding in his hand. "Come on, Richard, give me the glass," Colin said with a frown—but Mister Friel, clutching his glass to his vest, waved Colin away with his free hand. "No, no, this is fine," he said to our host, and then, to the young man on his left: "I sense you wish to keep your distance," as Colin rolled his eyes and walked off to the kitchen with a discouraged slump to his shoulders, as if he realized it was too late now to avert the catastrophe. "I sense in your novel, that is," said Mister Friel, "it is very evident there, that you are indeed *de afuera,* that this fact provides the entire tone of your book. But now to meet you and find that you are so affable, so charming," he said, waving his hand. "This fascinates me."

The novelist was rescued by the arrival of Sarah, who sat down on Mister Friel's other side, took his hand, and said: "Richard, what is this I hear about you slipping on a copy of an old *New Yorker* and having to go to the hospital emergency room?"

Mister Friel, already slightly tipsy, beamed, and looked at her with damp, sparkling eyes as he closed both his hands around hers, and gently squeezed it.

"Never, never leave a *New Yorker* on the floor," he smiled. "They're very dangerous. Like glass. It's the glossy paper. You need ice skates."

"Richard's apartment is unbelievable," Sarah said to the other guests as he held her hand. "He sleeps on back issues of the *New York Times.* I mean his mattress support is literally stacks of reviews by Walter Kerr he has never been able to throw out. And there are old magazines all over, as well," she said. "So, one night last month he got out of bed in the middle of the night, slipped on the *New Yorker* and ended up at St. Vincents!"

"This could have been tragic," said an Iranian designer of opera sets with a frown.

"As everything is, if you wait around long enough," Mister Friel snorted. "As the divine Racine said: 'I have completed my tragedy. Now I must simply write it down.' Though even Racine could not write in this heat," he gasped, reaching for another of the half-filled glasses on the table. There was a momentary silence, punctuated by the wheeze of a bus outside, and the shriek of a distant ambulance. "You would all of course rather be in Sag Harbor or Water Mill," he said. "But we are not. We are in the city. On the hottest weekend of the year so far. And since we are, I would like to make a toast," he said, raising his glass.

And then—as he paused to remember some couplet from *Phèdre,* no doubt—a small roach appeared at the cuff of his shirt while he held his glass on high, crawled to the very edge of his cuff link and waved its antennae, as if it had come out to see who the guests were, one of whom, before it could retreat, flicked it onto the floor with her fingernail, where Colin immediately smashed it beneath his foot, gathered it in a napkin as if it were a live coal, and marched it off to the kitchen.

Mister Friel put down his glass. "Did I bring that with me?" he gasped.

"I'm afraid so," said Sarah in her matter-of-fact voice.

"And it's not the first time, Richard," said another of the guests, a Frenchman who translated at the United Nations. "You've taken lots of insects on summer holidays. Even to my house in New Jersey. You bring them in your luggage."

Mister Friel sighed, and tossed down the remains of another vodka and grapefruit juice, then said: "Mea culpa. The truth is, at a certain point in summer, I give up my battle with the insect world. There is too much heat. They need to get out, too! They move into areas forbidden them in winter. I cannot exterminate roaches. I do not think we have the right to destroy what we cannot create. Even roaches are God's handiwork. They constitute Life. I only ask that they stay out of sight. Until the odor becomes noticeable, and then I admit, I call the exterminator, who these days seems always to be a lesbian. Now, there's a novel," he said, turning to the novelist. "The life of a lesbian exterminator. Who will tell that story?"

"Someone already has," said the novelist, "in both novel and comic book form. All the stories have been told, I'm afraid. And that's why our civilization is going to disappear, vanish at its height, like the Mayans. Because we've told all our stories. There are no more stories!"

Mister Friel waved his hands about excitedly, rocked back and forth in his chair as he heard these words, finally put his fingers in his ears as he always did in the subway when the train came into the station.

"No, no!" he said. "I cannot bear this! Of course there are stories! There are a million stories in the Naked City! I had to watch one last night while standing in Keller's, even though it was as painful as witnessing a crucifixion!"

"Whatever do you mean?" said Sarah.

"I mean, I was standing by the window looking out at that throng of gay men in leather and little else who hang out on West Street on Sunday afternoons now, in a sort of herd such as you see on the Serengeti," he said, "when what do I see but a young man in his late twenties come walking up with a terrible frown on his face, a *grim* expression, and behind him, their heads hanging, a woman in an A-line skirt and white printed blouse and big white handbag, and a man in blue pants, pale blue short-sleeved shirt and glasses, following along. His parents! I did not know whether to cringe or cry! This demented young man had somehow decided, out of some misbegotten obsession with the truth, or a desire for revenge, or a promise to his shrink, to show his parents the world in which he now is living! To say: 'Hey, Mom, hey,

Dad, this is me. And these are my friends, my favorite bars, what I do every Sunday afternoon after calling you long-distance.' He was showing them his life. He was rubbing their noses in it. They did not even know where to look, they followed him down West Street, through the crowd, in and out of Badlands, Rawhide, Peter Rabbit's, like two rabbits being led to the chopping block. I have never seen anything so sad! Believe me, there are stories, and that was one of them. There are tons of stories. Stories are all we have! You above all, should not think we are out of stories! You are the storyteller! Do you really believe all human behavior has been portrayed? Must we content ourselves with films about robots, aliens, extraterrestrials, and spaceships? Am I the only man in America who thinks the Christ imagery in *E.T.* was blasphemous? Has the last word been said on Love?"

"Of course the last word has been said on Love," said the novelist. "Thousands of years ago. Yet I'm expected to write novels about it, when I'm not sure it even exists. All I see around me is the desire for love, the hope of love, the assumption that it exists—I see very little Love itself. Perhaps between parents and children. Perhaps at the onset of infatuation. But most of the time, you have to admit, people who go out looking for Love end up with sex instead. And even that they can't get. People want sex, dream about sex, look for sex, far more than they actually have it. I think people looking for Love should be grateful for a reliable supply of sex, because even that is hard to find."

"Mother of God!" said Mister Friel. "To think of being this jaded, at your age! I read somewhere that your generation has finally separated sex and sentiment—which they made sound like the discovery of radium—but I'm not sure this is a discovery to be proud of. I can only hope your entire speech is a response to having been left behind in the city in this awful equatorial heat!"

Everyone smiled. But Mister Friel had a point. There is a certain social humiliation to being in town on weekends in July, the kind that causes people to explain their presence in Manhattan the way you explain an accident. The following day was supposed to be even more humid, and even the novelist's speech on Love—which might have been stimulating on a cold night—was just another noise that afternoon, like the wail of distant police sirens, the whir of a helicopter passing overhead, the voices of people passing by on the sidewalk outside, the baseball game the super's radio was turned to. Everyone was grateful when our host entered to tell us lunch was ready.

"Salve, Regina," said Mister Friel, taking my hand in his, like a priest with a parishioner, as we walked out. "Colin is the most wonderful cook. He serves a salad with five kinds of lettuce, or used to. I just read a clever article in the *Times*—the social history of lettuce—tracing the various fads that have swept the city, from Bibb to radicchio. Talk about decadent!" he snorted. "You've heard of 'Radical Chic'? Well, this is lettuce chic. At the moment it's radicchio, though of course that won't last long—like so much else in this wonderful town," he said, beaming as he patted my hand, and then let me go as we came to our chairs. I was already seated when I heard a commotion, looked over, and saw that Mister Friel had entirely missed his chair.

He was lying on his back on the carpet like a roach when it's turned over, his arms and legs flailing gently, as he looked up at us with an astonished expression on his face, as surprised as anyone that it had happened.

"Richard!" cried Sarah, in an alarmed voice, as she rushed over and knelt to help him up.

"It's nothing, nothing," he said.

"But I heard your head hit the chair leg!" said Sarah. "I heard a crack!"

"It's really nothing," he continued to murmur as Sarah helped him roll over to one side, and he got up on his knees, then stood and grasped the back of his chair.

"Richard," said our host, at the opposite end of the table, in a gloomy voice, as Mister Friel sat down carefully on his chair. He stared at his hamburger man, with distraught eyes, reminding himself, no doubt, that this was why he was a hamburger man; angry that Mister Friel had been able to get vodka in the confusion of the glasses. "Are you all right?"

"Yes, yes," said Mister Friel in moist little gasps. "I'm perfectly fine." And he began to eat his antipasto.

"He mustn't get any drunker," said Colin to Sarah in a low voice, "because once he does, he falls down. And you can't get him up. We're very lucky he stood on his own. Three years ago I had to call an ambulance."

"An *am*bulance?" whispered Sarah.

"It is like trying to move an elephant," said Colin. "You need a sling. *I had to call an ambulance,*" he said.

"An ambulance!" repeated Sarah. "That's incredible!"

"Not really," said Colin. "Richard is a big man." And we all looked at Mister Friel, who, at the other end of the table, was murmuring to the novelist on his left as he held his fork, festooned with a piece of prosciutto, in the air, "Of course, some people have a wall around them, but it's usually because there is nothing inside the wall, and they do not wish this to be found out, whereas in your case, I sense paradoxically the presence of an enormous warmth, a love of life and people, so I am thrown back again on the central paradox—why? Why is there this wall around you, or your character, whichever you prefer?"

The novelist stared at Mister Friel coldly, then turned to the man on his right and said: "I hear you were just in Greece."

"Yes, we had a wonderful time," said the man on the other side of the novelist (as Mister Friel murmured, "This peculiar wall that keeps out other people . . ."). "We had a little house above the harbor, I even had an affair with a shepherd."

"An affair with a shepherd?" gasped the novelist, who leaned forward, eyes dancing with dreams of Theocritus. "A real shepherd?"

"What do you think?" murmured Mister Friel into his melon. "A pseudo shepherd? A faux shepherd? I have friends who dress as cowboys, construction workers, even Canadian Mounties, but I know of no one impersonating a shepherd." As he finished these words, he looked up, beamed at me, and squeezed my hand.

"Yes," said the man recently returned from Mykonos, "and it was wonderful. I went with him into the hills every day, we made love beneath olive trees, though you mustn't tell John about it," he said, referring to his lover. "Aside from that, of course, the island was crawling with European queens."

"You do not mean the kind that gather in Estoril," muttered Mister Friel. "Deposed and throneless."

"No, I mean the kind that gather in the Mineshaft," he said.

"An affair with a shepherd," said the novelist dreamily. "I once had an affair with a gondolier, in Venice."

"An affair with a gondolier!" said the man who claimed an affair with a shepherd.

"I was staying with a rather rich friend," said the novelist, "working on a novel that was never published. I would write in the library all day before a fire, with a blanket over my legs, and then at five o'clock the gondolier would call for me. It was the happiest I've ever been in my life." He smiled.

Mister Friel sighed. "Why do I never have an affair with a shepherd, *or* a gondolier?" he said. The entire table regarded him for a moment—struck dumb by the question. "Why do I never have an affair even with the Arab who sells me my newspaper at the store? Why do I never have affairs, period?"

Sarah laughed and put her arm around his shoulder. "Because you are too much of a romantic," she said, "and because you would probably rather sit at a table like this and talk about affairs with gondoliers because you have decided all that is behind you for some reason."

"A very good reason," said Mister Friel. "I am fifty-six this autumn—don't ask me my sign. I cannot bear that nonsense," he said. "The appearance of drugs in our high schools, the fact that my fourteen-year-old niece is an alcoholic who only likes to shop—none of these convince me that America is on the skids. But when an otherwise intelligent friend plans her trip to Egypt according to the position of the planets, *then* I'm convinced we are in an age like that of Rome when eastern religions began to be adopted. Don't ask my sign," he said. "Though I am fifty-six this fall. Which gives me the right to inquire," he said, turning to the novelist, "why is there this wall around you?"

"I really don't know," said the novelist with a smile. "Don't you think there's a wall around everybody?"

Mister Friel cocked his head and squinted at the ceiling, as if the answer were a little fly up there. "No, no, I don't," he said when he returned his gaze to the novelist. "Most people have no reason to put up a wall. But you are different—that is why I'm extremely curious about what you will write next. In fact, I have never waited quite so eagerly for a second novel. Tell me," said Mister Friel, turning to him with a forkful of melon at his lips, "when may we hope your next novel will be published?"

The novelist shot up, toppling his chair, tossed his napkin on the plate of Brie, and ran out of the room. We heard the bathroom door slam. Nobody spoke. Finally Mister Friel put a napkin to his mouth, his eyes wide, and said, "What was that all about?"

"What did you say, Richard?" said our host sternly from the head of the table. "What did you say to John?"

"I asked, I merely inquired," said Mister Friel, "when we could expect to see his next book. And he—jumped up, ran out, and slammed the door behind him! I know the pressure of the second novel is intense, but I never expected—a quite casual question, asked by a fervid admirer—to produce . . ." He patted his lips with his napkin, and then put his face in his hands. Then he pushed his chair back, and began to get up. "I must apologize," he said. I helped him stand as Colin said in an annoyed tone: "Oh, Richard!" Mister Friel tottered for a moment, and then went through the doorway, where I followed to make sure he did not lose his balance. "John," Mister Friel said against the bathroom door. "John, I'm so sorry, I didn't mean—that is, it's of no importance *when* your book—I mean," he sighed, "won't you please come out? I think Colin is about to serve dessert. They're waiting for you."

Mister Friel put his head to the door and listened for a response. Then he said: "Colin always serves the most wonderful desserts. His specialty is dessert." Silence. Then Mister Friel tottered to the doorway of the dining room and said, "Colin, forgive me, but what is the dessert?"

"Pears *en croute*," said Colin.

"Oh!" said several of the guests appreciatively.

"It's pears *en croute*," said Mister Friel against the bathroom door. The door opened, and the novelist looked at Mister Friel, who went quite pale, and held his fingers to his lips, like a child about to be punished. "You must never, ever ask me that question," the novelist said evenly. "You must never, ever ask any writer that question. It is extremely rude. Everyone asks me that question. I have no answer. Because I don't know when it's coming out. I just threw away what I was working on all winter long. So let's never mention my second novel again," he said, holding Mister Friel's elbow and gazing at him with the intensity of a gangster telling a bartender he had better be out of town by midnight or he will be killed. "I do not mean to criticize you," he said. "It is not your fault. But let's just go on with lunch, and never, ever refer to that topic again, all right?"

"Certainly," whispered Mister Friel, his hands now pushing up his cheeks, staring with wide eyes at the novelist. "I will talk about anything but that. We can talk about Venice if you like. We'll talk about Venice, Venice is sinking, I'm told." And he tottered back to his seat, behind the novelist, who sat down with a composed, placid expression and regarded his fellow guests as if daring them to pretend anything at all had happened. "Pears *en croute*," Sarah said as the dessert was placed before her. "How lovely."

"Pears *en croute*," said Mister Friel, as white as a sheet, fanning himself with his napkin as the dish was put in front of him. "I feel so *de afuera*," he hissed, turning to me. But no one noticed his remark, not even as an excuse to mention Joan Didion again; the table fell into one of those strange silences when each person is reminded that he or she is all alone in this world, and begins to think already of what they plan to do after they leave, till a woman who worked at the Met said: "Any word from João? Is he back in school, Colin?"

"Yes," said Colin, looking down at his pears. "In Pôrto Alegre. Starting school next week. I don't know why he insists on finishing—I can't see him practicing medicine—but he insists."

"Will you be going down there?" she said.

"I'm not sure," said Colin. "Chloe Wilson has a house in Acapulco, well, north of Acapulco, she's offered me. I may go there instead. I'm getting to the point where I don't like really long flights. It must be age. And Mexico is somewhat closer than Brazil."

"But I adore the flight to Brazil," said Sarah. "Flying over Puerto Rico in the moonlight and looking down. So romantic! The Spanish Main! And then I just go to sleep," she said to Colin.

"You're lucky," said the man who had been to Greece and had the affair with a shepherd. "I can't. I've just accepted the fact—I cannot sleep on a plane."

There was another silence, the clink of cutlery against porcelain, as if we were all in the dining room of a small ship pushing its way through the noon-bright sea. Then Sarah said: "How long will you stay if you go to Acapulco?"

"Three months," said Colin. "I wonder if there's enough to do for three months in Acapulco."

"Oh, you'll love it," said the novelist. "The coast is very beautiful, and when you need sex, you can go into town."

"Yes," said Colin. "Well." He stood up. "Shall we have coffee in the other room? Is anyone having tea? Herbal or otherwise?" In the confusion of voices requesting tea or coffee, the scrape of chairs as the guests stood, I left the table and went into the bathroom off Colin's shadowed bedroom. I was washing my hands when the door, which I had not bothered to fully close, opened and Mister Friel appeared behind me and hissed: "Is it here? Is it in here?"

"What?" I said.

"A photograph of João," said Mister Friel, looking at the snapshots tacked to a corkboard above the toilet. "They were so wonderful together. They were together in Brazil, in England, here. Just last fall, I went out to Fire Island, it was late October, to visit. I'll never forget—it was the last house in the Pines, a stormy day, almost dark when I walked in. There they were beside a fire—João, staring at the flames while Colin sat beside him, *knitting.* I will never forget it. Something only an Englishman, never an American, would do. The brazenness, the honesty, the indifference to image of those needles! Not the only kind in Colin's repertoire, by the way. We spent the evening together. João was so handsome, so sweet. He told me I had beautiful feet! One of those remarks I will carry with me till the day I die. João thought my feet were beautiful! Of course, *every*thing on him was. Though he was very shy. No doubt because he did not speak English well. Perhaps in Brazil he won't shut up. Who knows? But he was grave and silent here. And when he did speak, it was in a husky, melancholy voice. Those are so rare!" he said. "Truly romantic voices! Most people have voices as tinny, as shallow, as their characters. João had a voice like the echo of a waterfall in the depths of the Mato Grosso! And now he's gone back because he didn't want to be Colin's kept boy, back to whatever provincial dustbowl he came from, to finish his education. We will never see him again! He'll get married. Colin doesn't even want to discuss the subject, he's so brokenhearted. As am I! *I* miss João so much that when I came here tonight, I thought I would at least find photographs to remind me of how handsome he was. And you know something?" he whispered as we stood in the center of the bathroom rug. "There isn't one! Like Hatshepsut, his image has been removed from all temples! Photographs and photographs everywhere, of all sorts of people, and not one of João! *Why?*" said Mister Friel. "Why is there no photograph of João?" he said. And then, focusing on me suddenly, "And what are you doing when this is over? Do you want to walk across the park and see the new Courbet at the Met? A lovely walk through the park? I'm also invited to tea with Jerzy Kosinski's secretary, if that would interest you, and a reading at which I'm sure La Sontag will appear. Then dinner with a friend of mine who happens to clean Elizabeth Hardwick's apartment. And then we could go to Roxy, though I'm far too old for that sort of thing now, even though I'm still comped and can get you in for free if you like!"

"Oh thank you!" I said.

"Dear boy, I would thank *you* if you would come," he said, opening the medicine cabinet and looking at the contents. "Though *why* you would want to get in," he said as we entered the bedroom, "I'm not entirely sure. The music is so fast these days you need pogo sticks to dance to it. Everything in our culture is accelerating. Music *and* sex. You know what Eliot said: 'In the end there will be Beethoven and Bach, but it will still be the end.' "

"Did he really?" I said.

"He said something *like* that," said Mister Friel as I watched him rifle through a stack of papers, and then what looked like an address book, and finally a Filofax on the bureau. "Watch the door for me for just a moment," he said, and I turned to face the other way. Five minutes later I felt his hand at my arm and I was gently propelled through the doorway into the dining room, which now was empty, everyone having moved to the living room, where some people were passing a joint around and others preparing to leave. It was going to be that sort of an afternoon. Through the window I could see, across the street, the open doorway of a restaurant kitchen where the sweating dishwashers had perched to take a break, squatting on their haunches, while behind them the clouds of steam issuing from the dishwasher itself was the exact color of the sky. Mister Friel told stories about the soprano Zinka Milanov, and then Colin announced he was going to the zoo to see the polar bears, and we all said good-bye to him in the street. "It's like an Eric Rohmer film," said Mister Friel after putting Colin into a taxicab. "The final scene—Colin going to look at the polar bears to ease his aching heart. Because he's still not over João," he said. "He'll never be over João. I'll never be over João. Someone like João comes along once in a lifetime! There are cynics who say that the only true love is the man who dumps you. But it's not that simple," he sighed as we walked toward Central Park at a very slow pace to accommodate Mister Friel's shuffle. He had lately complained of neuropathy, the sense that he was walking on egg whites, but whether it was this sensation or his more leisurely approach to life (the feeling that companionship—friends and conversation—were all that really mattered) or his habitual inability to bring anything to a conclusion that involved good-byes, I could not say. Whatever the reason, we seemed to move at a glacial rate, as if this were another century, another place, and Mister Friel, patting his forehead, stopping for no reason I could see, and then resuming, reminded me at this point of not merely a priest but a bishop, making his progress through a congregation—in this case, myself on one side, and the novelist (realizing his arch-tormentor was now drunk and harmless) on the other. "The problem is," said Mister Friel, "some people are worth loving. Some people *are* perfect. They're rare, of course, and they almost never happen to love you in return, but they do exist. For a while João did love Colin, I'm sure, and then—something happened."

"What?" said the novelist, staring at Mister Friel the way he had stared at the novelist earlier.

"João realized he didn't want to sit around apartments like the one we just had lunch in," said Mister Friel, "and waste his life. Only aristocrats like Colin have the nerves of steel required for doing absolutely nothing with one's life. For the middle class it's torture. João was middle class. That's all there is to it. So he went back to Pôrto Alegre, where Colin met him five years ago while changing planes. Leaving Colin with the polar bears," he said, "animals accustomed to roaming the pack ice in the Canadian Arctic—confined to a space that is probably no larger than Yoko Ono's apartment! It's not right. It reminds one that life's unfair. Even cruel. That's why Colin is going to see them. To look at animals as trapped as he is—by the pain of losing João. As the song says, dear boy—'loving you isn't worth the pain of losing you'! So often one finds the most profound wisdom in the middle of a dance floor."

"But perhaps he's not there at all," said the novelist. "Perhaps he did it just to get rid of the guests. Perhaps he took a cab not to the zoo but to a movie theater, or just around the corner, and back home. Perhaps he just wanted us to see him getting *into* the cab, and in fact he's already back home washing dishes."

"Perhaps," said Mister Friel. He beamed and looked over at our fellow guest. "Leave it to a novelist to imagine motives and a plot! Two things so obviously missing from our theater. The British are, of course, nothing if not polite, and—it goes with manners—terribly duplicitous, so your theory may be quite correct. Auden was more straightforward. Auden, you know, used to have an alarm clock, and when it went off at table, that was it—the evening was over, good night! People grumbled but I thought it made perfect sense."

"Do you, did you know Auden?" the novelist said.

"I knew them all," sighed Mister Friel, patting his forehead with the handkerchief. "It's only recently that I became a hamburger man. I've known them all. If only I had kept a diary. Then the diary would be keeping *me*. Do you?"

"Keep a diary?" said the novelist. "Yes. But only for my tricks. I'm trying to analyze each experience to see if I can find any general laws about the whole business. Plus, I figure it will be nice when I'm old and can't get laid anymore, to take it out and remember each one." He raised his arm to flag a cab. "I wish I'd been able to meet this Brazilian guy you rave about."

"João?" said Mister Friel. "Oh, he was entirely faithful to Colin. João was not promiscuous." The novelist got in the cab that had come to a stop in front of us. "I've never met anyone who was not promiscuous!" he said as he got in. "A few times."

"That's why you don't believe in Love," said Mister Friel as the cab shot forward. "So cynical, the young," he said, turning to me. "Always confusing sex with Love."

"But it's the opposite," I said. "It's because they've separated the two that people like him feel the way they do!"

"Dear boy," he said in a silken murmur as he shuffled along, "they merely think they have. In truth, every time they walk into a back room, or alley, they are only looking for Him."

"Him?"

"João," said Mister Friel. "The wonderful one. The true love. The real thing. And they so seldom find it, of course. That's why the novelist is, I bet you, already forming in his mind the wonderful story he will write about a handsome Brazilian doctor who broke an English opera director's heart. Like Henry James when told the anecdote that led him to write *The Ambassadors,* he has found his little story, the piece of dirt the oyster will make into a pearl! While in real life Colin's with the polar bears, poor boy, or back in his apartment, cleaning up this futile attempt to distract himself this afternoon. Colin knows—he'll never get another João."

"But why, really, did João leave him?"

"He didn't leave him," said Mister Friel as he saw the bus coming to a stop at the corner; a bus I knew he could not catch, given the pace at which he now walked. "He left that milieu. He didn't want to waste his life, you see—as so many of us have. That's the real horror. Not the drugs, or the houses in Acapulco, or the small talk—the waste! Of energy and talent, love and ambition! As the Church has always known, dear boy—there are a thousand ways to fall, and all so easy!" And with that, he put his hand on my arm and said: "But would you like to see the new Courbet?"

SOMEONE IS CRYING IN THE CHATEAU DE BERNE

MARTIN MCCLENDON HAD THE MOST BEAUTIFUL HAIR—he went to a barber on Astor Place who charged very little (Martin loved a bargain, and could afford little more), but his hair was so thick and luxuriant, he always looked better than the people who paid much more at Sebu. There were those who, out of envy, or cynicism, or both, claimed he was the only person they knew who once stayed in bed for three days with a bad haircut. It is hard to imagine this happening; but what they meant by this tale, of course, is that Martin was shallow, too sensitive to his appearance. But who has not, on some days, considered his barber only a shade less important than, say, his doctor? Martin was always a pleasure to look at, and when I caught sight of him at Grand Central Terminal one morning last March, on our way out of town to visit friends of his, I noticed as I got closer that the color of his sweater—a cinnamon crew neck with touches of gray— matched the color of his hair. The effect, as he looked up from his

newspaper with a warm and reassuring smile, was striking. "Darling!" he said to me, and held out his arms.

"No longer late for trains," I murmured as we embraced.

"No longer late for trains," he said with that dazzling grin,
"and smart enough to travel with very few things." He hoisted his
canvas overnight bag. "And considerate enough to bring gourmet
cheese and appropriate books for our hosts. God!" he said, holding up an illustrated survey, *The English Garden,* "in the old days
I was awfully rude, but now I'm so thoughtful I could puke!"

It was true—though even in the old days I would do just about
anything he asked. Only Martin McClendon, I thought, as he
took my arm and led me toward the gate to our train, could have
produced me on the spot with but four hours' notice; only Martin,
despite my deep affection for the country, could have persuaded
me to visit the house of people I did not even know; for whenever
Martin McClendon pulled up on his motorbike, or telephoned,
out of the blue, to ask for a loan, or a coat, or my company at a
party, I always said yes. There was something about him I could
not resist.

"Which side of the Hudson do they live on?" I said as we sat
down in our seats and he removed a stack of magazines, newspapers, address book, and letters—received and in progress—from
his canvas bag. "The gay side," he said, squeezing my hand. And
with that he settled back to read an issue of *L'Uomo* and the train
lurched forward and began to slide out of the station.

The journey was up the Hudson—into the countryside north
of those crumbling, mellow towns along the river, whose mansions are now open to tourists who come up on Sunday into that
peaceful farmland dotted with reservoirs—lakes on which no sailboats sail, no swimmer intrudes, since they contain Manhattan's
water—that look like the covers on packages of butter; the beautiful purlieus of Rip Van Winkle, where horses, farmers, and homosexuals retire when they have been too long in city pent.

The journey takes an hour and we read the entire trip, exchanging magazines, newspapers, letters from mutual friends, with the comfortable silence that is one of the legacies of a long friendship. So pointless did talk seem, Martin merely handed me his calendar for the month—March 1978—and I read the news that way. His calendar was unique. Not only was each event—dinner, opera, cocktail party, date—noted, but rated in the bottom corner with an "Ugh!" or "Golden!" I asked why he did things which were an "Ugh!" He said: "Well, one doesn't know in advance. If one did, one wouldn't. But sometimes you find yourself in a loft in Soho with two video artists, waiting for three hours for a hustler with a ten-inch dick to show up and tell his life story. You know." I handed him the calendar and said: "Of all my friends, Martin, you're the only one who hasn't changed. You still go out to parties, you still have your heartthrobs, you still go to Soho and wait for hustlers with ten-inch dicks!"

"*And* he had a pimple. Here," he said, pointing to his cheek; and with that, the train came to a stop in Brewster. It was snowing lightly, and there was no one to meet us. We called a taxi company and sat down on a bench. "How like them to meet us at the station!" he said. "How courteous, how thoughtful!"

He turned to me and said in a suddenly serious voice. "I suppose I should give you a little history. You know that in all my years in New York, I've never felt I *really* belonged. I never fit in with any group. Well, this is a case in point. I don't want you to panic," he said, taking my hand, "but let me be quite candid—these are *not* my favorite people we are going to see, *if* the taxi ever gets here. I met them all years ago when we were doing summer stock in New Hope, and we all wanted to be stars of stage and screen. Well, you know where *that* ends up. Not one of us made it, of course, and we all ended up doing different things. But one summer they took a house together on Fire Island and forgot to include me, until I begged, and ever since I've wanted to belong to their little family more than anything on earth. Even if—don't get me wrong—they're still perfectly nice people, if truth be known, I find them the *teen*siest bit dull now. And since moving to this house in Brewster, they're even duller. Wilcox is fun," he said, "and Roger I adore, but the rest—well, I'll say no more. Because no matter how I feel, every year—the way other people go to San Francisco, or Provincetown, or wherever—I go up to see Roger's new lover. He always has one, and he's always worth the trip. So we'll just meet the lover, stay overnight, play charades or something, and leave, and anyway, you *do* enjoy the country, don't you?" I assured him that I did. He patted my hand and said, "Well, it's all right then," and at that instant the taxi appeared.

We were silent as we drove through forests of fir, over hills that gave us views of little lakes, and finally to a white clapboard house that sat at the end of a long driveway in a gloomy stand of pine trees. "Hello, Martin," said a rumpled man with half-moon glasses and a magazine in one hand, when the door opened. "Welcome to Casa de las Reinas Muertas. A name too silly to translate. There's just the two of us now—Roger and Nick are out, and Wilcox is asleep. Let me show you your room." We went upstairs to a bedroom whose two windows looked out on an enormous oak. "Oh, Clayton!" said Martin dramatically. "This is *sim*ply stunning!" Then, the minute the door closed behind our host, he turned to me and said in a low, grim voice: "Isn't this ghastly? Look at this bed! I can tell without even touching it I won't get a minute's sleep. I have to have a very firm mattress for my back. *I'm* sleeping on the floor," he said.

"The floor?" I said.

"Absolutely," said Martin. "Otherwise I'll have lower back pain for weeks."

(It was not my first contact with Martin's likes and dislikes, though it brought to mind a remark made by a man who did not even know him, but who said, on learning I planned to attend Martin's birthday: "You mean you still have Geminis as friends? I got rid of my Geminis years ago!" When I asked why, he said: "Well, they're all very charming, but so inconsiderate!")

Our bedroom was in a wing of the house overlooking a small formal garden with a birdbath and a statue of the Egyptian god Osiris; the topiary had long since gone to seed, or whatever the phrase is for hedges that have not been pruned for so long they've lost everything but a faint suggestion of the shape they used to hold. One could not say the same thing for our bedroom; it was like a room in a museum—so stuffy and dusty that Martin and I both went to the windows to open them and get some fresh air in the place, only to learn they were not only locked but further sealed by storm windows, so we gave that up and stood instead in the middle of the room looking around in wonder. There were two canopied beds; silver hunting cups on the mantel and ledges above the doors and windows; framed photographs; arrangements of dried flowers; Delft plates and bowls; swagged curtains; a marble-topped bureau; a complete set of the works of Washington Irving, Charles Dickens, and Pearl Buck; several needlepoint panels; a statue of the *Dying Slave*; even one of those little beds the colonists put babies in to rock; and enough potpourri to stuff a mattress. "It's every bed and breakfast in P-town, Key West, *and* New Hope, in one room," Martin said in an awed voice, just as there was a knock on the door. "Come in!" he called, and in came Clayton, a basket of yellow rose petals in his hand. "Don't be intimidated by the boudoir," Clayton said when he saw us standing there, stock-still, in the middle of the room. "We had a B and B seizure our second year, and decided to turn the place into the *only* guest house east of the Alleghenies," he said, removing handfuls of petals with a mechanical air and sprinkling them on top of the tables and comforters. "However, like the formal garden, it came to naught. Wilcox was the only one with the patience and stamina—the training in the theater—to finish his assignment. This room," he said, scattering rose petals upon the dusty surface of an Empire writing desk and, finally, inadvertantly, on us. "That was our anal-compulsive year. Whenever a guest left, if we found a single petal of one silk peony ripped, we wrote *nasty* letters! But," he sighed, "now that we've cut out saturated fats, booze, and sugar, and begin every day with an hour's meditation, we couldn't care *less* what happens to the potpourri!" he said, upending the basket of rose petals into the tiny crib (which made a charming effect).

"Well, then," said Martin as he brushed the petals off the shoulder of his sports coat, "you've made progress."

"Of a sort," said Clayton as he stood there, cradling the empty basket. "I've even given up sex."

"Given up sex?" said Martin in an alarmed tone.

"Two years ago," said Clayton. "It just got too complicated. I became addicted to a truck stop on I-95. I was drinking, and one night nearly froze to death. So I decided to take a break, and got some temple bells."

"Temple bells?"

"At Kmart," said Clayton. "*Wind* chimes. Not the tubular, modern kind. Faded turquoise temple bells—like the ones in that Tibetan shrine on Staten Island. You remember, Martin. We went there one Saturday on acid to meet Ram Dass."

"How could I forget!" said Martin.

"Exactly," said Clayton. "After giving up sex, I installed temple bells. You couldn't round a corner without banging into a pair or two or three hanging somewhere. It was lovely for a time—after I stopped thinking of them as testicles," he said. "And that brings us up to the present moment."

There was a silence; then Martin took a deep breath and said, "Well! Thanks for a history of the house!"

"My pleasure," said Clayton in a dolorous voice. "Now do

make yourselves at home! Though," he said, pausing in the doorway, "I'd appreciate it if you used the Ivory soap in the bathroom. The hand-carved soaps—relics, really, of the anal-retentive past— we've decided to sell to a guest house on the Cape." And, with a wan smile, he closed the door and left us to ourselves, at which point, we rushed into the bathroom and came to a dead stop before four shelves of bars of blue soap carved into little pigeons and camellias. "Relics," Martin gasped, "of the anal-retentive past. What about the anal-retentive *present*?"

There was no answer in the scene that greeted us when we finally changed to more comfortable clothes and went downstairs. The flurry of energy, the wave, the ripples caused by the arrival of guests, had already subsided, and a silence as deep, as vast as that of a windless ocean pervaded the house. Sunk beneath the sea of their own inertia, they had stopped living in terrestrial terms—though metaphors seem beside the point; concrete details should suffice.

To briefly describe life in the house its occupants had christened Casa de las Reinas Muertas (a name I won't bother to translate either) let me simply say that that afternoon—after gossip had dwindled to silence—I looked up to see Harry sitting in an old red armchair as he stared into the fire with a perplexed expression on his face. "What are you thinking about?" I smiled. He looked over at me. "In all honesty, I was trying to remember if I've masturbated today," he said. "I don't *think* so—but I can't remember. Oh well," he sighed, and went back to his history of the house of Savoy.

Martin looked up next from the scrapbook on his lap—he loved scrapbooks more intensely than anyone else I knew—and said: "Here's Joe Clark! I haven't seen him in years! I wonder how he's aged."

"He's dead," said Clayton. "He fell off a cliff in Hawaii."

"I see!" said Martin briskly. Then, after a moment: "Who got his apartment?" Clayton looked at him. "That divine rent-controlled two bedroom on Twelfth Street. Who got it?"

"I haven't a clue," said Clayton.

"What a steal that place was," said Martin. "Six rooms for a hundred and nine dollars, and trees on both sides of the block."

"Martin," Clayton said, removing the cigarette from his lips with the slow, measured dignity of a man who deplores haste, "is it true you collected money for a Christmas tree fund from all the people in your building, and then gave a dinner party with it instead?"

"Well," said Martin, "it doesn't take news long to travel from city to farm, does it! It's true," he said as he looked up from the scrapbook. "But I had no choice. I was destitute, I'm a McClendon, I *must* entertain, especially around the holidays! Besides, I *got* the building a tree—a perfectly beautiful tree I took from the lobby of the Emigrant Savings Bank on Fourteenth Street just before closing Christmas Eve."

"Was it a pretty tree?" said Harry.

"Very," said Martin, putting down the scrapbook. "A girl's got to live, don't you see! I must say I used the building fund quite shrewdly. I bought every white poinsettia in the Village. Simple. Classic. I had twelve for sit down, twenty-four for charades, and got nothing but raves. I've saved all the thank-you notes! I've put them in my scrapbook. Wish I could remember the cutest," he said, as he stared off into space. "But I have no memory."

"You still have no memory?" said Harry.

"For most things," said Martin. "I can remember every vein of the wrist of the boy I spent last night with. Every one! To recall each vein on Pablo Correa's wrist, the neurons *rush* to collide with one another. Not for *Hamlet*. But then, you were there for *Hamlet*."

"Act one, scene four," said Harry.

"Mmm," said Martin, standing up. He ruffled the back of his

thick, beautiful hair with the fingers of one hand and said, "It's three o'clock."

This fact elicited no response.

"Would you like to take a walk?" I said.

"Oh, why not?" said Martin, and started up the stairs. "Let me just get my shoes."

The moment Martin disappeared, Clayton sighed, and said, putting down his copy of *The Persian Boy*: "Where would Martin be without his hair?"

"I beg pardon?" I said.

"Where would Martin be without his hair? That magnificent head of hair?"

I had never thought about it, but when Martin descended the stairs, I could not stop thinking about it; indeed, as we went out into the snow I stared at his magnificent hair and wondered if it did *not* explain his extended youth. It was impossible to imagine Martin bald, and it was evident he never would be. As we walked down the snowy road, the wind parted his hair briefly, like the fur of an animal blown into tufts by a breeze, and then it fell back into place. "To think," said Martin, "I once wept that I was not included in that group! I used to see them in their blazers walking down Ninth Street on spring evenings with daffodils and champagne in hand, on their way to dinner! While I was on my way to the Upper West Side to give some old man a massage! Well, weep no more! Don't get me wrong," he said, turning to me, "I know there are far worse things to be—they are not mean, or selfish, or cruel, but darling, they are *dull*. Do you know, they even watch a soap opera?" he said.

"Which one?" I said.

"*The Young and the Restless*," he said. "Two things they'll never be! And that's why I live in New York! In New York you *are* young and restless. You don't watch a soap opera. You sleep with the actors!"

He threw out his arms to embrace life.

"Martin," I said, "what happened in act one, scene four of *Hamlet*?"

"Oh, nothing much," said Martin, making a snowball. "I forgot my lines. But I don't think they have ever *quite* forgiven me for it," he said, and tossed the snowball against a tree. A sparrow rose up from one of its branches, flew around, and then returned to an oak limb to watch our progress. The air was sharp and clean. I took a tree branch and shook it and watched the snow shower to earth. Martin pulled a train schedule out of his pocket and said, "I don't know about you, dear," he said, "but I'm going to take the one o'clock tomorrow."

"Oh, Martin, no!" I said. "You have to relax, they're all very nice, you have to undergo a sea change and give the place a chance."

"A sea change?" he said.

"Yes," I said. "New York is so fast that it takes a while for you to slow down, to get into this other rhythm. You see, we're—or at least, you're—still going sixty miles an hour, and they're all going ten. But it's so beautiful here," I said. "Look at the hills in the distance! Breathe the air! How clean it is! Feel the cold on your face, look at the pheasants grazing there!"

"*Aren't* you good," said Martin in a grim voice. "Aren't you the perfect houseguest! I suppose I should give it another go," he sighed.

But when we returned to the house after our invigorating walk, filled with energy and good spirits, our hosts were in the same chairs, and seemed to have hardly changed position since we left; nor did they even look up from their reading at our entrance, or at the appearance of Wilcox at the top of the stairs as we stood in the hallway unwrapping the scarves from our necks. Wilcox—a tall, stringy redhead with freckles and green eyes—held out his arms to us and said: "Dar-*ling*."

"Sleeping Beauty!" said Martin, holding out *his* arms. "Were you awakened by a kiss?"

"Gas," said Wilcox as he descended the stairs. "We eat nothing but bean sprouts and I fart day and night. When did you get here? What time is it? What *day* is it? What is my *name*? And where *are* we, precious?" he said, embracing Martin.

"We're in Sleepy Hollow," said Martin, "in a town called Coma." He stood back, with his hands on Wilcox's shoulders and said: "Don't you look *stunning*! Having lots of sex?"

"Never enough," said Wilcox, and we entered the living room, just as Harry was saying to Clayton: "Do you think happiness is virtue or sensation?"

Martin and Wilcox looked at each other—years of madness between them—and Martin said: "*I* think happiness is a pair of silken balls, resting on my chin. If you want *my* opinion."

"Well," said Wilcox with a smile. "I couldn't go quite that far. I'd say it's the right sweater on my way to Tea Dance."

And the two of them sailed off to the kitchen to gossip about people Wilcox had not seen in months. Silence now descended on the house. Martin came back to the living room to retrieve his cigarettes and, after lighting one, whispered, "Will we ever get to Moscow?" rolled his eyes, and went back to the kitchen. A log shattered in the fireplace. The deep domestic peace deepened. Around the window seats stood baskets of flowering azaleas, bright pink against the snowy panes, and African violets. A white cat dozed in the corner. A birdcage filled with a stuffed parakeet, two walls of books, and little alcoves in which a comfortable old chair and a floor lamp promised hours of happy reading completed the decor. It was an old farmhouse, and even the fact that the floors slanted was charming—like the imperfection in handmade lace. Wilcox went up to look for more scrapbooks and Martin fell in with the regimen by leafing through old copies of *Barron's*. "Martin, can you cook yet?"

"I've never *really* got beyond Jell-O," he said in a somber tone.

"Who's cooking tonight?" said Harry.

"Roger," said Clayton. "He and Nick should be back soon. He's doing chicken Marengo. It's delicious. And organic. He raises his own chickens!"

"I'll say," said Martin. He put down his magazine and said, "Tell me. What is the new lover like?"

"Like all the others," said Clayton.

He elucidated this remark no further, but Martin mimed a silent shriek behind the newspaper he held before his face. We both knew that, in his opinion at least, all the others had been outstanding.

"He's very quiet and very sweet," said Clayton. "He loves the outdoors. He knows a lot about plants. He knows, for instance, that a waxy begonia requires partial shade. I just learned that today."

But this was all he offered. And as the silence resumed, Martin picked up the *New York Times* and read parts of it he never glanced at in town—the business section, sports, science, national and foreign affairs—and the log in the fireplace hissed and popped. The white cat rose, arched its back, and, receiving no inspiration from the humans around her, lay down again in exactly the same spot—as if, its day's exercise complete, it could now go to sleep. The light grew dim in the room, and when I looked outside, the sunlight lay in long, low, slanted bars across the snow. The trunks of two oaks glowed a ruddy brown in its light, and then they faded to pale gray, and the early winter darkness arrived.

Just then there was a piercing shriek, and we ran upstairs to the room from which it had come. Wilcox stood in the center of his bedroom examining himself in a bright light before the mirror on the wall. "Another *wart*!" he said. "On my neck! They're sprouting all over me, like cabbages! I hate them! By Halloween I'll be such a crone I won't even have to wear a costume!" He turned to Martin and said: "I already have to spend an hour every week clipping my ears! Next I suppose I'll grow a tail! Why does it happen overnight? Why isn't it more gradual? Why am I turning into a werewolf at the tender age of forty-seven? Why do I feel I'm about to be whisked offstage by one of those hooks they used for bad vaudeville acts?"

"Dar-*ling,*" said Martin in a gentle voice, staring into the mirror with Wilcox. "I've always said there are two things a well-bred woman doesn't mention—hemorrhoids and age. Both may be torturing you, but do *not* discuss the fact with others."

"Well," said Wilcox, "sometimes I get disgusted."

"So do we all," said Martin. "But it's a dreary fact that calling attention to only makes worse—so let's remember, and repeat after me," he said, taking Wilcox's hands in his, "these *are* our golden years."

"Martin," said Wilcox, "you said our twenties were our golden years."

"Wilcox," said Martin, "they're *all* golden. Life just gets better and better."

"You've been a big help," said Wilcox, and sat down at his vanity. "Now get out of here." And he picked up some scissors.

"I feel like I'm in a gay insane asylum," Martin whispered as we went down the hall to our bedroom to nap. "Or the mansion of a mad old widow whose silver I want to buy. I've just come to see the pieces, and then I've got to leave. But where *is* Roger? And his new beau? What's taken them so long?"

We lay down on the comforter and he began to recall the men Roger had loved in the past: the Japanese swimmer on a scholarship to Columbia, the Argentinian cabdriver who had just left the seminary in Buenos Aires, the carpenter from Colorado, the clarinetist from Cleveland, the naturalist from Oregon, these silent blonds, so rare on eastern shores, with whom Martin, too, had always fallen in love. "They were so special, you see, because they had a quality, a quiet masculinity, a lack of pretense," said Martin. "They were not always brilliant. I remember the boy he met in Montauk in—1968." He sighed. "I once had to spend the day with him, and found it a chore. But the others—the others were all, let's face it, gods."

There was a noise downstairs and we raised our heads: voices in the kitchen, stamping of boots. We sat up and listened. "It's Roger!" Martin said as I heard a hearty voice asking if we'd come. We got off the bed and bounded down the stairs, like children about to meet their father. "Hello!" said Roger. "Hello, Roger, hello!" we warbled while a young man with curly blond hair on which snow was still dusted came through the door and stopped. A single drop of water zigzagged down his temple, golden in the firelight.

"Nick, this is my old friend Martin, and Steve," said Roger, and—in the silence that occurred after Nick stepped forward and we shook hands and murmured greetings—one heard with utmost clarity the single pop of a log in the fireplace, and then the great, breathless quiet that often follows the apprehension of beauty, or the sudden realization (like the moment you feel you have caught the flu) that you have fallen in love. We turned to Roger and went on with life, as if the earth had not opened and swallowed us up. Martin behaved as if Nick were not there. He interviewed Roger about his teaching post, his car, his plans for the summer, and mutual friends now in Carmel, Key West, London. It was not until Martin and I were setting the table, and we were alone, that he put a knife between his teeth and bit it. "*Straight* from heaven," he whispered to me as we passed each other on the way to get more plates. When I returned I noticed Martin had gone pale, and sensed this might be more than the usual pleasure taken in a comely young man—a suspicion that was confirmed when, moments later, he put a hand to his temple and said: "I've got a *split*ting headache." Half an hour later he grimaced and touched his spine. "My lower back," he said.

"Next you'll have a fever blister," I murmured, by now familiar with my old friend's symptoms. Just before dinner Martin told everyone not to worry and retired upstairs. Nick went up with a tray. Downstairs we talked about New York until Clayton, coming in with a bowl of hot biscuits, said, "Who wants to take these to our sick friend?" and I volunteered. But the dialogue within our room stopped me cold just outside the door. "You must go to Flamingo at least once," Martin was saying, "if only once. I hardly go more than twice a year, myself. I used to go every week, but now there's Studio, too. And the White Party next week, and the Sleaze Ball after that, and the opening of Pravda. All of these are things someone your age *must* see, just as you must see Paris, Rio, the Sistine Chapel. They're wonders of the world! Imagine a gigantic space filled with perfect men at six in the morning, at nine they are *still* dancing, glistening with sweat! Everyone should experience it once, and who knows how long it will last!"

"I would like to go to the city," said Nick in a quiet voice. One could hear his smile. One could feel the joy flooding Martin McClendon (the wrong McClendons, a cousin of Martin's once told me) at that moment.

"You know, you're quite welcome to stay at my flat," said Martin. "I've almost always got a houseguest from somewhere, but it's no problem to find room for another. We'd have *such* fun! But you mustn't delay! In two months, it will all be over, and they move to Fire Island, which is a spectacle of a different sort. Have you ever thought of *liv*ing in the city?" he said.

"Well, Roger—"

But this was too much. I entered at that moment and yelled: "Hot biscuits, comin' up!" Martin shot me a deadly look. Nick got to his feet and said: "My food must be getting cold downstairs." "Has Martin been enchanting you with fairy tales?" I said. Nick smiled. Martin narrowed his eyes. "I hope you feel better soon," said Nick. He then excused himself and went downstairs.

"You *couldn't* have entered at a worse moment," said Martin in a gloomy tone, putting his hands to his temples.

"Martin," I said, "there are ethics. Roger is one of your oldest and dearest friends, and—"

"I *merely* invited him for the weekend," said Martin in that same deadly serious tone. "I think he should be seen. One rarely finds things like these in the boondocks. The boy is magic!"

"Earlier this evening, Martin, you delivered a line from *The Three Sisters*. May I remind you of another play by Chekhov? *The Seagull?*"

"Is that the one," mumbled Martin through bites of his chicken Marengo, "where the boy commits suicide—"

"And the girl falls in love with the sophisticated writer from the city, follows him to Moscow, and then returns, a broken bird, when he has tired of her."

"Darling, I'm not going to do that! I'm not sophisticated! I'd just love to have him for three days, and put his thank-you note—next to a photograph, of course, preferably nude—in my scrapbook. Some people collect butterflies. I collect thank-you notes. You know very well I'm not interested in the kind of long and deep relationship that is Roger's forte. I live for my scrapbooks! And I always will! The reason Roger has all these exceptional lovers, these gods, these angels—well, you must have wondered how he does it," he said, dropping his breast of chicken and picking up a buttered biscuit.

"I have," I said.

"It's simply that *he* is as obsessed with having an intimate relationship with a serious young blond as I am about having twenty-four for charades, and twelve for sit down. Now you must realize that because Roger *has* this genius, for that is what it amounts to, because Roger *can* give himself to these fellows, he is never without one! Simple as that! What most of us fail to realize is that each and every one one of us has a talent—"

"Which is death to hide," I said.

"Death to hide," he mumbled through his second biscuit, "and that we aren't *competing* with each other! And remember, dear, a young man *wants* to be attached to an older guy, he feels secure, he feels safe, he learns things, he meets people he never would otherwise—*people like us*! Remember how attractive *we* found older men when we were two and twenty? Forty-five was the *acme* of attractiveness. A graying temple, a slight puffiness beneath the eyes, was *heaven*! Now *we* have the graying temple, the bags under the eyes, yes, even the warts, and *we're* looking for a recent graduate of Long Island University! Altar boys! *I* can't give Nick what Roger can! I haven't the time! A weekend with me in the city is *hardly* the plot of *The Seagull,* dear! Try again." He finished his biscuit, licked his fingers, and sighed. "That was *ab*solute heaven," he said, looking up, as happy as a child. "I feel quite restored. Do you think if I went downstairs after coffee, we could persuade these girls to play a few charades?"

But this remained only a thought—even he decided they were too heavy a mass to raise to the heights Martin demanded in charades—and an hour later he was still beside me leafing through an issue of *L'Uomo* when I dozed off. I was awakened by his hand on my arm. "Shh!" he said. "What is it?" I said.

"Someone is crying," said Martin.

I listened harder, and discerned the sound; it grew louder, then subsided.

"Someone is crying in the chateau de Berne," said Martin.

"What?" I said.

"Someone is crying in the chateau de Berne. That was the name of the house they all took at the beach the summer of seventy-one," he said. "I remember lying in bed one night after a marvelous party in this house filled with young, stylish, drugged beauties—and hearing that sound. Someone had just broken up with his lover. He wept. Who could it be now?" He turned to me with a frown. "Do you think Wilcox is weeping over the wart he found this afternoon?" he said.

"Of course not," I said.

We sat there straining our ears to catch the sound—which wavered like a radio station in the country, died away, and then returned, as if someone were sobbing into a pillow and then lifting his head; this mysterious, incongruous sound that Emily Post had written no instructions for, when heard by houseguests on a night like this. "Should we go see if we can help?" I finally said.

"Absolutely not," said Martin. "This isn't Kappa Gamma Delta, dear. We're all big girls now. These people have stock portfolios. They read the *Wall Street Journal.* They've made wills."

"But it's still sad," I said, "nevertheless. That beneath the conventions, the bravado required for daily life, the obligation in this country to always be *up,* there is still this secret sadness, this music of the heart that defies all optimism, that will not die away entirely, and cannot be cured by chemicals."

"Dar-*ling,*" said Martin, rolling his eyes. *"Get a grip!"*

And he returned to his reading. The house was still again, but for the tapping of an oak branch against our window. Martin, ostensibly absorbed in the issue of *L'Uomo* on his lap, sat upright, ears alert, listening for the slightest sound, like a detective in an English murder mystery; only it was not murder he wished to detect, it was grief. There was a knock on the door. "Come in!" said Martin. And in came Roger. His face was calm. He sat down on the edge of the bed and said, "Martin, I have a favor to ask. Can Nick go into the city with you tomorrow, and stay a few days? He's been wanting to for a while now, and I think the two of us should have some time apart."

"But darling, of course!" said Martin. "How could I not do any favor you asked of me? I'll show him all the sights, we'll have a marvelous time!" There was a silence. Then Martin put down his magazine and went pale. He said: "Roger, I must be quite candid.

May I be perfectly frank?" He took Roger's hand in the palm of one hand and laid his other over it.

"Of course!" said Roger with a smile.

"I *invited* Nick to stay with me, and urged him to come to the city, and told him he'd have a good time."

"I know," said Roger.

"You do?" said Martin.

"Yes. He just told me."

"Oh. Well, let me just say I in no way wanted to cause a rift between the two of you. I would never forgive myself! I do find him dead attractive, as who does not—the angels weep!—but all relationships, rare as they are, are sacred to me, and—"

"Our relationship is over," said Roger.

We gaped. "*No!*" said Martin.

"Yes," said Roger. "You'll be doing me a favor, actually, by taking him into the city. We've simply been alone out here for so many months, we've devoured each other. Totally. I'm grateful to you for your invitation," he said, squeezing Martin's hand. "Thanks for your concern."

Martin sat forward and embraced Roger and said, "What's a friend for?"

Then Roger stood up, said good night, and closed the door. "*Now* I know why I was asked this weekend," Martin said in a fierce whisper. "Roger knew this would happen."

"Know what would happen?" I said.

"This! I wonder what's wrong with him."

"With whom?" I said.

"Nick! I wonder *why* Roger is finished with him. Kind of like buying a house, don't you see. You always want to know *why* the owner is selling."

"Roger *isn't* selling Nick to you," I said.

"Of course he isn't, dear," said Martin as he put an index finger to his lips and frowned.

"Martin," I said.

"Yes?"

"You shouldn't think of Nick as a used car."

"Well, one *does,* don't you see," said Martin with a sigh.

"What exactly *are* your plans for the boy?" I said.

"Nothing unusual," he said. "Just take him around. The week-end was all I had in mind, although it would be so easy to fall in love with that one. His eyes—I simply swam in them. Did everything but wear flippers and a face mask."

I broached the wisdom of painting the city in such bright colors; in describing positively a life whose limitations we all saw very well by now; in leading him to believe that there was happiness to be found in such places as Flamingo, or at the White Party, or the Sleaze Ball. "Oh," said Martin, "I won't send him to the Sleaze Ball. *I'll* go to the Sleaze Ball. These things must be done in stages. I'm not sure he even shaves every day! *He'll* go to the White Party. And anyway, you say all of these things are empty and meaningless and emotionally void, but, dear, you didn't think so when you were twenty-three! They were fabulous! They were ecstasy! You had a ball! I find it very amusing that all you girls suddenly decide in your middle and late thirties that the life you lately led was silly, sordid, and a waste. Easy to dish the host, dear, *after* you've left the party! Anyway, that's your opinion of it, not mine. *I* think it's still divine. *I* want to die on my knees in a back room with dead babies oozing from my lips!"

There was a crash in the corridor—I leapt up, opened the door, and found Clayton kneeling among the tea things, which lay around him and an overturned tray on the carpet. "I was just . . . putting these away," he mumbled, and, after helping him replace everything on the tray, I returned to bed. "Well," I said to Martin, "even eavesdropping has its risks. So tell me—what do you think happened to all of Roger's previous lovers?"

"They're probably buried in the basement," said Martin with a wave of his hand. He turned out the light. "At any rate, it's clear to me who was crying."

"Roger?" I said.

"Nick," he said. "He's scared, probably, of leaving what is, no matter what else it may be, a very stable home. But the breakup was not our doing. It never is. My conscience is clear, my calendar for next week *black* with entries. I shall take Nick everywhere!" And with that he sighed and—as only he could—fell asleep at once. Martin could fall asleep in discotheques. He snored beside me in noisy slumber, oblivious to melancholy, regret, nostalgia, or concern over the meaning of life.

In the morning we ate blueberry pancakes, and shortly afterward, caught our train back to the city, as Nick told Martin the story of his life, thus far, and Martin composed draft after draft of his thank-you note as he listened.

I did not see Martin for several months after our return. He owed me four hundred dollars, but I could not find the words to tell him so, even when that summer I saw him in Central Park. "What happened to Nick?" I inquired as we sat down on a bench near the bandshell. "Nick?" said Martin. "Roger's boyfriend from Brewster!" I said. "The weekend in January!" "Oh, *Nick!*" he said. "He's living with a record producer and his mother in Brooklyn," he said. "He was so handsome," I exclaimed. "But *very* dull," said Martin. "The magic wore off pretty quickly, dear, and thank God I placed him with someone who loves him." "Martin, you're not talking about a pet," I said. "I know, dear," he said. "But the man is very rich, and has already bought Nick ten thousand dollars' worth of stereo equipment. And a BMW. Nick stays at home with the mother, who adores him. They're all Greek, and she's a great cook, and Nick is as big as a house. And you know what? He wrote me the most charming thank-you note after he left! I have it in my scrapbook, next to a nude photograph of him, when he was skinny!" And with that we parted—he was on his way to sneak into the New York State Theater for a performance of *Giselle*—and went our separate ways.

Eventually I came to see very little of Martin, except from a distance, on the street, and on those occasions I did not stop him to ask for my money, my lamp, or my parka. Of Martin a friend had once said: "He's so shallow he has depth." But the friend who said this has long since disappeared up the Hudson, to one of those sleepy little towns with an abandoned factory beside the train station, on which the light becomes a ruddy gold on those quiet autumn afternoons when you step down off the train, and stand astonished by the silence and the beauty. He lives now in one of those little towns that recall the stories of Washington Irving, where the bricks of the buildings are faded and the aqueduct that runs down to Manhattan forms a bridle path between slender sycamores shedding their leaves on a warm October day, and the river is flat and blue and somnolent.

He lives there now—as do I—and only Martin remains in the city; so that when Martin comes up for a visit, whole households from other towns seem to drop in, just to listen to him read from his calendar of the month before, like an itinerant storyteller in ancient Greece—since Martin is the only person we know who still goes out, and people still want to see his hair.

⌒ INNOCENCE AND LONGING

THE HISTORY OF THE TOWN WAS THE HISTORY of its grocery stores—when his family moved there in 1961, there was only one, on the main street, a shabby place used mostly by people from Jacksonville who had summer houses on the lake; the floors were strewn with sand, and there were only two refrigerated lockers containing ice-cream bars beneath a scrim of sweaty glass; on the shelves canned goods gave the store the air of an imaginary grocery small children create with whatever their mother gives them so they can play store. People drove to other towns to buy serious food. Then the town grew, and a brand-new grocery was built, a block east of the main street, which seemed extremely up-to-date in comparison, with its own bakery and delicatessen counter, and generous hours of business. He would walk there around nine-thirty at night so he arrived just before closing and buy a candy bar as a treat. The place was usually empty of customers at that hour; a single checkout girl looked at him in surprise when he walked through the door; the bag boys were restocking the shelves, sweeping the aisles. They were all young, still in high school, he presumed, they all wore white shirts and black bow ties, and had about them an industrious, Horatio Alger air he admired, in contrast to the louts who hung out in a nearby parking lot beside their trucks and cars—a floating social club that seemed to move every few months to a different part of town, one he always disliked having to walk past, some memory of bullies rising up in him, even though he was almost thirty years their senior.

It was the bag boys he was glad to see: their youth, their industry, their innocent faces staring at him as he walked in ten minutes before closing while they swept the floors. He confined himself to a mere "good night" when he left with his Milky Way—though once, after dropping a jar of strawberry jam that shattered on the floor, he had to go tell one what he had done, and stand there apologetically while the bag boy swept up the shards of glass and jam, assuring him that it was "no problem, no problem," when in fact he imagined the broken jar was his heart, shattered in aisle six by the beauty of the young man dutifully cleaning up the mess. Afterward he walked home eating his Milky Way under the real Milky Way, full of admiration for the youth, and all the other bag boys, reflecting that no matter how decadent the culture and the country seemed, parents were still raising good kids who appreciated the value of hard work and wanted to start earning money even before they'd graduated, the way he himself had the summer he was an usher at a movie theater. The year he walked to the grocery store late at night was one he regarded fondly afterward because of the bag boys who seemed to be waiting for him, in a blaze of light, like angels in heaven.

Then that store closed, too, and became a hardware store and a brand-new, even larger supermarket was built in a brand-new shopping center about two miles out of town, and he could no longer walk there late at night because it was on a two-lane highway. And a year later yet another supermarket opened on the opposite side of town, about a mile and a half away.

The two could not have been more different after a year or so of operation. The first was the more upscale of the two, had better produce, and more prosperous customers; even the bag boys' uniform, of black slacks and dark blue polo shirts, was more becoming. The other, on the south side of town, was more louche; signs on the automatic entrance doors, handwritten, stressed the fact that after seven o'clock, the cashiers did not keep money in the register above a certain amount, and that no beer or wine was to be sold. Still, it was open twenty-four hours for the first year, and one could go there at three in the morning if one wanted. When you did, you felt you were at some fish camp at a nearby lake; standing in line at any time in that store, the people were in bare feet or sneakers, with cut-off Levi's, and tank tops, clutching twelve-packs of beer and food stamps, while small children played with each other around the cart, and the checkout girl had to hold up the line to wait for the supervisor to settle a disputed price, and two obese women behind you commented with cheerful contempt on the characters in the soap-opera magazine they were leafing through while they waited to check out. The clientele was poorer, alcoholic, working class, sunburnt, and fat. But the bag boys—while fewer in number, and not quite so all-American— were attractive in their eccentric way.

He would go into that store at eleven at night, when there was just one cashier on duty, and the whole store had a bright, empty sense of peace and quiet and boys were restocking the shelves; the handsomest was in produce, putting out the pears or cabbages or broccoli with hands enclosed in plastic gloves—not the sturdy chemical-resistant kind, but more temporary ones, clear, thin, disposable. The boy in produce never looked up. He was five feet six or seven, had classic, even features, a neat, short haircut, and a faint flush of sunburn. He never saw him say a word, except the night he asked him where the rice was. When he turned to answer the question, he saw his face up close for the first time; the eyes were small and bright. His habitual silence, his ruddy cheeks, his neat haircut and shaved neck—as if he'd just walked out of the barbershop, and the talcum powder was still on his skin—went with the small, bright, pale gray eyes. He was like a mouse; an animal that kept to itself, quietly arranging the rows of eggplants, his hands in their transparent gloves. Besides the occasion when he told him where the rice was, he never saw him speak to anyone again; he seemed to be left alone to do his particular job in produce, though sometimes he saw him sweeping the floors.

Hence it was a shock one Monday when he went to the other grocery and found him there, dressed in neatly pressed khakis and a fashionable short-sleeved white shirt made of thin cotton with three buttons and a crew neck. Even his belt and loafers seemed expensive. He was in the produce section of this store, too, but this time a plastic shopping basket dangled from his wrist as he stood there perusing the red-leaf lettuce. He wore loafers with no socks. His butt was a bit broad. He was utterly mute. He looked as if he had just come from the barber. He may have been there simply to check out the competition. But something different about him—the good taste of his outfit, the way he held the shopping basket—made him think immediately, with a certain excitement: He's gay!

He was so excited by the revelation that he went home and phoned the only other gay man he knew in town, a retired businessman he called when one of the bag boys made such a strong impression he had to share it with someone. That was how they relieved the pressure of their admiration for the occasional man they saw around town. Their tastes did not always coincide. They differed on the bag boys; Henry did not think the man in produce

as wonderful as he did; nor did he think the boy at the delicatessen counter in the better grocery store as superb as Henry said he
was. They did agree on the prison guard who lived across the
street from Henry with his wife and teenage son; a big, well-built
man with black hair, mustache, and glasses who wore, for some
reason, very short shorts that exposed his muscular legs. Then
there was the pair of brothers who lived in a house a few doors
down; and the young schoolteacher in the rented house no bigger
than a garage who Henry claimed was gay because there were
lace curtains at the window and he seemed so nice and sensitive
when they spoke when Henry walked his dogs. For a while they
both agreed he was, and when he took his walk at night past his
little house, he always glanced in to see him reading or working
at his computer in the hot little living room, shirtless, beneath a
naked ceiling light. This youth confounded them both by marry-
ing another schoolteacher and fathering a child soon afterward,
however; now when he saw him returning from a run, still slender, slight, handsome, and they greeted one another, he found it
odd that the young schoolteacher was a father.

Then there was the man whose wife made him smoke outside
the house, who stood on his steps, backlit by a porch light, every
night he walked by on his constitutional; a nearly bald man with
glasses whose silhouette, on the top step, was charged with a
sexual magnetism. He did not know whether to attribute it to
the man himself or the pose and lighting. In that town, at that
hour, so deserted were the streets and sidewalks, so great was his
frustration, the mere sight of this man on his step, smoking his
cigarette, watching him go by with legs slightly parted, assumed
the drama of a relationship. One night it was so hot the man
stood there with no shirt, exhibiting a powerful if slightly sagging
chest, and he thought: He looks like my father. A bald man with
glasses and a big chest—that's why I'm attracted to him. He held
his cigarette the way his father had, too—turned inward, cupped

in his right hand—and the stillness of the summer night, the isolation of the two of them, the fact that his wife was nowhere to be seen, implied, in his mind, a certain possibility, if not a sexual bond between them; it was a shock when he saw the man with his wife one night, saying good-bye to another couple in their driveway, and he had to admit—as he'd had to with the young schoolteacher who had the lace curtains—that the man, at the very least, had a heterosexual life. Still, he looked for him each evening when he walked past, and when he reappeared, alone, shirtless, his legs spread slightly apart, entirely still, calmly surveying the street as he smoked, in silhouette with the porch light at his back, it was like having sex to walk that long block under his mute gaze, which raised goosebumps on his arms and made him think it was only a matter of time before the two of them consummated the contract they had implicitly signed with each other with the regularity of this nightly tableau.

Farther down that street was a big garage where three handsome men were often working on a boat when he walked by; he would stop and listen to their voices as they discussed the engine they stood around, like surgeons about to operate on a patient; and then he came to the tennis and basketball courts. The tennis courts, if lighted, were very bright; the basketball court, next to them, was lighted with the spillover, which threw the bodies into a certain chiaroscuro. He did not know when a stranger glancing at a basketball game became a homosexual ogling the players; so he generally looked straight ahead. Sometimes there was just one young man, playing in the darkness, with the radio in his car to keep him company. Sometimes there were only skateboarders whose size and height contrasted oddly with their mode of transportation—not all teenagers had cars—and as he crossed the park to the main street, he would watch them leap over the prone body of one of their friends, with the grace of Cretan youths balanced on the horns of a bull on some ancient fresco. On that street, in the five-and-dime, on weeknights, he also passed a tall teenager who sat reading at the cash register in an almost always empty store. And then there was the gym.

The gym was in a row of storefronts on the main street of town and could be used twenty-four hours a day by anyone who had a key that cost twenty-five dollars a month. Small, it had only old-fashioned equipment, free weights, incline and decline benches, a big old fan in one corner, and trophies in the window; but you could see, through the lettering on the window, and the crude painting of two dumbbells, the people inside—mostly men, mostly solitary—from the sidewalk across the street. He always made a point of walking past if the light was on, and a truck or car parked outside. Sometimes it was a middle-aged man, lying on the decline bench, staring at himself in the mirror, between sets, momentarily suspended in that mood that can come upon a person when he or she, in the midst of some physical activity, in the silence and the oddness of the place and hour, comes face to face with some profound self-assessment, or makes a decision to have a wart removed, or a different hair color used next time. Teenagers were always active, bustling around from weight station to weight station, often in pairs. One was always more beautiful than the other. Some had bodies that no weight lifting could have created, or even improve; others had torsos that, no matter how hard they worked, would never achieve the natural grace and proportion of their friend. But there was something about the solitude of the place—especially on a Saturday night, at ten o'clock—that seemed to him poignant; like the little motel down the street with nine separate cottages, where he saw one night a handsome man pull up the blinds on the screened porch and stand there, shirtless, in a pair of jeans, surveying the ceiling in what looked like preparation for a paint job; or the tall man with a big mustache and thick brown hair who stood outside another unit when he drove by one morning, also shirtless, in blue jeans, with a protruding belly and the weary air of someone trying to wake up, and get on with another dull, difficult day.

Then there was the hardware store whose staff seemed to have been handpicked for their looks—and the building which used to house the hardware store before it moved to the one vacated by the grocery store, a building now used, so far as he could tell on his nightly walks, for meetings of a church that still had no church building of its own. One night, on the same dais where he usually saw a preacher exhorting the people in folding chairs, he saw a young man with a blond crew cut playing his electric guitar; it was a warm night—he wore no shirt and the maroon cloth strap lay across his golden chest—and he stopped in the shadows of the consignment store across the street to stare at the youth, head bowed, playing chords of an awful, incomprehensible nature. At such moments he thought: There is no place I'd rather be than this little town; where else could I see a sight like this? The key to it all was solitude; his own, the boy playing the guitar, the rest of the main street dark, shut up, except for the dresses in the lighted window of the consignment shop, the bleak light at the rear of the drugstore. And finally the little motel with the nine separate cottages and the occasional lighted window covered by venetian blinds.

All these images gave the place an erotic character he was unable to decipher—which is another way of saying he had become a voyeur. The other term for this crossed his mind but he rejected it: Peeping Tom. Peeping Tom was somehow too reductive for what he felt when he walked past the occasional lighted porch and saw two young men lifting weights behind the screen with grunts and clanks and groans. Peeping Tom was somehow not right for what he felt when he saw the young man playing the guitar in the hall uptown, with the maroon cloth band across his golden chest, or the married man standing with his legs apart on his front steps smoking a cigarette before turning in. He didn't crouch in the bushes after all and stare at anyone; he didn't lie in wait; he didn't want to see anyone undress, although that would, on consideration, probably be thrilling. He didn't even like the word "voyeur." He knew there was a Freudian explanation for it but he didn't want to be reduced to that either. He assumed he was drawn to windows because he was lonely; because having been cooped up in his house all day by himself, he was curious about what other people's rooms looked like; and because there was something beautiful in the sight of people going about their business with an unself-conscious concentration—the men working on the boat engine in the garage, the youth practicing his guitar, the man lifting weights—and because it was a form of intimacy. He realized it was a peculiar form of intimacy. But it was still intimacy, predicated, no doubt, on the insane hope that one of these windows, one of these men, would be accessible in a way he could not foresee.

One day he was driving out of town with a friend from Gainesville on their way to the ocean when he told him about the men in the houses they were passing: the prison guard, the married man who had to go outside to smoke, the youth who played the electric guitar—and what pleasure it gave him to just see them, nothing more. "But that's silly," the friend laughed. "It's like wanting to buy a house that has no for sale sign outside it." In other words, why want something you could not possibly possess?

But people did drive around towns just to look at other people's houses, he said, they did fantasize, and there was pleasure in the beauty of someone you could never touch. The entire film and advertising industries were based on that. The whole world lived on such images, in fact. He wondered what would happen if at the end of every day, people who had inspired desire in others were presented with a list of the names of those who had seen them that day and felt a sexual longing. It would never happen, of course, but it would at least be honest.

On the other hand, he also wondered if the desire he felt for these oblivious men he saw around town was based on the fact that he could *not* sleep with them; that they were not homosexual. When he stopped going to the gay bar in Gainesville he told himself it was because he was too old to be doing that, but it wasn't just that—it was that other homosexuals had become banal, predictable, all too familiar at this point in his life. He was looking for rarer quarry—men in their native habitat; on the steps of their own houses, as if the context itself might supply the intimacy he wanted. In the bar, in the city, men were flowers that had been cut and shipped somewhere; in the town they were plants in the ground—a specific plot of ground, like the one the man smoking his nightly cigarette surveyed from the top of his steps: much more evocative, rich with association, than a mere body encountered at the baths. He was in this town because he was afraid of sex, no doubt, or at least disease, but also because he was tired of mere sex, and wanted a deeper connection; even the one he felt watching the young man practice his guitar all by himself in the deserted hall at nine o'clock on a Tuesday night.

And that was why he admired the bag boys—wondered when they came to work with a black eye, or bruised forehead; worried, especially after seeing their photograph in the paper the week of graduation, whether they felt this was a dead-end job but didn't know what else to do. The bag boys, the man in produce carefully arranging the artichokes with plastic-gloved hands, were one of life's dependable pleasures. Even the man whose wife made him smoke outside could not be counted on—there were many nights when he wasn't there at all—and he could only stare at his car in the carport, his lighted window, as he walked by.

One night he walked by the house when the man was not to be seen, passed the empty tennis courts, and the park, and turned onto the road that dipped into a little ravine opposite the public beach, when a Volkswagen slowed down on the curve and the driver asked him if he wanted a lift. Determined to complete his exercise, he said, "No thank you," and kept walking. A few corners farther he saw the Volkswagen turn around on a side street; instead of reversing its direction, it stayed right there as he approached, and blinked its headlights twice. Finally, through his reverie, and the deadening carapace of habit, the realization that he was being cruised struck him, and he walked over to the car. Inside a man his age sat, stroking an erect penis as straight and hard as the gearshift beside it. "Get in," the man said. They drove clear around the lake to the man's rented cabin on the other side. He was so startled, and so grateful, to meet another man in this town he could sleep with, he began talking and did not stop till they had driven round the lake; all his solitary walks, the sound of his footsteps on the gravel and the sidewalk and the sand, the silence of the men he caught only glimpses of, came rushing out; he gushed about the beauty of the man who smoked his cigarette on the steps, the people in the little gym, and finally the bag boys at the grocery stores, and how innocent they were. "Innocent?" the driver said.

The man—a nurse who delivered oxygen to invalids at home—told him he had given blow jobs to several of the bag boys; that he offered them rides home after work, and when they accepted, it was tantamount to an agreement to have sex; that the earnest young men he saw striving, Horatio Algerlike, to earn money, graduate, and move on into real careers almost all enjoyed getting stoned and having sex in the car. He did not ask which ones the man was speaking of—or if his favorites were included. They undressed, went swimming naked in the black lake, then had sex in the cabin. When he was driven back home he decided that what he had learned would not alter his own conception of the town; he knew he would never have the nerve the male nurse had in flashing his headlights at him, or asking the bag boys if they wanted a lift home; as far as he was concerned, they were just as chaste and off-limits as before; his conception of them was quite different from the nurse's. Months later, shortly before Christmas, feeling especially lonely, he drove over to the nurse's cabin on the other side of the lake; but when he parked, got out, and looked in the windows, he saw that it was empty; the man had moved somewhere else. He was gone. Then he drove to the grocery that stayed open late and found the handsome man in produce with his thin plastic gloves arranging broccoli on a bed of ice. He lingered not far from him, pretending to peruse the squash; the man with the plastic gloves did not look up; after trying to think of a question to ask him, he gave up, and walked off to buy some chicken breasts in the store whose bright, empty aisles, and rows and rows of cookies seemed to restore a sense of moral order to the universe; then, after staring at the man with the plastic gloves, now unloading bags of carrots, he took the change from the checkout girl, and went home with his bag of groceries. In just a few weeks he had restored the town to innocence and longing.

⌒ DELANCEY PLACE

IN 1970 THE BARS I WAS TOLD TO GO TO in Philadelphia were all conveniently located within two or three blocks of one another near the intersection of Spruce and Broad Streets downtown, and it was possible, the moment you got bored, to walk out of one and go to the next to exchange one roomful of faces for another. Of course, as with all social life, there was a sequence in which one did this: One went to the Allegro around eleven, the Westbury around midnight, the Steppes around one A.M., an after-hours club at two, and then—if all of these failed to yield the customer a companion—a block of town houses people circled on foot or in automobiles. This sequence ended with dawn rising in the east, and the birds starting to chirp, at which point the seeker of love went home feeling very much like a cockroach when the kitchen lights are turned on, stripped off his clothes, too tired to even masturbate, and finally fell into bed, turning over everyone he had been interested in, and everything he'd said and done that evening, his last thought before oblivion a vow to do better the next night.

I had that summer a nearly inexhaustible capacity to spend hours in bars myself, since I had only discovered them that spring; when I got home at two or four or five in the morning, the threads of my maroon Lacoste stank of that peculiar amalgam of cigarette smoke, beer, and the very hours I had just spent in their enchanted precincts—as if Time finally had a perfume: the smell of cigarette smoke. The next night I lived only for the night; waited until the appointed hour after performing the unimportant errands of the graduate student dropout (laundry, gym, part-time job typing for a professor of linguistics) and then walked down-town through the deserted city as if I were walking into a page of *A Thousand and One Nights*. The minute I entered the Allegro each evening, often as the jukebox was playing a song by the Undisputed Truth called "What You See Is What You Get," I felt an extraordinary surge of hope and happiness, a feeling that finally I was where I wanted to spend the rest of my life. That long, red room with the staircase at one end leading to a second bar upstairs, the mirrored wall, the vase of gladiolas by the cash register, the handsome bearded bartender I was so transfixed by I often followed him after the bar closed to a little coffee shop on Panama Street and watched him eat an omelette, the vague atmosphere of a Gilded Age bordello, were all bathed in a roman-tic silver and red gloom. The bartender—calm and masculine, absorbed in his work, above the petty battles waged by the pa-trons whose habit of pretending not to notice one another drove me crazy—even looked, with his large blue eyes, and beard, and long, narrow face, like Jesus Christ. He might as well have been that summer, for I felt I'd stumbled, after many years of repres-sion and loneliness, into Paradise. When a new friend who had led me around to all the dim rooms in town where homosexuals of different sorts had segregated themselves (elderly, macho, hippie, black) said, "I used to stand in bars for hours, but now I can't bear them for more than ten minutes," I could not imagine what he meant, especially since people like he were so kind in giving me advice those first few weeks—from the practical (I should keep my beard, and wear red) to the psychological ("Remember, you're going to have to speak to the person after you've had sex"). Even the last did not seem like a problem—what would be difficult about that? When the bars closed, I was still so enthralled with this brand-new world of cruising that I moved on to the next stage of the night like someone at a delicious buffet, and walked down Spruce Street following other gluttons to the next platter of shrimp—the block homosexuals called with perfect accuracy "The Merry-Go-Round."

That is just what it was—besides being one of the most elegant blocks, perhaps the most beautiful row of houses, in a historic city. The houses on the Merry-Go-Round were Federal, and they regarded the street with a reserve so complete, a dignity so immense, their aristocratic aloofness seemed to demand that no one should ever enter or leave one of them. A Nobel Prize–winning novelist, the president of the University of Pennsylvania, and the Rosenbach Museum could all be found on that block. But only once did a woman open her door and ask me to sit elsewhere. For the most part the block was absolutely quiet—even the homosexuals sat in their parked cars as still as mannequins. The same men walked round and round as if in a trance. Occasionally a car whose radio was playing passed with an hysterical burst of music. From time to time the police drove by, and the still figures on the stoops suddenly moved; but, when the police car disappeared around the corner, the figures brought to life by their appearance all instantly resumed their poses on the various staircases, and all was quiet again. Perfectly quiet: a hushed summer evening between midnight and dawn. Hushed and filled with unbearable suspense at the same time—provided by the presence of the Italian American seated in his Chevrolet convertible parked on the corner; so handsome, so aloof, he merely looked at people's reflections in his rearview mirror, like the lady of Shalott, as they walked by, without ever turning an inch to gaze directly at the passerby.

It was a fellow student at the University of Pennsylvania who compared this man in the convertible to the mirror-bound woman in the poem by Tennyson: a young, stocky, law student with thick glasses and neatly combed brown hair whom I had become acquainted with after running into him one evening leaving the apartment of another graduate student (in English) I was on my way to visit. Later, when we compared notes, we learned the man writing his thesis on Virginia Woolf had tried to seduce us both, and in exactly the same manner; even the menu he served us was the same (beef Stroganoff, poached pears), and the fact that after coffee he had put on a recording of *Tristan und Isolde,* and then insisted we lie beside him on the sofa while the music played. It hadn't worked in either instance—alarmed by the music and his pawing of our persons, we'd both stood up, made excuses, and bolted. The law student seemed, if anything, more skittish than I about these things—though this did not mean he spent any less time on the Merry-Go-Round, even if it was more of a sacrifice for him to do so. He came from a long line of attorneys in Carlisle, Pennsylvania, and was going to law school out of a sense of duty so strong he often brought a book with him, and sat reading it under the faint light of the street lamp, marking from time to time passages that were important with a Magic Marker, or briefing the cases in it on little notecards. Then, when he heard footsteps, he would look up, lower his reading glasses, and, after the man had passed, resume his studies. Apparently he saw no reason to waste any more time on this than one had to; I gathered he disliked the whole irrational and enigmatic nature of cruising. One night he arrived at the stoop and said to me: "I had an idea last night. I'm going to make up a questionnaire for people who reject me," he said. "So at least I know why. I'll just hand them a mimeographed sheet of questions. Am I too young, or too old? Too innocent-looking, or not innocent enough? Do you like men with glasses, or without? Should I wear contacts? Grow a mustache? Was my opening line a turnoff? Or should I have pretended to not notice you at all? Was my voice too high? My shoes wrong? Would you prefer my pants to be jeans or corduroys? Did I wait too long to make a move, or not long enough?" He stepped over the blond youth with bad skin smoking a cigarette two steps below me and sat down on the stoop beside me. "You see," he said, "the trouble with being rejected in the bar is, you never know why. And if you don't know why, how can you learn from your mistakes? How can you improve? It's demoralizing. This friend of mine was rejected by the State Department last year and was never told the reason. They don't have to tell you! She went into depression, and I can tell already it's going to drive her crazy for the rest of her life. Of course she was neurotic to begin with, very insecure—that's why they turned her down, no doubt. But I'm not neurotic," he said.

"Maybe that's your problem," said the blond with bad skin in a languorous, drawn-out voice that one could tell instantly was an act of pure will; a cover-up for the most nervous and emotional of personalities.

"What do you mean?" said the law student.

"Well-adjusted people don't do well in the bars," he said in that flat, languid voice that jarred with the bright, bright eyes and nervous cigarette smoking. "The days I go out in a really bad mood, the nights I go out suicidal, I have to beat them off with sticks. You have to be in a really rotten mood to get cruised. A friendly, open face interests no one."

"Why not?" said the law student.

"Because people aren't looking for nice guys when they go out," he said.

"Then what *are* they looking for?" he said impatiently.

"Someone a little complicated, a little dangerous, a little depressed, even nasty," he said. "Someone who's neurotic."

"But I don't want to be neurotic!" said the law student.

"You will be if you keep going to the bars long enough," said the blond in his nasal, deprecating drone.

"But," said the law student, "it doesn't have to be this way! If we could just be honest and straightforward! The way it works now, it's like going to the supermarket to buy bread. You stand there looking at hundreds of loaves and then leave without one. Even though you came to get bread. That's what going to the bars is like."

"Tell me about it," droned the blond from Cherry Hill who still lived with his parents.

"In fact," said the law student in an emphatic voice, "next time I think I'll just go up to whoever I'm attracted to and say: 'I find you very attractive and I'd like to suck your cock.' "

We looked at him. Then the blond said: "I did that once. My first night in a gay bar. And you know what? It worked. The guy said, 'Okay.' And we left together. But I was never able to do it again. I lost my nerve. So here I am, on the steps with you."

"It would save so much time," said the law student. "It's the only rational solution to the whole mess—the waste of time. It would eliminate the posing. I'll just do it."

"No, you won't," said the blond in a sharp voice.

"Why not?" said the law student.

"Because you can't tell someone you want them," he said. "That's the one thing you can't do. I don't even look at the person I want."

"Why not?" said the law student.

"Because he'd know I want him!" said the blond.

"This is why I despise the bars," said the law student. "This is why going to them is so completely counterproductive. You go to a bar to meet a man and spend the night *not* looking at the one you want."

"That's right," said the blond.

"Not telling him you want him."

"Exactly."

"Then why do you go to the bars?"

"To give attitude," said a man sitting on the bottom step.

"But that's insane!" said the law student.

"It's all insane," said the blond. He flicked the ash of his cigarette onto the steps of the Rosenbach Museum—a town house with a famous collection of manuscripts whose presence only a few yards away from us emphasized the point. How easy it would have been, I thought, to call for an appointment at the Rosenbach Museum and go inspect the letters of Emily Dickinson or a draft of *Leaves of Grass.* How impossible to get the Italian seated in the convertible at the end of the block to take me home. It was just what the law student called it. For if the evenings on Delancey Place were initially tranquil and soothing—one sat down full of hope, like a patron of a theater, and watched as the actors came onstage—they almost always ended in humiliation and distress. Since eventually the sky began to whiten above the trees, and the birds awakened to insult us with the news that day was beginning, we rose from the stoops and scurried home, feeling very much a failure and a fool.

And yet the next day—when I dressed and hurried to my job typing letters to insurance claimants for the Western Penn Company in a large room downtown filled with women connected by plastic tubes to Dictaphone machines—I was animated every moment of that long fluorescent morning by the suspense of waiting for night to fall. The prospect of erotic love is so thrilling when you are young, it made no difference to me that I was typing form letters whose main thrust seemed to be telling policyholders why their contracts did not cover that particular claim.

Outside, the steamy, humid city beyond the thick plate-glass windows of the skyscraper contained, beneath the deceptive normalcy of the people going about their business down there on the brick plazas, or sitting down in seersucker suits and cotton dresses to watch the pigeons clustered near a fountain, a world of intense erotic pleasure only waiting for night to fall and a certain doorway to be entered. My mornings, spent typing replies to people who had made the impertinent mistake of asking their insurance company for money, were irrelevant—as were my afternoons, spent in an old brick mansion in West Philadelphia typing up a professor of linguistics's long manuscript on the use of the word "anyway" among street gangs. In the garden my window overlooked—the grass uncut, the flower beds gone to weeds—there stood, just beyond the shade created by a magnificent copper beech, a single sundial—the classic symbol of passing Time—but it didn't threaten me. The time I was wasting typing that abstruse monograph, or the letters to the insurance claimants, was no loss, because that night I would scurry down to the bars. My daytime existence didn't matter—because when dusk fell and I looked up from my books and saw the lights come on across the plaza beneath my window, in a moment the world began to change into something deeply romantic. At seven I took a swim in the university gymnasium. At eight I washed the chlorine—and the day—off my body in the shower room beside the other swimmers whose beauty no longer upset me because now that I had discovered the bars, I needed only rush downtown to find facsimiles of them I could touch. After a solitary supper, I spent at least an hour trying on various combinations of T-shirts and pants till I had the right outfit. Then I set out, like an actor going onstage.

The building I left was full of graduate students studying their subjects with a dutifulness that I could no longer approximate, and my heart pounded as I went down in the elevator, as if I were a Communist ballet dancer defecting to another country. My skin felt too small for my body, till I left the dormitory—but the instant I was out in the warm, windy night, I was free. It was night. It was summer. The last thing I saw was often the law student, standing in line at the convenience store on the corner, clutching his bag of Swedish Kreme cookies and bunch of bananas—the stuff that would enable him to spend three more hours studying torts before he went down to the Merry-Go-Round. I could not even do that anymore; I had withdrawn from school the previous spring; the dean had assumed I was dropping out to become a journalist—in fact, it was to go to the bars.

A sickly sweet odor permeated the air as I rushed downtown— the effluents of the large refineries in South Philadelphia— perfume to the barfly as I walked the deserted sidewalk under a sky filled with neon-pink clouds, over industrial gullies, railroad beds, past dark warehouses and empty factories, under the billboard that advertised Chock full o'Nuts coffee and gave the exact time. I felt I owned the city. The bar was the anteroom, the foyer, the parlor in which men from all parts of this vast metropolis and its suburbs came together; leaving a single room in West Philadelphia, one could, through the medium of the bar, wake up the next day in a converted carriage house on the edge of an apple orchard in Wayne with a handsome, middle-aged accountant. Or a doctor, or a nurse, or a gymnast, or a bartender. Even more important, I might find, standing beside the jukebox, one man in particular. For I had discovered not only erotic life, and the rooms in which my potential lovers gathered each evening around the meaningless tableau of the pool table, but a man named Joe Myzlanski.

I was not sure what Joe did for a living—he worked in a hospital doing something—but I knew he lived in an apartment on Panama Street, and had a friend who also worked at the hospital, a black man who was always beside him in the bar. Some evenings Joe looked tired, and pale, and sleep-deprived—a broken angel with shadows under his eyes; most evenings, in fact. He was about five feet seven. He had dark, curly hair and gray eyes, a stocky, muscular build, and there was an air of perpetual fatigue about him. He was taking penicillin, I learned when I first over-heard him talking to his friend, as I stood behind them by the jukebox, because he had just learned he had syphilis, but this information, off-putting in someone else, only deepened his al-lure, confirmed my impression that he had a rich erotic life, fueled perhaps by his exposure to so much illness and death at work. He was used—like sheets that get softer the more one sleeps on them—a broken angel, because his profile (with its head of black curls) and open, clear-eyed gaze resembled that of a seraph on a canvas by Raphael at the museum of art.

He was also, on a more psychological level, one of the few people in the bar who seemed relaxed. It might well have been that, coming from a shift at the hospital, he really did unwind in that roomful of men in a way those who went there to score could not. He bought his beer, took up his position beside the jukebox, and exuded an air of such friendliness and composure that one was reminded of the original purpose of a bar: conviviality, cama-raderie. In that forest of petrified men he seemed the only soft and pliable figure. Yet the rumor was he wanted, like the rest of us, people he could not get. "People," my informant said, "who would surprise you if you saw them. Joe likes sleepers. The ones nobody looks at twice. The ones in the far, far corner, who look like they just got off work at Kmart, and live with their mothers in Chestertown." (That seemed to describe a man who was inter-ested in me that summer: a fellow about twenty-six who worked in a shoe factory and lived with his parents, and seemed as fixated on me as I was on Joe Myzlanski.) "Of course he's right," the man continued. "Those people are the best. The ones who are grateful you go home with them. Not these showgirls who know they're gorgeous," he said, looking at the Italian American whom

I would see sitting in his convertible on Delancey Place, a man who was—to put it bluntly—that unreal thing: perfect. "They're always lousy in bed. They expect you to do all the work. It's like licking a Rodin." Then the man next to him said that was all nonsense: Joe Myzlanski was interested only in black men, and Fred, his constant companion, was, in fact, his lover, though they refused to admit it. "You gotta be a black guy from the projects with ten inches, minimum, for Joe to sleep with ya," he said, before finishing off his beer. "Though he'd never say that."

Yet Joe couldn't have been more confiding; or so it seemed when he spoke to anyone, since he had a habit in that noisy bar of putting his mouth right up against the ear of whoever he was talking to, so that he would not have to raise his voice. Often he was looking over the shoulder of the person he was speaking to, but it looked as if he was establishing a certain intimacy with each person. When he did this to me, a chill passed through my body as I felt his breath against my earlobe, and his oh-so-solid body next to mine, the raised blue vein on his pale white forearm that caused me to think that if I could only trace its undulation down his arm with the tip of my tongue, I would be happy. The next moment, however, he had put his mouth beside Fred's ear, and he was saying something just as banal to him. Most of my exchanges with Joe were mere pleasantries—the weather, the bar, the weekend coming up—though one night he turned to me at the jukebox, put his lips beside my ear, and surprised me by asking why I never went home with anyone. "I guess I haven't met the right person," I said.

All of these people in the bars had histories. The law student and I were novices. That was, no doubt, one reason the bar was so deeply interesting to me—why I felt such elation walking down there, and such dejection when the lights came on (as they would later on the Merry-Go-Round at dawn) and we had to leave. Till that depressing moment I was utterly absorbed in trying to figure out the men around me—especially those who hung around Joe, a coterie that ran the gamut, from his fellow hospital worker Fred to a man who often came to the bar in a dinner jacket or black tie with Serena, the locally famous drag queen whose racketeer lover had backed her in a restaurant down the block so she'd have a place to perform. He obviously knew Joe quite well, so it was with a feeling of particular excitement (that I was getting nearer to the source of happiness) when I began to notice this same man come out of his apartment on the northern end of Delancey Place to exercise each evening I took my place there on a stoop after the bars had closed.

This man jogged late at night, when it was cooler, presumably; he would come out of his apartment in Bermuda shorts and white polo shirt (and sometimes a red foulard), and smoke a cigarette as he waited for the cab he had just called. That's how he began his run—by getting in a taxi on the northeast corner of Delancey Place; half an hour later he would reappear on foot from wherever the cab had dropped him, run down the west side of our block, then back up the east side, holding his cigarette, and stumble to a stop precisely where he'd caught the cab. Then he disappeared, showered, changed clothes, and often returned to sit down on the steps, with a cigarette. He had an apartment down the quiet alley that abutted the eastern end of Delancey Place, where flats with French doors looked out on the rooftop gardens of converted carriage houses, so in a sense he was simply taking the air in his own neighborhood before turning in.

His age was indeterminable: Though he was bald, his face was as smooth and unlined as a baby's. He had small, bright eyes, a rosebud mouth, and with two perpetually raised eyebrows, he looked like a Pierrot. Like Pierrot, he was blank—neither happy nor sad, just very cool as he sat there smoking his cigarette and watching the pedestrians and cars go by on a fragrant and breathless spring night. "Doesn't this cast of characters ever change?"

he finally said the night he sat down with us, in a silken voice whose accent was neither American nor British but something equipoised in between, as if at any moment he could tip one way or the other, depending on what was required—an ability that made sense, I suppose, since he was planning, he said, to move to Barbados that summer.

"But what will you do?" I said when he told me this.

"You mean, how can I live by myself? Very simple. I'll read and garden and swim. Aren't you beginning to see the same faces over and over again in the Westbury, anyway? Don't they all remind you of Madame Tussaud's? Don't you realize they're all alcoholics?"

"That's why we're here," said the law student.

"Waiting for Al?" said Pierrot, nodding at the handsome Italian American sitting (so gorgeous he might well have been made of wax) in his Chevrolet convertible, watching people pass in his rearview mirror. "Al's in a coma," he said in his smooth, silky voice. "The only person I know who can go in and out of a coma. *And* drive. That's the real trick. Al will never move, much less acknowledge you. Give me five bucks, and I'll stick a pin in his arm and show you. No reaction. I promise." He turned to look up at us with that cool, childlike gaze. "Actually, he's an inflatable doll," he said. "It's all done with a bicycle pump."

"Yes, but," said the law student, raising his finger, "he has the single most valuable thing you can have in this game."

"What's that?" said Pierrot.

"Universal Appeal!" said the law student. "I bet he could sleep with anyone in Philadelphia he wanted to."

"I'll bet you're right," said Pierrot. "But that's no big deal. *I've* slept with everyone in Philadelphia."

"Have you really?" said the law student in an awed voice.

"Everyone who interested me," he said.

"Then tell me about Joe Myzlanski," I said.

"Well," he said, "he's older than you think. When he wakes up in the morning, for instance, he has bags under his eyes."

He looked at me as if he'd just given evidence of armed robbery in seven states, but I said nothing, for this did not in the slightest diminish my interest in him.

"I heard he's being kept," said the blond. "By a bishop, on Rittenhouse Square."

"That's Freddy Goodwin," said Pierrot.

"The tennis player with the big chest?" said the blond, even his carefully controlled, uncommunicative voice betraying surprise.

"That's right," said Pierrot.

"Well, who's keeping Joe?" said the blond.

"I am," said Pierrot.

"*You* are?" said the blond, dumbfounded.

Pierrot looked up at us, his cigarette held at a jaunty angle beside his mouth, pleased at the reaction his remark had produced: all three of us sitting there with our jaws hanging open. I wasn't sure who he reminded me of now, with the silk foulard at his throat, the cigarette in its small black holder—the society dame in a film noir who leads the detective into trouble, or an extra in *The Philadelphia Story*. "At least I'm trying to get him to go to Barbados," he said now. "But I doubt he will. Joe's happy right here, I'm afraid. He wouldn't even go to New York."

"Were you going to New York?" said the blond.

"I thought of it," he said. "For a while. But then I realized I could never live in Manhattan the way I do here. Maturity is accepting limits—including the limits of one's trust fund. Besides, there's nothing in New York as nice as this," he said, looking out at the beautiful street.

Silence fell over the group; as wonderful as Philadelphia was—I could not imagine a more beautiful block than the one we sat on every night—the spectre that hung over it was the knowledge that in New York there were even more gay bars, filled with even handsomer men. "He's moving to New York," Pierrot said, nodding at a handsome man unlocking the door of a house on the east side of the block, who never once glanced at anyone when he came home, very late, always in a suit and tie. "Is *he* gay?" said the law student now. "Yes," said the blond. "But he won't sleep with anyone because he has a small cock." Pierrot laughed. "Oh, queens," he said. "The exact opposite is true. He won't sleep with anyone because he's got a boyfriend in New York. Which is where he's moving because he's already starting to get so much work as a model." "Oh," said the blond, crestfallen.

"Anyone else you'd like to know the actual facts on?" said Pierrot, standing up and flicking his cigarette ash over the banister onto a bed of daffodils.

"Joe Myzlanski," I said.

"Joe Myzlanski?" he said, turning to me with his smooth white face, the upturned nose, the small gray eyes. "Joe Myzlanski's simple. Everyone wants to sleep with him. And he'll oblige. He'll sleep with anyone—just once," he said, walking down the steps, at the bottom of which he stepped on his cigarette, and then looked back at us. "Which means I wouldn't fall in love with him if I were you. It would be like falling in love with—the bartender. And we all know the first thing you learn in this life is: Never fall in love with the bartender."

"Give us some more tips," said the law student.

"Never sit around waiting for someone to call—not even Joe Myzlanski. Never pursue a person—if he wants you, he'll let you know. Never assume that beauty has any relation to character traits. And never allow expenses to exceed income." He raised his eyebrows even higher and smiled. "Good night," he said, and strolled off in the direction of his apartment.

There was a silence, a beautiful silence, and then the law student said: "Of course you should pursue a person. How else does he know you want him?"

"Joe Myzlanski doesn't have to pursue anyone," said the blond. "They come to him. He always has a lover. I wonder why he even goes out at all."

"I haven't seen him at the bar all week," I said.

The blond stepped on his cigarette. "He's been home sick with a cold," he said. "His friend told me."

Only their presence kept me from stealing off to Panama Street at that moment to keep a vigil; their presence, and the sudden commotion of a car stopping in front of Pearl Buck's town house and two young men getting out and slamming the doors as they argued about something that had just happened in the bar. They got back in the car just as suddenly, and the car accelerated noisily, screeched to a stop at the end of the block, turned right, and disappeared. Then, like people at a tennis match, we looked in the opposite direction at the sound of voices, and saw a pair of men who always came here together, one of them a very handsome, well-built factory worker with wavy brown hair and a broad chest who always wore jeans and a white T-shirt. His companion, half his size, was completely unprepossessing in dirty sneakers, pants, baggy sports shirt, and thick, black-rimmed glasses. No one could understand why they always went out cruising together, the two as glued together as a shark and a pilot fish, the nature of their symbiosis a complete mystery.

And then the male nurse appeared—a mop-topped blond with glasses who walked down the sidewalk after his shift at the hospital with an introverted expression on his face, looking neither to the right nor left—the defense someone who actually lived in a basement apartment at the end of this block had to adopt, since every time he left his room or returned to it he had to run the gauntlet of us interlopers, who had come to cruise. Then Pierrot came out of his town house as a cab pulled up before it, got in, and was driven off, as he waved to us with cigarette in hand, for another destination. We were becoming fixtures of the neighborhood; at such moments we felt we lived there, courtesy of the invisible souls who lived in the houses at our backs. Their windows were all dark; only the Rosenbach Museum across the street kept a light on, like the votive candle in a temple, through the night. Finally, the male model who was moving to New York came out, and without a single sign that he'd noticed anyone, picked up his mail and disappeared again.

"Next weekend's July the Fourth," said the blond. "Everyone is going to Atlantic City. There's a big party one of the bars is throwing down there. The whole crowd is going. I've got a room at the Hotel de Ville for two nights, if you want to come. My cousin's spending the night, I think, but if you wanna day-trip, you can use my place to change and shower. I'm sure Joe and his friend will be there," he said, turning to me.

Atlantic City in the early seventies was a strange place to visit— still in a state of pre-casino deshabille, like a middle-aged house-wife in a soiled print nightgown clipping flowers in her backyard, glimpsed as the train goes by. The big, old hotels with the elegant English names (the Marlborough-Blenheim, the Exmoor) still rose, dingy and dignified, above the brown beach and mud-colored waves, but on the boardwalk itself no pretense to anything aristo-cratic existed. Stores sold taffy, fudge, and cheap souvenirs the length of the boardwalk, which featured gazebos with benches like the one on which we sat watching a large family from Balti-more consume its meal of fried chicken and potato salad, drop-ping the bones at their feet, so that when they rose and walked off they left behind them a little heap of avian skeletons. "There you are," said the law student as he looked at the bones, "after Joe goes to bed with you." Joe was, of course, nowhere to be seen. Further proof of the irrationality of gay life, in the law student's eyes, was this inefficient scattering of the people we could see far more easily on Delancey Place among the various bars, restaurants, and sunbathers on the beach here in Atlantic City. When we went to the blond's room to shower and rest up for the next phase of the evening, the law student lay down and sighed. "This is all so inefficient. I wish they would all stay in Philadelphia."

But they would not—even the hotel was another venue in which they searched for one another. The hallways of the De Ville seemed to go on so far they visibly sagged several times on their way to a single window's rectangle of blinding light in the distance. Guests left their doors on these long corridors ajar, and admitted, or refused passersby, as they lay on their beds smoking cigarettes, with one foot on the doorknob. Only the sudden slamming of doors—like a slap across the face—punctuated the briny white silence, the drowsy atmosphere. The heavy air of the sea had no effect on the law student, however. His sense of duty was so strong he sat up, opened his book on property, and began to study on his bed, while the blond with bad skin sat in a chair looking out the window and smoking a cigarette as the branch of some shrub outside the room knocked against the hotel with a slow, rhythmic insistence in the ocean breeze. "What does that remind you of?" the law student said, raising his head from his book, as if to no one in particular. "George Unger's dick when he slapped it against my face," said the blond.

The law student gasped.

"Well, you asked," said the blond, and the law student went back to his book, blushing. That evening as we strolled the boardwalk between dinner in a diner and the hour at which one could expect to find people in the bar, he said: "Sometimes I think this is the most horrendous waste of time in the world, and sometimes I think it's the only worthwhile use of time there is. I mean, the question is—if the bomb dropped today, what would you want to be doing? This. Wouldn't you?" he said. I nodded. "But if the bomb doesn't drop, we've wasted a great deal of time." He looked at me and smiled. "That's law school for you—you can look at everything two ways. For instance, you could view this as a lovely, deserted time of day on the boardwalk—there's more of a breeze, it's cooler, the sun has finally set. Or," he said, his voice intensifying, "you could just scream: 'Will everybody please go to the bar *now*?' " But he did no such thing. Instead we continued walking, and he continued to talk. "Of course the reason we go to the bar is so that we can find someone and never have to go to the bar again," he said. "The only problem is why we can't find that person. I think the only rational way to approach this is to want only whoever finds you appealing. If we were attracted only to people who found us attractive, then everything would make sense. The trouble is, most of the time A wants B, B wants C, C wants D, et cetera." And: "You have to admit this is really a tough business. If we were straight, we wouldn't be doing any of this—we'd be at our in-laws' right now, eating blueberry pie and watching the game on TV." And: "What if Joe Myzlanski leaves Philadelphia—moves someplace else? Would you follow him?" He was still continuing to turn these problems over as we rode back on the bus to Philadelphia later that evening through the bright moonlight, past a state park, which, the man across the aisle assured us, was a heavy cruising spot; a fact that only elicited a brief expression of disgust from the law student. We were too tired even to stop for dinner on Spruce Street when we got back; instead, we went straight to Delancey Place—dear Delancey Place, so quiet, so civilized, so lovely in comparison to the beaches, bars, hotels, rest stops, where men roamed looking for each other. Why couldn't there be just one place: this block? It was very late. The bars were closed on Sunday night. Confirming our loyalty to this particular spot, and my affection for it, the people in the town houses had in many cases put out pots of geraniums on their stoops, as if to welcome us back. Alas, we were the only ones to appreciate the flowers—exhausted by the long weekend, everyone else had gone straight home, and after a few hours, we rose to say good night also, when who should appear but the man we had gone to Atlantic City hoping to see.

He came walking down the street in his usual outfit of faded jeans and T-shirt that suggested he did not separate whites and colors when he did a wash, and waved when he saw us. What I admired about Joe Myzlanski was the fact that he was so comfortable with people—my own legs were shaking so much, I was grateful to have a stoop to sit back down on when he stopped. He'd had to work that weekend and had gone to the bars (mostly empty) and listened as we told him about Atlantic City; then, belatedly, I introduced the sunburnt law student in his plaid Bermuda shorts, his hair standing straight up in tufts, stiff with salt, his black-rimmed glasses held together with a paper clip, a striped short-sleeved blue-and-white button-down shirt half open to reveal his featureless chest. I was worried, for a disloyal moment, that whatever stock I had in Joe Myzlanski's estimation had just sunk in value because of the company I was keeping. But that was my own snobbery—Joe Myzlanski could not have been more gracious, or more friendly, as he paused to speak to us before heading home—an apartment, I knew, not far from here. "Some night I'm gonna cook for you—I make a pretty good lasagne!" he called back to us from the corner, turning once before disappearing. I was so excited as we walked back to West Philadelphia that the law student had to calm me down from the incident by reminding me of Pierrot's rule that one should never make pursuing someone your primary goal (as we had in going to Atlantic City); one should just live one's life, and perhaps you will run into him—something, he said, even Katharine Hepburn had advised in an interview in *Parade* magazine. "So," I said, "you do read something besides torts!"

"Of course," he said. "And that's the only stuff I remember. I can't remember a single thing about the law."

And with that we both fell silent for the rest of the journey, exhausted by the sun and sea, and our desire to meet men.

The July Fourth weekend seemed to mark a real change in people's habits; the summer began unraveling very quickly after that. In the sticky heat, perfumed by petroleum by-products, I walked downtown to the bars not so much to admire the men as to get into the air-conditioning; it was so hot by the end of July that the Chock full o'Nuts sign seemed to be a different color, a much harsher red than it was in winter, and sitting on the stoops of Delancey Place was uncomfortable after the frigid air in the bars. Pierrot stopped jogging, even late at night. The blond got a new job that prevented him from staying up late. The beautiful Italian in his convertible at the end of the block vanished altogether, probably to the shore. The law student said it was too hot to study outdoors and stopped coming; I saw him a few times in the back of the Westbury, seeking the relief of the air-conditioning, like me. Worst of all, Joe Myzlanski was nowhere to be seen, which made me think he had changed his shift, as hospital workers often do. One night, in despair, I went home with the man who seemed as taken with me as I was with Joe—to reverse roles for a change, to grant him what I could not obtain—but it was a big mistake; I lay there as still as a stone, aware that I was being selfish, unresponsive, unkind, and helpless to pretend otherwise, crushed by the fact that life does not allow us to love whom we should. Then, in the middle of August, I went home with a short, muscular, Italian-American doctor who lived just a few blocks from the bar in a high-ceilinged town house on Spruce Street; when he told me to get on my knees, all fours, and started to penetrate me, I started laughing—not only the position, but the whole idea of it, seemed silly. Angered, he sat back on his haunches; five minutes later, I was on the street walking to Delancey Place.

There was never anybody there of interest these days—the male nurse with the dirty blond Prince Valiant haircut and the disheveled clothes continued to come home every night around two A.M. The male model moving to New York had evidently moved to Manhattan. The rest of the scene was a hodgepodge of people I'd never seen before, a crazier, more high-strung sort in big cars that needed mufflers, playing their radios too loud as they went by, making me wonder when the people in the houses behind me would complain to the police and have the whole block put under surveillance. Miraculously, they never did. Perhaps they were in Maine. It occurred to me, sitting by myself on the stoop on Delancey Place, that the law student and I had been, perhaps, a bit arrogant—subjecting all this to a rational critique. Our middle-class notions of sensible behavior seemed to no longer apply. Perhaps it was the heat, the surreal quality of mid-August, the sense that the city had been evacuated by the people who had made the Merry-Go-Round and the bars interesting that winter, but whatever the reason, I began to lose that sense of superiority I'd felt while sitting with the law student—as if we, fresh, new, unspoiled, could survey the scene, refuse to participate in its insanity, and get from it what we wanted, and no more. Now the law student was gone, and without his commentary, his disdain, I felt myself sinking to the level of the people squabbling in cars as they drove slowly down the street, to loud music, gunning their engines at the end and making the tires squeal as they accelerated around the corner. It was no longer enough simply to be in the bars. The thrill I had felt all winter whenever I walked into the dim, red-lighted interior of the Allegro, or Westbury, or stood beside some handsome man in a white polo shirt while the O'Jays sang "Backstabbers," or, even more delicious, the song "What You See Is What You Get"—a title I now realized that most assuredly did not apply to that place—was gone. The enchantment had faded. It was just a roomful of men, though I wanted to go home with one—just to prove I could. A few weeks after laughing at the Italian-American surgeon in his house on Spruce Street, I saw him in the Allegro again; this time I was so desperate that when he left, I ran out of the bar after him, and caught up with his muscular figure halfway to his house. "Listen," I said breathlessly, "I'm sorry about last time, I'd like to try again."

He shook his head and smiled. "No," he said.

"But *you're* going home alone, and there's nobody in the bar *I* want," I said. "Why don't the two of us go home together?"

"Because I've got to get up very early in the morning," he said, resuming his walk home.

"But what are you doing out now, then?" I said, walking with him. "I mean, why did you go out in the first place?"

"To relax, and have a beer," he said. "Sometimes that's what a bar is for, you know. I'm going home now to get a good night's sleep," he said, unlocking his door and going in. "You got a lot to learn, kid," he said, turning to me just before the door shut. "Good night."

I was left standing on the sidewalk in a state of frustration and chagrin—where was the law student when I needed him now? Only he would appreciate the absurdity of what this man had just done. It was worse than the law student even claimed, I thought as I walked furiously down Spruce Street, my face stinging as if it had been slapped. It was perverse. At that moment I saw Pierrot, in a white dinner jacket and tie, turning onto Spruce Street a block ahead of me.

"Where have you been?" I said, grateful to find someone I could talk to. "I haven't seen you in weeks!"

"Well, for most of that time I've been in Barbados," he said, looking at me with that face that seemed at once so childlike and so cold. "But just now I was at Joe Myzlanski's at dinner."

"*Oh!*" I said. "How was it?"

"Charming," he said. "I always like seeing Joe."

"What did you eat?" I said.

"Pot roast," he said.

"Oh!" I said. And: "Was it just the two of you?"

"The two of us and your friend the law student. It was a good-bye dinner, I was astonished to learn."

"For whom?" I said.

"For them. They're moving to Atlanta on Sunday," he said, stopping to flick a fallen leaf off the sleeve of his dinner jacket.

"I don't understand," I said.

"Neither do I," he said.

"I haven't seen either one in weeks!" I said.

"That's why," he said as we resumed our walk. "That's always the reason when someone disappears. Apparently, they went home together one night about three weeks ago, and the two of them have been quite joined at the hip since then. Your friend is actually dropping out of law school to move to Atlanta with Joe."

"To do what?" I said.

"To open a gay bar," he said as we sat down on the stoop of Pearl Buck's town house.

The feeling that the summer had entirely escaped me was suddenly raised to a panicky pitch—a feeling that must have been visible on my face, for Pierrot actually took my hand and patted it. "You see why I'm moving to Barbados. It's just me, the cook, and the hibiscus." He looked at me with one raised eyebrow and a rueful pursing of his lips. "Would you like to go to Barbados with me?" he said. I sighed and shook my head. "But thanks for asking," I said. "Well, good-bye," he said. "Good-bye," I said, and watched him walk away through the glistening, humid air beneath the carriage lamps. There was not a single soul in sight after Pierrot disappeared till shortly after two, when the male nurse appeared at the far corner and walked down the sidewalk with his compact body and introverted air. I must have watched him so intensely this time that he came to a stop at the foot of the stairs, looked up at me, and said, "Hello." Five minutes later we were undressed in his stifling basement room, his lean, smooth body silvered by the light of his little refrigerator as he stood before it getting us a beer, and when he came to the bed on which I lay waiting for him, dappled with the light of Delancey Place that came through the shrubs outside his window, I thought I had never seen anything so beautiful in my life.

JOSHUA & CLARK

THEY WERE INSEPARABLE FRIENDS. One was homely, but had a big dick; the other was handsome, but had a small one—so they were both discarded for different reasons. In the end it would have been hard to say which one had more sex; the pretty one had more partners, who had him just once, and that was enough—the homely one had a few people he had sex with repeatedly, since once they'd broken the barrier of his looks, the penis was one they were glad to go back to. "It's all about dick," said the pretty one as he sat eating French fries in a booth at Tiffany's on Sheridan Square, where they would go for dinner after their workout at the Sheridan Square Gym. "Let's face it. If two homosexuals arrived in New York from wherever they came from, you could predict exactly what sort of experience each one would have by telling them to just pull their pants down." "What if they were the same?" said the homely one in his flat voice. "Then you'd have to get into other factors," said the pretty one. "But you don't have to be Susan Sontag to figure out what men want in this town. What makes them happy." The truth was they were happiest with each other—intellectually, at least—in a booth at Tiffany's; sexually, they were always on the prowl for potential lovers, as was everyone else in the city, it seemed.

The pretty one had almost Victorian ideals: monogamy, fidelity, romantic love, though couched in the obscene, cynical terms of a once bookish person who had stumbled into the Eagle's Nest one autumn while writing a dissertation on William Blake at NYU. He was looking for brains. "I want someone who can quote Rilke, *and* eat my ass till his face falls off," he liked to say. The homely one had dreams just as romantic but lived in such despair of their ever coming true, he sounded even more cynical. He liked going home with couples, he said, "so I can suck all that love out of them." In the meantime, he had sex as often as he could. "What's your idea of happiness?" the pretty one asked him, the very afternoon they met (by accident, at the Strand Book Store, looking for the same novel by Machado de Assis). "Getting my kitten punched for a long, long time," he said. ("Getting my kitten punched" was an expression he used for coitus.) When that wasn't happening, they went everywhere together.

They went to Flamingo every Saturday and danced, and the Ramrod the next afternoon; they ate dinner in Tiffany's every night after their workouts at the gym; they worked the buses to Fire Island in summer, serving drinks; they went to Broadway and off Broadway, lectures at the Ninety-second Street Y, Charles Ludlam plays, Balducci's, Brooks Brothers, Canal Jeans, Georgette Klinger, and all theme parties. You never invited just one to dinner; you always asked them both, even though they were not lovers—they were inseparable friends. There were a few differences. The pretty one went to more theater than his friend (he loved the stage). The homely one went out to the bars much more than the other. ("The bars *are* theater," he said.) The pretty one,

in concert with his Victorian ideals, had a strict social sense of
where one should be seen or not seen, and was careful not to
overexpose himself. The homely one had no such reservations.
The homely one had been raised in a small town in West Virginia,
and experienced an adolescence so forlorn, he told his friend soon
after they met, he used to take walks every day up the dirt road
his high school used as its lovers' lane, pick up the used condoms
on the ground, imagine the football players he was in love with,
and put them to his mouth. When he finally escaped to college,
he spent those four years driving from bar to bar in Charleston,
Pittsburgh, Nashville, and Memphis, crammed into an old VW
with five queens in ball gowns and high heels; four years of driving the Midwest in a beige VW, past fields of corn whose husks
scraped against each other in the bitter wind, on their way to
Chicago; four years of snow, and gas stations, and gay bars, till
he got to the city he really wanted to be in. Since moving to New
York he had not stayed home a single night. He seemed to need
less sleep, for one thing; for another, he had moved to Manhattan
to go to the bars, so that when people went to the Eagle's Nest,
people who felt guilty at going to the bar so often (Am I overex-
posed? Isn't this a big waste of time? How many hours do I plan
to waste in these places, before going home alone?) opened the
door, looked up, and saw Clark standing there, they thought:
Doesn't he *ever* stay home? And: Does he realize how ugly he is?

It was hard to say which offended the people who did not know
him more: the fact that he was always there, or the fact that he
was ugly. The two things somehow went together. The fact that
someone else is out every time you go out, of course, only reminds
you of the fact that you are going out every night, too, and Clark
had the same effect on people that William Wilson's dopple-
gänger had in the story by Edgar Allan Poe. He became their
ghost, conscience, mirror image. He disturbed, rebuked, accused
people just by being there beside the jukebox every time they

walked in. *He's* here again, they would mutter silently. (And the corollary: So are you.) As if one's mystique were all an illusion one had to maintain by not appearing in these places too often (precisely the view the pretty one subscribed to), an illusion ruined by the presence of this implacable, silent witness. He seldom spoke to these people. They simply looked at each other during that brief instant the new arrival came through the door and met his eyes—because he had put himself right where he would be the first to see whoever entered.

The people coming through the door had often manufactured rationales for stopping in: The bar was on the way home from their gym, it was air-conditioned on a hot summer night, it was pleasant to listen to the music on the jukebox for an hour before turning in. Not Clark. He was there for one thing: to get laid. He seemed determined to defy the fact of his face, determined to crash this fraternity composed of men who went to the Eagle's Nest because they were handsome, determined to hang around, a fly on the wall, every night till closing, and then linger in the street outside where the snobbery of looks dissolved in little puddles of need beneath the West Side Highway. And his determination—so plain it was obvious—destroyed their face-saving, since even if in a very large city like New York you rarely have to worry as you do in small towns about seeing the same people over and over when you go out, when you walked into the Eagle's Nest and found Clark there beside the jukebox every time, you could not say, "There but for the grace of God go I," because, at that moment, there you were, in the same bar.

Had he been handsome Clark might have supplied a different rebuke ("You can't have me"), might have even made the place, the night, more glamorous; but the fact that he was homely only increased people's feelings that this was an off night. Like a very old man who goes to the baths, an old man who has to pause on the dimly lighted staircase, one hand on the banister, the other

holding his towel, as he carefully sets his foot down on the next
step so as not to fall, and in so doing holds everyone up behind
him, Clark's presence actually irritated people. For one thing, it
was hard to imagine anyone wanting to sleep with him. In a
culture that values good looks, there was Clark dressed in the
regulation uniform of jeans, white T-shirt, and black leather
jacket, with a face that resembled that of a creature on a canvas
by Hieronymus Bosch. He had no chin, for one thing, or at least
a very recessive one. He had bad skin, for another: pitted, scarred,
pockmarked. He had what appeared to be a broken nose, and
small, gray eyes, and lead-gray, thinning hair that was lank and
greasy-looking at the same time, combed forward over the top of
his high, shiny forehead in little Napoleonic wisps. The head itself
was, furthermore, too small for his body, and oddly shaped. He
looked prematurely aged; he looked like something in a medieval
painting—the stable hand in breeches and leather jerkin slopping
swill for the hogs while the prince rides past on a white horse; he
looked colorless, light-starved, malnourished. He was the blade of
grass that turns yellow lying under a pot. He was a creature
starved for oxygen in the womb. He was a shock. When he was
amused, his lips drew back to expose the gum above his uneven
yellow teeth, and he laughed so hard he sprayed the air with
saliva that caught the light of the jukebox at his side as he was
bending over at the waist.

But he did not think himself off-limits and so he wasn't. The
issue of his looks did not deter him, and worked in his favor with
people who took the admiration of others for granted—among
them a bank teller from Queens, a mulatto with a perfect face
and body, and a deep, resonant voice, many people wanted and
could not get; a beauty bored with his own beauty. Clark was
never bored with beauty. "Oh, he's beaaaaaauuutiful," he would
say to the pretty one about a man they knew, with the starstruck,
romantic fervor of an adolescent; that was why he was in the city.

That was why he went out. Beauty was the greatest joy, sex with Beauty happiness; so he went out hoping to find it every night. No matter how many trips to movies, discos, restaurants, theaters, the pretty one planned, the homely one would always have to slip away at a certain hour to prowl; he had about as much commitment to the devotion the pretty one felt for him as a wolf or coyote feels for its captor. He always put sex first. He did not even try to explain the hold it had on him. Once, when Joshua asked him, the way the hostess of a salon might have asked one of her guests to discuss electricity, for his definition of good sex, he confined himself to a single comment: "Bad sex leaves you depressed," he said, putting down his cheeseburger with a solemn expression on his face. "Good sex leaves you suicidal."

In the summer he followed the men in the Eagle's Nest out to Fire Island, where he wore the same uniform he wore in the bar (ripped jeans, leather jacket, white T-shirt)—though it looked completely out of place in the sparkling sunshine, the cheerful harbor of the beach resort where everyone was strolling around in shorts and bare feet. Sunlight, water, blue skies, salt air, made no impression on Clark; he was bound, with his six-pack of beer, from the grocery to the Botel, to obliterate the gorgeous day in his rented room till night fell, as if sex was the only aspect of nature that needed to be worshiped. He was not there for the beach; he was there only because They (the men in the Eagle's Nest) spent their weekends on Fire Island. At Tea Dance, he removed his leather jacket; the outline of a single nipple ring visible beneath his snug white T-shirt, long before such things were popular. With his jacket slung over his shoulder, his body proved to be powerful, barrel-chested, almost voluptuous—but it only made his small, wizened, oxygen-starved head seem even more allegorical. His presence here was more incongruous than in the bar. But, though there is a kind of self-censorship in places like the Pines, there he was, standing among the throngs of all-American guys in their Speedos or khaki shorts, their hair brushed back from the forehead in imitation of the models in *L'Uomo*. And there he was dancing that night.

He always danced with the pretty one, who took a share in a house every summer with four other short, muscular men like himself who formed his dancing pod. They were good dancers and they knew it; they took dancing very seriously. The pretty one became so absorbed, so oblivious to his surroundings as he stabbed the air with short, staccato thrusts in time with the beat, that once he managed to undo the string holding the halter top of a woman walking by as he was rising to the climax of "Don't Leave Me This Way," with a series of arm thrusts in the direction of the ceiling. The homely one danced with no expression on his face, head down, crouched in the pose of the hard-driving disco queen, so that his eyes met no one else's. The pretty one seemed to be on stage, and would stop, between one song's departure and the next's mix, with one hand to his throat, as if surveying the crowd through an invisible lorgnette, or wondering if the bouilla-baisse needed more salt, and then, when he decided the new song was worth his art, he would bend over and begin the pile-driving, air-slicing, halter-top-undoing crisscross of his short, muscular arms through an imaginary sphere around his body. They never left each other's side. Even when they took a break, they stood together in the same corner of the deck outside, the pretty one talking to friends while the homely one stared wordlessly at the beautiful men around him, like a child on Christmas morning. They always danced till closing. Then the pretty one would walk home along the boardwalk, reciting, in the breathless tone of the ingenue, poems by William Blake as the sun came up, while the homely one (who always had a place to sleep in his friend's bed-room, who became the pretty one's "official permanent guest") kept going right down to the Meat Rack—the reality beneath it all. The pretty one would not have been caught dead in the Meat

Rack, but kept a place for his best friend on the blanket he and his house took to the beach later that day; when, sure enough, around two or three, the homely one was seen marching up along the blue, blue water's edge, the black leather jacket slung over his shoulder, a kind of testament to the pornographic ideal, the world of the bars, the sex he would describe in a flat voice from which all traces of emotion had been carefully removed the moment he sank down upon the blanket next to his friend, after which the pretty one would turn to his housemates and say: "I told you he has more sex than God. And I can't find anyone I even like who isn't married." And he'd insist the homely one show everyone his cock ring, composed entirely of car parts.

Eventually the homely one began coming out every weekend with the pretty one—a bit sheepishly, since he knew he was getting a bed for nothing, but then the two of them were best friends and shared everything and everyone in the house adored him, though the bond between the two struck some of their housemates as odd—at least, the things they would laugh about; the shared sense of humor that seemed not so much black as nihilistic. The week in late July they spent out at the beach together there was only one other person in the house, a librarian, who would come upon them cooking together as they watched a little television on the counter. Clark made a wedding soup Joshua declared the best wedding soup in the world, and as he stirred the pot, the two of them would convulse over some story on the six o'clock local news—the more lurid, the better—about a woman in Brooklyn who had thrown her baby out the window because she thought it was the devil, or, one evening as the librarian was making his own supper, put it in a frying pan to cook it. "Next time," Joshua said, "next time, use just a *lit*tle oregano!" while Clark droned in his flat, nasal monotone: "She could have at least breaded it first. I mean, a real cook takes pains. Doesn't Julia Child have a whole *chap*ter on breaded baby?" And the librarian, watching them laugh so hard they started to cry, wondered just what vision of life it was that bound these two together.

In October, back in the city, Joshua even went to the bars with Clark the first weekend, and they stood together beside the jukebox at the Eagle's Nest, riding the tide of good feeling the people who've been on Fire Island carry into the city every fall, as if they don't quite want to give up each other's company. Joshua, surrounded by his housemates, talked in a theatrical, animated fashion while Clark stood there looking slightly annoyed by this injection of the social note into a milieu he knew would be much more sexual in a month. Till then he knew he could use Joshua to find out whatever he wanted to know about the men he admired, for Joshua knew them all. In a bright, crisp voice, while the person walked past, Joshua would say to Clark: "Huge dick, likes to get fucked, his best friend is Bobby McMasters, you know the guy who gave the underwear party on Shore Walk. The blond with the dimple and the scar who *says* it was from a motorcycle accident but everyone knows he wouldn't know a motorcycle from a hair dryer and it was really a suicide attempt. He had this, like, breakdown, like Scavullo, and started smashing *mirrors*." News which caused Clark to burst into laughter; his lips drew back to expose the gum above the teeth, and he laughed so hard he bent over several times, like a marionette, as the blond walked by. This only lasted a few weekends; then Joshua stopped going to the Eagle's Nest and confined himself to sporadic visits to the baths.

He was saving himself, guarding his mystique, looking for what he called a Hot Daddy. He was attracted to age, experience, brains. He flirted with men in the Eagle's Nest who were CBS executives, psychiatrists, professors; though more often than not these men, in their mid-forties, already had lovers, had had lovers for ten, fifteen years, and were not about to leave them now. He refused to consider sleeping with them, anyway, the moment he learned they were part of a couple. He would express his shock, as he sat in the booth at Tiffany's with Clark, discussing his night at the baths. "I may be *wild*ly old-fashioned in this matter," he said one evening, "but I must say I find it very questionable that they go there at all. And not very nice to their lovers."

"Oh, Joshua," Clark said in an exasperated voice, "he just wants to get his kitten punched. You get tired of the same person all the time."

"I wouldn't," said Joshua, carefully putting a spoonful of ice cream to his lips, "I'd be as faithful as a dog."

He was faithful only to his best friend, however; when he did meet someone, and the man wanted to get serious, he inevitably found fault with him. "He's *cute*!" Clark would say. "Oh please," said Joshua. "He's clinically obese! He has love handles the size of Botswana! He believes in astrology, for God's sake! He asked me my sign! I can't sleep with someone who has to stop himself after the third cheesecake, and thinks the most important book he's read in the last year was Linda Goodman's *Love Signs*." Clark leaned forward and keened: "He has a beaaaauuuutiful, thick beard, his skin is perfect, I've seen his cock at the gym, the head is as big as a Ping-Pong ball, he's got really thick eyelashes, and he loves you!" "Which tells you a lot about his IQ," said Joshua with a short, hard laugh. "Like, I wonder how he ties his shoes." "Oh, Joshua," said Clark, "you go to all this effort at the gym to look good, and then when someone falls for you, someone whose piss I would build a wine cellar for, you think they're crazy. What do you think the lat machine is *for*?" "Well, what about you and Jerry Babson?" said Joshua, naming the mulatto bank teller from Queens. "Everyone is dying just to meet him, and he's yours for the asking! You've got him sitting by the phone!" "He's sweeet," said Clark, with a grimace, "but—maybe that's the problem. He's sweet." And he started laughing; which broke Joshua up.

Indeed, while they were both ostensibly looking for lovers, the two of them spent more time together, and took more pleasure in each other's reactions to things than most lovers do. Whatever happened to each one did not really matter until he had told the other about it. They loved to analyze. And while Clark loved to go home with couples because they were couples, and bathe in the affection between them, Joshua loved to go home to West Virginia when Clark went back for Thanksgiving or Christmas, and spend four or five days with his best friend's extended family in the hills west of Charleston. It was like being in *The Waltons,* Joshua told a friend when he got back. His own family—orthodox Jews who lived in Queens—had ostracized him when he told them he was gay; at least his mother had told him to leave home since his father's heart condition meant he should have as little stress as possible. Of course people never knew quite what to believe when they listened to Joshua, not even Clark. He made things up. Once, when Clark asked him why he fabricated stories about people, he said: "Because real life is so dull." This included, apparently, Clark. Though Joshua, like a student in some debate club in school—which he had been—could take either side of an argument with equal fervor, praise someone to the skies, then dish them a moment later, rave about a book, a show, and then reverse himself the moment you said the opposite, as if he had long ago decided that the world and everything in it was far too subject to change for him to grant it the dignity of permanence, as if he truly were some wandering Jew who might be driven across the border tomorrow, a citizen of nothing—the one guiding light, the fixed pole, was his unqualified admiration for his best friend in the world.

Indeed, he could hardly talk about him without appending a litany of honors. "My best friend, Clark," or "My best friend in the whole world" was the most brilliant, witty, sexy, accomplished man/cook/dancer/lover in the world; this nine-to-five employee of a reference book publisher in midtown Manhattan had opinions that were the last word on everything. ("My best friend, Clark, thinks Joan Didion is *it*," he would say. Or "My best friend in the world thinks Armando is the *only* deejay," and "My best friend in the world's had sex with Frank Post, he's had sex with everyone, he's such good sex the word gets around," etc.) And when, that fall, Clark went to the opening party at the Saint, and decided that disco was now dead, Joshua decided the same thing. "But why?" someone asked him at the gym. "Because my best friend in the whole world says that when the special effects upstage the dancers, it means it's over. Didn't you notice how everyone spent the whole night looking up at the dome? Nobody was looking at each other. When Jerry Sanchez asked Clark afterward what he thought of the Saint, he said: 'It gave me a stiff neck.' Which means it's over. I'll give you my membership card if you want— I'm never going again. My best friend and I will go to movies. Or we'll cook. Dancing's finished." And, like a convert to a new religion, he never once looked back. "My best friend, Clark, always knows when something's over," he said. "He knew it after one hour at the Saint."

In fact, much of Joshua's theatrical testimonials to his wit and sexuality embarrassed Clark; so that when people who'd heard this extraordinary being's praises sung for months finally, one night in line at the movies, actually met "my best friend, Clark," and it turned out to be the man beside the jukebox at the Eagle's Nest, their mouths fell open in astonishment, and Clark, knowing why, blushed. That was one reason he was happiest on a week-night standing by himself in his corner at the Eagle's Nest, or in a clutch of men under the West Side Highway. Sex was what mattered to him. After Clark used the money he got by selling his Saint membership to visit San Francisco one week in January, he told Joshua when he got back that he wanted to move there. Joshua asked why. "To improve the quality of my promiscuity," Clark said with a sardonic laugh. "But you can do that here!" said his friend. "Oh, Joshua," Clark said in a tone almost of despair. "In San Francisco you have sex. In New York you wait for people to come." "Oh God," gasped Joshua, filing away another aphorism he could use to prove his best friend was the most brilliant wit in New York.

"And they have these incredible butts," Clark added in a tragic drone, "from climbing hills. You know how the machines at the gym, all those squats that are probably destroying our spinal column, can *never* give you a bubble butt? Well, you can *have* a bubble butt in San Francisco," he said, "just by walking to the *bars*." He put his suitcase under the bed and said: "I'd rather work on my glutes *that* way."

"Oh God," said Joshua, with exaggerated awe, one hand to his throat, his eyes wide, as if Clark had just revealed the cure for cancer.

Things changed after that—thinking it made no difference now, since he intended to move to San Francisco, Clark gave up his apartment to save money and moved in with Joshua on St. Marks Place, in the apartment he shared with an editor at Scribners. They were hardly ever there, however. Their lives became even more identical. Their schedule—work, gym, restaurant, movie or play—sent them out at eight in the morning and brought them back seldom before eleven or twelve; and then Clark changed clothes and went to the bar. The next morning they set out for work in their clothes from Brooks Brothers— another pleasure Clark spent his salary on, along with restaurants, movies, books; beautiful Harris tweed jackets, and cashmere sweaters and Italian ties. Neither one kept any money in a savings account. They spent their salaries on Christmas and birthday presents for each other (dinner at La Caravelle, orchestra seats for *A Chorus Line,* Swiss binoculars, tickets to the Black Party). They went to San Francisco in March and when they got back, Joshua told someone at the gym: "I actually felt attractive there. Me.

Men looked at me. I was—a sexual being. Clark's right, as usual."
But when asked if he would move there, he replied: "I can't. I
love the theater too much. I'm taking Clark to *Hedda Gabler* tomorrow night." In fact, the things they did together accelerated,
now that they both knew Clark was going to move to San Francisco. They had never been closer. The editor didn't understand
how two people could spend so much time together, could share
their lives this much, and not engender some resentment. But
then he hardly saw them. They were perfect roommates. Once,
when the editor came home from a trip to Chicago and found
blood and shit on the comforter on his bed, Joshua—wanting
to forestall any trouble—sent the comforter to the dry cleaner's,
apologized to the editor, *and* bought him a new one at Bloomingdale's. The editor told him not to worry. The editor assumed it
was Clark's doing—that, despite Joshua's efforts, there was something in his best friend that, finally, could not be domesticated.
Still, it was a surprise when the editor came home one day and
found Clark—usually with Joshua at the gym at that hour—
standing in the middle of the living room with a dazed look on
his face, and the tie he had just removed still dangling from his
hand. "I'm sorry about the comforter," Clark said. "He was a
stage set designer I've always had a big crush on. I ran into him
on the corner of Second Avenue and we had nowhere else to go.
He's *soooooooo* beautiful." "That's all right," said the editor. "I'm
moving out anyway," Clark went on. "I just took a job in San
Francisco," he added in that flat, nasal, self-deprecating, disillusioned voice that implied his having done so could only be a disaster. "You're kidding!" said the editor. "I'm not," said Clark. "I
haven't told Joshua yet." "He'll be devastated," said the editor.
(He could say this calmly because he was attached to neither one
of them the way they were to each other.) Clark screwed up his
face. "I don't know," he said. "You know the worse thing about
Joshua?" "The lies?" said the editor. "The exaggeration?" "No,"

said Clark. "It's that fifteen minutes after something happens to him, it's as if it hadn't happened."

"Well, I'm not so sure about that. You're a huge part of Joshua's life. Joshua says you want to move there to improve the quality of your promiscuity," said the editor with a smile.

"That's not the real reason," he said.

"What is?"

Clark looked out the window with a smile that creased his lips at an angle, a face as prematurely old, and pitted, and scarred as someone who had been in a train wreck, and said, as he folded his Countess Mara tie: "To get away from Joshua."

"Ah," said the editor. All Joshua said when people learned Clark had moved to San Francisco was: "The only problem is, I'm totally color blind, and Clark picked out all my ties for me. Who's going to do that now? Clark is the only person who really knew how to shop. He had perfect taste."

Shortly after Clark left town everything began to change and Joshua stopped going out altogether; a strange new cancer had appeared that some people said you could get just from touching the sweaty bodies of men dancing at the Saint. Once again, Joshua said, Clark had known when something was over; and what to do next. He had left Manhattan just when it was about to collapse. For the first few months they spoke on the phone every night; then the phone calls became letters, passages of which were so witty Joshua would read them to friends at the gym. The theme of the letters Joshua read from were the same: Out there in the mother city of homosexuals he was having a wonderful time. "Clark's having an affair with a drug dealer," Joshua said to the editor one night, after folding up the letter he had just received. "He says the sex is only good when they take acid, but when they take acid he gets his kitten punched for a really long, long time. Gee," he said in a musing voice, "I wonder what that's like—having an affair with a drug dealer," and he put the letter away in a little inlaid box in which he kept all of his friend's letters, like a nineteenth-century widow keeping the correspondence of her son, off trying to make a life for himself in South Africa or Zululand. The truth was, he was beginning to look like a woman in mourning, and people did treat him as a sort of widow—not knowing quite what to say when they ran into him, at the gym, at parties, without Clark; though as the year passed, he began going out less and less, as if Clark had been the key, the magic passport, which had enabled him to have fun. "Work is prayer," Joshua would sigh when he came home in the evening now, and settle down to some freelance copyediting of yet another paperback original with titles like *Shalom, My Love.* His clothes, his habits, his demeanor, were all subdued. The editor wondered if he were even playing a part; his suits got darker and darker; he made a pot of tea and stroked the cat when he came home, as he sat at his desk working in a large gray shawl, looking, the editor thought, like Whistler's mother, though he said nothing. He wasn't sure what the cause was—the changes in the city, or the departure of his best friend; the two things seemed to be related, as if Clark had been, in the end, just a superior consumer who knew when he'd had the best of a place and should move on—leaving Joshua behind. Ostensibly things were booming; the Saint was a success, the lines down Second Avenue every Saturday night all the way to Seventh Street, the baths just as busy. But friends were getting sick at the gym. The things Joshua had done with his best friend he stopped doing. He went to macrobiotic cooking school instead, and then learned sign language, and acquired, momentarily, a new set of friends, and then dropped them all. Then all he did was work. He said he would be going to San Francisco but then he got a freelance assignment and took his vacation time to do it instead. Meanwhile, the shawl was used—no matter what the temperature in the apartment—the cat was given attention it had never received before, the shelf got covered with a hundred varieties of herbal tea, the letters from San Francisco were folded and put away in their box, and he would mumble a new aphorism out loud over a manuscript when he made a mistake: "Commas, like nuns, travel in pairs." Then a year later Joshua received a letter from West Virginia: Clark had gone home the previous month to his sister, who wrote in her letter that the end "wasn't pretty." He'd asked her not to tell Joshua he was sick. "Gee," Joshua said in a faint voice as he folded the letter, "Clark died without telling anyone." A year after that—after Joshua had taken a course in Portuguese, and then signed up to cook for cancer patients—the editor came home from another business trip to the Midwest and found something else on his comforter: Joshua's body, in a puddle of bodily fluids, some of the pills he had been hoarding still left in a vial on the night table. The superintendent asked why Joshua had done it and the editor didn't know what to say, but he thought part of the reason may have been that something had deeply depressed him—perhaps his best friend's getting sick and dying without telling him, like a suicide who leaves no note, like Joshua. Perhaps it was just loneliness, he thought, as he took the comforter out to the cleaner's.

⌒ THE HOUSESITTER

THAT FALL HE WAS LIVING OFF EAST END AVENUE, a block from Gracie Mansion. A writer who had been flown over to London by the BBC to do some interviews on "Literature in the Age of AIDS" needed someone to watch his two cats and dog while he was away for three weeks; Morgan gladly accepted the offer and moved in. The apartment was next to the Chapin School, and he could hear, as he walked by with the dog on his way to Carl Schurz Park, that noise girls make when they are swarming: the high-pitched, shrieking sound of seagulls rising up in alarm— pure manic energy, the life force, as wild as the sea itself. Workmen were repairing the facade of the building that October, and the scaffolding that turned the sidewalk outside the school into a damp, fragrant, echoing tunnel only magnified the sound coming from a large room on the ground floor where the girls were gathered, either for recreation or a meal, he could not tell as he walked by: the sound of excitement at being together, between classes, separated from their desks, in a single, intense mass. The workmen heard it every day. For that reason the men clambering over the refuse in a Dempster Dumpster and conferring in an office inside a trailer seemed to ignore the joyful noise. So did Emma. Emma was excited by the prospect of reaching the park. Morgan, who liked dogs, and had grown up with them in Pennsylvania, carried a piece of newspaper with which to remove her anticipated poop because he had been frightened by his experience on their first outing, when, while lighting a cigarette, he failed to notice Emma defecating, and, before he could exhale, he found a meter maid in front of him threatening to fine him a thousand dollars. Morgan didn't have a thousand dollars; that was why he was house-sitting; he had only the prospect of some unemployment checks, and a bill from the IRS he was still paying off in small installments, and the determination to make it through the winter sober until he resumed his job hosting at a restaurant on Fire Island next spring.

It seemed to be a time of year for walking to and from the park—and so, after examining the books in the apartment, the invitation to the author to dine at the White House, which he had found on the desk, Morgan spent the next week either walking Emma to and from the esplanade on the East River, or, after performing that duty, walking alone to Central Park. Central Park, the autumn of 1997, was in better shape than he'd ever seen it. "Remember what it was like in the seventies?" Morgan said as we entered the park the first morning just south of the Metropolitan Museum. "Patches of grass with huge expanses of dust? Graffiti on everything? Bethesda Fountain was dry, filled with litter, the bathrooms were, of course, locked, and the Great Lawn looked like the dust bowl. But I came here anyway whenever I could to get away from it all. I used to walk through it at night, even, when people said it was too dangerous. It wasn't dangerous—because there was no one in it. They had all been scared off by the muggers, so the muggers didn't come because there was no one to mug. Fear had emptied the entire park. I had the whole thing to myself at night," he said, exhaling another puff of the cigarettes he chain-smoked. "And look at it now, all cleaned up. Look at the fresh sod. Look at these benches. Look at Bethesda Fountain," he said, stopping at the top of the stairs. "It's actually on. There's no graffiti. There are flowers in the flowerpots! It looks like a movie set! Why did we put up with the boom boxes, the graffiti, the dry fountain, all those years? Why did we not complain?" I had no answer. "Do you think he's gay?" I said, watching a handsome man coming toward us with a small child in a stroller.

"No," he said. "He's got a kid."

"But that doesn't mean anything anymore," I said.

"I'll bet he's an actor, or model, but straight," said Morgan as we watched him stop to talk to a beautiful young woman with a small girl in hand. We listened for a moment. "Oh," said Morgan. "He's French!"

We fell silent as the man walked by, carefully avoiding our eyes. "So how's the apartment?" I said as we sat down on a bench near the band shell. "Are you enjoying it?"

"I love it," he said. "It's perfect. It's the perfect New York apartment—just the right size. Cozy, books, tree-lined street. And complete silence. The loudest thing is the girls when they leave school—that incredible noise they make. The only problem is Emma. She won't leave me alone. If I want to sleep an extra half hour, she poops. She's a great dog, though. The cats are cats. They broke into the bag of cat food yesterday, it was all over the floor when I got back. But there's really no problem. I have to make myself leave the apartment. If it weren't for Emma, I'd be lying on the sofa all day watching CNN."

"Is that what you watch?"

"Yes," he said. "After a summer in the Pines dealing with

queens, you just want to lie there and watch the crisis in the Middle East. And this summer we had a lot of French people. French queens are incredible. After dealing with French queens with attitude, the West Bank is very relaxing."

"And where will you go next month, after this?"

"Well, when the writer comes back, I'll stay with Peter. But I can't stay there very long. Like, one night, I think—he's very strange. After Peter, I'm going to the Cape. My friend Iris bought a house up there."

"Who's Iris?"

"She's a nurse, working in a treatment center near Hyannis. I knew her in New Orleans. It will be just the three of us. Iris, Jack, and me."

"Who's Jack?"

"An old boyfriend of Iris, though they haven't had sex in five years. He's a nice guy. Had a trust fund, the trust fund ran out, now he's a roofer. On methadone. He's been on methadone for five years, and Iris is getting a bit fed up."

"Do you get along with him?" I said.

"With Jack?" he said. "Oh, yes. Very well. He gets up at five every morning, drives clear across the Cape for his methadone, goes to work, and doesn't come home till four. Iris leaves about nine and comes home at six or seven. I'm home all day, or I was last winter, watching TV."

"So it's nice," I said.

"Yes," he said. "Though watching TV all day is not a life. But it's very pretty there. It looks like the Hamptons. Beautiful woods, rock walls, little lanes disappearing into the forest. I take walks with the dog."

"And you all get along," I said.

"We do," he said. "We've known each other since New Orleans. We get along very well. Why not? We're all the same. Three emotional cripples on the Cape."

"Don't say that."

"But it's true," he said.

"You're not an emotional cripple," I said. "You're a survivor!"

"What's the difference?" he said, looking over at me.

I looked at him and he started laughing.

"Look," I said, "you mustn't be hard on yourself. You're sober now, two years. You got through last winter, you're going to get through this winter. You're doing very well. It's already late October and you haven't had to pay any rent. What would be nice is if the writer would stay in England a bit longer, and you could just live there."

"That would be very nice," he said. "But he's coming back Tuesday."

"What about your sister—can't you stay with her?"

"No," he said.

"Why not?"

"Pride," he said. "The last time I was on my way to visit her, when Bob and I were still together, I asked if it was all right if Bob came, too, and she said no, because of the children."

"How old are they?"

"Five and eight," he said. "Or they were at the time."

"Well," I said, "I can understand that. People, in this country, are very funny when it comes to children—though I think five and eight are hardly ages to worry about that."

"Worry about what?" he said.

"Oh, you know," I said.

"No, I don't," he said. "When she came to visit me in New York, when I had my own apartment, did I ask her not to kiss her husband in front of me or hold hands?"

"Not the same," I said.

"Why not?"

"Because in her case there are children involved."

"So?" he said. "You're just as bad as she is! The point is, we are considered sleazy, sub rosa, because we're gay—that's all it is. We will never be accepted. All this so-called assimilation is only because of AIDS. We wouldn't get any sympathy at all if we weren't dying. Happy, healthy fags—*that's* offensive. Like rich blacks. Everything that's happened the last twenty years, the acceptance of gays, is a, superficial, and b, because we are dying. As we should be, in their logic."

"You're being too harsh," I said. "That has been the means by which the information was assimilated, but it's not the reason— the reason is, Americans are basically a happy people who want everyone else to have a crack at happiness, too."

"That's what Dan Riley says."

"Who's Dan Riley?"

"The friend I stayed with last week in Sag Harbor. He's in his mid-sixties, we had dinner together in New Orleans, remember? Tall, handsome, silver hair? His lover was a concert violinist? Died two years ago? Dan's all pink now. He's using this ointment that peels your skin to get rid of skin cancers. It strips your skin for about three weeks, then you look normal again."

"It's so hard to keep up."

"Tell me! Halfway through the summer I realized all these forty-year-old men in the Pines with the twenty-eight-inch waists—they'd all had liposuction! Can you imagine submitting to surgery to lose weight? Dan's house is perfect."

"Really?"

"Yes," he said. "It's on a narrow lot between two big estates— well, not estates, but two-, three-acre lots, each one with a big old house. His is modern, Frank Lloyd Wrightish, it's built like a railroad flat, you enter into a long living room with plate-glass windows on both sides, then at the back, off to the left, is a kitchen, and an herb garden, and at the end of the garden a little guest house with two bedrooms. Everything is landscaped, in flawless taste."

"But doesn't it clash with the Victorians, or whatever, on either side?"

"No," he said. "It's built into the vegetation, and has a fence on three sides covered with ivy so you don't see the fence. It's perfect. His lover, the violinist, left just enough for him to live on, invested. He doesn't have a lot of money to spend. But he has a nice life. He was just in China for three weeks with his new boyfriend."

"What new boyfriend?"

"This Italian lawyer in his thirties who still lives with his mother in Queens. Bearded, handsome, proud of his pecs—at least that's what I got from the picture of him I saw. The lawyer has a house of his own near Bayshore and gets together with Dan on the weekends. Dan says it's the best sex he's had in his life—as good as the sex he had in *his* thirties, when he was seeing some Cuban."

"Imagine that," I said.

"What?"

"The lawyer in his thirties."

"He went to China with him for three weeks."

"What did he think of China?"

"He said it was awful. Drab. People everywhere."

"That's what I imagine. Do you suppose they had sex there?"

"Why not?"

"Imagine sex in China!"

"Why would sex in China be different from sex anywhere else?"

"I don't know. Because it's China. People have been having sex in China for thousands of years. There's been more sex in China than anywhere else on the planet. That's why there's over a billion Chinese. So you had a nice time at Dan's."

"Not really," he said. "He lectures me. He lectures me on all the things I lecture myself on—I'm getting old, I have to start looking for a real job, I have to get my teeth fixed, and take care of my skin cancers. I had to listen to all that. Plus, I can't smoke at Dan's. I have to go outside to smoke, and it was very cold and rainy all weekend."

"So you had lectures and cold cigarettes."

"Yes," he said, "and by Sunday I couldn't wait to get back here, where I can smoke. Life simplifies itself as we get older, don't you think? Fewer and fewer things become important to you, but the things that do become *very* important. Like being able to smoke," he said, puffing on his cigarette.

"I've forgotten—where did you say you will go when the writer comes back?" I said.

"To Peter's," he said. "Though he won't let me stay more than one night. It's incredible. On the Island he came over to my room a lot, he would climb in bed with me when his housemates were noisy, he calls me every day—but when I go to his apartment it's very clear he doesn't want me to stay."

"Maybe it's because he can't bring tricks back when you're there," I said. "Is he still having sex?"

"Yes," said Morgan. "He likes Puerto Ricans. He had one who came to his apartment once a week and let Peter blow him. For twenty-five dollars. But then the guy disappeared. Now he has to go to Times Square and look for another."

"That's not good," I said.

"He doesn't think so either," he said. "But not for the reason you imagine. He has cats, and he told me he's afraid his trick might kill him and then the cats. It's the cats he's worried about, not himself," he said.

"How many does he have?"

"Five. He wants two more, he says."

"Uh-oh," I said. "That way lies madness. Pretty soon he'll have ten, then twenty. Then they'll die on him, in places he can't reach. I've seen it happen. It astonishes me how people are attached to their pets. Everyone on my floor has dogs. They go to work and leave them shut up all day. It's not humane. It's cruel. I sit home listening to them bark all day. I sit home listening to all this paranoia and loneliness. Everybody's got a dog now."

"On Fire Island they bring them to dinner, and then talk about how cute the dog is, how well-behaved, what shots they got and who their vet it. It's like the dogs are their children. It went on all summer. I got real tired of it. The bragging. Emma is ruthless—if I don't take her out, she shits right on the bed. She's not about to miss her walk."

"Good for Emma," I said.

"I like Emma," he said. "I don't particularly like cats. Here's what I'm going to do when I stay my one night with Peter. I'm going to be sitting by the window when he comes home from work. I'm going to hide the cats in the hamper, and then, when he asks where they are, I'll just glance at the open window. He'll have a nervous breakdown."

"Because he'll only let you stay one night."

"Because the last time I visited he took the day off from work rather than leave me alone in the apartment with the cats!"

"Well, this is neurotic," I said. "He obviously has a problem. Perhaps you shouldn't take it personally."

"Well, I do," he said. "I really need a place to stay."

"Men get very strange, living alone," I said. "The cliché is true: Don't live alone, you get used to it. We're all very set in our ways."

"He's beginning to look like a bird," he said.

"What do you mean?"

"He's beginning to look like a bird."

"What sort of bird?" I said.

"A parrot," he said. "It's his nose, primarily. He's beginning to look like a parrot."

When we went back to walk Emma, the girls were just getting

out of school—more subdued now, at the end of their day, in small clusters, on their way, we supposed, to ballet class. They looked crisp and alert in their uniforms, a sight you see only on the Upper East Side. "Oh," said Morgan to one of them waiting in front of his building, "you're reading his book."

"Whose book?" she said.

"The man whose apartment I'm staying in," he said. "He wrote that book."

"Really?" she said.

"Yes," he said. "He's got it upstairs in about nine languages. He's got all the translations. Is it a good book?"

"It's okay," she said. "It's a little depressing, but beautifully written."

"Well, I'll tell him," said Morgan. "I'll leave him a note." And he went into the building.

"Have your read the book?" I said.

"Yes," he said. "It's very depressing. It's a gay story but all the characters are straight—he belonged to that generation when gay men wrote parts for women. It was his only real success. I can't imagine why they're giving it to a girl her age to read. It's very bleak. It makes Jean Rhys look like Rebecca of Sunnybrook Farm." He unlocked the door. "But why not?" he said. "He knew how you end up—with two cats and an elderly dog," he said as Emma ran up to him and started wagging her tail, "and maybe an invitation to the White House."

"So next you go to Peter's," I said.

"For one night," he said.

"And then to the Cape," I said.

"For two weeks," he said. "Then back here to sign for my first unemployment check, then back out to Sayville."

"To rent a room."

"Yes. Though the room I rented last year is no more—they sold the building."

"But you can find another."

"Yes. If not, I'll go back to the sober house."

"But you hated that!"

"I didn't hate it," he said. "It was a bit noisy at times, the guys were a bit crude, but I didn't hate it. I ended up being the most popular person in the place. Even when they found out I was a fag. You can't use the 'f' word anymore, you know, the same way you can't use the 'n' word. Social engineering! These homeboys from Long Island would not let anyone use the 'f' word in my presence. They loved me."

"And will you get a job in the diner this year?"

"No," he said. "The diner was too depressing. Dealing with all the drunks. And those teenage brutes. It's not very nice to have a fifteen-year-old girl tell you to eat shit. Oh look," he said, at the window. I went over and saw a young man walking down the sidewalk, across the street. "I followed him the other day all the way to Lexington," he said. "It wasn't intentional, I just happened to be behind him, walking at the same pace. I kept thinking: That's how I used to look."

"Some of them are so handsome," I said.

"Here come the cars to pick up the girls," he said. We leaned out the window and watched the line of Mercedes town cars begin to form outside the school next door. Young women in solid hunter green skirts, white blouses, and book bags came out, got in the cars, and disappeared. "You know, I envy them," he said.

"Why?" I said.

"I've always envied kids who went to school in New York. You know the room we pass on the ground floor when we walk Emma?" he said. "I often hear them in there doing aerobics or something, and the music is so hip, it's the stuff they play in the Pines! And the stuff they throw out—the books, and tape cassettes—is incredible. I find it in the Dempster Dumpster. These girls are getting the very best education the world has to offer, an incredibly sophisticated education. I'm sure they come from divorced parents, and have their insecurities and miseries, but they're getting this fabulous education. Wouldn't you like to be a sophomore at the Chapin School?"

"But you know very well it doesn't guarantee a happy life," I said as we watched the girls come out and get into the glossy black cars. "You know very well some of them are going to fall in love with the wrong men, get divorced, become alcoholics, or something worse, become disillusioned with much of what they were taught here, and end up looking back on this period of their lives as one of the happiest. Or worst, who knows? Don't envy these girls. They're on a conveyor belt to oblivion."

We walked out of the apartment, took Emma to Carl Schurz Park, then took ourselves to the Rambles. The leaves had not yet begun to turn, but the weeds, with thick magenta stems, were high along the paths; it looked overgrown and barren at the same time. Still, the sun was shining and people were out cruising, in that viscous medium of watchfulness, that slow, glutinous patience as characteristic of men looking for sex as the substance slugs emit as they move along. Looking at the scene, you would have thought nothing was going on—merely a few people sitting on benches, or walking slowly around the periphery of the meadow. "Nothing changes," said Morgan as he lit a cigarette on the bench. "Absolutely nothing. Look at these guys, walking around and around, hoping to meet someone and go back to their apartment. Or do it in a bush. It's another generation, doing the same thing. I remember meeting a guy from Boston here one Sunday in the early seventies. He was blond, average height, compact, and he had a room at the West Side Y. I was on my way to Donald's, I think, so I made a date to be at the Y at five, and on my way over I started running because I was late. It was very hot, the middle of August, and I was running through the Rambles with a bottle of poppers in my pocket, past all these kids with boom boxes, and I could hear the drums they used to play around Bethesda Fountain. I was streaming with sweat and I was so happy, on my way to sex. I remember thinking: I'll never be this happy again."

"And were you?" I said.

"I suppose," he said. "The next summer I went to the Pines for the first time, and I was the hot number that year—the one everyone wanted to sleep with. Now I won't even take my shirt off in public." He laughed. "I had two queens from California last month, standing in line one night waiting for a table, and one of them comes up and says to me: 'Can we go back to our room to get a sweater, and not lose our place in line? We're very cold because we don't have any body fat.' And I thought: What is the point of all that's happened? Apparently there is to be no progress, nothing new, no evolution. We'll never regard each other as anything but fantasies, we'll never integrate sex with the rest of our lives, we're just going to keep on going to gyms and dance clubs, taking drugs, dancing, and cruising the Rambles. I mean, it's staggering when you think about it! Nothing changes! The only thing different about the Pines is that I think it's all a bit duller," he added in a lower voice, flicking the ash from his cigarette.

"Do you?" I said.

"Yes," he said. "It's all become so predictable. Self-conscious and bourgeois. They're so concerned with the right resumé, the right dog, the right amount of body fat—it's like the whole generation is art-directed. There's no craziness anymore, no characters, no spontaneity or sense that things are being done for the first time. It's all become ritualized. They don't evolve, or find new ways to relate to one another, they just keep doing the same old things," he said, his voice slowing down and lowering at the same time as the scene before us finally secured a hypnotic hold on him. For a few moments the Rambles was utterly peaceful—

the silver sky, the leaves strewn across the grassy oval, turned patchy by games of soccer and volleyball that summer, the figures on the benches opposite us utterly immobile. Then, all of sudden, two young men stood up on the rock above us, like pop-up figures in a book. They stood there surveying the scene below, their shirtless torsos still brown from the summer, wondering, no doubt, where the sun had gone, or who was on the walks; then, having seen what they wanted, and declared their own beauty, they lay down again and disappeared amid a flurry of laughter. There was a silence. Then Morgan turned to me and said: "Of course, why should it change? It's like expecting straight boys and girls to not date or get married because it's been done. Of course nothing changes. Because sex doesn't! Because being young and beautiful doesn't!" he said, and with that we got up, rather stiffly, and left the park, as if a problem had been solved.

☞ AMSTERDAM

SOMETIMES I HAD TO LOOK FOR THE BOOK—although the first night it was in plain sight. I'd come back from the sauna late, he was sleeping downstairs on his little bed, and when I tiptoed up the stairs which so resembled those of a ship, and my head emerged into the attic room where I was to sleep that week, I saw a small reading lamp on the floor in the corner. Beneath that, on a pillow, like some altar offering, or wedding ring, a notebook. Even then I wondered if he had left it out on purpose for me to read. Taking all things into consideration, I decided he had not. I knew he'd come up to the attic room earlier that evening to smoke marijuana. He'd opened the windows so the wind would disperse the odor (he was afraid his landlady, an elderly woman who lived beneath him, might smell the smoke) and, by the time he had finished writing in his journal, I surmised, he was so stoned he forgot to put it away before he went downstairs. Proof of this came, I thought, a few nights later: The journal was nowhere in sight when I returned to my room, and I had to search downstairs the next morning, while he was out shopping, to find it among the papers on his desk.

If I was wrong, and he did leave it out on purpose, then I must say—despite the rather creepy calculation that hypothesis implied—the first day's entry was kind. It began, in fact, with a sentence saying it was "so nice" to see me. It went on to say my jacket was "scrofulous" (the lining was quite tattered, it had been hanging in my closet for years, food for moths) and that I had body odor and halitosis (I'd been on jet planes for more than ten hours across the Atlantic and the Channel) and that I had become, like him, "a rabid eccentric, à la late Auden"; but these remarks did not hurt my feelings. No, the first night's entry I was relieved to read.

I was relieved because the minute I'd entered his room that afternoon, ushered in by the landlady's son-in-law, who'd answered the doorbell of the tall, narrow, brick house, I sensed he felt invaded. There was no embrace, no handshake—he stepped back, separated from us by a low, round table, and stood there without even meeting my eyes, his shoulders drawn up, his hands frozen, as if backed into a corner.

Of course, his last letter had been an explicit warning—that he'd had words with the two guests preceding me, that he was afraid he'd "disappointed" them both, and that because he was going through a period of very low energy, I must not expect him to do much with me. There's nothing wrong with that, I thought when I read the letter; it was the sixth year of his knowing he carried HIV, and he'd complained of low energy levels before. It was rather the tone of the letter that made me uneasy: a flat, affectless prose that one would not even call weary, but rather bone weary, weary beyond any desire to camouflage itself or to pretend one cared about anything. It was matter-of-fact, businesslike, and beady-eyed. And it was the first letter I'd received from him in months.

Before that I'd received and written many more—he was, in
fact, over there in the Netherlands, the recipient of virtually my
daily diary; the perfect epistolary confessor to whom I could pour
out my frustrations, failures, impressions of the life I was leading
in the small town in North Carolina that he'd abandoned to rent
an apartment in Amsterdam. The first few months of his new
existence there, my letters received letters in return—long, handwritten letters, intimate, confessional, frank. They described his
daily life in his new city—his joy on finally finding a doctor he
felt would be reliable until the end, including the end, which, for
him, meant a euthanasia unavailable in the United States. Many
things amused him—including the way his landlady washed his
clothes by tossing the entire laundry bag into the machine un-
opened—"keeping them separate, though included, a perfect example of my status here." Then there was his joy in meeting a
young Dane at the Nightsauna—an architect who lived in Paris
but seemed much taken with him—a joy he had not thought he'd
experience again, at his age, in his situation. For weeks he worried
how to tell the Dane he had HIV; then he told him, and the
Dane never touched him again. A period of silence ensued, like
the time he had stopped coming by or telephoning the two weeks
after getting his diagnosis; a cessation of communication that
made me think I had done something wrong, offended him in
some way. Then, a few weeks later, came an apology for not
having written. And then the letters began to change; no longer
descriptions of the flower market, the landlady, the grocery, the
streetcars, the Dane, his joy at being over there, but rather the
rooms, the apartment itself, the linden tree outside in the backyard, the piano he sometimes heard the landlady playing, the sky
and rooftops through the window, and I thought: He's turned
entirely inward, reduced everything to a room, a white room in
Amsterdam. In other words, he'd become really depressed.

In subsequent letters he wondered what he was doing over

there, and said he felt purposeless, alone, confused, and of no value to anyone. He walked by the bars on the Amstel, he wrote, saw the men congregating outside them on warm June evenings, and kept going, thinking, "I have nothing to offer them, I'm diseased meat," and scurried back to the two rooms in the rear of the canal house owned by a woman whose daughter, son-in-law, and two grandchildren lived downstairs. "What more is there to say?" he wrote in the last letter I got from him that summer. "I feel I've written everything. It's hard to manufacture raptures when you feel the way I do." What followed that letter were simply postcards; postcards that seemed a shrinking not only of his correspondence but of himself, his spirit, his ability to live, as the depression encroached and obliterated other aspects of his life. Still, I was not prepared for his reply to the letter I ended by saying that despite everything, I admired his having made the move, found the flat, started a new life in a foreign city; that in the end I was hoping he had found some modicum of satisfaction—"Little Gloria, happy at last."

"Little Gloria, happy at last." Who could have known it would earn the letter it did? "You asshole," he wrote, "all my life people have been accusing me of being selfish and spoiled, simply because I was, through no fault of my own and the considerable shrewdness and effort of my father, left enough real estate so that I did not have to earn a living beyond managing these assets intelligently and with as much foresight as I could. Which I have done, despite Their desire to see me fail. I don't need you or anyone else to lay a guilt trip on me, which people all my life in that town have been trying to lay on me out of envy and disapproval of my 'lifestyle'—i.e., sexual orientation—and sheer hatred. *Happy* in Amsterdam? Are you nuts? How could you think I was? If I do have any satisfaction over moving here, it's only because They can't get to me over here, i.e., the ones who have laid that mean, judgmental, small-town crap and envy on me all my life. So please in the future refrain from your usual superficial glibness in characterizing the happiness or unhappiness of people whose lives you know nothing about with inappropriate and inapplicable phrases picked up from the abattoir of pop culture. There is a permanent hole in your vision of the world that will forever prevent you from understanding anything about me."

This letter changed forever our friendship—not so much because I'd chosen a poor metaphor, but because that error had released a stream of bile and disdain so out of proportion to the imagined insult. The anger had not come out of nowhere, I had to conclude; it had to have been lying beneath the surface crust for a long time, like the remains of ancient forests and swamps that explode upward in a gusher of oil. It was as if he had been waiting for some time to turn this torrent upon me; or at least that all his life he had been tortured by what I had represented with the use, entirely inadvertent, of an innocent phrase.

One does not write drafts of a letter to a friend, but this time I did—careful not to use another phrase that would, like some drill, or grenade, produce another explosion. His next letter— replying to my own expression of dismay and shock—apologized and described, with moving simplicity, the depths of his own sadness. After that it was back to postcards; until, a week before I left, the letter arrived warning me not to expect much energy in him when I arrived, though he was still, he wrote, looking forward to my visit, a visit postponed so that two other friends could visit first.

These friends I queried before I left. Both told me they had argued with him—the first over the manner in which he'd been forwarding his mail to Holland, the second over the issue of how they were to live together over there for two weeks. The second was a young man, in his mid-twenties, who wanted to go out and do things every day—something Roy, at fifty-eight, said he did not have the energy or desire to do. They had a fight about that.

The young man called him a lazy old man. "Which I am," Roy wrote me in the last postcard sent just before I left, "and once we got that established, that he was to do things on his own, and not expect me to accompany him everywhere, everything was all right, and we had a fine visit. I don't want you to depend on me either." Well, I didn't. I went over with that uppermost in mind: I would not depend on him, I would do things by myself; I would avoid the arguments he'd had with my predecessors. So when I came home that first night, tiptoed up the stairs, and found the journal, sitting like an illuminated manuscript on a queen's prayer pillow, I was relieved to read I'd passed the first test. Halitosis, body odor, scrofulous coat aside, at least he felt it was "nice to see" me. The next day I showered, bought mouthwash, and tried to repair with some tape the tattered lining of the coat.

The following night I went to the sauna without him; he told me, on arrival, he had a sore throat and had to lay off for a while. His custom, I knew from his first letters, was to go either to the Daysauna or the Nightsauna every day for a few hours; besides euthanasia, the reason he was living over here after all was the availability of pot and sex. But when I arrived he was out of commission. After advising me to buy the six-pack (six visits for the price of five), which he could use if I did not, he touched his long, slender fingers to his throat and said: "What happened was someone in the dark room got a bit too enthusiastic, so now I've got a little lesion in my throat, which I suppose could be syphilis, which is why I'm going to the doctor tomorrow to find out. But I doubt it. It's just that one forgets how hard a dick can be when it's young," he said, sitting in the chair upstairs and smoking his nightly joint, and calmly discussing his situation in a polite, measured voice. "*Steel* hard. I don't think they mean to hurt you, but they get carried away—thank God—in the back room, at least. The orgy room. You'd be as*ton*ished," he said, "at what goes on in the dark room. I've learned that's where they all end up, even the great beauties. All that walking around the halls outside is merely posing. When they want to have sex, to be touched, they go into the orgy room, and honey, they don't care who puts his mouth on their dicks. I've had demigods in there! Absolute demigods! When you go to the Rijksmuseum, look for a painting called *The Massacre of the Innocents*—that man in the foreground with the marble ass! I've had dozens like him, in the dark room, and it's not just slam-bang, thank-you-ma'am! On the contrary! A great deal can be communicated—affection, even—with a penis. It's astonishing how much! I know. It's been my salva-tion—because *no* one was coming into my cubicle before I hit the dark room, dear. I don't know what will happen when you go, but I couldn't get *arrested* in the hallways. However, now that I've moved my act to the dark room, I'm having *all* the sex I could possibly want, I've found Valhalla!" He laughed, rocking forward and back. Rain began pattering on the windows; he took another puff of the joint, allowed the smoke to be completely absorbed by his lungs as he looked off into the distance, and then his voice began issuing not from a human mouth but from the granite lips of a satyr in the corner of some neglected winter garden, dense and cold, as his pent-up urge to speak to a friend gave way. "Two weeks ago," he said, leaning forward, as he touched the side of his lip, "I was panic-stricken. I came home from the Nightsauna and found this small purple bruise next to my mouth. Oh God! I thought, it's finally happened! Kaposi's sarcoma! But when it turned yellow a few days later and went away, I realized it was just a bruise," he said, laughing. "It was a love injury, from all that *battering* my mouth had received in the dark room! Needless to say, I took a rest until it healed, which is what I'm going to do now, now that someone has literally ripped the lining of my throat!" He laughed. "And meanwhile I'll gargle with this mar-velous new mouthwash I got Dexter hooked on when he was over here, the one I bought for you this morning."

The mouthwash—Dutch—sat on the table between us in a small orange-and-brown bottle; Dexter had told me about it before I left, to prove his statement that there was no way one could bridge the gap between a person who carried HIV and one who did not. One morning this past spring, when Dexter found himself alone in the apartment, he went downstairs to shower and brush his teeth before going to a museum, picked up the bottle of mouthwash, rinsed his mouth, and then realized, on putting it down, that he'd picked up Roy's bottle, not his own. His mind raced toward a sensational conclusion. He had just brushed his teeth, abraded the gums, then used Roy's mouthwash; ergo, he had given himself HIV. At that moment the gulf between them closed—its depths visible only now that he thought he had joined Roy on the other side—and he realized his sympathy till now had all been egoistic, condescending, based on his own presumed escape. When we spoke of his panic—a panic he eventually reasoned his way out of—I told Dexter I thought he was only half right about the gap between the infected and uninfected. Part of the chasm was Roy's own personality, which had incorporated the HIV into his general view of life—a melancholic, melodramatic, at times even apocalyptic prism that had caused Dexter to refer to him for some time between ourselves as "Cassandra."

"You're right. But Cassandra has now got HIV," said Dexter that day, "and we cannot possibly know what that is like. But I'm sure it's at the root of his unhappiness. And he's very unhappy. He went to Amsterdam to die! And now he's not dying, and he doesn't know what to do. And he's much too proud to admit a mistake. And the disease is still for him the final insult! His whole life he's been condemned by his mother and all the women in that town he grew up in for being homosexual, and his mother, believe me, could be incredibly cruel. They went for days without speaking to each other. She was *not* easy to please. She told me I was the *only* one of Roy's friends she liked. And now I'm not speaking to him."

"Why?" I said.

"We had a horrible fight our last night, in a restaurant—ostensibly over how I'd been forwarding the mail. I just couldn't take it any longer."

"So what I have to do is avoid the argument," I said. "Be very careful what I say."

"Whatever you like," said Dexter. "But remember—be patient. Be kind. The man is sick."

"But his last blood work was very good!" I said.

"I know," said Dexter. "But that doesn't change the fact that he's still furious."

"But don't you think the function of a friend may be to let the person express his anger by using him as the object?" I said.

"No," said Dexter. "I've had friends scream at me the day before they died: 'You should be dying, not me!' I didn't know what to say, because there is no answer to it. Life *is* unfair. But still, there are limits. You don't have to be a doormat."

"You don't?" I said.

"No," said Dexter. "Although God knows I've come close. You have to be firm with him. Draw the line. Don't let him cross it. Otherwise he will. And remember—as you reminded me, you are dealing with Cassandra, and Cassandra has a reason now to be apocalyptic."

But she always had, I was thinking as Roy took me around the city that first day, even before HIV; during the eighties, he had predicted incessantly that the Reagan presidency was going to lead to revolution in the streets, barn-burnings and African-American riots. It was hard to say where he had developed this apocalyptic view of things. He had been raised in the mountains near Asheville, in a small country town whose Baptist strictures my friend had fled the minute he finished school till, years later, parental illness required his presence at home again. Then, shortly after his parents' deaths, the discovery that he had HIV sent him flying once more; determined not to let anyone in that small town whose mores he despised watch him suffer the fate they believed people such as he deserved. He still looked hale and handsome, nevertheless, a tall man with shoulder-length hair that was more blond than gray, and clear green eyes, and a land inheritance— long since converted to shopping malls—which gave him the ability to live wherever he wished. Not with a clear conscience, however. The wealth he'd inherited from his parents, the land that had become so valuable as Asheville spread outward, increasing his net worth as he slept, induced only guilt in him. "American capitalism," he told me as we walked down Utrechtstraat the next day after taking money out of an ATM machine, "is a *complete* failure!" The Dutch had better health care. Their enlightened view of euthanasia was only part of a system that was superior in every way. (He was so grateful for this, I think—that there was such a society, a city, a place on earth where he could have this option—that the relief and gratitude spread a sort of radiance over every aspect of Dutch life.) The Dutch did everything more sensibly than we, he said as we strolled to the flower market. They were not falsely polite, they did not mince words, or pretend things they did not feel; they were blunt, honest, plain-spoken. Nobody said those hideous words: "Have a nice day." They wasted no time pretending things they did not feel. They had no land, no space, and therefore no words to waste. And they were so handsome! The complexions, the hair and skin, the physiques! The baths were unbelievable here! The acceptance of all types— the absence of game-playing—the straightforward expression of desire! The Dutch had all the good qualities of the English and Germans, none of the bad, and they were far superior to the French. It sounded to me, as we walked along, and he showed me the cash machine, the streetcar lines, the grocery, the magazine shop—all the things I might need—like the fervent faith of the recent convert; the small-town Southerner who'd felt himself a misfit back home because he was homosexual but who, like some jazz musician or minor opera singer, had finally found a new life in Europe, where, it occurred to me, nobody cared what he did so long as he paid the rent and all his other bills. Amsterdam, city of merchants, had simply taken in another customer.

It had also given him a new identity, the sophisticated American abroad. "There are other versions of this now," he said to me when, leaving the apartment, he watched me put on the blue hooded sweatshirt I wore beneath my leather coat. "Since you're going to London after Holland, why don't you go to Burberry's and get something like this," he said, indicating the double-breasted khaki raincoat with a red-plaid lining he wore. "It's really not that expensive," he added as we went out the door. I had to admit he looked more dignified than I did, in my ancient cruising outfit, which seemed—as we walked around through crowds of people who all wore the sort of outdoor gear you find in Land's End catalogues—like a relic from the past; my last trip to Amsterdam, in fact, six years earlier. He looked, on the other hand, with his glasses, his thick mustache, his umbrella and Burberry, like a Dutchman—a professor of zoology at the University of Amsterdam, say, walking to his office. He was different over here. Whatever had made him feel like a freak in his own hometown was gone. "Look," he said, pointing to the advertisements, on the wall of a tram stop shelter we were passing, of the American actor Eric Roberts grinning at us in a pair of very brief underwear, "all these actors who'd never do this in the States have huge advertising careers over here." Like Eric Roberts in Europe, Roy had another life.

It was a quiet and simple one; after taking me around my first morning, he left me on the steps of the Rijksmuseum and went on to get a massage in another part of town, then home to cook supper on his hot plate and watch an interview with the duchess of York, peddling her book on *Larry King Live.* That was how I found him when I returned. "She is beyond any *con*cept of humiliation!" he crowed, eating a bowl of soup as he watched the TV. "There is *nothing* she will not do!" He doled out a bowl of soup for me while rain fell past the windows. I was charmed. Like the rooms in the houses on the canal I loved to walk by at night, peering into their lighted windows at people making or eating dinner, working or watching television—or the seventeenth-century paintings in the museums—his was a Dutch interior. Like the postcards his letters had shrunk to, these two white rooms connected by a little set of wooden stairs, the cyclamen in flowerpots, the lamps, the wicker basket, the simplicity, seemed a conscious paring down, an abandonment of many material possessions for this quiet cell in the rear of a canal house; a house presided over by an elderly grandmother who reminded him, he'd said more than once, of his mother. "Do you know, the number thirteen and number five tram still stop outside Anne Frank's house," he said to me as we ate our soup, "and the bells of the Westekerk that kept her up the first few nights she went into hiding still drive people crazy," and I wondered for a moment if he felt that he himself was hiding, like her, not from Nazis, but from people who had judged him.

Of course it was only a friend at his door when I returned to the house, but still I wondered if I was the enemy now as I ate the soup he offered me—the silence, and the solitude, of this room, with a view of the gardens behind all the houses, hitting me for the first time. There is nothing stranger than the way a long-awaited trip, a reunion, a meeting of two friends can collapse so quickly into nothingness. Never meet someone you've corresponded with, someone told me years ago; it will only spoil the correspondence. Sitting there I could hardly swallow the soup, so suspicious was I that this man, my friend of ten years, wished I was not there. Yet he was politeness itself. He gave me homemade cake, fresh bread he'd bought that morning, his favorite Gouda, a dish of yogurt and pears, and chocolates from a shop he said made the best chocolate in the world. He told me about an exhibit of photographs he thought I would enjoy at a museum I had never heard of, he gave me the address of a shop where I could rent the bicycle I'd talked about, he told me about the Stripkaarten I could buy that would save me money on the streetcars, asked me what sort of music I wanted to hear before putting on a CD by a blues singer I'd not heard before; and all the while I sat there, spooning the yogurt into my mouth, like a dog being fed who eats his food not knowing if he will be struck next, afraid to say anything—though I agreed to go with him to his weekly meeting of the English language group.

He'd told me about this in his letters, a group of people of all ages and nationalities who met once a week at the gay and lesbian center simply to help each other out with the difficulties of living in Amsterdam, and provide some feeling of family in a very transient town. "The facilitator is this Israeli queen," he said in a cold, imposing voice, as we walked down the Herengracht in the crisp November chill, "who's really a bitch. He tried to drive me off. When I went back the second time, he said to me: 'Oh *you're* here again?' " Roy laughed: a short, dark bark. " 'You bet, honey,' I said, 'and you ain't drivin' me away!' " And then Roy laughed again. Upstairs at the gay and lesbian center an odd lot was assembled: two beautiful young Finnish women, a slight Scotsman, his Asian-looking Dutch boyfriend, a bearded cook from Arkansas, two American musicians, a third American jazz singer, another woman from Helsinki. ("I sense something truly honest, and spiritual, about the Finns," he murmured, before the meeting was called to order. "I wonder if they don't have to be investigated. Because these women have a certain quality, a spirituality I find very attractive.") We were, in our fifties, by far the two oldest people in the circle, and might well have felt out of place. Roy sat there with his arms folded across his chest, looking like

Father Time, or Santa Claus, or some Norse god, though there was, when I glanced at him, an expression of such sadness on his face that even though he was taking an antidepressant, the Prozac could not mask the hurt visible in his eyes. Like a man in a prison cell in some ancient dungeon, filled with seawater when the tide came in, he'd had to make sure his depression did not drown him utterly—not to mention his sex life, whose orgasms the Prozac dampened, so that he had to balance the two things . . . lower the dosage in order to reach a climax, raise the dosage in order to be able to leave his room for the sauna.

"Why did you come to Amsterdam?" everyone in the English language group was asked the evening I attended. Everyone gave his or her reason—to earn money, or a degree, to start a career as a singer, or violinist, to live life in a gay environment—the dreams of youth. When it was his turn, Roy simply said in a morose voice, his arms folded across his chest: "Because there is no language barrier, and because I can smoke dope." Everyone laughed, and I thought: At least he is honest. (Though he did not say: "I came here to die.")

About the English language group I kept my thoughts to myself after we said good-bye and walked away from the center—they'd seemed to me a dull, pathetic group of souls, as lost, as forlorn, as any young expatriates could be; the blandness of the conversation had been shocking; but Roy obviously held the group in some affection. They were, I surmised, the people he identified with now. So it was a surprise when he said to me as we walked away: "Dexter found them poisonously dull. He was furious I'd brought him at all."

At the Leidesplein we had a hamburger at Burger King. "You have to eat more, you're anorexic!" he said, turning to me as we stood in line. "Not to mention the fact that you're going bald. You need the vitamins for your hair." Then we prepared to part in the Kerkstraat, he to return to his nightly joint and journal, I to the Nightsauna. "You know, the wonderful thing about Amsterdam," he said, eating his hamburger on the street thronged with people, "the reason I love it so much, is it has both the *Night Watch and* the Nightsauna! Have fun!" he said, and walked off, a big raincoat tinged with neon. I hardly wanted to go to the sauna but it seemed the only way to separate; once there, wandering the halls upstairs, I was conscious only of the fact that They were still as good-looking, as wondrous as I'd found them the last time. In the empty, dark room I stood for a moment trying to imagine Roy lying on one of the pallets. Then I crawled into one of the cubicles that lined the hallways and lay there in a dark corner and watched the oblivious messengers of Time go by till two and then went home, where once more I found my host.

He was asleep, his arm thrown across his face, on the sofa downstairs, turned to the wall like a child who has been punished and has cried himself to sleep; a motherless child, I thought as I looked down at him, a long way from home. I tiptoed to my garret, dejected and tired, slid the wooden panel shut over the stairs, got in bed, and saw the notebook, sitting on its pale green pillow under the reading lamp, not ten feet from my bed.

Should I have left my bed and crawled over to it and started reading? No. A gentleman, now that he knew this was a private journal, would have turned his eyes away, gone right to sleep with the diary not ten feet from his pillow, without a second thought. But I rationalized my second breach of manners with a medical excuse: He was my friend, I was concerned about his state of mental health, worried that he had exacerbated his depression by living a recluse's life over here, that the letter describing his feeling that "They cannot get to me now" was that of a man burrowing deeper and deeper into paranoia. In fact, it was the sight of my name in the first line that made me abandon any pretext of manners; I knew well I would have to find and read it every day till the day I left, like a playwright reading his reviews.

Unfortunately, the first day's entry (the pleasure of seeing me, despite my scrofulous coat, bad breath, and body odor) had been followed by a less favorable notice. The second night, even after what seemed, on the surface, at least, a pleasant outing together, had been a disaster. "He is such a mess," he wrote, "he is painful to look at—fragile, anorexic, agoraphobic. I obviously make him ill at ease, he seems quite terrified, and I have no way of changing that. He looks like a frightened monkey. I cannot imagine what people passing him on the street must think." I put the journal down, turned off the light, and drew the covers up. Snow was falling past the windows. The room was a ghostly white. It was like a nine-year-old's tree house, with flawless modern decor. The pots of cyclamen on the windowsills, an expensive stereo that would have provided music had I wanted it, the chair in which he got stoned and wrote in his journal—unless he did that lying on the floor, with the notebook on the green pillow—the small bookcase, the wicker baskets for his laundry, the view of the rooftops and terraces and gardens were all so civilized. Still, it was a stage set, a nightmare now. The next day, trying to make sure my face did not look like a frightened monkey's, I went downstairs and had breakfast with him, the cereal sticking in my throat, and then, after a morning shower, I set out for the day.

The excursion he'd taken me on the first day was the only one we took together—having done his duty, pointed out the places I might need, he retired to the life he'd been living before my visit: napping, eating, reading, watching television, going for a massage. "I can't be a tour guide anymore," he said. I was the tourist, not he; each morning I closed the door of the house behind me, the person foolish enough not to have moved to Amsterdam, and set out on my walk.

O Amsterdam! I walked to the usual places. It was late November. The weather was exhilarating: clouds, rain, sleet, hail, snow, then shafts of sunlight piercing the clouds, till another gust of rain came, followed by hail, followed by rain, and the cycle began again. It was the light of the landscapes in the Rijksmuseum, where, in my attempt to stay away from the apartment as much as possible, as any considerate guest in my situation would, I spent more time than I ever had on previous visits. Rooms I'd never bothered to enter before I now examined every object in: wood carvings, altarpieces, jeweled chalices, ivory saints—the Middle Ages had never seemed so lovely and so enviable, now that I had the time to peruse objects like the tiny *Flight from Egypt* carved from alabaster. Then I looked at paintings I'd not studied before. Everything was drenched in the sadness of the end of our friendship—even a canvas that depicted the god Content, the card beside it said, "a god the people worshiped to the exclusion of Jupiter himself until the father of the gods, annoyed at being slighted, sent the god Discontent down to them." That was all I could say about what was happening to our friendship: the god Discontent (who knew he was a god?) had been sent down to our decade of intimacy. And the change was shocking. Life is like a painting, Pascal said—for a certain while, you are too close to it, for another, too far away; but at one point, you are exactly the right distance, and see it clearly. That was our problem, I thought as I shuffled along in the dim light. He and I were suddenly seeing everything clearly.

Certainly, the beauty of the Dutch—the people I saw on the canvases (Adam and Eve, Judith, Holofernes, Saint Jerome, Apollo, Mars, Aphrodite; the man with the marmoreal butt in *The Massacre of the Innocents*) were there the moment I left the museum, walking up and down the rainy streets; the same cream-and-gold complexions, the same well-proportioned limbs. An old woman, silver-haired, with finely wrinkled white, white skin, and dark brown eyes floated past me in the Vondelpark, the only one who fixed me with a steady gaze, a Rembrandt ringing her bicycle bell. There must be something on my face, I began thinking, that made everyone else look away.

We dress carefully, after all, select our clothes, the colors of our clothes, we cut our hair a certain way, assume an expression on our faces for the faces that we meet, and then—They see something else, something we may not even be aware of, something we have tried unsuccessfully to hide; that we are, in fact, unhappy, lonely, depressed, profoundly lost. It was possible to walk from the Vondelpark to another park and still another park as the rain came and went that day; a necklace of green spaces that led from the central city to the suburbs and finally a footpath to the town of Haarlem running along a crowded expressway. I could see the spires of Haarlem on the horizon, but walking beside the constant traffic was unpleasant, so I turned back. Gradually the emptiness of the paths began to change. Dog walkers and men playing soccer and couples pushing baby strollers and students returning home from school appeared. So great was my distaste at having to pass another human being, I made a point to look at them long before we reached each other, like gunslingers walking toward each other at high noon, from opposite directions, to hold the gaze till their own eyes dropped or glanced to one side; over-compensating for my self-consciousness, looking too hard, too long, because I did not want to look at them at all, all the while, no doubt, asking them a question: What am I doing here? How am I going to spend the rest of my life, with everyone I love already dead? Where should I go, what can I do?

At night there was no problem—it was dark—and after crossing the bright lights of the Leidesplein, where I ate a fajita at Burger King, I started walking toward the Amstel. In the darkness—if you stayed away from the bright commercial streets that run like veins of mica through the otherwise dark city—you did not have to prepare a face to meet the faces that you met. There was no self-consciousness as I walked through the cool, wet air along canals on whose black water the streetlights wavered like reflected candle flames; just a general sadness over what was happening. We were like two men drowning, I thought as I walked, neither one could help the other. Instead of comforting, joking, laughing, commiserating and encouraging, we were going our separate ways. How foreign the sound of laughter was, the click of heels on the pavements, the voices of people leaving a restaurant or apartment building on the corner. The little bridges lined with lights—a carnival touch that might have made sense in summer—looked garish now, like something at an agricultural fair, like all the touristed streets that ran along the streetcar tracks, with their decorations for St. Peter's Day fluttering forlornly in the wind like plastic pennants at some used-car lot, till one turned off, as I did, onto the darkness of the Amstel, into the cold wind chafing its surface, the only lights those brassy-colored flames reflected in the water.

Depression is like carbon monoxide—it extinguishes more and more of your sanguinity with no visible signs or odor. You do things to escape it that end up reinforcing the mood. One of the bars mentioned in Roy's letters came into view. A handsome man with short, dark hair and a bushy mustache sat in the window two floors up at a little counter with a vase of flowers, looking down onto the street and river with a beer in hand; the exact image of the man I'd been pursuing for thirty years. But what was the point? Moments later I passed a corner where ten years ago a tall young man who'd just left a leather bar had stopped to look at me. He was not there now. So I crossed the Amstel and wandered into a part of town I was not familiar with, my sole criterion in charting my course the darkness of the street, the absence of pedestrians coming my way, till I turned back and decided I could not possibly go to the Nightsauna in this mood, I would go back to the apartment even if it was but eleven o'clock.

He was playing solitaire when I walked in. To my surprise I got what seemed to be a warm welcome; in a thick, rich, resonant voice that suggested he'd already smoked his joint, my host, seated at his desk, waved his arms when I came in and said, "Oh good, you're back, come look at these photographs I just had developed, some of them I think actually work!" and I went over to look at his latest project, and praised them. Then, after eating the bowl of soup he offered, I went upstairs, where he followed me a few moments later, to smoke his last joint of the night. His throat was better, he said, he was preparing to go to the Night-sauna. "I feel I've stayed away long enough," he said in a sonorous voice. "It has its own etiquette, you know, which I mustn't violate. People rely on me, like a gas station or a public telephone. I feel I am expected to be there in my usual spot at the appointed hour. I am a fixture, I think, at this point—a public convenience, a tram, a place where people can make a deposit after the bank has closed. I am a mail drop, I am the number five, I am a statue in a traffic circle, a bakery that stays open late, a cash machine that is expected to be there. So I shall be," he said. As he got stoned, he became warmer, friendlier, more expansive. We talked of mutual friends, including one in San Francisco who, I said, had become hooked on speed. It was awful, I said, what drugs did to people; not thinking it necessary to draw the distinction between crystal methadrine and the marijuana he was puffing on. "Dexter was on speed once," Roy said, "when he lived in New York in the seventies. Now he's clean and sober," he laughed, "but he's so fat he can hardly get through doorways, and as for watching him get on and off the streetcar, it was like waiting for a third-rate soprano to hit high C. He moves very slowly now, he has no choice, since he gave up sex ten years ago out of sheer terror of AIDS and decided to eat himself into oblivion. Well, he's achieved his goal. Unfortunately, he still has these delusions of grandeur that may have made sense when he was a slim, young, handsome man working for Geoffrey Beene in New York, but now are simply crazy! I can't tell you the things he said in some of the antique stores," he said, his face crinkling, "where, of course, they all understand English perfectly! I can't show my face in some of them!" he chortled, and began rolling another joint. Then, after reiterating how much he loved Amsterdam and how worried he was about what he'd do when he went back home this January— which sounded, the way he expressed it, like a death sentence—I asked why he couldn't stay here permanently. He looked up at me; his eyes narrowed, and he fixed me with a brief but snakelike look. "Because I have a *house* to take care of," he said with a sharp, nasty tone in his voice; and I flinched beneath the covers, as if I'd nearly tripped the wire that would cause the explosion waiting for a fool to set it off. A few moments later amity seemed to be restored, and when a gentle rain had begun pattering against the windows, making perfect the domestic coziness of our presence in that neat, dry, snug, little space, I thought this might be the best moment to try to talk about the situation that lay beneath his being here, to finally puncture the ice that had frozen our conversation, it seemed to me. "Tell me," I said, as the rain thickened, "do you think about the future? Are you pessimistic about everything?"

"No," he said, carefully rolling the cigarette on his lap, "not really."

"Do you think in terms of Time?" I said (a euphemism for: How long do you think you'll live?).

"Ten years," he said. "But then I thought that when I was diagnosed six years ago. It still seems to me ten years from now. It's always ten years from the present. And, honey, I mean to get me as much dick as I can before my ten years is up!" And with that, he stood up, put his marijuana plate on the table, and told me I might enjoy putting on the radio; the station here played wonderful classical music you didn't hear in the States.

I doubted that, but I did enjoy wishing him luck after he had gone downstairs, wrapped a scarf around his neck, and called up from below: "Lulu's back in town!" With a high-pitched cry—the shriek of a warrior going into battle—he left the apartment, and I lay there with a smile on my lips after what had seemed an essentially friendly exchange, almost like the old days. The next morning, after he left for a massage, I found the journal under some papers on his desk, following a search of the apartment that lasted almost half an hour. "I have been *humiliated*!" I read. "I can no longer even smoke dope in my own house! I got a *nasty* crack last night about what drugs do to people. He is a total tight-ass incapable of having any pleasure without guilt, or any real closeness with another person, or friendship, for that matter. I continue to find it a terrible strain to be with him. His insincerity, fragility, selfishness, and agoraphobia are matched only by his inability to form any sort of connection with the proletariat. He is a textbook example of the narcissistic personality. His vanity is so tedious at this point that all I can do is remind myself to be kind. Be kind. He's more to be pitied than anything else."

I got my coat and left the apartment. The only charge I could dismiss without first examining it was my inability to form an association with the proletariat. What did that mean? I put my head back and laughed, and a woman with a shopping bag looked at me strangely. Go to the train station now, I told myself, go right to Paris. But to have gone to the train station and taken the next train to Paris—or to have moved to a hotel—would only draw attention to my reading the journal, I thought, so I went to the Concertgebouw instead. There I sat with my jacket on, pressing my arms to my sides, fearing an emission of body odor, beside a kind old man who proudly pointed out his daughter, a violinist, onstage; the daughter smiled at him, a note of human affection that reminded me that not all life was like the apartment I had just fled. After the concert I walked into the park, looking forward to departure, and the fact that, after the perfectly worded thank-you postcard I would send from England, thus discharging my last duty, I would never, ever speak to this man again.

And so I walked on from park to park, surrounded by the Dutch in various congeries of familial relation—handsome young fathers with children on their shoulders, grandparents, young lovers—grateful that babies did not burst into tears when I passed. The weather was sympathetically vile. In the middle of the Vondelpark I had to run out, when a lightning storm began cracking right above me, and found shelter on the porch of a house, where I watched some workmen, who also looked normal and kind, restoring a mansion across the street. Then the rain let up, and, determined to stay away from the apartment till midnight, I walked west till I was in Osdorp. This is where I want to live, I thought as I walked through the nondescript suburb, the well-planned streets, with trees, small parks, and low apartment houses all on a human scale. I wish I were waking up on one of these quiet streets with a man I'd met the night before. I want to live with a Dutch boyfriend in a small flat near the Sportspark, going for a swim in the public pool on this wet, windy, stormy day. It was Sunday, the Dutch were home relaxing, reading the paper, cooking, watching soccer on the tube, planning a trip to the Maldives, or whatever it was they did that made their domestic life so comfortable. If I really do care about the friendship, I thought as I tramped along, I should confront Roy with what I've read, and we would have it out, discuss what he thinks, and go on, at least honestly, perhaps even salvage what is left of the last decade's closeness; unless there was nothing left—that was the shocking thing—and the whole friendship had been a sham, flattering to each other's vanity, and nothing more. This is how marriages end, I thought, all of a sudden, with no warning, they just give out. Boom! If I wanted to continue as his friend, I had to tell him what I'd read. But the moment I considered this, I realized I couldn't. I could not bear a voice raised in anger, much less the bile that would flow once I said I'd read the journal. And so I kept walking till I was on a footpath along a vast, open field where I met three young women, who stared at me unabashedly, leading miniature horses as I went by. Above the field I stood beside—dotted with sheep and seagulls under a low, wet, gray sky—the airplanes that would deliver me from hell were rising into the sky. Perhaps I *am* an agoraphobe, I thought. The gray skies, the seagulls, the absence of people, soothed me deeply. Walking back into the city I felt a sense of despair. My project was to stay away from the apartment till I went to bed; to kill time I walked now to the Central Station to inquire about trains to Paris. The woman in the window seemed impatient—even though I knew her job was a tedious one, the slightest coldness in anyone I dealt with now seemed connected to the journal; after she gave me the information, I turned away and thought: Paris will make me even more self-conscious. So I walked up and down the Amstel on both sides for another two hours in the blessed darkness and then went back to the apartment.

Roy sat at his desk arranging photographs in the lamplight. He looked up as I came in: a cold, beady-eyed expression. "A long day," was all I could say in an exhausted voice. "I'm beat. Good night!" And I went up to bed. I lay there, as he worked downstairs and the rain gently blew against the window, and tried to think of something I could go downstairs and say, something that would heal the breach, break the silence, restore the friendship, but, like people who were ending an affair, it seemed there were no words available. The rain hit the windows. He hummed downstairs. I could not decide whether he wanted me to talk to him or preferred I did not. In the morning I found the journal next to the television. "The most shocking selfishness and cruelty. Came home, went upstairs without a word. This stubborn self-reliance, this pride, this insane determination to go his own way, all alone. What does he prove? I can scarcely imagine his day after he leaves the apartment. He is surely past the point of meeting anyone on the street—or of going to bars for that matter, and having one person look at him—looking as he does. He is fit mostly for vultures at this point and I haven't seen any of them wheeling in the skies over Amsterdam. He must be terribly alone. One of those sad creatures who finally know their life has evaporated when they weren't looking. It is all coming to an end for him. He has lost his looks and doesn't know what to do without them. He has nothing to fall back on, not youth, or charm, or even a profession. He is a frozen shriek, dangling in space, a man who has hung himself out to dry. Yet he is far too proud to accept help from me, or anyone. He can only go on, like some mechanical doll, pretending he has someplace to go each morning he leaves the apartment, pretending he is not suicidally lonely, and *very* close to cracking up. So uptight, so controlled, so bitter, it's no wonder he tested negative! And he's flatulent! The truth is he is no longer worth the effort—at least any I can make." So, I thought as I put the journal back, I *should* talk to him when I come home at night.

Instead I asked him to come with me to see the Vermeer in the Hague when he returned from the grocery store—and he agreed. We set out after two bowls of yogurt. It was raining lightly as we left the building, closed the door on the shrieks of the landlady's granddaughters playing "Für Elise" on the piano on the ground floor, and headed up the Herengracht. Ten minutes later I looked around and saw that he was gone. I stopped, turned back, and saw him standing on the corner, in his big double-breasted Burberry, beneath an umbrella. "I'm not going if I have to keep up with you," he said. "It's not worth it. I'll go back and work on my photographs." I was stunned. But I said, "All right, but I'll be back by six, and I want to take you to dinner." It was a matter of pace, I thought as I continued on: We simply move at different speeds. I did not go to the Hague. I went to the Daysauna instead, crawled into one of the dark cubicles and spent the day there. That evening my impatience got the best of me as we were walking up Utrechtstraat in a much stronger, driving rain—and at the corner, unable to restrain myself, I stepped round him and proceeded on ahead to the Rembrandtsplein, where he said the restaurant was; then, just as it had happened that morning, I looked around and realized I was alone. I stopped and looked up and down the street; I could not find him. I walked twice along a frieze of restaurants on the square, with no luck; my heart began to accelerate with the apprehension that this was the final break—he'd ditched me in public, had finally expressed in action what he was doing in his journal—when I looked toward the park and saw him standing there. The rain had stopped. His umbrella was furled. He was waving the folded umbrella like one of those men on an airport runway directing an airplane to its gate—with a weary air, not even speaking. Ah, I thought as I rejoined him, he's not even rebuking me this time; he simply doesn't care. And with that we sat down to a quiet dinner in a little gay cafe, like a married couple who have been together for so many years that they have nothing to say to each other at dinner in a restaurant.

But I refused this image, and, as the rain streamed down the glass of the enclosed porch, I talked of Vermeer and Rembrandt and my regret that I had not gone to Paris. "Paris!" he said. "What on earth would you want to go there for? It's just another city the automobile has completely destroyed! And the rudeness! I refuse to go there and be humiliated!" The rest of the dinner we resuscitated the stale topic of the few friends we had left in common, and I watched him devour them one by one like the roasted chicken on his plate. George was a user who could think of no one but himself; John was addicted to Percoset; Ron was a neurotic faculty wife always retreating into a nervous breakdown when his turf was threatened; Bob should have had a sex change years ago since even antidepressants could not provide him with a personality. "And when does your next guest arrive?" I said.

"Tuesday," he said. "It shouldn't require much effort. Rudy is an old friend from our theater days in Miami."

"Well, that should be fun," I said.

"I don't know how much *fun* it will be," he said, his voice as cold and hard as wet stone in winter. "I've warned him not to expect much from me."

"Well, he'll like Amsterdam," I said, toying with my flan.

"Perhaps," he said. "If he goes out at all. But Rudy's pretty much a recluse at this point. Or at least he's damaged goods. In fact, all you can say about Rudy at this stage in his life is that," he said, "he occupies Time and Space."

"The truth is, that's all any of us are doing now," he intoned. "Occupying Time and Space. And a mat in the orgy room, thank God. The fact is, we are all desperate souls devising strategies to stay at life's restaurant, even when the waiter has evidently presented the check, and the table is wanted by other customers," he said as the waiter brought ours. "I'm losing all my friends for a simple reason. They cannot bear my Truth. And if people cannot bear the Truth," he said, standing up and taking his umbrella from the back of the adjacent chair, "then I don't have time for them. Because that is *all* I deal in at this point, baby—Truth!"

And with that we went out into the night. Careful not to repeat my mistake, I matched his pace all the way back to the house on the canal. The canal was dark and quiet, like death itself. The city seemed quieter, too, and harmless, like any place you are leaving in the morning. When we passed the plump, cheerful, gray-haired landlady in the narrow hall she said to me, "What do you think of the weather?" I said, "Exhilarating!" and we went upstairs, where, before going to the Daysauna—though it was already nine o'clock, I was determined not to leave him a single coupon—I sat down across from him as he rolled his joint. "Going to the baths?" he said. "Yes," I said. "Good for you," he said. "Because God only knows we should do these things while we can. Because it's only going to be worse next year. And the year after that," he said. "Because at this age," he said in a cold, calm voice, fixing me with a piercing stare, "nobody wants us. Nobody really cares. It's that simple. And when you realize that," he said, spreading his hands, "you're liberated. When you realize you are traveling completely solo, and the most you can expect in life is service for payment rendered. Which is all *I* want when my time comes." He picked up two cigarette papers and said: "I've not run anyone off in the last ten years I regret running off, and I wouldn't take back a single thing I've said to them. I just got tired of disappointing people—I'd rather stay away from them. And when I become sick and helpless, I don't want *friends* coming into the room—I'd prefer kind, professional help. I don't want friends coming and feeling superior, thinking they've survived, which, believe me, I've got news for them, they haven't." He started to laugh as he rolled his cigarette. "It's all so funny, really," he said. "*I'm* dying. But what are *you* going to do?" He shook with laughter, licked the paper of his cigarette, closed it, put the plate to one side, and stood up.

I could think of nothing to say—so stricken was I with fear of saying the wrong thing, I merely watched him as he stood there. He regarded me with a benign smile, amused by his own comments, and then said, "I'm going downstairs and take a shower. Do you need the bathroom for anything?"

"No," I said, "I'll shower at the sauna. I just want to finish packing."

"All right," he said in a pleasant singsong, and then he went slowly and carefully down the narrow stairs. A moment later I heard *The Four Last Songs* of Strauss: the anthem of melancholy queens. I stood in the center of the room, heart racing; I knew, if the pattern held true, he was writing in his journal at that moment. I knew, too, it was my last chance to read the journal—it would be impossible in the morning, before I left; so I packed, unpacked, arranged, then rearranged my things, kneeling down to peer under the bed, going through the magazines and papers

I'd accumulated at my bedside all that week, making sure, more conscientiously than I ever had before, that I'd left nothing behind. (I'd left a great deal behind, and because I knew that, I was even more determined that the room should bear no trace of my ever having been there.) Ten, then twenty, minutes passed. Then I heard the door downstairs open and close. I put on my coat and went down the wooden steps. The notebook lay on the desk. I opened it. "It's over," he'd written. "And when something is over, there is nothing you can do. He will attribute it all to the marijuana, but it's not the marijuana. It's that it's over, and when it's over, it's time to move on. As Miss Alma said: 'People change and forget to tell other people.' " I closed the notebook, left the apartment, to the sound of his singing in the shower, and walked to the Daysauna.

The Daysauna was too cheerful, too full of light, for my tastes during the afternoon, but an hour before closing—at ten P.M.—I found a dark cubicle upstairs and lay in the corner where no one could see me. The pleasure was strange and bitter. I could see a stream of men walking by, a few of them coming to a stop in the alcove directly opposite to lean against the wall and wait for a passerby to approach them; I could watch their expressions of disdain or relief when someone finally stopped and fixed his mouth on a nipple. Or, if I moved to another corner, I could see across the linoleum floor another cubicle in which two figures were bobbing up and down above each other, could hear their grunts and whispers, the sighs, the "Where are you from?" I could watch it all undisturbed—a pleasure that was so tedious after a while, I was about to crawl out of my cave, my nonexistence, when a young man came to the entrance of my submarine chamber, stopped and arched his body forward so that his torso entered the realm of darkness in which I lay, offering himself, like some foolish skin diver investigating a reef—and I, to my amazement, moved forward like an eel, began to tongue his body, and took him in my mouth; at which point he climbed into the cubicle and let me feed.

It was what my host had been doing in the dark room of the Nightsauna—the solution to his age and clinical depression (what used to be called despair); a solution that had sounded pathetic to me, even as he laughed while praising its joys. Now that I was feasting, however, I did not care; it seemed to join the two of us together; and it was one way to have a young man without the risks entailed in the usual seduction—a young man who did not care, apparently, what I looked like—an arrangement that lasted till he stood up and withdrew from the cubicle without a word. Astonished, wiping my lips, I lay there wondering what it meant to have sex like this, till my diver returned—and I resumed my adoration, wondering why he, in the outer world of sunlight and appearances, could not find what he wanted, and had come back to me for appreciation. Then, when we were through, I watched him wrap the towel around his waist and vanish; whereupon, suddenly impatient, I waited till there was no one in the alcove outside and I could leave my lair unseen, dash downstairs, dress, and depart. When I left I felt a strange mixture of shame and exultation as I stood at the checkout before the handsome young clerk with a crew cut, glasses, and intelligent eyes. Casting the key onto the counter, I immediately realized it seemed as if I'd flung it at him with a certain contempt—a gesture the handsome clerk imitated perfectly by flinging the drawer with my wallet in it back across the counter to me. Ah, I thought as I picked up my valuables, these men have had so much experience with people like me, flinging their keys in ways that express their anger, sadness, and despair; and they give it right back, calibrated perfectly. "Thank you," I said to him, to cancel the rude impression. "You're welcome," he smiled. "Please come back."

 In September, the Light Changes

In September, the light changes, he thought as he walked out onto the deck at the rear of the beach house. It was the day after Labor Day. A sense of exhaustion and peace lay over the island. He sat down on the edge of the warm wooden planking and stared at the lush green underbrush that stretched between the dunes to the blue horizon and the tip of the weathered brown roof of a house whose occupants he did not know. He waited, secretly, patiently, devotedly, each year for this moment. It seemed to him that he was not the only creature emitting an audible sigh; it seemed to him the whole world—the sky, the leaves of the holly tree shining in the sun, the flat blue bay—all exuded a uniform sense of relief. The breeze was blowing off the ocean—there was always a breeze in September—fluttering the leaves of the grapevine on the trellis they had put up, and the sunlight fell gently, ever so gently, on the plate of toast, the coffee cup, the pot of jam the owner of the house had left there on the red-and-white-checkered tablecloth in his haste to catch the boat that morning, to get back to the city to work. He lay back to feel the sun on his body, lifted his head to look at the light shining on his legs—because he could not get over the fact that in September, the light changes. Now everything—his legs and stomach, warm in the sunlight while flies (still thinking it summer) buzzed over the pot of jam, the green underbrush, the roofs of the houses on the horizon—was annealed by a delicate silver light, the most beautiful light of the whole year, a light that was both warm (if one lay in the sun, as he did now) and cool (if one stood in the shade). He knew that if he went into the dunes today and lay in a hollow he would soon be drenched in sweat. He knew, too, there would be clouds of monarch butterflies floating above the goldenrod, and, across the wind-chafed bay, the steeples of the churches on Long Island would stand out in perfect, sharp detail, and the whole scene—the bay, the clam boats, the churches, the clear, shallow edge of the water where it lapped the shore, the gray, flat expanse of bay reflecting the clouds passing above when the wind died down—would seem like some engraving of the Peaceable Kingdom, everything, birds, fishes, fishermen, and sailors, exhaling upward a great thanks unto God.

It was worth waiting for, this day. It was worth holding his breath till the last person in the house had gone back to the city—and he would, out of revenge, or a small sense of triumph, wander through the rooms trying on their clothes, the bathing suits they had worn all summer, the shirts he had admired, the caps and shorts—all of it his now, in peace and quiet. But now all he wished to do was lie there on the warm wooden planks, with a breeze on his body, and the sound of the still-droning flies, and finally, after an entire year—it always seemed—relax. When he got up he would harvest the basil, and clean up the kitchen, and put out the rugs to air in the wind, and then walk down the beach two miles to the grocery and come back to a solitary dinner at dusk on the roof and watch the migrating geese flying south over the bay, and the smaller birds dipping and swooping in the twilight over the dense, low shrubbery only a few yards from his dinner plate. And he would gradually discover over the course of the next few days the people who were on the Island with him, the ones who had stayed, like him, because it was the best time of all.

He hoped at the moment they were few—that was the pleasure of this time of year, it distilled a crowd down to just a few persons. It astonished him slightly each fall when the crowds, at a stroke, went back to the city, that this gorgeous weather continued at the beach, like the sound of a tree falling in an empty forest, or a kingdom unplundered by white men. Were they really creatures of such habit, that summer ended for them with this one holiday, when so clearly it went right on? He was deeply grateful they were, if that was the case. He could hardly believe his good fortune. He got up, stretched, felt drowsy again, his whole body heavy, and walked round the house, through the cool shadows on the west side, where the water pump dripped and the tree shade was heavy and dense, and little sunlight penetrated even in August, to the wooden walk bordered by pine trees, and the beds of petunias his friend had planted in worn weathered boxes half-eroded of their paint. To his right, the gray bay was covered with white caps; to his left, the horizon was a blaze of wind and sunlight mixed inextricably into a brilliant radiance that made one lower one's eyes as one walked toward it, a protective gesture that induced a sense of reverence. The breeze and the light blew over his body as he walked. He bowed his head into the wind and came to a stop at the head of the stairs and looked at the beach. It was the harvest, this beach, of a whole summer's labor by the sea. What had been gouged away in the winter, reduced to a strand so slender and steep people spoke of the dunes being breached, was now immense, rich, heaped up, plenteous, so wide it took ten minutes after descending the worn wooden stairs to walk to the point at which the sea spray had dampened the sand. The surf was roiling: jade green, and glittering, glazed in the light, the wind throwing back mist from the crests of the waves as far as the eye could see in either direction. There was not a single human being anywhere to be seen on this beach that yesterday had contained so many little human dramas, feuds and friendships, romances ending and beginning, gossip and disclosure. He broke into a run. Oh, sea, he thought as the wind at his back blew him down the beach, I am yours, oh, sky, I am yours, oh, day, holy day, I am yours.

He made vows, he made plans, he tried to figure everything out, he wanted to come to conclusions as clear as the light on the sea, and then he gave up, it was pointless, he would simply turn into a shell in whose hollows the wind whistled, when he held it up to his ear, and watch the monarchs in the goldenrod resting on their flight to Mexico. He went back and forth from surf to dune, and, like a sailboat tacking on the bay, worked his way down the beach till he realized he was near Point o' Woods, and turned back, this time into the wind, which reduced him to a figment of itself, the sandpipers skittering out of his way on the flat, shining skein of water as the tide receded, pecking at their prey burrowing into the sand. He did not return till the sun was setting, and the whole sky turned a leaden crimson, as if behind it some plume of ash from a distant volcano were tingeing the sunset. And the sky above the underbrush when he finally climbed wearily back up the stairs he'd descended that morning was low, lurid, surreal, and the whole group of houses that constituted the town was utterly dark, and the only sound a bell, forlornly ringing in the wind, and he ran into the dark house and lit the kerosene lamps. That night he slept on the roof under the stars and woke around dawn. The next day he saw people.

He was seated on the roof reading one of the old magazines he had found in a wicker basket by the fireplace—magazines one hardly had time for in the city, but which here, at the beach, seemed like the precious flower of centuries of civilization. (The bookcase was filled with children's books and reports on shipping during World War Two.) As he turned their pages over in the morning sunlight, reading about haircuts, clothes, beauty tips, he heard voices, looked down, and saw them. They were two men in their thirties who owned a small house at the opposite edge of the town, who rented it during the season, and came out themselves only in spring and fall. They were both extremely handsome artisans who restored ceilings and molding in mansions up and down the East Coast. One was tall, the other short. Both were hefty, extremely well built, as solid as caryatids supporting a porch, or a chariot, or a bridge. If one had to choose the handsomer, it would probably have been the shorter, who had black hair, green eyes, and a face that stopped just this side of being swarthy. The other had blue eyes and dirty blond hair. Both wore crew cuts— crew cuts which, in an earlier era, were the style of a young man growing up in a Midwestern city, but which here, at this time, looked art-directed. Their hair was thick enough to stand straight up without the aid of any cream or gel. They labored in the rarefied world of restoration; they knew the way to paint faux water stains on faux marble, not to mention trompe l'oeil, and everything about them, despite, or especially, their resemblance to football players in Muncie, Indiana, circa 1952, was the work of a sophisticated taste and a conscious effort to be attractive. Yet this last seemed impersonal—nothing more than an exercise in taste, the same sense of design and beauty they brought to their work restoring ceilings and crown moldings, or the little beach house in the hollow which, when they purchased it, had been painted and decorated in ways they immediately removed so that it looked now like merely a weatherbeaten shack that seemed to have been at the beach for decades, abandoned by everyone.

And though they clearly were vain, and meant to be handsome, it seemed, again, for no other purpose than the expression of their taste in design, for neither one seemed interested in anyone but his lover. When you saw them, you felt that a certain aesthetic propriety had been achieved: two men as handsome, as meaty, as stylish, as sensuous as these two deserved each other. They both had thick legs, big hands, broad chests, and full lips. They both reminded you of stone figures holding up lamps on certain bridges in Paris, in part because all of this flesh might as well have been made of stone. That is, they gave the impression of being amiable but cold. They kept to themselves most of the time; they visited other houses only with a purpose (to confirm some gossip about the town, which affected them as house owners), never simply to sit and visit. They had each other. They needed no one else. "Do you have any basil?" they asked him now, and he said, "Help yourself," and pointed to the herb garden still flourishing at the rear of the house in a sunny spot on the back deck. And there they went, as he followed them with his eyes, down the narrow walk along the edge of the house, speaking to one another in low voices.

The herb garden was well-known in the little town—like the goldenrod that drew butterflies, it drew people they would never have met otherwise. One day he had been kneeling in the garden pulling up weeds when he heard voices, looked up, and saw a man and a woman standing above him with the sun at their backs—two models he'd seen till then only on the pages of magazines—and they said the same thing: "Do you have any basil?" He chided himself for feeling as if, like someone in a mythological tale, he had been asked directions by a god and goddess; but then that's what they looked like that day, as did these two fellows now: more earthy, these, demigods, perhaps, connected to some dell or clump of woods; centaurs rooting, the way the deer did when no one was there, in the clumps of herbs.

He was glad they were there—he approved of whoever had selected them for this glorious week at the beach—but after holding up the basil they'd taken to show him, and saying, "Thanks," they wandered off into the salt-thickened sea mists toward their house without another word. During the next sunny days, he would look up from his lunch or his book as he sat on the roof—feeling quite like a king, able to see both ocean and bay, to the left, to the right, and the green spine of the island laid out before him, his only company the birds that flew over the top of the shrubbery—and see them wandering along the beach, or rummaging in the piles of abandoned wood for nails or window frames they might use. They were frugal, they were clever, and they looked—the two of them, that week, from his roof—like two boys on a Saturday morning wandering around town in search of junk with which to build a treehouse. Perhaps that was it. The bond between them could not be merely physical—it never was with lovers; especially at this stage of a relationship as domestic as this, involving joint ownership of property, and a business. It was some complete union of taste, and temperament, ambition and outlook. "He sees the world the way I do," said a friend of the man he had been with for thirty years. That was it. They were content with one another, and he respected their solitude as being like his own, in their case peopled with two, in his with just one.

In love with the season, the days, he felt no need of any human connection—this was the dispensation of autumn at the beach; the lovers receded into the scene, like the butterflies, the sea, the light on the dune grass, so silver, so sharp. There was a rumor about the tall one he recalled—that he liked to choke people during sex, especially as his orgasm approached—but other than this he knew nothing about them as individuals; they were simply fellow devotees of autumn at the shore.

At night he lit the hurricane lamps and read by the fire, or went to bed early, dragging his mattress out onto the roof so that he could fall asleep under the starry sky and awaken in the morning to the sunrise. Then he walked down to the next town, purchased the newspaper, and walked back to have his breakfast. On his way back on Thursday, he noticed the clouds massed over Long Island, and by the time he got back to the house a fine rain had begun to blow on the bay, and, as he shut the windows he saw it begin to darken the moored sailboats and flat, gray water till it was puttering on the leaves of the shrubbery around the house, and he went out to the kitchen and looked through the back windows at the dunes. It was a storm. He went out to the beach that afternoon to see the ocean boiling under a golden-brown foam. The seagulls stood lined up in the driving rain, their feathers fluttering in the breeze, just out of reach of the hard, crashing waves that shot up the steep slope of sand with astonishing speed, and fell back just as fast. He wore a yellow slicker, and so did the lovers when he ran into them on the soaked and slippery walk and they asked him if he had matches. Inside the kitchen, their hoods pushed back, their faces pale and wet, he wanted them—but he sensed this was absurd. He had a friend who went home with lovers the way a bee attaches itself to a flower; it was the love between them his friend fed on, and wanted, it was their intimacy he wanted to witness, when, after feeding on the stranger, they inevitably turned to each other, and, their fantasies spent, they renewed their commitment in view of this third party. "That's why lovers go home with third parties," he said. "To make them remember they want each other more than anyone else." But looking at the two centaurs, the two caryatids in the kitchen, their broad, deep chests, and handsome heads, their damp mustaches, he did not think such a need obtained here. These two were different. Even when he began to run low on food, he did not want to intrude on their privacy. He used cans of soup that had been on the shelves for more than one season, and ate pasta with marmalade on it. The storm continued to throw rain against the windows and walls for three days. At four in the afternoon it looked like night, and at night it was a bit claustrophobic—there wasn't anyplace to go. He had read all the magazines and given up on the idea of replanning his life and now a certain gloom entered him. He loved storms at the beach and as he went through the house he kept imagining someone in each room. But there was no one. He had arranged his life, he realized, to be alone, and the world had granted him his arrangement, like a child the rest of the family lets stay in his room at dinner. He considered going back to the city—taking the last ferry of the day; but he let it leave without him and watched its silhouette move across the bay from his roof.

Usually this sight induced a feeling of gladness and relief—that one was once more cut off from the mainland, alone under the stars, by the sea for another night—but this time the decision depressed him instead. The storm was not letting up. He was too alone now. I am a professional homosexual, he thought as he sat staring at the fire; I lecture, write, think about homosexuality, and I sit here alone while they are chopping tomatoes together four walks away in their little house. They had each other. He had no one. He wondered how his life had led him to this point and whether they knew something he did not.

He wondered if the storm entitled him to visit, not to borrow matches or food, but simply to have human company. Had they not been lovers, there would have been no question. He'd go. A woman and her daughter, a straight family, an elderly couple would have been fun to drop in on—they could laugh and share their experience of the storm. But these two, so forbidding in their sensuality and reserve, made such an innocent foray impossible. The fact was, he did not even like the short one; it annoyed him that he found him compelling. He had seen him in the city; he lived in his neighborhood; he'd noticed him one night at the newsstand on their corner waiting for the truck that brought the *New York Times* between eleven and midnight. Even in the crowd on Second Avenue there was something about him that conveyed a certain self-regard, a lack of interest in the people around him. He gave the impression that he wanted no one to look at him even though he knew people were. He was like a closed city one cannot visit, the closed city of Gorky. He was there that evening on St. Marks Place not to be picked up but merely for the paper. Now the rain was blowing against the house and he was thinking of this man in bed. What did they do? Did the tall one strangle the short one? He supposed that at this point they probably rarely had sex, their lives having meshed in every other way; but the idea of them in that cottage began to obsess him. He sat up and decided to visit. He could no longer watch them scavenging the town from his roof. He could no longer expect them to call up to him: "Can we get some basil?" He no longer knew if both of them were on the island; when it grew dark he went upstairs and looked out the window and saw, with relief, the lights in their house. He put on his slicker, and went out in bare feet, and walked down the slippery walk to the harbor. There he turned right, walked up the boardwalk over a hill, and down into the hollow where their weatherbeaten shack sat, trying to think of something to borrow. He could see the kerosene lamps on the table through the porch window; he walked up the steps and knocked on the door.

The tall one answered the door—smiled, and said, "Come on in!" The short one smiled, too, from his perch on a couch, as he put down the magazine whose pages he'd been turning. There was a cat in the corner, a pot on the stove whose cover was ajar to let the steam escape; the two lovers wore gray woolen socks, jeans, and sweaters—and looked in the light of the candles the way more and more homosexual men looked to him these days: like models in a menswear catalogue. There was in the house, too, the same almost unbearable domestic charm: the kerosene lanterns, the pot on the stove, the faded jeans and old sweaters, one dull red, the other dull green. Even their hair was parted and combed, even the kitten was pretty. He told himself that were he their contemporary, he would still feel intimidated by the attention to detail, the perfect taste; but being older, he now wondered if it was his age. But all he said was: "Have you got any vegetable oil? I'm all out and don't have the energy to go down to the Pines." The tall one asked how much he needed, and the short one asked the tall one if he still needed a phone, and when the tall one shook his head, he explained: "I was going to come over and borrow your phone today, and then I realized I didn't have to. Are you getting along all right?" "Yes," he said. "Till I ran out of cooking oil. Oh, that's plenty," he said as the tall one handed him a carafe of oil. "What a nice, cozy house this is," he said, looking around.

"It needs a lot of work," said the tall one.

"I think it's wonderful, just as it is," he said, and then—after the smallest of pauses—he realized they were not going to ask him to stay. He would have, in the same circumstances, had their positions been reversed. But they were not. So—slightly amazed—he thanked them for the oil, and, after a joke about getting swept off the boardwalk, he went out with the carafe, hunched against the gale. Were they really so self-sufficient, he wondered, or just dull? Wouldn't anyone else have enjoyed a visit? Was their reserve so absolute, their contentment so complete, they did not need another human being? The cat and the candles, the pot and the African violet, their freshly scrubbed faces, the bodies beneath those old faded sweaters with the reindeer in a silhouette! "I can't *stand* it!" he screamed into the wind. When he got back to the house, it seemed cold and creaky, dark and damp, full of ghosts and failure. He went straight to bed, got up the next morning, and walked down to catch the first boat back to the mainland. In September, the light changes—as he crossed the bay, it was once more beginning to break, in long, beautiful shafts, through the clearing sky—but not the human heart.